the House Swap

BOOKS BY JO LOVETT

The First Time We Met

the House Swap

JO LOVETT

Bookouture

Published by Bookouture in 2021

An imprint of Storyfire Ltd.
Carmelite House
50 Victoria Embankment
London EC4Y 0DZ

www.bookouture.com

ISBN: 978-1-80019-508-0
eBook ISBN: 978-1-80019-507-3

To Charlie

Chapter One

James

'I understand that James has a very special gift for Emily and a very special question for her.' Emily's mother directed a coy smile at James, replaced the mic in its stand, stepped back and ushered James forward.

James frowned. This wasn't what he'd been expecting. What did she mean by 'special'?

He looked at the mic on the stage in front of him, and at the sea of expectant faces below. There had to be a good hundred and fifty people down there.

He glanced upwards. There were helium balloons bumping against the ballroom's high ceiling. They weren't three- and zero-shaped, as you might expect for a thirtieth birthday party; they were heart-shaped.

Special. Hearts.

Was he expected to ask Emily to move in with him or something?

Surely not. That would be ridiculous; they both knew their relationship wasn't that serious.

How long had they been together now? Maybe nine months? But only loosely together. They didn't talk a lot. They went out sometimes, they slept together; that was about it. They barely knew each other's friends, and they were light years away from anything like exchanging an I-love-you. Except, what else would 'special' mean?

James looked sideways at Emily, standing just to his right. She was wearing a floor-length, shimmery-green, silky dress, very tight all the way from the strapless top down to around shin level, where it flared out at the back. Kicking room. Her hair was mainly up, with a few strands down round the sides. She was wearing a pearl choker and diamond earrings. She looked stunning.

His gaze moved back to her mother, standing just beyond her, holding a glass of champagne and beaming. What was the woman's name? Nope, he couldn't recall it; that was how close he and Emily were.

Like everyone else in the room, Emily's mother was looking at him.

People were starting to murmur.

He caught a movement out of the corner of his eye and glanced down. Emily had inched her left hand towards him, with her ring finger proffered.

What? No. Couldn't be. Was she expecting him to *propose*?

Emily's mother's words replayed in his mind. *Special*. No. He really hoped not. *Surely* not.

He took another look at Emily. She actually looked quite bridal, in a green way. And her mother's outfit looked pretty mother-of-the-bride.

Unbelievable.

Maybe if he hadn't been running late and preoccupied by the god-awful day he'd had at work, he might have registered some of these details when he arrived. And run for the hills.

Emily, still with the proffered finger, raised her eyebrows and jerked her head slightly in the direction of the microphone.

James didn't move.

'It's probably time to make the announcement.' The acoustics of the room were terrible. Emily's words were still bouncing off the walls whole seconds after she'd said them.

And everyone was still waiting for James to speak.

Except there was nothing that he wanted to say, other than *Goodbye*. And maybe *Help*. Clearly, Emily had completely mistaken where they were at in their relationship. Getting married was in no way part of James's life plan. He was pretty sure that he was a good friend, godfather and uncle. He didn't want any commitment beyond that, and he always made that clear to girlfriends from the word go; there was no point upsetting people unnecessarily. He'd definitely made it clear to Emily. Surely.

She'd cooed over babies in buggies when they'd walked through the park a couple of weeks ago. She might have talked recently about selling her Central London flat and wanting to buy a house with several bedrooms out in Wimbledon. He also had a vague memory of her saying something about getting a dog. But, really? Should he have extrapolated from that to this? It was a big leap from there to here.

'James?' Emily's voice had a nasty edge to it now.

The guests had upped the decibel level of their murmuring.

He'd better do something.

He gave a small smile around the room, reached into his pocket, pulled out Emily's present and held it out to her.

She didn't immediately take it, probably something to do with the fact that it was long and thin, rather than a square, Tiffany ring-shaped box.

He didn't actually know exactly what was inside it. Presumably a necklace, given its shape. He'd given Dee, from the concierge company that he used, what had felt like a pretty generous budget – although obviously, because he wasn't getting engaged, nowhere near what you'd spend on an engagement ring – and had asked her to buy jewellery. Dee did all his present shopping and people were always pleased with what she chose.

Emily finally took the gift. James stood staring at the wall opposite. He could hear her tearing at the ribbon and paper and clunking the box open.

'Is this a joke?' she hissed in his ear.

Nope. Hadn't been. Dee had told him that Kate Middleton owned the same piece of whatever jewellery it was and had been photographed wearing it to polo matches. That had sounded ideal for Emily.

Some of the guests were sniggering. He took a sideways look at Emily. Her mouth was pinched and her cheeks were scarlet. Still beautiful, but angry-beautiful.

Her mother's Botoxed forehead was creasing a little.

The guests were all talking quite loudly now.

Okay. James needed to wrap this up and go home. He wanted to be inside his flat, with the door closed on the rest of the world, so that he could forget that this day had ever happened. There seemed to be only one obvious way to do that.

He leaned into the mic, gave it a little 'check the sound's working' tap, cleared his throat, nodded at the band, made a big conducting motion with his hands in the direction of the guests, and started to sing, '*Happy birthday to you…*'

The band obligingly struck up the tune and a lot of the guests joined in.

'You bastard.' Emily spat the words.

James carried on singing, staring straight ahead. There didn't seem to be any alternative. He'd apologise and make his escape as soon as the song finished.

Emily slapped his face on the 'dear' of 'dear Emily' and, while he was still reeling – the woman had some serious strength in that arm – dug her nails into his cheek and scratched, hard, on the 'ly' of 'Emily'. Impressive; he saw stars briefly.

James moved out of her reach while Emily's mother put her arm round her daughter's rigid shoulders and said, voice brittle and high, 'You were supposed to be proposing.'

'There must have been a misunderstanding,' James said, which was extremely polite considering that Emily had just assaulted him.

The mic was obviously still on. Someone at the back of the room started cat-calling and cheering, and a fair few people joined in. Some of the other guests started booing.

In retrospect, he should have left immediately after Emily's mother asked him onto the stage.

'Good evening,' he said into the mic, and walked off the stage and out of the room, to what sounded like a pretty fifty-fifty mix of cheering and booing.

*

Home. Thank God.

James really needed a whisky. He rarely drank by himself – in his experience, when you grew up around an alcoholic you either went that way yourself, or you were very careful to do the opposite – but today had been a shockingly bad day, this evening the icing on the crappy cake.

He sank into his favourite armchair with a glass, cradled it in his hands for a moment, then took a large sip, leaned his head back and rolled his shoulders while the fire of the alcohol spread through his body.

He looked out of the long windows over the end of Campden Hill and into Holland Park. He loved this view at night, the streetlights and sometimes the moon illuminating the park's majestic trees, their outline sharp tonight against the black sky. Today had been one of those crisp, cloudless April days that reminded you that summer was just round the corner and how great this part of London was during those summer months.

He also loved his gloriously tidy and orderly flat – a long way from the chaos of his childhood. And he loved living alone. Just one of the many reasons that he wasn't planning to get married.

He definitely hadn't said anything to lead Emily to expect that he was going to propose. Or even that he was in love with her. He was certain he hadn't. And was she really in love with him? Surely she didn't know him well enough. It had to be his flat and his lifestyle that she'd fallen for.

He took another sip. Yes, this was good. He could hunker down for the weekend and re-group. Thank God for peace and quiet.

Right. Some TV and then bed.

A clicking sound from behind him punctured the silence. What? It sounded very similar to a key turning in a lock. And a door opening. Again, what?

'James.' It was Emily. In his flat.

He stood up so fast his whisky spilled onto the floor.

'What are you doing here?'

She walked across the room towards him, smiling. 'I came to apologise. I overreacted. I just thought that now would be the perfect time to get engaged, being our one-year anniversary.' One year? Really? That long? 'When we met in the club last year it was my birthday party.' Her smile and voice had both hardened.

James shook his head. 'How do you have a key?' There were four spare keys to the apartment. He kept one in a drawer in the kitchen, and the other three were with his cleaner, the concierge company and his best friend, Matt.

'You gave me one at the weekend, remember.'

'No, I didn't.'

'James. You did. When I left the restaurant.'

He worked back through Saturday evening in his mind. Oh yes. They'd been at a dinner in nearby Notting Hill with a group of Emily's friends, and Emily had told him that she'd left something in the flat. He'd offered to return himself for it, in fact he'd tried to insist, but she'd insisted harder, saying that she also wanted to pop to the loo and didn't like the ones in the restaurant, and was more than happy to come back by herself.

'You borrowed my key to pick something up,' he said. 'And then you gave it back. How do you still have it?'

'I got one cut,' she said, like he was stupid.

Right. Twenty-four-hour London. Normally a good thing, but not in this instance.

'I'd like you to give me the key.' He put his hand out. Emily put it inside her dress, down her cleavage.

'Come and get it.' She lowered her head and looked up at him from under her eyelashes. Really? Did she seriously think that she could set him up to propose to her, hit him and reveal that she'd obtained a key to his flat by deception, and then flirt for two seconds and they'd have sex?

'I'm sorry, but it seems that we have different ideas about what we wanted from this relationship. It's over. Could I have my key, please?'

The remainder of Emily's smile dropped from her face and she launched herself at him. This time James was more prepared. She got in one – again impressively hard – slap to his temple before he caught her arms, spun her round and marched her to the door. He had the door closed and the deadlock on before she'd managed to get the key back into the lock.

She stayed outside, smacking the door and screaming like a banshee. Very disturbing. She hadn't seemed drunk, but maybe she was. Hard to explain this otherwise.

Despite the way she'd ambushed him, it was hard not to feel sorry for her, but he couldn't really see how he could help her; better to keep the door firmly shut and hope that she'd calm down soon.

Chapter Two

Cassie

'So we're agreed that you're going to come over to London for a week or two. Soon.' Jennifer had a very piercing voice. Strident. Cassie winced and turned the volume on her phone down. 'And then we can finalise where you're going to set the books. And finally meet.'

'I'm not sure.' Cassie looked at the beautiful, calm, shimmery sea through the trees at the end of her garden. What would that shade be called? Cerulean? Azure? If she could get rid of Jennifer quickly, she could get a swim in before lunch. 'I'm really sorry but I don't think I can set any books in London. I don't know it at all.'

'Really? I thought all Brits knew London.'

'No. I've only ever been about three times and the last time was about ten years ago.'

'But you were a lawyer.'

'Yes, but all my clients were in Scotland.'

'And you never lived in London. Ever?'

'Nope. Before I moved here I spent my entire life in Glasgow and Edinburgh.'

'How did I not know that?' Probably because Jennifer didn't ever do touchy-feely small talk. 'Well, not a problem. Maybe you don't have to know London to set your books here. You can use the internet and your imagination.'

'I really don't think I can. I know Glasgow, Edinburgh and Boston very well.' Cassie had rented an apartment in Boston for a few months after she left Glasgow, while builders made her new home on Hawk Egg Island, Maine, habitable. 'That's how I've been able to write about them. If I wrote about London, my readers would spot my mistakes. I mean, the books are supposed to be semi-educational.'

'Cassie. This is a fantastic deal. Six more books in your series. Huge. TV rights guaranteed. Huger. And a mega advance to match. If you need to get to know London, you're just going to have to spend some time here. Move here for six months.'

'Right.' Cassie remembered too late that sarcasm was usually wasted on Jennifer.

'Great. So you're going to come soon? Next couple weeks?'

Seriously? Of course not. No-one decided at the drop of a hat to go and live on the other side of the world for any period of time. And Cassie didn't want to go and live in London. She didn't want to go to London for even just a few days. What she wanted was to stay on the island and go for a swim this morning. The weather forecasters had stated with great confidence that today was going to be the last day of this once-in-a-decade April heatwave. Snow was a lot more usual than sunbathing weather at this time of year in Maine. It probably wouldn't be warm enough again for weeks.

'Maybe.'

'Maybe definitely?' Ouch. Near-perforated eardrum. Jennifer was getting more excited and her voice was getting shriller.

'I'll think about it.'

'Think fast. We don't want to let this opportunity go.'

'Okay. I'll think soon and I'll call you back.' Obviously she *should* consider it properly. From a personal perspective, it really didn't appeal, but from a professional perspective, she couldn't ask for better.

'Today?' Honestly. Always so demanding. 'This is going to be even bigger than your Scottish books. Edinburgh and Glasgow are great, but this is London we're talking about. Think film rights, even more merch. That's going to be a lot of money.' Jennifer was big on exaggeration, but it *was* good money and it *would* be a very exciting project, if it didn't involve an enormous and unpalatable lifestyle change for the next few months. 'So we'll speak later? You know what? Why don't *I* call *you*? This afternoon. Four p.m.?'

Cassie closed her eyes. This was why Jennifer was a very successful agent. She was also, occasionally, a nice person. Cassie should remember both those things and not judge her. 'Okay. Great.' Wonderful. Well, she'd think about it. Actually, maybe they could compromise. Set the new books in a different big city, like New York.

Jennifer hadn't finished. 'And don't tell me that we could set them in your backyard. It has to be London. Your Scottish ones sold a lot better than the Boston ones. They want British. That's the deal.' Mind reader as well as super-bossy. Irritating. 'Later.'

Cassie pressed red on her phone and looked out of the kitchen window at the sea again. Realistically there was going to be no time for a swim now.

Right. It was too early for wine. She needed chocolate and she needed a list.

Pros:
Perfect book deal
IVF – London fertility clinics

The money
Which would cover a lot of IVF cycles – very lucky to be able to afford
Fab to meet up with family and friends in London
Interesting to live in a city again
Especially London
Sightseeing
Extensive in-person shopping opportunities
Restaurants
Theatres

Cons:
Don't want to go back to the UK
Leaving the island:
Friends
Laura's 80th
Amy's 18th
The animals
House and garden
So much hassle
Expensive to rent somewhere nice

It was a lot easier to think without Jennifer shouting on the other end of the phone. Writing all your points down showed you what you needed to focus on. And that was the beauty of a list.

She stood up and opened a cupboard to grab a bar of raisin and almond chocolate.

Clearly, if she wanted to, she could sort the logistics of a move. She might get homesick and she didn't fancy having difficult memories triggered by being back in the UK. But actually, she should probably just give herself a mental slap and do it. Four years was a long time not to have been back.

The book deal was very tempting. It would be a dream to add another six books to her MacDuff Twins series.

And being close to fertility clinics was also very tempting. It would be so much easier to be staying down the road for the duration than to be on the island and having to take numerous trips to Boston, some of them overnighters and at short notice. What if she needed to go to the clinic but there was no ferry? Plus, if she did it in London she wouldn't have to tell anyone about it. If the whole experience reminded her of losing the baby four years ago and she started to fall apart, she'd have space to get herself back together.

God, now she was welling up. Pathetic. She put two squares of chocolate into her mouth and stood up again, to get a glass of water.

She'd just turned thirty-seven and she'd love to have children. Given the absence of attractive men beating down her door, it was looking like IVF with donated sperm was her best option. If she wasn't spurred into beginning treatment this year, she'd no doubt faff around for the next few months, like she had last year, and then tell herself that it was silly to start it during a snowy winter.

She took the water and chocolate out into the garden to go and see the animals. The bloodroot blossom smelled amazing. And her fruit and veg were shaping up to be fantastic this year. But they'd be great next year too.

Fred, the youngest alpaca, nudged her shoulder with his face and tried to snaffle the chocolate from her hand.

'Cheeky,' she told him.

She was going to miss the animals.

Oh, okay, wow, so apparently she was going to do it. It felt a bit mind-boggling, but it did also feel like the right decision – the career opportunity combined with how much easier it would be to do IVF in London than here.

Jennifer's shrill levels were going to be through the roof.

Cassie needed to start googling rentals. Good ones. The last time she'd been to London, she'd stayed in a very cheap hotel in Streatham, which had had an infestation – either large beetle or small cockroach, it had been hard to tell – round the radiator in the bathroom, a few stray short, curly hairs on the sheets, and some grim brown stains on the ceiling above the bed. In an ideal world, she'd rent a very nice and very clean flat in an appealing area of London, except that would presumably cost a fortune, and it would seem a waste not to end up with greater financial security after agreeing a lucrative deal, because writing wasn't exactly a consistent source of income. Maybe she should let out the house here and use that money to help pay for somewhere swanky in London. And as a bonus, if she got a good tenant, that would take care of a lot of the worry about the house and garden.

Cassie gave Fred another hug, went back inside, opened up three tabs on her laptop and typed in *London fertility clinics*, *Sperm donation UK* and *London leafy neighbourhoods*.

And… it was the middle of the day so the Wi-Fi was down. She'd have to google later.

*

'Cassie.' Three fifty-nine on the dot.

'Jennifer.'

'Made your decision?' So loud.

'Yes, I actually have. I think I'm going to do it.' It was as though Cassie had entered some kind of parallel reality. It still felt unbelievable that she was planning to move to London for the entire summer and hopefully start IVF. 'I'm googling rentals as we speak.' The Wi-Fi had sprung into action suddenly.

'Fantastic.' Woah. That sound. Cassie's *ear*. 'How soon can you be here? Next week?'

'Next *week*? Er, no? I have a lot to organise. I think I'm going to rent my house out, and I need to work out what area of London I want to be in and then find somewhere to live. Google tells me that the world's moved on since I last got involved in renting property.'

'You know what you should consider?' Jennifer's voice was down to just moderately hideous levels of shrillness. 'SwapBnB.'

'SwapBnB?'

'As it sounds.'

*

Cassie took a big, calming breath, and a big, calming slurp of her wine. She was nowhere near the end of a very long and very frustrating day.

Working out which things she 'required' in the swap she was looking for and which were 'desirable' had been difficult and boringly time-consuming, a *lot* less enjoyable than choosing an actual holiday. Cassie was fairly sure that she wanted to set her books in Hampstead and around the heath there, so she should probably rent there. Although Sod's Law she'd arrive in London, do a bit of sightseeing and discover that she wanted to set the stories around Wimbledon Common or Blackheath or who knew where – maybe somewhere she'd never heard of – and have a one hour-plus schlep every day to check places out. So maybe she should go for somewhere central. Also, she wanted to be at least reasonably close to the clinic or hospital she was going to go to for her treatment. Did she want to be in a modern block or a period mansion? Would she rather have access to a garden or be closer to the nearest Tube station? There were a lot of variables to consider.

Writing the one-sentence blurb for the SwapBnB ad had taken the three of them over an hour, which would have been ridiculous if it had been done by some semi-literate children, and was beyond ludicrous given that Cassie was a writer and Laura a retired headmistress, and Dina, another neighbour and very close friend, ran the most successful independent dolls-house business in the world from her attic.

'Okay. Read it to me again.' Cassie closed her eyes to help herself focus. The ad needed to scream *The perfect house swap for a luxurious London flat.*

Dina cleared her throat. 'Island house off coast of Maine with private beach, panoramic sea and headland views, three bedrooms, two bathrooms, state-of-the-art kitchen.'

'Do we *definitely* think it's okay that I just included the animals in the photos and didn't mention them specifically in the description? Do we think it definitely isn't mis-selling if I've alluded to them visually?'

'Again, yes.' Dina's glossy black retro-style glamour waves haircut remained firmly in place as she nodded her head emphatically. 'I think it's totally fine. I mean, it isn't like the swapper's going to have to look after them unless they want to. And people with land often have animals like deer or moose wandering around. So, if you pay someone else to feed them, they'll just be similar to wild deer or moose at the end of your large garden. For example.'

'True. And you'd think everyone would love alpacas and chickens. What about the *state-of-the-art* thing, though? Is that pushing it?'

'It's a wonderful kitchen,' Laura said. 'My mom always wanted a kitchen like this.' Maybe not the best indicator of modernity given that Laura was pushing eighty and had mentioned recently that it was the twenty-year anniversary of her mother's passing at the age of eighty-five.

'Well, thank you—' Cassie smiled at Laura '—but I think it's maybe just *nice* rather than state of the art. I can't say "nice" in the description, though. This is *so* hard. I could literally have written an entire chapter in the time it's taken to draft this.'

'I think just go with it.' Dina reached for the wine bottle and topped up their glasses. 'I mean, it says what we want. The photos and the location will be what really sell it.'

'And are we happy with the photos?' Cassie asked. Taking the photos for the website had been a nightmare, because, obviously, you wanted to make your house look as alluring as possible while not mis-selling it, but, also, she didn't want anyone other than the eventual swappee to be able to work out exactly where her house was or find out anything about her.

Simon, her ex, was a classic case of wanting what he couldn't have, and still tried to track her down occasionally via her cousins and friends, and she didn't want to speak to him. And fans of her MacDuff books and TV series were also sometimes keen to track her down, and Cassie didn't want to be famous.

'We totally are,' Dina said.

'Yes, I think we're done on photography for now, sweetie,' Laura said.

Yep. None of them had come out of the photo shoot happy. It had been fun at first but it had gone on for a *long* time. Laura had had to go home next door for a nap halfway through. Dina had had her nails shellacked during a trip to the mainland last week for her thirty-sixth birthday, and had broken four of them climbing up a tree for an 'aerial view' of the beach, and then one of the alpacas had pooed on her flip-flopped foot while she was herding it out of the way of a blueberry bush for a garden shot. And Cassie had got no work done all day and had ruined one of her favourite tops while crawling along the roof for another aerial shot. She should have got changed first.

'Okay. I'm doing it.' Cassie pressed Upload. She felt her heart rate pick up. Maybe she'd get hits immediately. Or not. 'Maybe no-one will be interested,' she said, while the computer did its thing, slowly.

'They will.' Laura patted her hand.

'Of course they will,' Dina said. 'Look at the hordes of summer tourists we get. And the house and garden are beautiful. And the beach. To die for. I mean, of *course* you will. No-one can resist a private beach. The question is whether you'll like any of their places enough to do the swap.'

They weren't going to find out any time soon.

'It's frozen.' Cassie waved the mouse around ineffectually. 'Maybe I should try uploading in "Small", "Medium" or "Large" instead of "Actual".'

'No, the photos are important. I think you need to have them in high def. I think you're going to have to do the three a.m. thing.' Dina cut more slices of blueberry pie and placed them on their plates. She was right. The one bad thing about living on the island was that if you needed to use a lot of broadband you had to make sure you did it when no-one else was competing for the gigas or megas or whatever. Cassie had forgotten to include that in her list yesterday. *London pro: unlimited broadband and Wi-Fi. London con: no easy excuse for avoiding your emails or social media.* 'You could maybe get away with two o'clock. It's been a bit better recently.'

'Maybe it's a sign that I shouldn't do it.' Cassie closed her laptop. 'Maybe the broadband gods are telling me just to stay at home. Tell me about your Saturday date instead. We've spent far too long talking about me moving. Let me get us some more wine.'

'Later. For the date lowdown, not the wine.' Dina eye-swivelled in Laura's direction and then raised her eyebrows suggestively. Cassie laughed. Dina liked an explicit conversation, while Laura did not. 'And no, the Wi-Fi is not telling you not to do it. Plus, haven't you signed the contract with the publisher?' Dina pulled the laptop over and re-opened it. 'But we should take the opportunity to re-check the ad. Laura and I both have nearly as much invested in this as you. We all need good neighbours.'

'I need to go home and check my online orders and sleep.' Dina looked at her watch. Laura had left them to it about an hour ago, saying that she thought she'd left her TV on and needed to switch it off. 'Wow. It's later than I thought. Nearly twelve thirty. The Wi-Fi might be working already. Try again?'

Cassie opened her laptop and started clicking. Yep, the island's normal-speed Wi-Fi had started early tonight. She had the photos uploaded within minutes.

'You all done?' Dina asked.

'No. I can't press it. It's too nerve-wracking.'

'But what's the worst that can happen?' Dina did a big hands-raised gesture, palms upwards. She had a very good point. The worst that could happen was that no-one wanted to swap with Cassie.

'*Do* it, *do* it.' Dina liked a chant when she'd had a bit too much wine.

'Okay. Doing it.' Cassie pressed Submit, and discovered that the Wi-Fi was still working, just as if they were on the mainland. She was 'live'. 'Quick, let's log in from our phones and view me.'

They had the website up on their phones within seconds.

They both stared at Cassie's house's web entry. For ages.

'Well,' said Cassie eventually, 'I kind of thought that something would happen immediately.'

'Honey, think about it. We're being stupid. It's the middle of the night here and still early morning in Europe,' Dina said. 'Things will definitely happen when they all get out of bed. By midday tomorrow you'll have so many wonderful offers you won't know which one to choose.'

Chapter Three

James

Ten o'clock on Saturday morning and James was barricaded, literally, in his apartment, screening his calls, with one eye on the angry emails piling up in his inbox and the other on the lucky, carefree joggers out in the park below. Probably on their way to get morning cappuccinos and brunches with friends.

It was looking like his breakfast might have to be the remains of Thursday's Deliveroo beef and shiitake mushroom in oyster sauce, which had been moderately nice at the time but probably wouldn't be that great this morning. If he went out now to buy food, though, there was the risk that Emily would be waiting for him outside the building or might even have got back inside again. He'd had the lock changed on Thursday but he wasn't fully convinced that that was enough to stop her.

He looked round his kitchen-living room. It was an estate agent's fantasy. Shiny appliances, greige paint, walnut floors, floor-to-ceiling windows with uber desirable views of Holland Park. And then there was the view he had through to the hall, of the armchair he'd wedged against the front door and the spaghetti ladle that he'd pushed through the key chain to stop Emily getting in.

Living the bloody dream.

Good to have finally found a use for the spaghetti ladle, though.

His phone was going nuts. So many messages.

They weren't *all* from people who wanted to kill him. For example, there was one from his sister Ella, and she was never anything but polite to him. He didn't feel like talking to her right now, though. Truth be told, since Leonie, his other sister, had died, he never felt like talking to Ella. Hearing her voice, so like Leonie's, stirred up too many emotions, plus there was the worry that she'd want to talk about Leonie. He didn't want to upset Ella, so normally he'd call her back and have a politely distant conversation; today, however, he couldn't face a duty chat. He'd speak to her in the next few days.

Another text landed. Matt. Yes. James hadn't told him about Wednesday evening yet but he did now feel like talking to his best friend.

Mate. I hear you ruined Emily's entire decade if not her life by not proposing the other night. Also hear she lost it. How's your face?

What? Unbelievable how news travelled. Surely Matt didn't know anyone who'd been at the party. Probably some Facebook thing. Matt was big on social media. James wasn't.

He took his phone into his bedroom and closed the door. He was pretty sure that the front door was soundproof, but just in case. If Emily was outside, he didn't want to make her even more homicidal. If she damaged his front door he could obviously ask Dee to find someone to fix it, but there was every chance it would involve a lot of hassle. He'd thought that Emily was done after Wednesday night, and she hadn't been back on Thursday, but yesterday evening there she'd been again, and she'd also knocked twice this morning. The building security guys were great for banter and taking deliveries and letting tradespeople in but not so hot on actual security.

Emily had sounded so out of control last night that he'd genuinely wondered if she'd be coming back with some kind of weapon or tool to get inside. Fortunate that your average Londoner would probably struggle to lay their hands on a gun or chainsaw first thing on a Saturday morning.

Matt answered on the first ring. 'So what happened at the party?'

'Basically, she thought we were in a serious relationship and I didn't realise. And also, she's a little unhinged it turns out.'

'Yeah. I've seen the video on Facebook. Did she draw blood?' Video. Marvellous.

'Yep. She has very strong nails.'

'You going to have a permanent scar?'

'Yep, think so.'

'Ouch.'

'Yeah. Then she turned up here after I got home and let herself in with a key that I didn't know she had.'

'Woah. Mate. What then?'

'She started hitting me around the head, so I moved her outside and barricaded the door. Security had to escort her out.'

'That's a bad evening.'

'Yeah. I'd had a shitty day, too. I had to make over two hundred people redundant.' On paper, James had just been doing his job, but, in practice, it was never comfortable witnessing the devastation of people who might not be able to meet their mortgages or pay their school fees.

On the one hand, it was arguably foolhardy to earn enough for a fancy lifestyle involving a big house, private schools and expensive holidays, but not save for a rainy day. If any of these people had had a childhood like James's, they'd probably have learned to be a lot more prudent. James's mother, and by extension her children, had frequently barely known where the next meal was coming from, let alone new clothes or a holiday.

On the other hand, you'd have to be made of stone not to feel sympathy watching a grown man cry. Plus, James didn't like to be reminded even slightly about unemployment or poverty.

'That's a bad day,' Matt said.

'Yep. With ongoing backlash.' How the hell had so many of these people got hold of his phone number? It was bad enough that a lot of them had found his email address, but the messages and the phone calls were ridiculous. And what did they expect James to do about the redundancies? He was just doing his job. Without that loss-making part of the business, the rest of the company his fund had just bought should survive. With it, the whole thing would almost certainly go under, and then a lot more people would lose their jobs. 'I'm wondering how so many of these people knew how to find me.'

'Facebook. I'm on there now. Emily's posted stuff online about you and she's given out your personal email address and phone number and linked it all to your firm.'

'Christ.' He should *not* have told her that he'd had a bad day on Wednesday. Never confide in anyone except your closest friends. If you confided at all.

'Yep. Sorry, mate. What're you going to do now?'

'Well, that's the question. How far will she go? She's been back a couple of times. Is she going to keep coming? And how many times is she going to get past Security? I obviously don't want to see her again. For a start, I don't want to have to manhandle her out of my way.'

'Yeah, definitely don't do that. She might claim you'd attacked her.'

'Exactly. But I don't want to call the police myself because, you know, you just don't, do you?' James was fairly sure that Matt didn't really know. James hated all things remotely sordid. They'd had the police round a few times when he was a child and he didn't want to revisit those memories. By contrast, it was pretty unlikely that police visits had featured heavily in Matt's childhood with happily married parents in a large house in a leafy suburb of Dublin. In fact, James would know if they had. Matt was an open book, which it was easy to be when all the pages of your life were as clean and wholesome as Matt's were.

'Fair enough,' Matt said. 'Did you take selfies of the injuries to your face? If not, maybe you should? Also, you have your one hundred and fifty witnesses. And I can save the recording from Facebook. She can't argue with that. What about, if she gets past your building security you just threaten to call the police and hope that does the trick? I think you also need to tell her you'll call the police if she posts your home address.'

'Yeah, I think you're right.'

'What are you doing today? Want me to come over now and check whether the coast's clear? Or you're very welcome to move into our spare room for as long as it takes. Becca's mum left yesterday.' James thought longingly of Matt and his wife Becca's spare room in their house in Clapham and even more longingly of Matt's frequent barbecues and Becca's tendency to insist on making large fry-up breakfasts for anyone in the house. And less longingly of their six-week-old, Charlie, and his tendency to scream the house down for half the night, according to Matt. Yup, he wasn't going to go. If he needed to move out, he'd sleep a lot better in a hotel.

'Thank you. Both very tempting offers but I'm big enough and ugly enough to look after myself, and I think you and Becca need your time with Charlie. I'll take your advice on the selfies and the police threat, and go out now to get some breakfast if she isn't there.'

'Not ugly enough, mate. That's your problem. The offer's always there.'

'Thank you.' Matt was a great friend.

James changed into running kit and then decided that he should message Emily sooner rather than later.

Emily. If you give my personal details to anyone else I will call the police. I would remind you also that a lot of people saw you physically attack me on Wednesday, and not all of them would be willing to perjure themselves in court, plus I have a video.

Two grey ticks but she didn't pick it up.

He poked his head outside the front door. No sign of her in the hall outside; hopefully he was safe to go out.

She was there, waiting outside the building, when James got back with a takeaway granola and a coffee after a satisfyingly pounding run. For a moment he considered leaving again, and then he decided that he wasn't going to be pushed out of his own home.

She held out a bakery bag as he approached. 'I brought you breakfast to apologise. I'm sorry I lost my temper. I shouldn't have shared your details online.' Right.

'That's kind, thank you,' James said, not smiling, 'but I've already got breakfast.'

'Could we talk?' Emily smiled at him and put her hand on his arm. James shook his head slightly. The contrasts between her moods were frightening.

He moved his arm away from her, and said, 'I'm sorry, but no. I have a busy day.'

Emily smiled again and said, 'Okay, later.' She leaned forward to kiss his cheek before he could step away from her, and then set off down the road. James shook his head again and went inside. He really hoped he wouldn't be talking to her later. After everything he'd experienced with his mother and his sister Leonie, he didn't ever want to be involved in a complicated relationship again. Or any kind of serious relationship, for that matter.

Forty-five minutes later, after he'd had his breakfast and a bracing shower, James sat down in his office to go through some work. It was clear from the mountain of emails and texts he'd received that Emily had done an excellent job of broadcasting his personal details far and wide.

He was going to have to change his phone number and his email address. It didn't seem like something Dee would be able to sort out without significant input from him, so he might as well just do it himself. Such a waste of time.

He actually would call the police if Emily posted his home address online. You couldn't easily change where you lived, and he really didn't want to. He liked it here.

Mid-afternoon, the doorbell rang.

On his way to the door, he took a look at the security camera to check that Emily hadn't somehow made it back in again. Nope. It was a man he didn't recognise. Probably a delivery. Sometimes people left parcels downstairs; sometimes they brought them up. Had he ordered anything online in the past week? Had he asked Dee to order anything for him? He couldn't remember. He swung open the door.

'James.' The man wasn't in normal delivery driver garb. He was wearing a suit. He looked vaguely familiar now. Probably late forties, maybe early fifties, shortish, pleasant face. 'I wondered if I could have a word? About the job?' His voice was shaking, and his eyes were staring. He had to be one of the employees James had made redundant this week. Clearly, he had no idea how many people James had spoken to. How could he seriously remember any of them as individuals? More importantly, how the hell had the man found James's address? Via Emily? 'Could I possibly come in?'

Come in? No, of course not. James's home was his sanctuary. He did work from home sometimes, in his study, but what work he did and when was his choice. He never invited anyone except his closest friends over. And, occasionally, women, and that had just been shown to be a huge mistake, so he wouldn't be doing that again any time soon. And he certainly wouldn't be inviting this guy inside. He could be as off the rails as Emily, for all James knew. He certainly had to be desperate, or he wouldn't be here, and James did not want desperation over his threshold again.

James patted his jeans pocket to check that he had his keys, moved outside and pulled the door closed behind him.

'I'm sorry. I can't talk. There isn't anything else to say, unfortunately.' He took a couple of steps round the man, to indicate physically that the conversation was over. The man turned so that they were still facing each other. James started to walk towards the lift. The man followed him.

'I don't know if you remember my name. Tim West.' Of course James hadn't remembered. 'I did some detective work to find your address. I hope you don't mind. It's just very important that I speak to you.' James did mind. It was better than if Emily had been sharing his address, but it wasn't great.

'I hope you understand that like everyone I have to have a line between work and home, and I can't have people calling on me here in person.'

'Not to worry,' Tim said. 'I wouldn't tell anyone else and they won't find you. I actually went to your office yesterday and followed you home and noted the address.' Woah. Stalker-like and *admitting* to it. Doubly unnerving.

Tim was ploughing on with his obviously pre-prepared spiel. 'I've been working at Leadson's for twenty-nine years. I love my job. More importantly, I'm good at my job. I have ideas about how we can improve the business. I understand that some streamlining's necessary but I think you're making a mistake in letting the entire division go. It never works as well if you bring outside management in without retaining some of the people with knowledge.' His voice cracked. 'And I need this job. I don't know how I'd get another one. My knowledge is very specific. I'm at twenty-nine years and eight months. After thirty years of service I'd have been able to take early retirement and access my pension.'

Christ, if you allowed yourself to think about things like this and you weren't shaken by the invasion of your personal privacy, you could feel very sad. But you couldn't let sentiment into business. Ultimately that made for poor decisions, lower profits and more job losses in the future.

James pressed the button for the lift and cleared his throat.

'Sorry, sorry,' Tim rushed on before James could speak. 'I didn't plan to mention the personal side of things. That's irrelevant. What's relevant is that I can help you and you're making a mistake in letting me go. Please? Could we at least talk this through?'

James hadn't made a mistake in making Tim redundant; he'd made a rational business decision. He did make a mistake in looking down at Tim's face and seeing the pleading in his eyes. Hard to ignore that.

'I can't intervene personally, I'm afraid,' he said. 'I hope you understand that I wouldn't be able to do this for everyone, so I can't do it for anyone. Your best bet would be to work on your CV and submit it to HR. There's a possibility that some who are at risk of redundancy will be considered for other roles within the business. Very few people, though. Please don't get your hopes up.' The lift door opened and James nodded at Tim. 'Goodbye and good luck.' He stuck his hand out.

Tim shook it fervently and said, 'Thank you,' before he got into the lift, which really didn't make James feel good.

'I'll speak to HR on your behalf as well,' he told Tim as the doors closed. James shook his head. He'd had no choice about the redundancies last week. It was hard not to feel awful, though, when you witnessed the fallout.

*

James arrived early for beers that evening with Matt and a couple of other university friends.

He'd received a message from Emily's mother late afternoon telling him that he was 'a shocking commitment-phobe' and 'a wolf in a handsome sheep's clothing' and that he'd 'ruined Emily's life'; and had decided that he'd rather be in the pub than at home.

He chose a table for four in a corner and sat down with a pint of low alcohol lager and a packet of smoky bacon crisps.

He hadn't felt like this in a long time. Not at ease in his own home and his own daily life. Time for a holiday, maybe, except he was only just back from skiing last month and he was very busy with work. He and his private equity partners had discussed recently the idea that one of them might spend some time out in the States, working with their Boston and New York offices. There were a lot of opportunities out there that they wanted to look at, including ecotourism.

Maybe he should think seriously about a stint in the US.

He munched crisps, staring at a very odd picture of a crowned frog on a cushion above the mantelpiece. He probably should broaden his horizons. Thirty-five years old and he'd lived his entire life in London. He'd come a long way since childhood, from the small high-rise flat in a crowded estate, but by distance it was actually only about two miles.

Yeah, a temporary move to the States was genuinely tempting.

'You should, mate,' Matt told him later on when James had finished describing where his thoughts had taken him. 'And rent the flat out. Give you peace of mind.'

'Tricky to find the ideal renter, though?'

'Swonbee.' Josh spoke through a mouthful of half-pounder. He swallowed. 'Sorry. SwapBnB. You literally swap properties, with some obvious caveats. We've done it three times. Some great places on there. You start by putting a ballpark rental value on your own property but you can go higher or lower if you and the other party agree. Where are you looking at?'

'Somewhere commutable to both Boston and New York, but probably somewhere rural. I want to look at investing in some ecotourism businesses.' The whole idea was sounding more and more appealing.

'Two of the three swaps we did were in the US. Both great.'

'Thanks, mate. I'll check it out this evening.' James was liking the sound of SwapBnB. Really liking it. If there was a great-looking house on there in a good location he might genuinely go for it.

It turned out that Emily had been back while James was out. Henry, on security, had been primed, so she hadn't made it inside; but she'd left a bottle of wine for James. He passed the wine to Henry.

He was liking the idea of a US sabbatical more and more. A sabbatical involving calm, solitude and no women.

Chapter Four

Cassie

'Goddid,' Dina slurred. 'Totally got it.'

Cassie blinked and shook her head. Serious googling was hard work on the island. You either had to stay up late or set your alarm and get up in the middle of the night, or you had to sit in the garden to get reception and squint at your phone. Tonight it was raining, so they'd gone for the staying up option. They'd combined it with wine and now Cassie's eyes felt *heavy*.

'Got what?' she said, still blinking.

'You were *asleep*.' Dina pointed an accusatory finger in Cassie's face.

'No.' Cassie shook her head again. 'I was just resting my eyes. They hurt.' They'd been staring at the screen for a *long* time plus it was four o'clock in the morning. Of *course* she'd been asleep. And now she was really, really aching because a kitchen chair for a mattress and her forearms on the table for a pillow were a poor substitute for her lovely comfortable actual bed, and when forty wasn't that many years off you *really* valued your own pillow for not getting neck-ache at night. Maybe she'd take herself back to bed in the morning for a bit more sleep once she'd got the chickens up and sorted their water and feed.

'Anyway. Look at this.' Dina moved round to Cassie's side of the table, pulling her laptop with her. 'Got to be him. James Grey. Director of a company registered to the same address. He looks like a *stud*. I'd be totally happy for you to swap with him. He looks like he'd be a *great* neighbour.'

'You cannot tell whether someone would be a good neighbour by *looking* at them,' Cassie said. She peered at the photo on Dina's screen. Oh. Okay. No, she'd been wrong. You could *totally* tell. 'No. He'd be a shit neighbour. I mean it. And I don't want to swap with him.'

'What? Whaddya mean? He's got the most amazing apartment *ever*, in what looks like an amazing location, he wants to swap for the right length of time, and he's got a smart haircut and a good suit so he's probably someone who'd be anal and look after your property well. He's the dream swappee. And he's *hot*.'

'He is not the dream swappee. Someone *looking* neat and tidy means nothing. You can't judge a book by its cover. I think he'd be a terrible swappee. I think he'd be unsupportive, untrustworthy and, basically, horrible, and I don't want him in my house.' Whoops, Cassie's voice was shaking.

Dina was staring at her. 'Honey, are you okay? You're sounding a little nuts. You don't know him at all, right?'

'I know his type.'

'But you just said you can't judge a book by its cover. Honey, what's wrong?'

'He looks very similar to my ex.' Simon had betrayed her when she was at her most vulnerable and she didn't like to be reminded of that time.

'You do know that two people can look similar but be very different? This man is not your ex, he's a completely different person.'

'I suppose so. I mean, obviously, yes. I suppose he doesn't look *exactly* the same. It's more the impression he gives. That blond, good-looking, swaggery look.'

'Two things. You cannot see a swagger from a corporate headshot. And you cannot dislike all blond, good-looking, confident-looking men for the rest of time. It isn't good for you disliking people on sight.'

'Not always good for you *liking* everyone on sight.'

Dina was looking for a happily ever after and had a tendency to like men very quickly, and it often ended in tears.

'Honey. I get a lot more sex than you do and that's a good thing. But I tell you what: you stop *dis*liking gorgeous men on sight and I'll stop *liking* them on sight. And do not cut off your nose to spite your face. Please? This is the perfect apartment for you. It's the perfect swap. And it's not like you'll ever have to meet him anyway.'

Yeah, maybe Dina was right.

*

'I just got an email from James.' Cassie gave her coat to Dina, put her phone back in her bag and took the glass Dina was holding out. 'Thank you.' She took a big sip. Wild blueberry sparkling wine was a relatively new speciality from a southern Maine vineyard that Cassie and Dina had visited on a wine tasting last summer. It was delicious, at least as good as champagne or Prosecco. Oh, God. Cassie was really going to miss her life here. 'This wine is *so* good. So anyway, he wants to speak before we sign on the dotted line.'

'Sounds reasonable.' Dina chucked Cassie's coat onto a sofa in her sitting room, pulled the door closed and led the way through the hall towards her kitchen, where the rest of the Hawk Egg lobster festival committee were assembled.

Cassie screwed her face up. 'There's no real point in us speaking,' she told Dina. 'I mean, we know a *lot* about each other now. He's been very anal in checking my background.' If they spoke on the phone rather than by email, there was a chance she'd end up snapping at him if he asked yet more questions. It seemed the basic SwapBnB checks hadn't been enough for James. In the end, Cassie had, in the space of forty-eight hours, provided him with passport and driving licence details, proof of her dual British and US residency (she'd been born in the US before moving to Glasgow as a baby) – apparently he suspected her of some kind of visa scam – plus a bank reference, proof of ownership of her property, various health details, all manner of things. Frankly, it had been a surprise that she hadn't had to supply her dental and vaccination records. She'd been on the brink of pulling out several times, but each time had remembered that his flat looked *perfect* – location, layout, size, niceness, everything – and none of the other options she'd found had looked remotely right for her.

They went into the kitchen and Cassie distributed hugs and hellos to her friends before taking another slurp of her wine. That was good.

'It can't hurt to speak to him, though, can it?' Dina asked, as Cassie joined her at the side of the room to gather snacks to carry them to the table.

'He's very annoying. Very demanding.'

'People often come across that way in writing and are sweethearts in person, though.'

'That's true.' Cassie chewed her lip. 'And it would be good to be on friendly terms with him. I just don't want to discover that I can't stand the man who's going to be living in my house.'

'Honey—' Dina reached round Cassie for bowls '—you're swapping homes. He isn't an ogre. He's a regular human being. If he *isn't* a regular human being, you don't want to swap homes with him. Speaking to him will be totally fine.'

Cassie nodded. Dina was probably right.

'You know what?' Dina waved a pretzel in Cassie's face. 'By the end of the call I bet you'll be the best of friends.' She handed the pretzel bowl and one containing cheesy crackers to Cassie. 'Guaranteed.'

*

Cassie huddled into her coat and pulled her faux-fur-lined hood closer. She squinted through the bright-blue fluff of the fur at the steel grey clouds above the sea. She should have given James her landline number. Her mobile almost never worked inside the house, so she had to be outside to speak on it, and, even without the rain that was threatening, this afternoon wasn't *the* most pleasant for sitting in the garden. She checked the time. One minute to go.

And approximately sixty seconds later, her phone rang. Not a surprise. You'd guess from his photo and emails that James was punctual. Anal. Not a hair out of place. Not a reference un-asked for. To be fair, Cassie did like punctuality, but not to a ridiculous extent.

'Cassie.'

'Hi, James.'

'Thanks for agreeing to a call. I had a couple of points I wanted to discuss that I thought would be easier by speaking rather than emailing back and forth.' He had a deep voice with a bit of a rasp, and was both extremely London and extremely confident-sounding. It was the kind of voice a lot of women liked. Cassie herself had gone for that type of man in the past; now she was older and wiser.

'Okay, great,' she said, not meaning it. There'd be a lot to say once the swap started, obviously, because they'd want to tell each other how things in their respective houses worked, give each other advice, all sorts of things, but there was no point going through any of that now, because they'd just forget.

'Firstly, I thought it would be good to touch base, just really to confirm that we are who we say we are.' What? He still didn't believe she was definitely who she said she was after conducting possibly the most anal pre-house-letting due diligence of all time?

'Right. Well, yes, I am me.'

'Great.' There was a pause. Maybe he'd just realised how ridiculous he sounded. 'And I am me, of course.'

'Excellent,' Cassie said. Honestly.

'The other main reason that I wanted to speak to you was to agree the start date of the swap. We should probably actually have done this before exchanging all our other details.'

'Okay, no problem.' When they'd filled in their online forms, James had said that he could start any time and Cassie had said she could start in about a month's time. She wanted to be around for Dina's daughter Amy's eighteenth, plus it would take time to pack. She'd started preparing the house and she'd started on some notes for James, as and when things occurred to her, but she was in no way ready. So, since James could do any time, they would presumably start when Cassie wanted to. Ideal. 'Thank you for being flexible.'

'Sorry, but I'm not flexible.'

'You aren't?'

'No. I'm afraid that I need to start the swap immediately,' he said.

'But you said on the online form that you could do any time starting now.'

'The form was badly constructed in that sense. It didn't give me the opportunity to say exactly what I meant, which is that not only can I start the swap soon, I do need to start the swap within the next week.'

'But I can't start for at least three or four weeks.'

'Is that due to work or family commitments?'

James wasn't coming across like someone who'd be sympathetic to her being a slow packer and wanting to be around for a birthday party and, if she was honest, just needing a bit of time to get her head round the whole big-move thing. Maybe it would be better to be vague.

'It's for a number of reasons,' she said.

'And there's nothing you can change?'

'Not really.' Cassie went for her best assertive tone, the one she used when the alpacas wouldn't do what she wanted. 'Sorry.'

'Apologies, then,' James said, not sounding that apologetic. 'I need to start the swap immediately. If you can't commit to starting within the next week, perhaps we should both look for an alternative.' *Noooo.* Cassie wanted to stay in James's flat. But it would be a nightmare getting ready for the swap that quickly. And there was the party.

'I can do three weeks from now,' she said. She could go straight after the party.

'Too late, I'm afraid. Not a problem. I'm sure we can both find other swaps that we like. Apologies for having wasted your time.'

There was no way Cassie was going to find another place that she liked as much. She didn't want to spend several months knowing that if she'd just foregone one party and got her packing skates on she could be living somewhere so much better.

'When's the latest you could start the swap?' she asked.

'Next weekend.'

'Right.' Cassie stuck her middle finger up at the phone. Very satisfying actually. 'Fine. Okay. Let's do that.' Crap. She was going to have a *lot* to do this week. And she was going to miss the party. She *could* stay for it. Dina would definitely happily have her as a guest for a few days. But no, it would be too weird living next door to her own house. It would be better just to take the hit on the party and go. There'd be other parties.

'Thank you.' Not a hint of a smile in his voice. Honestly.

*

The following weekend, having moved mountains to get everything ready, Cassie heard wheels crunch over the stones in the drive, gave the flowers in the vase in the hall a final nudge into place, and grabbed her coat and bag.

By the time James had parked, she was outside the house, wearing her best welcoming smile. Which he probably wouldn't be able to see, because, after a beautiful morning, this afternoon's weather had been rain, rain and more rain, which was currently so heavy that visibility was almost as poor as if it were night-time, plus Cassie had her hood pulled tight round her face, because there was far too much wind for an umbrella.

'Hi, James,' she said as he got out of his car. Leaped out, really. He was a lot bigger than she'd expected – both tall and broad – rugby-player big. He wasn't dressed like a rugby player, though. Through the rain, she could just about make out that he was wearing smart jeans and a cashmere-type jumper, with suede loafers. His hair was blond and sharply cut, and definitely gelled. His handsome face held a polite but aloof smile.

'Good afternoon. Excuse me for a moment.' He gestured at the rain and turned and reached inside the car for a very new-looking khaki-green waxed jacket. The kind that your rich city-dweller might imagine that a country-dweller wore but which in fact they did not wear. Cassie wondered whether it was properly waterproof. James would know the answer to that within a small number of minutes if they stood outside for too long. His feet would be soaked, too.

'Why don't we go inside?' she said, loudly, so that he'd be able to hear her over the downpour. 'I can show you around outside later, when it stops raining. I know that this seems very heavy, but according to the forecast it's only a shower, and there's blue sky over there. The weather can change remarkably quickly here. I think it'll be dry and sunny within fifteen or twenty minutes.'

'Inside? Apologies. I didn't catch your name.' Who did he think she was?

'I'm so sorry.' Should she go and shake hands with him? He seemed like quite a formal person. Best not, actually; it was far too wet. 'I should have said. I'm Cassie.'

'Cassie? Cassie Adair?' He frowned. 'We did agree today?'

'Oh, yes, we did, I just thought it would be nice to stay and show you around. I mean, I left you some notes, but, you know, I thought maybe I should talk you through things.' She took a couple of steps towards the house. James didn't follow. He just stood there next to his hire car, his hair now completely wet and the shoulders of his coat already dark from the water. She'd bet good money that some of the water had already soaked through the coat onto his jumper.

'Stay?' he asked, with barely a hint of a smile now, and his eyebrows raised.

'Oh, no, not here,' she told him. 'I moved out yesterday. I'm staying with my neighbour and good friend, Dina. You'll meet her soon, I'm sure.' He was actually pursing his lips slightly. 'I'm leaving tomorrow.' It suddenly felt important to clarify that. 'I just thought it would be useful to meet and run through a couple of things in person.'

'That's very kind, but I think I'm good. Pretty sure I can work everything out for myself. If you could just leave me the keys, that would be great.' He smiled only very slightly, and turned his back on her, like he was dismissing her, opened the boot of his car and started taking out very new-looking smart, dark-grey luggage. All matching.

Cassie glared at his back. She'd bent over *backwards* to accommodate his request to start the swap a good two to three weeks earlier than she'd wanted. She didn't expect actual thanks but she also didn't expect him to be *rude* to her.

Right. Well, she should just go, then.

No. She shouldn't just go. She'd moved on in the past four years, and she was no longer a woman who took this kind of crap. They were obviously going to need to be in touch while they were living in each other's houses. She wasn't starting their swap relationship like this. She was going to tell him what she thought.

Chapter Five

James

James walked round Cassie and over to the porch outside her front door and placed the first two of his suitcases on the dry ground there. Hopefully, by the time he'd got back to the car to get the other two cases, she'd have buggered off back to the neighbour's house.

He was an adult. He didn't need to be shown round the house by its owner; he needed to look around and unpack in peace. The drive up from Boston to Maine via the scenic coastal route had been glorious, but the long queue for the ferry out to the island had been pretty un-glorious, as was this bloody rain. He clearly didn't want to talk to a complete stranger right now.

The complete stranger was ranting at him, he realised, as he turned round. He couldn't hear a word that she said, due to the rain and the fact that she was about fifteen feet away from him. He also couldn't see her face, or anything of her other than some long dark hair escaping from her hood and the fact that she was quite short, but her body language was clear. She had one hand on where her hip would be underneath her enormous coat, and with the other was gesticulating in a finger jabbing kind of way.

Whatever. If he didn't engage, hopefully she'd just go away. The only thing he needed from her was the front door key.

'Great,' he said, when she'd finished her inaudible tirade. 'Is the front door open?'

She took a couple of steps closer to him and said, 'Great?' Okay, so she was within earshot again.

'Yes. Is the front door open?'

'What do you mean great?'

James shook his head slightly. He turned back round to try the door. It was open. Good news. He would need the key, though.

He turned back to Cassie. 'This is great,' he said. 'Fantastic. Thank you. Kind of you to welcome me. Could I get the key?'

'Frankly, that's a poor apology.'

'Sorry, what am I apologising for?'

'As I *said*, I moved heaven and earth to change my dates for you, and I think a lot of people would have acknowledged that.' She had a very attractive accent. He'd noticed it on the phone and again now. Scottish. Or Irish. He could never tell the difference, which he knew was shocking, especially given that Matt was from Dublin, but in his defence he was pretty sure that there were a lot of similarities. Her voice was attractive too, warm and soft. Her attitude, however, wasn't that soft. She'd been snippy from start to finish. She'd been reluctant to provide the extra documentation he'd asked for – very reasonably, surely, in that they were entrusting each other with their homes. She'd been awkward about the start date for their swap, with no reasonable explanation given. And now she wanted 'acknowledgement'. Her face was obscured by the ridiculous bright-blue fake fur all the way round her large hood, but at a guess she'd be looking angry.

Well, fine. He'd both apologise and thank her, and hopefully she'd just leave, immediately.

'I'm sorry and I'm very grateful,' he said. 'Thank you. Very kind. If I could just get the key?'

Cassie pulled it out of her pocket, took a couple of steps forward and plonked it into his hand.

'Have a great stay,' she said. 'Let me know if you need anything.'

'I'm sure I'll be fine,' he said. 'Thanks again. Have a good flight.' He hoped she was leaving tomorrow.

'Thank you.' She didn't sound like she meant it, which made no difference to him. Hopefully they'd never speak again.

'Bye,' he said. His feet were soaking. These loafers were new, and they were probably ruined. If Cassie hadn't been here, either he'd have waited in the car until this shower blew over – if it was indeed short-lived – or he'd have got himself inside quickly. Either way, his shoes would probably have survived a lot better.

'Goodbye.' And, thank God, off she squelched.

By the time James had all his luggage inside the flamingo-wallpapered – yes, really – hall, the rain had, as Cassie had predicted, suddenly stopped. Probably a good idea to explore outside now, in case another shower started.

The setting was as perfect as Cassie's photos and Google Earth had indicated. When Cassie had quibbled about the start date, he'd nearly pulled out. He'd had his eye on another couple of options, one in Vermont, in the mountains, and the other by a lake in New Hampshire, but he'd liked the idea of island living, and the tourism business opportunities it might present, and now that he didn't have Cassie in his face, he could see that this was looking great.

It didn't seem likely that he'd be disturbed by neighbours, which was ideal. Cassie's plot was on the tip of a headland at the end of the island furthest away from the little ferry terminal, down a lane from the centre of the nearby village, in a cluster of five or six houses.

The house itself was low, wide and wooden. James walked round the side of it and found a large and beautiful garden. The views from the garden were stunning – the ocean, some other islands, or fields and woodland, depending where you looked. He nodded. Idyllic at first sight.

He continued through the garden towards the ocean. And, yes, there was an actual gate onto a little beach. The beach was the stuff of fantasies, particularly those of investors in the tourism industry. Fine white sand. Blue ripply sea. Great views including nearby uninhabited-looking islands. Silence apart from sea birds, lapping water and an odd animal clicking kind of sound somewhere to his right. Essentially unspoilt and yet easily accessible from the East Coast of America. Pretty spectacular. There had to be some great business opportunities here. People loved holidays in this kind of environment.

James pulled his jumper off over his head – incredible how much warmer it was now that it had stopped raining – and turned to walk back towards the house. Time to check out the interior. Maybe he'd unpack and then go for a swim if the weather stayed like this for the rest of the day.

Wow. He hadn't focused on Cassie's garden furniture on his way towards the beach. Now he was seeing it in its full psychedelic glory. On a patio outside double doors at the back of the house, which appeared to lead into the kitchen, were metallic chairs and a table in a riot of purple, orange and pink stripes merging into each other. Where could you even buy stuff like that? And *why* would you buy stuff like it?

The colour theme continued inside the house. Seriously. Cassie really loved her colour. The flamingo wallpaper was pretty muted by comparison to some of the rooms. No wonder she'd included mainly photos of the garden and its surroundings on the swap website. Too many up-close images of the interior could definitely scare some potential swappers off.

The woman also loved her books. There were full bookcases everywhere, with no discernible filing system. On one shelf alone she had *Golf for Beginners, The Portuguese Cork Industry, Harry Potter*, a couple of Mills & Boons, Charles Dickens and some modern fiction, with block-coloured spines and authors James didn't recognise.

One shelf was completely clear, and very well dusted, presumably ready for him to arrange his non-existent collection of 'Books I cannot travel without and have therefore transported from London to this island'. Even if he read more than about two non-fiction books a year – he'd read no fiction since school – he wouldn't have brought them with him, would he? And didn't most people have Kindles nowadays?

Upstairs, all three of the large double beds were made, with starched-looking white bed linen and bright – of course – velvet bedspreads. There were also piles of sparkling white towels on each bed.

Why hadn't Cassie had the beds left stripped, as he had in his flat? He'd had his cleaner and the concierge company put all the flat contents other than furniture and kitchen basics into storage. Who wanted to sleep in someone else's bed linen and use someone else's towels?

James certainly didn't. After a childhood in an often dirty flat, with grubby sheets, sometimes with unappealing strange men staying with his mother, he had an extreme aversion to mess, dirt, and sharing personal items with strangers. It was alright in a high-end hotel where they had industrial washing machines, but in a domestic home? Not so much.

Speaking of which, where were his parcels? Dee had ordered all the necessities he could possibly want for his stay on the island, and had texted earlier to say that they'd arrived and been signed for. Presumably it was Cassie who'd signed for them. He should have asked her. No way was he getting in touch with her again, though. He'd find them.

He'd noticed a couple of envelopes with his name on them downstairs. Maybe she'd left a note saying where she'd stored the parcels.

The first envelope, on a sideboard in the hall, next to a vase with big fresh orange and red flowers in it – thoughtful of Cassie, yes, but completely unnecessary – contained several typed pages.

Cassie was welcoming him to her home, as though he were a guest, and had made a list of instructions and suggestions. Like he was lacking in common sense and unable to use Google. Clearly a woman with time on her hands.

She'd listed 'useful information' about the house and the village and the island, and even the mainland, by category. She'd grouped things into an actual index. It looked like she'd included details about every conceivable part of life here, and also some inconceivable parts, like clubs – bridge, not night – and social events. There were a lot of events for such a small place. There were probably a lot in London too, for people who were bored enough.

James skim-read a couple of the pages.

The annual lawnmower race was taking place in a month's time. Cassie imagined that James would like to go, and had included details on where her lawnmower was and how it worked so that he could *join in*. There were pages and pages of information. A lot of lists. The vast majority of it pointless.

She kept alpacas and chickens in the field at the end of the garden. What? She'd lined someone up to feed them but he'd be welcome to feed them himself if he liked. Nope. Obviously not.

He hoped she wouldn't be disappointed that he hadn't made any lists for her. But they weren't friends. They were effectively renting each other's properties. Estate agents did not leave you lists of your neighbours' telephone numbers or details on when the next full moon would be because night-time kayaking was blissful. Even if he wanted to, James wouldn't have that kind of information to share. Like your average Londoner, he didn't know his neighbours and he didn't get involved in niche clubs and activities. He worked, he worked out, and he went out with his friends, not his neighbours.

He put the list back down on the hall sideboard and wandered into the kitchen. The other envelope he'd seen was on the kitchen table. What more could Cassie have to say?

'Bugger me, the woman loves a list.' He'd pulled the notes out of the second envelope and was flicking through them. It looked like these covered different aspects of life from the ones in the hall. Thorough wasn't the word. Cassie had included so many things it would take him a week to digest all this information, if he wanted to. She had a master list. She had sub lists. She had sub-sub lists. She'd literally even pointed him in the direction of her cookery books. Which, unlike the ordering chaos of all her other books, she had arranged by cuisine and by genre of cooking (starters, meat, fish, Scandinavian, New England, French; the list could and did go on).

She'd also left him a fridgeful and a cupboardful of fresh food and he was welcome to anything he liked from the freezer. She'd stocked it with meals in one-person portions for him because he wasn't likely to want to go shopping immediately, she thought.

'Bugger me,' he said again. Clearly they'd had different ideas about what a house swap entailed.

'Language,' said a woman from somewhere behind him. From inside the room. She sounded elderly, very Jessica-Fletcher like.

He turned round, clocking as he went some copper saucepans hanging from the timbered ceiling. Just on the off chance he needed a weapon.

The woman on the other side of the kitchen did look as though she'd stepped out of *Murder, She Wrote*. Elderly and very small, although upright, and wearing a red twin set. And holding what looked like a cake tin.

'Hello?' he said. It didn't seem like the copper saucepans were going to be necessary. A map might be, though. Had she wandered in here by mistake?

'I'm Laura. I live next door. I brought you a blueberry pie and I have packages for you at my house. They were delivered this morning. Cassie was out running last-minute errands, so I took them in.' The cake tin wobbled in her hands. James stepped forward and took it and put it on the table. A fruit pie? He didn't eat dessert.

'Hi, Laura. Thank you. That's very kind.' She wasn't moving. In fact, she looked like she was eyeing up a kitchen chair, like she wanted to sit down and chat. 'Shall I come and get the parcels from you now?'

'Any time you like.' Still not moving.

'Now would be great if that's alright by you. I have some necessities in there.'

'Of course.' Laura started to make her way slowly out of the room. 'We can get to know each other on the way.'

Really?

James's phone beeped as he and Laura emerged from the house. He took it out. Matt. After he got back with the parcels, he should take a photo of the view from the garden and the beach and send it to him.

Several other messages pinged in at the same time as the one from Matt, which was either a big coincidence or a sign that James didn't have a great signal inside the house. He really bloody hoped that wasn't the case. It was one thing choosing to leave London for a while, another having an enforced digital detox.

Laura wasn't joking about getting to know each other, and there was ample time for it. Next-door neighbour here was not the same as next-door neighbour in London. Even at James's pace it would have taken a good ten minutes to get to Laura's house. At her pace, it took nearly half an hour, and she put that time to good use, definitely capitalising on the fact that from James's perspective it felt off being short with an elderly person. She had a lot of questions, and James struggled to avoid answering them.

'So you're thirty-five. Any children?' Laura was asking as they finally got inside her house.

'No children,' James said. 'I should take my shoes off.' He bent down and made a big performance out of the shoe removal, to try to shake her from her interrogation.

'Would you like to have children?' Seriously.

'No plans,' he said. Did she really think that he was going to discuss things like this with her? He'd already had to evade questions about his family.

'Future plans, though? Are you looking for a wife?' Yes, seemingly she really did think that he was going to talk about these things with her.

'No plans at all. Not on my agenda. I should really pick up those parcels. Thank you again for holding on to them for me.'

'Why don't you join me for a cup of tea?' Laura said, making no effort whatsoever to point him in the direction of his parcels.

'I should really get back,' James said.

'Are you busy?' she asked. No evident snideness, just – a lot of – interest. Was he busy? Not really, but he wasn't keen to be interrogated any further.

'I have some work to do,' he said. 'Been on the road a long time. No opportunity to get anything done.'

'But you said you worked in finance? Is that a weekend job?'

'It kind of is,' he said. 'Never stops.' Laura nodded. He smiled at her, hoping that the questioning wouldn't re-start.

'Okay, then. I'll get those packages.' She started moving, painfully slowly, towards a room at the back of the house.

'Why don't I help you?' James moved to follow her.

'That's kind, but there's no need.'

'Okay. Thank you.'

James looked around her hallway while he waited. It was like a scene from an old-fashioned TV show. In fact, it could be Jessica Fletcher's hallway. There was even a dial phone on a little table, complete with notepad and biro. As a child, he'd always wished that his home was like that. Half the time they hadn't had a phone line at all, because his mother hadn't paid the relevant bill.

'Here we go.' Laura was lugging parcel after parcel into the hall. He should have driven here. If he took them back on foot, he was going to have to go back and forth at least twice. 'What do you have in here? Some of these are heavy.' Astonishing curiosity. Who asked you about the contents of your shopping? For all she knew, he could have sex toys in there, rather than towels and outdoor clothing.

'You know what? I think the best thing is for me to get my car and drive them back round.' He bent down to pull his shoes back on. 'I'll put them all outside and then I won't need to disturb you.'

'There's no need to do that. You won't be disturbing me.' Very kind of her, but he'd had a long day and he really just wanted a bit of time to himself to settle in.

When he got back with the car, Laura was right there, waiting, questions at the ready.

'Thank you so much,' James said over the questioning. 'I'm incredibly grateful. I'm sure I'll see you again.' Hopefully not too soon.

'My pleasure. You just let me know if there's anything else I can do for you.'

James nodded and smiled his way into the car as fast as he could. He checked his mirror when he got to the gateway to her drive. Yep, she was watching from her doorway.

The woman was far too friendly, possibly for her own good. What if he'd been an axe murderer or similar?

Despite how long he'd spent with Laura, there was still enough light for a quick swim before dinner. The water was bracing, but a great temperature once he'd got going, and the views were fantastic.

He felt less positive when he got back inside and remembered that he was going to have to make his own bed. Better to do it now, before dinner, so that he could relax while he ate. Stripping all Cassie's sheets from one of the beds and wrestling on his own new ones took a fair amount of time. He'd better make sure a cleaner would be coming regularly.

The steak and veg he'd bought earlier in the day on the mainland were good. The lack of phone signal and apparently wavering Wi-Fi signal were less good. He hadn't thought through how little there'd be to do on a Saturday evening somewhere quite remote without any of your friends. Well, there were outdoor activities and business opportunities and he'd get a lot of work done while he was here. It wasn't forever.

*

Jetlag was a bugger when you had a relatively empty day ahead of you. Sunday. 4.30 a.m. Wide awake.

James might as well get on with some work now. Catch up from the couple of days' holiday he'd taken for the coastal drive up here. He could go for a swim later on, and then maybe for a long run this afternoon, explore the island.

As the day went on, the clear skies gradually clouded over, and a few minutes into his afternoon swim the heavens opened. James didn't mind swimming in the rain, but it wasn't to everyone's taste. And it wasn't that pleasant trying to wrap yourself in a soaking wet towel that you hadn't had the forethought to leave somewhere sheltered. He'd need to take the weather into account when he was thinking about tourism opportunities in the area, and check out rainy day activities.

God, the towel was absolutely sopping. There was no point in using it at all. He put his feet into his sliders, squeezed some water out of the towel and slung it over his shoulder and started back towards the house.

'Oops, sorry.' Cassie was immediately recognisable due to her enormous coat and blue-edged hood. What was she doing here? Hadn't she said she was leaving today? Where had she sprung from? They were walking in the same direction so she had to have come from the end of the garden rather than up the drive.

'I was just saying a wee goodbye to the animals,' she said. 'I hope you don't mind.'

He did mind. But excellent news that she'd been saying goodbye.

'Not at all. What time's your flight?' Just to make sure.

'Eight this evening.'

Perfect. She'd have to be on the ferry soon.

'Have a good one,' he told her.

'Thank you. How was your night? Is everything alright? Did the notes make sense?'

Kind of her but she really didn't need to behave as though they were friends.

'All good, thanks. Have a great journey.' He nodded at her and gave her a small smile and took a couple of steps towards the kitchen door, turning his back slightly as he went.

'Thank you. Bye then. Obviously call me or email me if you *do* have any problems. And we'll no doubt speak soon.'

'I'm pretty sure I'll be fine, thanks, and I think everything in the flat's pretty self-explanatory. Enjoy your stay in London.'

'Thank you.' And off she and her coat went round the side of the house. Finally.

Chapter Six

Cassie

'Oh my goodness,' Cassie said to Dina, as the ferry that was going to take her away drew closer. 'This is so scary. I don't know if I can do it.' It was like the island and her friends here were a cocoon, a comfort blanket. What had she been thinking? She wasn't ready to venture back to the UK and to city life.

'Well, two things.' Dina pulled her into a big hug. 'One, you kinda have to, because there's a strange man living in your house now.'

Strange *hot* man, Cassie thought, remembering him in his swimming kit. And strange *grumpy* man, she thought, remembering everything else.

'And two,' continued Dina, 'you totally got this, babe. You're going to have an amazing time in London. In fact, you're probably not going to want to come back.' She squeezed Cassie hard. 'Please do come back.'

'Of course I'm coming back. I'm missing you and the rest of the island already.' She wasn't joking. This was going to be hard.

*

The great thing about a very long journey was that it did transition you from one location to another and lessen the shock of the change.

By the time Cassie had driven a hire car down to Boston and endured all the airport checks, she was just desperate to get on the plane. And after an almost entirely sleepless flight with poor bathroom facilities, she was just desperate to arrive at the flat, so her arrival at Heathrow kind of passed her by. She'd expected it to be weird being surrounded by mainly British accents again, driving on the left-hand side of the road, seeing British architecture, but she didn't really register any of it.

She did take in her surroundings when she finally got out of her taxi outside James's building. The road was amazingly peaceful for somewhere in the middle of a big city. It was a quiet cul-de-sac, between Notting Hill and Kensington High Street, ending in a footpath leading to Holland Park. This was a fab location. For this, she could forgive James's unfriendliness.

The contemporary mansion block in front of her was the one. Cassie picked up two of her suitcases and moved forwards. She buzzed on 'Reception', per James's instructions, gave her name, the main entrance door clicked open and, as she pushed it, a man – dressed in what looked like an actual uniform bordering on livery – came towards her through the foyer.

'Good morning. Can I help you with your bags?'

Yessss. The thought of schlepping up and down with them by herself at the end of what had been a very frazzling journey had not been appealing.

'Yes, please,' Cassie said. 'Thank you so much. I'm very grateful. I'm Cassie.' She stuck her hand out.

The porter looked at her, a little open-mouthed, and then shook it. 'Henry.' He had an excellently gold-toothed smile. Should she tip him? She had no idea. She also had no pound coins on her, so it was kind of academic.

When they'd stepped out of the lift together and had all her suitcases outside the door of the flat, she said, 'I'm so sorry. I can't tip you because I have no cash on me at the moment but I *am* very grateful.'

'No tip necessary.' Henry flashed another gold smile. 'An absolute pleasure. Anything else you need, just give me a shout.'

Cassie's hand was a bit shaky as she put the key in the lock. The area was incredible, the building was swanky, in a good way, and the flat had *looked* nice in the photos, but it might not be. What if it wasn't clean?

It was sparkling. Literally. Cassie could see that as soon as she opened the front door. She kicked her suitcases inside and closed the door behind her. There was a big open-plan kitchen/reception room ahead of her. The dark wood floor was extremely shiny. The floor-to-ceiling windows were so clean it was like they weren't even there and the view out of them was spectacular in a London kind of way. She could see immaculate buildings and trees to one side, and ahead of her into Holland Park. Wow.

She really needed to wash her hands and face. The floor plan had been easy to memorise, because the whole thing was just a loo, a small utility, a study, the kitchen/reception room and three en-suite bedrooms, and she knew that the loo was the door to her right in the little hall.

As promised by the SwapBnB photos, the loo was very nice in a boutique hotel way, with dark brown and gold shimmery paper, dark brown matt stone tiles – the type that looked as though they'd been hand-delivered straight from a difficult-to-access Andean quarry – wall-hung toilet and a swish basin with funky taps. It looked smarter, less bland, in real life than in the photos. Very sophisticated. If James had chosen this décor himself, he wasn't necessarily going to *love* Cassie's style.

Where were the towel and hand soap? There were cleaning products in an – actually quite cool – almost-invisible, recessed cupboard in the wall but that was it. There was at least a loo roll, thank goodness.

Cassie dried her wet-but-not-soaped hands on the loo paper and went to investigate the rest of the flat.

The sitting room, like the loo, was very boutique-hotel. Tasteful artwork and a geometric, maybe silk, rug in shades of dark grey. Two enormous pale leather sofas, covered in lime-green cushions, and a grey velvet armchair were angled towards a gigantic wall-hung flatscreen TV. The dining table to one side of the room was modern and wooden, and the eight velvet dining chairs were the same colour as the sofa cushions.

She lowered herself down onto one of the sofas. Wow. That was a lot less comfortable than it looked. Like it was for show only.

Cassie's stomach rumbled loudly. She hefted herself off the sofa to go over to the kitchen area.

It was all stainless steel. Cassie should definitely not have described her own kitchen as state-of-the-art. *This* was state-of-the-art. The appliances were incredibly shiny and unused-looking. How did anyone maintain that? The inside of the oven looked as though it had never seen a stray splash of anything.

In the middle of the – obviously shiny and sparkly – black granite island there were three bottles: champagne, red and white, with expensive-looking labels.

She found the built-in fridge after only three false door-opening starts. It was remarkably bright white and spotless inside. And remarkably empty of food. As was the freezer. There was in fact no food anywhere. The only food or drink of any kind in the entire flat were tap water and the wine, unless James kept food in the bedrooms, study or utility.

The utility was as smart as the kitchen and did not contain any food.

The study had another lovely view, brown panelling and grey wallpaper, a large desk and, obviously, no food.

The bedrooms were all enormous, with identical, modern, glossy-tiled shower rooms. They also obviously did not contain food. Or, unbelievably, *bed linen*. Or *towels*. All the cupboards in the bedrooms and utility and hall were almost entirely empty, other than of cleaning products and a vacuum cleaner. There were at least glasses, crockery and cutlery in the kitchen, and one (small) saucepan, a cheese grater and a spaghetti ladle.

So after having been on the road for about twenty-five mainly wide-awake hours, Cassie could sit on an uncomfortable sofa, she could lie down on a sheet-free mattress, and she could have a glass of water, wine or champagne. And she could do some cleaning or vacuuming.

But before she could eat or sleep or have a shower, she was going to have to go bloody shopping.

Honestly. Yes, the flat was perfect and you couldn't help feeling grateful to someone when they'd left things in such an immaculate state, and provided wine, but would it not have been normal for James also to have left some milk and bread or something? And sheets and towels. Surely? Maybe when he'd been asking her to confirm that her passport was valid, she should have been checking whether or not he was planning to strip his flat bare.

Right, well, she was starving. She needed to have a shower and then she'd better go and find a supermarket.

Maybe she'd just drop James a quick text first, to ask him if there were any sheets or towels. Maybe they were in a cupboard that she hadn't spotted. She could ask for café recommendations too, and whether there were any instructions for the appliances.

The shower was fab – powerful and hot. She used her dressing gown to dry herself, which worked less well than she'd thought it would because, while the dressing gown was made of towelling fabric, it was a lot less absorbent than an actual towel.

She wished she'd remembered to bring an adaptor for her hairdryer. It had been a really bad decision to wash her hair. It was usually her favourite thing about herself but today it wasn't working in her favour. There was too much of it and it was still dripping down her back. Maybe she could borrow a hairdryer from a neighbour. And that was an idea she would have been better to have had *before* she got in the shower.

'Hello?' The next-door neighbour was a very dapper man, probably in his early seventies, with a neat moustache and wearing a yellow V-necked argyle jumper and what Cassie would have to describe as slacks. He was looking at her blankly.

'Hello. I'm Cassie. I've done a house swap with James next door. I don't know if he mentioned it?' The dapper man wasn't looking remotely as though he knew what she was talking about.

'I'm sorry?'

'I've moved in next door. James and I have swapped homes for a few months. So I'm your new neighbour. Cassie.'

'I see. Hello. I don't think I know James.' That wasn't a surprise given that a lot of averagely friendly people didn't know their neighbours in cities, and James seemed a lot less friendly than average.

'He owns the flat but I'm going to be living there for the next few months. I was wondering if I could ask an enormous favour. Could I borrow a hairdryer, if you have one? And maybe you'd like to come over for a cup of tea in the next few days?'

'I'm Anthony. I live here alone.' He put his hand out and Cassie shook it. 'Great to meet you and yes to both. How nice to have a friendly neighbour.' Exactly. Unlike James.

A reply from James came through as she was going back into the flat. He'd had new bed linen and towels delivered to the island and had presumed she'd do the same for herself in London. And he recommended a café called Luigi's. He didn't mention the appliances.

Cassie had *already* bought expensive new bed linen for James and had nearly broken her back making all the beds in one morning. Hard not to find that annoying.

It was what it was, though. There was nothing she could do about it now, other than go shopping this afternoon, and for now go and check out James's café recommendation.

Luigi's was quite near Notting Hill Gate Tube station, but on a side road out of the way of all the bustle. Inside, it smelled deliciously of warm bread and pastries.

Cassie sat at a table in the corner, next to the windows, with a herby squash and chickpea salad, some very moreish olive bread and her Kindle. James was right; the food was great. And the café was great too. She had an excellent view of passers-by and the pastel-painted terraced houses opposite. This would be a great place to work with her laptop.

Right now, it was very relaxing sitting here, reading a little, watching the world go by, reading again. This was something you didn't get on an island where you knew everyone. By the time she was eating a delectable raspberry tart for pudding, she had the sensation that she was on an enjoyable weekend city break. London was great, and the flat was extremely clean and well furnished – ignoring the sofas – and in a great location. She'd probably been too harsh on James.

*

Five, literally *five*, hours later, after trips to the supermarket and a department store, and a nightmare journey back on the Tube grappling with an enormous duvet box and pillows as well as the sheets and towels, she was standing in the bedroom in the flat, sweating – actually sweating – from trying to get the bloody sheet onto the incredibly heavy mattress, and she knew that she hadn't been harsh *enough* about James.

Making the bed wasn't going to work. She'd bought a fitted sheet, obviously, because she wasn't a masochist and she didn't want to be ironing sheets, but it did not in fact fit. She'd definitely bought the right size, but the sheet wasn't going on, because the mattress was deeper than the seams on the sheet. She got her phone out. And Google confirmed that there was such a thing as an extra-deep mattress, for which you needed extra-deep sheets. Maybe, *maybe*, James *could* have bloody mentioned, *knowing* that she was going to be buying bed linen, that she needed deep ones.

She really wanted to say something to him. She shouldn't. Sod it, she was going to. She was really tired and, yes, she felt cranky. She sent him a quick text. And immediately regretted it. It was easy to forget to mention things.

The doorbell rang as she was staring at the 'deep fitted sheets' page of the John Lewis website.

A tall, blonde woman was standing outside the door. Her clothes were conservative and expensive-looking: navy narrow-legged trousers and a navy silk top, with a cream jacket. She was beautiful but definitely suffered from 'resting bitch face'. Unless she'd arranged her features like that purposely.

'Are you the cleaner?' She really did not look friendly. Cassie hoped she wasn't a neighbour.

'Nope. I'm living here for a few months.'

'What?' Now the woman had a moving bitch face. 'Where's James?' She didn't wait for an answer but pushed past Cassie, through the hall and straight into the sitting room.

Cassie followed her in, fast. 'Excuse me. James has moved out. He left last week and I'm now living here.'

'Nonsense. Where is he?' Wow. The woman's voice was trembling and, from the looks of her screwed-up face, it was with anger.

'It isn't nonsense. He doesn't live here at the moment.' Why was Cassie engaging with her?

'What? Where the hell *does* he live?'

'I don't know.' Cassie didn't want to be giving her own address to this woman. 'James has moved out and I've rented the flat. I'm sorry but could you leave?' Seriously. So ridiculously British of her. The woman had barged in and was swearing at her, and Cassie was using the word *sorry*.

She'd definitely been too British about things. The woman wasn't moving towards the front door; she was walking towards the bedrooms. And flinging doors open. *Wardrobe* doors. She was literally searching the flat.

'Please stop,' Cassie said. This was awful. Normal life didn't prepare you for a seemingly deranged woman hunting through the flat you'd just moved into. She had no idea how to stop her. *Now* the woman was riffling through the piles of John Lewis bags Cassie's new bed linen and towels were in, like any kind of remotely average-sized man could be hiding under them. 'I'm sorry but I'm going to have to call the police if you don't leave.' The police. *Security*. Cassie had a buzzer. 'And security.' She was already on her way over to the button.

Henry answered immediately and told her he'd be straight up.

He was fast. The woman was still checking out the study when he arrived, while Cassie stood in the hall saying, completely ineffectually, 'Will you please stop that?'

Henry got the woman out of the flat in well under a minute and then knocked on the door and put his head round it when Cassie said, 'Hi, Henry, thank you.'

'I can only apologise,' he told her. 'She must have got past me when I was signing for a delivery.'

'Do you *know* her?'

'Yes. Emily. Mr Grey's ex.'

'Wow.'

'Yeah.

'Well.' Cassie *really* wanted to ask Henry for every detail he had. Obviously, she couldn't. Not until she knew him a bit better, anyway. 'Thank you so much for your help. That's the first time I've ever experienced anything like that.'

'Would you like me to call the police?'

'I don't think so. Although is she likely to come back?'

'This is the first time for a while.'

'Maybe we *should* call the police. How many times has she been?'

'Six or seven, I'd say. This is the first time she's got back up here. I'm very sorry.'

'Honestly, it really isn't your fault. You really shouldn't blame yourself.' Surely James should blame *him*self, though, for not mentioning his stalker to Cassie.

Chapter Seven

James

James turned towards the shore to begin the sprint finish to his swim. There was a woman there, waving manically at him. She was shouting. Something about neighbours. James didn't really want to spend his Monday morning speaking to someone who might be great to talk to but might equally be a younger version of Laura and bombard him with personal questions.

How was it possible that in a large city you could avoid your thousands of neighbours but on a small island they were in your face the whole time? He waved, turned round and swam away from her.

When he got back, the woman had gone, good news.

He checked through the messages on his phone on his way through the garden to the house. There was one from Ella, meaning that he now owed her about four texts or calls. Guilt, again. Maybe he'd send her a message later, with some photos of the beach for his nieces.

After a shower he discovered that the Wi-Fi was still on the blink. It had been erratic all morning apart from first thing.

Okay. He could get round this. He could work in the garden and hotspot himself from his phone until it was up and running again.

Working in the garden wasn't bad. Incredibly different from sitting in a London office. Something to consider in promoting get-away-from-it-all tourism opportunities to workaholics.

Yeah, this was great, really.

No. What was that? It was a raindrop on his screen.

It was a bloody deluge. James grabbed his laptop and sprinted for the house. Extraordinary how fast that rain had come. Laura hadn't been wrong when she'd said, 'If you don't like the weather here, wait ten minutes.'

The Wi-Fi was still down. So what the hell was he going to do now?

He was going to find some shelter for his phone just outside Cassie's study window so that he could continue the hotspotting but work inside.

A golf umbrella, a large bowl and a rock worked well as a phone shelter but now he was on the other side of a wall from his phone. Christ, this was frustrating. Bloody countryside.

He went outside at lunchtime to check his phone. He had a message from Cassie. About bed sheets, unbelievably. Another one came through as he was holding his phone. What now? Another housekeeping question? Should he have bought her toothpaste? Left her details of local knitting clubs and piano recitals?

Oh, Jesus.

Emily came round. Asked if I was your cleaner. Barged straight into the flat and searched for you. I had to call security.

Shit. So unacceptable. He was going to have to call Cassie.

'Hi, James.'

'Hi. Cassie. I'm so sorry about Emily. Are you alright? What happened?'

'I am okay, thank you, but if I'm honest, it wasn't very pleasant. She wouldn't believe that you'd moved out, and started hunting through the flat for you. She actually started going through all my stuff, like you'd be hidden in there. She didn't leave until Henry escorted her out.'

'That's awful. I can only apologise. She's been before but I didn't think she'd come back, because I threatened the police if she did anything else.'

'I kind of wish you'd warned me if there was even the tiniest chance of her coming back.'

'Yep, again, I'm very sorry. I really didn't think she would but I take your point,' he said. 'I'll call Security and speak to them and I'm happy to call the police.'

'Thank you but I've already done it. I made a complaint but I didn't press charges. I think Emily was really shocked when she realised that she'd barged into a stranger's home and she knows that I called the police, so I don't think she'll come back. And I had a long chat with Henry. He felt awful. I told him obviously it wasn't his fault.'

'Well, thank you for speaking to Henry and the police. I'm incredibly sorry that this happened and that you had to deal with it.'

'Thank you. No problem. Well, I mean, it was a problem, but I do realise now that it wasn't really your fault.'

'Hopefully that's the end of it,' James said.

'Yes. Okay, so goodbye then.'

'Apologies again,' he said. 'Goodbye.'

Damn. Cassie shouldn't have been dragged into his sordid nightmare-ex situation. He should probably ask Dee to send flowers.

Dee picked up the phone immediately. 'Flowers,' she said. 'Absolutely. What's she like? Any particular preferences?'

What was Cassie like? Unreasonable at times – although she could have been a lot angrier about Emily. She had a nice voice. She was overfriendly when she wasn't being unreasonable. She liked colour and lists.

'Colourful ones, I'd guess,' James said. 'Whatever you think, really.' Dee was fantastic at presents. 'Actually, she needs bedsheets for deep mattresses. Super king-size. Could you possibly take them round tomorrow?' Cassie probably wouldn't want another unexpected visitor today.

Right. Polite gesture sorted. He'd like to think there'd be no further need for him and Cassie to speak.

*

James was going to have to call Cassie. He was furious, or about to be. He needed to know.

The Wi-Fi had been great again at the crack of dawn today, like yesterday, but at around eight thirty this morning, it had just stopped working. Like it had yesterday. Today there'd been constant heavy rain, so he hadn't been able to sit outside at all, so he'd been separated from his phone all morning for the hotspotting. Having to get raincoated up or soaked in order to check his messages had not improved his mood.

And now it was lunchtime and the crap Wi-Fi situation had been going on for several hours.

He really needed to know if it was always like this.

Actually, Cassie might have mentioned it in her notes. That way he could find out without having to speak to her.

Yep, 'Wi-Fi and internet' was one of the lines in her weird index.

She'd said that if demand on the island was high, Wi-Fi could 'quite often be slow'. And the best time to be sure of it was in the middle of the night when everyone else was asleep – as he already knew from his early rising. It seemed like 'quite often' was a euphemism for 'all the bloody time during normal waking hours' and 'quite slow' was one for 'completely bloody dead'.

In whose parallel universe was it okay that she hadn't mentioned straight-up, in her SwapBnB entry, that the Wi-Fi was erratic at best? Right now, he could be living in an Alpine-style chalet in the mountains in Vermont with working bloody Wi-Fi.

Outrageous.

And the lack of phone signal inside the house as well. Again, she should have mentioned it.

He dragged on boots and a coat and went outside to call her. He normally kept his temper tightly under control – as a child he'd seen enough anger-fuelled arguments at home to realise that if you wanted a good life you needed to avoid acting in anger – but he was *furious*. It was a big deal leaving your home city and moving halfway across the world for a few months. He'd *trusted* Cassie. And seriously, who pretended to be thoughtful and left a freezerful of food for you, but lied by omission about Wi-Fi?

'Hi, James.'

'Cassie. The Wi-Fi. I'm speechless. I can't understand how you can have thought it was acceptable not to tell me until after I'd arrived here about the lack of phone signal inside the house and the lack of reliable Wi-Fi.'

'I'm really sorry. I forgot to mention it before I wrote the notes. It was all a bit of a whirl. It all happened so quickly.'

'Forgot? That's ridiculous. It's a huge deal. You should have mentioned it in your SwapBnB post.'

'Again, I'm sorry. I forgot.'

'*How* can you have forgotten? I mean, you effectively entered into this swap under false pretences.'

'I did *not* do anything under false pretences.' Her voice had gone very high-pitched.

'You should have mentioned it.'

'I'm sorry that I forgot to mention it but maybe you should have *asked* if it's this important to you. A lot of places don't have reliable Wi-Fi. I mean, a lot of people wanting to get away from it all for a few months might not feel the need to be fully connected at all times. Some people are actually seeking out a break from modern, connected life. And obviously, if you'd asked, I would have told you.'

'Are you joking? I live in London. I have a job. And we're in the US here. I didn't choose to go and live in a remote village in a developing country famous for its lack of internet access, did I?'

'I have a job too, and I don't have a problem with the Wi-Fi,' Cassie said. 'Surely the onus was on you to ask if you care this much?'

'Really? I mean, really? That's ridiculous. Wi-Fi's a basic necessity, like running water and central heating.'

'Well, I'm sorry. Although, we do have Wi-Fi daily, just not all the time. And, as I said, I have a job and I manage totally fine with it the way it is.'

James shook his head and raindrops splattered his face. 'You should absolutely have told me.'

'Like you should have told me about Emily?'

He gritted his teeth. 'I apologise for that but I did not know that Emily would come back.'

'I did not know that you would need constant Wi-Fi but would not tell me that.'

James muttered a couple of words.

'Did you just *swear* at me over the phone?'

'Yes, I did,' he said.

'I'm sorry but I am *so* annoyed. I *bloody* bent over backwards for you. I travelled earlier than I wanted to. I bought new bed linen and towels for you and apparently they weren't good enough for you. I cooked food for you. I left notes for you. I did everything I could think of to make this a good stay for you. You got to travel when you wanted to. I'm grateful for the wine, thank you, but you didn't even leave bread or milk for me and I had to buy sheets and towels the day I arrived.' She was almost babbling.

'Cassie. You're in the middle of *London* with everything you could possibly need on your doorstep. And everything you need is readily available. This island's the arse end of nowhere and what I need is working Wi-Fi so that I can do my *job*.'

'Are you *shouting* at me? And calling my home the arse end of nowhere?'

'Yes, I am,' he yelled.

'Right.' She paused. 'I'm going to apologise again for having forgotten to mention the Wi-Fi, which does actually work, just not all the time. And I think you should apologise to me.' She stopped talking.

James said nothing. He didn't want to carry on ranting at her but the Wi-Fi issue was *huge*.

'Really?' Cassie said. And ended the call.

James held the phone in front of him and swore at it. He really wished Cassie could hear him.

A message had come through while he'd been on the phone. Dee.

Just to let you know that am on way to deliver your flowers and gift to Cassie

Oh, for God's sake. Perfect timing.

Chapter Eight

Cassie

Cassie checked her watch. 6 p.m. A little early for a glass of wine maybe, but she *needed* one. Bloody James. And the bloody Wi-Fi. She should probably apologise properly, with no temper involved. Obviously she *should* have told him about it, but it just hadn't occurred to her at any point before she wrote the notes for him. She'd been too overwhelmed by the whole Eek-I'm-moving-to-London-far-sooner-than-I-was-expecting thing.

She found a bottle opener and poured herself a glass of his red.

She took a big sip. And that was good. James wasn't her favourite person but he had great taste in alcohol. Cassie sat in the sitting room armchair – the only comfortable seat in the flat – and wriggled her shoulders, feeling her tension begin to slip away. She took another sip. Yes, *very* good.

And then the doorbell rang. She jerked upright in panic. Was it Emily again?

Luckily, she leaned forward as she moved, so that she spilled her wine on the floor, not the chair.

No, of course it wouldn't be Emily at the door again. Cassie was just being paranoid.

She mopped up the wine with loo paper – she should have bought kitchen roll yesterday – and tiptoed – like the doorbell ringer could hear her – over to the doorbell camera screen. It wasn't Emily, obviously. It was, however, *another* beautiful woman. How many of them *were* there?

She checked that the chain was definitely on the door and said, 'Hello?', over the intercom.

'Hi. Cassie? James asked me to bring a small present for you. He said it was an apology.' Oh. Wow. She really hadn't expected that. So soon after their call, as well. He hadn't sounded apologetic at all on the phone. Well, that was nice. She was definitely going to apologise to him again too. She'd obviously misjudged him. And it was nice that he had close (beautiful) friends who would come round with presents, at the drop of a hat, even if he didn't know his neighbours.

The woman was even more beautiful in the flesh. She flashed a stunning smile at Cassie and held out a perfectly wrapped, rectangular gift and an enormous and gorgeous bouquet of flowers, deep purples and reds.

'My name's Dee, and James uses our concierge services. I've just popped my card in the bag,' she told Cassie with another perfect smile. 'You never know.' Oh, okay. It seemed remarkably flash of James to use a concierge service but it was a nice gesture.

'Thank you. The flowers are beautiful.'

'Not at all.' Dee flashed her perfect teeth again and she was gone.

Cassie closed the door behind her and went into the sitting room with the flowers and wrapped present, interested to open it. Was it something James had suggested or was it Dee's choice, something generic?

There was a card tucked into it, simply worded: 'Apologies. James'.

The present turned out to be two deep-mattress, fitted bed sheets. Which would have been an excellent apology if it wasn't a day late, after her one-and-three-quarter-hour round trip yesterday afternoon traipsing back to John Lewis and exchanging the other ones. And if you ignored the fact that he should have provided bed linen in the first place. Still, she'd better send him a text to say thank you.

She got two blue ticks immediately. He must be outside to have reception. Oh. Right. Yes. That thought demonstrated that it would be quite annoying to be in his position, thousands of miles away from his friends and contacts but with unreliable Wi-Fi and no phone signal in the house.

He'd replied.

Np.

Cassie *really* disliked 'Np'. Just say 'No problem', or 'No prob', or even 'No worries'. But, whatever, he'd apologised for their argument, and she was going to apologise too. Oh, three dots. He was typing again.

Just to be clear, the apology was for yesterday, for Emily's intrusion.

What? No apology about his Wi-Fi tantrum? The rude shit. She was tempted to send a sarky message back, but she was going to be the bigger person here. And now that she'd calmed down she could appreciate that having no Wi-Fi might be quite annoying.

Okay, well thanks. Apologies that I forgot to tell you about the Wi-Fi. I really did just forget because I was in a flap and I do now appreciate that it's very annoying for you and I'm very sorry.

One grey tick. Two grey ones, so therefore it had arrived.

They didn't turn blue. Rude.

Well, whatever. She was going to ignore him and get on with her evening.

Cassie really couldn't be bothered to cook dinner today and that was fine. This being a fancy London neighbourhood, there were more takeaway places with outstanding reviews within a square mile than you could possibly count. The only question was, what did she feel like having? Hard to decide, except it didn't matter; she could have a different one *whenever she liked*. On the island, you could only get takeaway from Joe's Diner, and only when Joe was in the mood.

Another thing, of course, that she could do here whenever she liked, was use the internet at wonderfully high speed, and order her takeaway online.

Half an hour later, she was forking up Chinese – to-die-for sautéed squid in black bean sauce, with cutlery because she was terrible with chopsticks – while checking out some facts about the Tower of London for her books on her laptop, occasionally glancing at the leafy views from James's sitting room windows.

A message did ping through while she was eating her dinner, but not from James. It was Dina.

Hey honey. Been teeming down outside today. Missing you babe. Alpacas missing you too. Chickens not so loyal if I'm honest. Just happened to pass by your place to check on the animals this morning while James was having a swim. OMG RIPPED :) :) :)

Not so friendly though – definitely tried to avoid me this morning. I'm planning to overlook the unfriendliness because he is HOT.

Yeah, if he was straight and single, Dina would have him under her thumb pretty soon.

Hello lovely Dina. Missing you too. DO NOT HAVE SEX IN ANY BED IN MY HOUSE. If that's okay. Take him back to yours. Please. LOVE YOU

She hadn't been comprehensive enough.

Me again. Also please don't have sex in my shower. Or in/on ANY sanitaryware in my house. Or on any furniture. Basically please don't have sex with him ANYWHERE in my house. Thank you :) xxxxx

When drunk, Dina had a lot of stories to tell about the different places she'd had sex. Cassie didn't want her house to be one of those places. If anyone was ever going to have sex in Cassie's house, surely it should be *Cassie*. Which it hadn't been once in the four years that she'd lived there and wasn't likely to be any time soon. Every date she'd had since she arrived in the US had been a one-off and an utter let-down, so none of them had made it past her front door. At least she'd had Dina to laugh with about her bad dating experiences, though.

A wave of homesickness washed over her.

She took another forkful of delicious squid and opened another tab to google Hyde Park. It was incredible to think that only a couple of hundred years ago there'd been sheep grazing there. She had to be able to work that into a scene.

No, she wasn't that homesick. She could totally do this. It was only for a few months, there were a lot of great things about being here, and she had a lot of plans. In fact, now she was here, her mind was buzzing with so many ideas and she was so ready to start writing that she was going to have to thank Jennifer and admit that she'd been totally right; of course spending a few months in London was the right thing to do.

Another text from Dina.

Babe. If we're overtaken by passion, we'll have no choice about where we do it.

And another one.

No, seriously, promise: I WILL 'date' him and I will NOT date him in your house.

Cassie laughed. Her friends were only on the end of a phone. She could *totally* do this London thing.

*

Cassie was the most wide-awake person in the whole of the northern hemisphere. Sleep was impossible. She'd eaten her meals at the right times. She'd avoided evening caffeine. She'd drunk warm milk. Nothing worked. Last night she'd been awake until three thirty UK time. Tonight was even worse. It was nearly four o'clock and she'd finished her book and she just *could not sleep*. No, that was okay, she was nodding off, she was. But, help, what if she overslept and missed her fertility appointment? Which was now in only seven hours' time. Oh, and now, *wide awake* again. Bloody *hell*.

She must have drifted off at some point because she woke suddenly on Wednesday morning to find someone *in the bedroom with her*, saying, 'I'm sorry, good morning.' Oh God Oh God Oh God, it was Emily.

Cassie couldn't get her arms out of the duvet. She was trapped. She was going to be murdered in her bed because she couldn't get her arms free.

The door closed loudly as Emily left the room. What was she doing?

Cassie opened her mouth and screamed, 'Help!' Would anyone actually hear her, though? How thick were the walls? She screamed again, as loudly as she could.

The door re-opened and Emily switched the light on. Cassie upped the screaming. Why wasn't there a panic button? Where was her phone? She should call 999.

'I'm so sorry.' Someone was shouting over her screams. It wasn't Emily. It was someone with a different accent and much better manners.

Everything was pitch-black but also a bit starry. Cassie realised that she had her eyes squeezed shut. She opened them. A pleasant-looking, and also distressed-looking, woman of maybe thirty was standing there holding a mop.

'My name's Ralitza. We haven't met. I'm your cleaner.' The *relief.* 'James told me you would be living here but I thought you'd be out.'

Frankly, it was a surprise that he'd thought to tell his cleaner about her. He certainly didn't tell Cassie things. Apart from how annoyed he was about the Wi-Fi.

Also, she didn't really want a cleaner but obviously she wasn't going to fire Ralitza because that would be awful. So she was going to be stuck with someone she didn't want. Irritating. She'd better text him to ask how much she needed to pay her.

The good news was that it was only nine o'clock and Cassie was now wide awake and pumped full of adrenalin and therefore definitely on course to arrive extremely punctually for her appointment.

*

Cassie looked around the waiting room. The other people there were three very couply-couples. All male-female. There was a lot of PDA going on. Two of the couples were holding hands. The other pair were sitting so close together it looked vaguely obscene. Fair enough, really, because they were obviously all about to go through a highly stressful and highly intimate experience together. *Together*. No, she didn't need to think now about how lonely her first pregnancy had been.

She did need to do something to pass the time, though. She should have considered that her usual practice of arriving in good time for things wasn't always the best way. It was great when you were queuing for a first-come-first-served ferry. Or anything first-come-first-served, in fact. It was also great when you had somewhere comfortable to wait *and* something to do. This waiting room was very nice, actually. Padded suedette chairs, low music, soft lighting, pleasant décor, large vases of vibrant orchids at strategic intervals. It almost felt as though the clinic were trying to get people in the *mood*. Which, in the case of the male halves of these couples, presumably they might need to be, for sperm production. Eurgh.

Anyway, the room was lovely as waiting rooms went. But it was *not* comfortable being here. She *really* needed something to do. She got her phone out.

She should have googled 'what to expect at your first fertility appointment' in advance. She'd kind of been blanking it out until now, when blanking was no longer possible, since it was *happening*. Thinking about anything ob/gyn-related brought back terrible memories of losing the baby. Her last appointment had been six weeks afterwards, and she'd had to have an unexpected internal scan (bad) done by a man (even worse). She'd then had a discussion with a female doctor who'd told her with an ill-placed big smile that all was well and you'd never know she'd ever been pregnant. *Especially because I don't have a baby to show for it*, Cassie had screamed. She'd thought she'd screamed it out loud and had then realised that the noise had only been inside her head, and had wondered if she was going mad with grief.

Actually, she'd moved on enormously from there, to be able to be sitting here perfectly normally.

And now she was finally reading what Google had to say about what to expect. Basically, it varied. Sometimes there was an internal scan to check your ovaries and uterus, sometimes there wasn't. Maybe the leaflets the clinic had sent would have told her but she'd been too stressed to read them. There was likely to be a lot of chat. Maybe some blood tests.

In summary, it was likely to be a crappy morning. But it would be more than worth it if things worked out.

Yep. It had been a crappy morning. Cassie walked up the steps from the clinic onto Harley Street. Funny how out here the world was just going on as normal, while in there such huge things happened.

A man in paint-splattered overalls bumped into her and said, 'Cheer up, love, it might never happen.'

And that was the whole point. It might indeed never happen. Oh God. Her eyes were filling again.

She'd spent the entire morning in there. She'd had a couple of blood tests and was going to have to go back next week to have some more on a different day of her cycle. As feared, she'd had an internal scan, which had actually been better than expected because the woman who'd done it had been very understanding and had said that she knew that no woman ever was keen to take her underwear off, hitch her dress up, cover herself in paper and stretch her knees 'wider please, if you wouldn't mind'.

As it turned out, those had been the *best* parts of the morning.

The bad part had been the 'chat'. Cassie had cried. She clearly wasn't the first, because they'd had tissues on hand and had seemed completely unsurprised, but still.

Now she had a headache and a lot to think about. If she was going to go ahead, she needed to choose her sperm, from a well-regulated supplier. And she had to attend 'implications counselling'. She needed to be aware that there was the risk of failure. Well, duh. And that going through pregnancy and looking after a baby by yourself were both hard. Again, duh; and also, yes, going through pregnancy by yourself would be a challenge, but, frankly, it would be a hell of a lot easier than going through it with a selfish, uninterested partner.

To be fair, there was a lot to consider. Doing it by herself would be very stressful and there could be a lot of heartache involved. Maybe she should explore adoption.

Too many thoughts.

What Cassie needed now was some carb and chocolate-heavy lunch and to distract herself with work.

She began the afternoon with a walk round South Kensington for research purposes, past immaculately kept white stucco houses in side streets, and then up Exhibition Road past the famous Science, Natural History and Victoria & Albert museums and into Hyde Park. She saw beautiful architecture, and beautiful trees and shrubs in the park. And, honestly, what felt like literally thousands of beautiful babies. Everywhere. In buggies, strapped to people's chests, being carried in people's arms, some older ones toddling around very gorgeously. And when she tried to look away from the babies, her gaze just encountered glowing pregnant women. Literally everywhere. It was like she'd been transported into some baby-filled parallel universe.

It had been like this after she'd had the miscarriage. Everywhere she'd looked there'd been happy parents with babies and young children.

If she did IVF and it didn't work out, it would be so hard. And now she was feeling physically sick to the stomach at the memory of when she'd realised that something had gone terribly wrong with her pregnancy.

Could she do it? Would she regret it if she didn't try?

A gorgeous nutmeg-brown Labrador ran past her, chasing a stick.

Maybe she should get a dog. She loved the alpacas and the chickens. Animals were great. She'd explored the IVF idea, which had been the right thing to do, and now she should move on. Having a baby would be a huge undertaking by herself. Island living was hard in the winter. She was lucky. She had a lot of friends and the animals. Better to move on from the baby plan and, yes, get a dog, and focus on the good things in her life, including work and her new books.

A text pinged through from James.

Cleaner – don't worry – I have her covered.

Okay, well that was nice. There was still something very irritating about him, though. And what was even more irritating was that every time she thought about him, she remembered how hot he was. It didn't seem right to find supremely irritating people attractive.

Chapter Nine

James

James picked his coffee cup up to head back inside after sending Cassie a quick text. If he was honest, he knew he should have replied politely to her Wi-Fi apology message but he'd been too angry, and now it felt like the moment had passed. Anyway, whatever, he was still paying for the cleaner and neither of them was going to get angry about that. The Wi-Fi situation was still really pissing him off but hopefully he'd be able to get it sorted soon.

'Hullo. You must be James.' A middle-aged woman carrying a lidded casserole dish had come round the side of the house. 'I'm Isla Brown, Don's wife.' She said it like James would know who Don was. There was a lot of extreme friendliness on this island. 'How are you doing today? I know Cassie left a lot of meals for you but she only cooks European food and her fancy Middle Eastern dishes. I thought you'd like to have a New England speciality. I have Maine-style clam chowder for you.'

'Thank you. Very kind of you.' It *was* kind of her, but he hoped she didn't want to question him the way Laura had.

'It's my pleasure.' She was beaming at him. 'We're so pleased that you're here. We were so sad when our wonderful Cassie said that she was leaving for a few months, and we already miss her so much, but it's great to have a new neighbour to get to know.' Wonderful Cassie. Really? 'Have you settled in? What do you like to do in your spare time? We have a lot of different activities on the island. 'There's something for everyone.' Isla looked like she was keen to linger. She was edging towards the kitchen door.

'That's great.' James stepped forward and took the casserole from her. 'Thank you again for this. I'd love to chat but unfortunately I have a conference call starting in a couple of minutes.'

'Another time. Perhaps at the weekend. Good to meet you. Enjoy the chowder.'

'Thanks.' James carried the casserole dish into the kitchen, telling himself that he really didn't need to feel any guilt about rejecting her obviously well-meant friendship advances because he was *busy*.

James sat back and stretched. Cassie's desk chair was fantastic, he had to give her that. He wondered what she did for a job, given that you could do pretty much anything remotely now. She'd said 'Writer'. That could mean a lot of things or it could be a cover. Chief exec of a major corporate. Underwear designer. Spy. He'd discovered via Google that her last job was as a solicitor in Glasgow. Her digital trail had ended pretty abruptly four years ago, when she moved here.

What time was it now? Good God. Only half four. Time was pretty much standing still today. Shocking to realise how much your phone and your colleagues distracted you, and also made your day go faster. Maybe he should have invited Isla in for a cup of tea. Nope. He wasn't that lonely.

Time to stretch his legs and check his phone.

It was raining but maybe he'd take a walk up to the end of the garden and to the field, take a look at Cassie's animals.

The alpacas were taking refuge from the downpour under a large, wide tree. They were clearly the source of the clicking he'd heard a couple of times.

Where were the chickens Cassie had referred to? It was hard to see. Would they have some kind of chicken house? Yep, there was an enclosure in the top corner of the field, containing a wooden hut surrounded by a large wire enclosure. The chickens must be inside, and who could blame them.

'Hey.' The woman's voice in James's ear was a shock. The sound of her approach had obviously been masked by the pounding rain. 'I'm Dina. You must be James.'

James took the hand she was offering for a sodden handshake.

'Yes, I am. I presume you're one of Cassie's neighbours?' She had to be the woman who'd waved manically at him a couple of times while he was swimming and who he glimpsed walking up the garden past the house from time to time. 'Are you the person kindly looking after the animals?' Why was he feeling grateful to her? They weren't his animals and there was nothing wrong with his choice to have nothing to do with them.

'Yes, I'm Cassie's neighbour and we're also very good friends. I live just around the headland. And, yes, I'm looking after the animals while she's away. It's great to meet you.' Dina was around his age and was wearing a lot of glossy, bright-red lipstick and a large smile. Applying serious make-up didn't seem like an obvious choice before going to feed animals in heavy rain, but maybe that was island life for you. Maybe this was going to be the highlight of her day and she was dressed for it. Or maybe her island life was a lot fuller than James's was shaping up to be, and she was on her way somewhere else.

'Good to meet you, too.' Sad to say, he wasn't lying. There was only so much isolation a person could enjoy. If he'd known how time was going to start dragging, he probably wouldn't have ignored her when she waved at him.

'I'm just here to collect the eggs. Wanna come see?'

James opened his mouth to say thanks but no thanks, and then thought about his plans for the evening. Work. The chowder – might as well eat it. Whatever there was on US terrestrial TV. Yeah, he could stand to spend a few minutes looking at chicken eggs with an attractive woman.

The egg collecting surprised James. There were more eggs than he'd expected, and they varied in colour and size a lot more than he'd thought they would. There were blue – properly blue – ones, some regular egg-coloured ones, some very pale ones. Apparently most of the chickens laid an egg most days, especially during the summer; and the gigantic ones were double-yolked and from the youngest hens.

'Does each chicken lay the same colour egg each day or do they vary?' he asked, genuinely interested in the answer. Really, almost nothing had happened in his life today.

Dina laughed. 'Spoken like a city boy. Each chicken lays pretty much the same coloured eggs each day.'

'And what do we do with all the eggs?' *We.* Like this was anything to do with him.

'Cassie gives them to her neighbours. There's a lot of that on the island. People sharing their produce. Laura contributes a lot of blueberry bakes.'

'That's nice.' In a weird, living-in-a-nineteenth-century-children's-story kind of way.

They were walking back towards the house now. Dina seemed like good company by any measure. Compared to having no-one other than

Laura to talk to, she was *great* company. James was almost tempted to ask her in for coffee, except she'd already told him that she was single and she'd been directing a lot of her red-lipsticked smiles at him. He really didn't need another dating-type misunderstanding in the near future. Maybe something could happen towards the end of his stay, when it would be obvious that he'd be leaving soon.

'So I'll maybe see you at the island dinner on Saturday evening?' Dina was hovering but he wasn't going to ask her in for coffee.

'Island dinner?'

'It's in the community hall, at seven. Everyone on the island goes.'

James hesitated for a second. Life here was not exciting. Saturday was going to be a slow day. But, no, going to a dinner with everyone on the island would really not improve the day. There was bored and there was desperate.

'Yeah, unfortunately I have plans,' he said. Plans? What plans could he possibly have?

'Okay, well, if you change your mind, you know where I am. Next door, that way.' Dina pointed, shot him another big red smile, and sashayed off round the side of the house.

In fact, checking out the chickens was the joint highlight of his day, along with getting a Wi-Fi engineer to agree to come out by the end of next week. *Next* week, and James wasn't even tempted to tear a strip off him, he was so grateful. Turned out telecoms engineers had an aversion to doing jobs on islands.

The low point was being bored enough to open an email from his father. He nearly didn't open it. He should stick to his resolve not to engage. Although when you were on the other side of the world, on a fairly remote island, with a new phone number that you'd only given to people you liked, it felt somewhat as though you were protected. If he read it, his father would never know. So he opened it.

It was the first time the man had been in touch since the death of James's mother nine months ago and he hadn't referred to her at all. He wanted to borrow some money from James because he was raising capital for an investment in an organic vineyard in the Greater Manchester area. James wasn't an expert in viticulture but he was pretty sure that all the signs were that this wasn't a great business opportunity. Also, over his dead body would he go into business with his father. He pressed Delete.

Bad idea even to read the email. He shouldn't have given his new email address to his father. The email had made him think about his mother, and that had made him think about Ella and Leonie.

He sent Ella a guilt message telling her about the island and the alpacas and chickens, for his nieces' benefit. She was up late and sent an immediate – very chatty – reply, with a couple of references to Leonie, which James couldn't deal with. He'd get back to her in a week or two, when enough time had elapsed for him not to need to refer back to what she'd written.

Not a great evening.

*

When Dina went past in the morning on her way to feed the animals, he was almost tempted to join her.

He flicked through the animal part of Cassie's notes while he was eating his breakfast. Extraordinary. The top part was actually an animal master list. There were sub lists. Feed. Exercise. Vet numbers. Egg collection instructions. Egg distribution suggestions. And so on.

The three alpacas and the eleven chickens had names. Of course they did. He was guessing that none of the chickens would be ending up as a roast dinner.

Maybe he should start helping Dina with the animals.

Yeah, maybe not.

The solitude was definitely getting to him. Good job he'd be going down to Boston and New York for the occasional night on business.

Early afternoon, after several hours of back-to-back Zoom meetings moving an uncomfortable (brightly coloured) metal chair around the garden the whole time to get out of the sun's glare, he took a kayak out.

This was the first time the sea had been calm enough for him to go far. Twenty minutes' hard paddling took him round the headland and into a bay with a shallow beach bordered by shrubs and woodland.

James paddled himself over to the beach and got out.

Wow. This was like a little piece of paradise. It was completely secluded. All he could see was the ocean in front of him and vegetation behind and to either side. This must be a wildlife haven. Tourists would love it.

Whoever owned the land and beach had to be sitting on a goldmine. *Or*, whoever found the owner and bought the land would be sitting on a goldmine. James needed to do some research. You could build an eco-hotel here and charge rich people a fortune to fly from the far corners of the world to take a green holiday. You could include a charge for offsetting on their behalf the carbon footprint for the flights they'd take. You could have them fish for their own supper and cook it themselves and thank you for it. In fact, you could charge rich people to come and *build* the hotel for you as an experience-vacation. This was the perfect project. Total serendipity that there looked to be an amazing business opportunity right under his nose.

It took several hours of digging to find the owner of the plot. C. Adair. Cassie, or a relative. Had to be; it was too much of a coincidence otherwise. If it was Cassie herself, she must be quite wealthy. Inheritance? Or whatever job it was she did? She'd really covered her tracks, like she really hadn't wanted anyone to know that she was the owner, which was slightly odd.

So far, he'd found her pretty annoying, and in an ideal world, he'd minimise conversations with her until they ended the swap, and then not speak again. But he knew he'd regret it if he didn't at least try to buy or lease the land from her. Unfortunately, they weren't on *great* terms, post the Wi-Fi argument. He was going to have to swallow his pride and improve relations between them.

The woman herself gave him the ideal opportunity the next day.

Hi James,

I hope you're settling in. Hope it hasn't been too rainy for you – it isn't normally that wet on the island, especially as we head into the summer, honest (!!).

I'm writing because there's a little favour that I'd like to ask that I didn't really want to put in the notes I left for you; and it's too long for a text…

Laura (next-door neighbour; you met her, she took your parcels in – yes the island grapevine does stretch across the Atlantic and yes the island grapevine does stretch to discussing

exciting matters such as parcel taking on behalf of neighbours)
is elderly and, while in excellent health, not quite as sprightly
as she once was.

Basically (and of course please do feel free to say no), I
wondered if you would be able to check on her from time to time.
Dina's around but sometimes very busy with work.

Thank you! (But please do ignore if you don't have the time.)
Best,
Cassie

Well, this was perfect. Cassie was apparently going to ignore their argument, clearly because she wanted him to do her a favour. And he was going to reply politely today, visit Laura tomorrow, and then call Cassie with a friendly, chatty update. And when they'd had a few conversations and established good relations, he'd call her again to broach the land purchase.

Chapter Ten

Cassie

Cassie twizzled her pen between two fingers and thumb and stared hard at the panelled wall above her laptop. She really needed to make some progress on her plans for Books 2 to 6. She'd never had a mind blank like this before. It was like London was too big and there were too many choices about settings. If she was honest, it was also because she kept obsessing about the IVF decision. She was having her final investigations on Monday, in case she wanted to go ahead. *If* she wanted to go ahead. Did she?

She *really* needed to focus. She was seeing Jennifer this evening for dinner, and a lack of concrete plans always made Jennifer tetchy.

It felt weird to finally be meeting her. Cassie, a Glaswegian in the US, and Jennifer, an American in London, worked together remotely. Cassie had become Jennifer's client and got her first book deal with a big London publisher, who she'd also never met, just before she left Glasgow. When she'd lost the baby, she'd just wanted to escape. Luckily, as a writer you could live anywhere. She'd bought the island house with an inheritance from her grandfather, the sale proceeds from her Glasgow flat and her publisher's advance. And then when she'd got her TV deal, she'd used the money to buy a wildlife haven on the island.

A message pinged in on her phone. Dina. Much more fun to be texting her than panicking about work, and clearly Cassie *had* to check that something bad hadn't happened to the animals.

Hey babe. How you doing? I've been busy – soooo much work the last couple days. My news: BEEN TALKING TO JAMES. Even hotter up close (AND PERSONAL SOON I HOPE). Little bit more friendly than I thought but turned down invite to the island dinner on the weekend – not gonna be popular. Laura's good. Tonight your agent dinner? Have fun xxxxx

It was a mistake on James's part to have decided not to go to the island dinner. *Everyone* went. He seemed so unfriendly. Although, to be fair, he'd sent a surprisingly nice reply to her – unashamedly arse-licking – email asking him to keep an eye on Laura. Maybe in fact he was just too busy to go to the dinner.

James himself called her just after she'd finished her text conversation with Dina and was reluctantly returning to her notes.

'Hey, Cassie. How are you?' That was an oddly warm greeting from him.

'Good, thank you. How are you?'

'Yes, great, thanks.' He actually sounded quite smiley. His deep voice was bordering on very sexy when he wasn't biting out grumpy comments. 'I thought I'd just let you know how Laura was.'

'Oh my goodness, is she okay?'

'Yes, she's absolutely fine. I just went round to check on her. She was up a ten-foot ladder, clearing ivy away from the top of a wall. I had to promise to drink a lot of tea and eat a lot of blueberry pie before she'd get down.' This was like talking to a different person from the grumpy man with the Wi-Fi issue. Very Jekyll and Hyde.

'Thank you so much for checking on her,' Cassie said. 'Kind of you.'

'Honestly not a problem. That's what neighbours are for.'

Really? Cassie had arranged to have tea with James's London neighbour Anthony at the weekend, and Anthony had repeated that he'd never met James. Well, whatever. It was great that James had visited Laura.

They exchanged a few more platitudes before ending the call.

Well. That had genuinely been pleasant.

*

'Come in, come in.' Jennifer was beaming at Cassie like nobody's business.

'Thank you so much.' Cassie stepped over the threshold into Jennifer's hall and Jennifer flung her arms round her, nearly squashing the flowers Cassie was holding. Fortunately, Cassie's biceps were more powerful than she'd suspected – must be all that kayaking recently – and she managed to hold the bouquet away from her. You didn't want a lily stain on a silk dress.

'Those flowers are gorgeous. Thank you. And I love Sancerre.' Jennifer took the flowers and wine from Cassie, led her through the hall and laid them on the worktop of the island that stood in the middle of the Tardis-like, quite narrow but gigantically long, kitchen. 'It's so wonderful to meet you.'

'I know,' Cassie said into another huge hug. Actually, so *weird* to finally meet. On email, social media and the phone, Jennifer was ferocious. The kind of woman Cassie imagined wore monochrome, edgy fashion and extreme lipstick, lived in an amazingly glamorous industrial warehouse apartment in a trendy location and could use chopsticks perfectly. And didn't cook. She'd be too busy going out for power drinks and dinners. The kind of woman who, if you *were* having drinks with her, would constantly be looking over your shoulder for someone better to talk to. The headshot she used on all her profiles definitely backed up all of those assumptions. Cassie had been astonished when Jennifer had suggested that she come over to her house for dinner. She'd thought they'd be going out to a restaurant.

In fact, Jennifer was dressed in a long, floaty, floral skirt and lived in a beautifully but traditionally decorated and furnished Edwardian semi-detached house in the lovely and leafy but not edgily trendy London suburb of Barnes.

And in the extended kitchen at the back of the house there were quite a lot of baby accessories. A playmat. A highchair. Some toys in a wooden chest. Jennifer had never mentioned children.

'Yes, I'm a proud mom,' Jennifer said, gesturing towards the baby stuff. 'Angela, my wife, is just doing Sammy's bath time and then she'll bring him down to introduce him, before he hopefully goes down for the night, and then we can eat without interruption.' Jennifer's face had lit up just talking about them. So at odds with her over-the-phone work persona.

Never judge a book by its cover. Which was what Dina had said about James, and until their phone call today he'd turned out to be *exactly* like he looked.

'Wow. I had no idea. How old is he?'

'Six months. Yeah, I kind of don't mix business and pleasure unless I'm going to meet someone in person. So I don't post about home stuff, or talk about it on business calls.' To be fair, there was a lot that Cassie didn't share with most people.

'Well, wow again. Congratulations. I can't wait to meet him.' Not totally true. She adored babies but, in the middle of huge indecision over whether or not to go ahead with fertility treatment, she was worried that she might actually cry or something if she met one today, and she didn't want to blub in front of anyone else.

No choice. A truly stunning woman walked into the room holding a gurgling baby dressed in a Babygro and waving a rattle manically around his head. He was *beautiful*. Cassie swallowed, hard.

'Hey, Sammy.' Jennifer walked towards him, arms stretched out, and he reached for her, chortling. 'And Angela, of course. Hard not to relegate your partner to behind the baby at times. Cassie, this is Angela. And Angela, this is my wonderful client Cassie.'

Angela smiled at Cassie. She had a gorgeous smile. Cassie had the strange sensation that she was looking into a mirror that massively improved the way you looked. She and Angela both had a *lot* of dark, curly hair and olive skin and dark eyes, but Angela was very tall and slim, which Cassie was not, and her hair was very under control, which Cassie's was not. And she had an air of swan-like serenity, which Cassie was pretty sure she didn't.

'Hi, Angela. So nice to meet you.'

'Likewise, I'm so pleased to meet you. And this is Sammy. Say hello, Sammy.'

'Hi, Sammy.' Mega heart-lurch. He was *so* cute. 'I love your tooth.' His wide, gummy smile, with one little front tooth just showing, was adorable. Sammy held his arms out to her.

'He likes you,' said Jennifer.

Angela lifted Sammy into Cassie's arms. He was so gorgeously chubby and cuddly. Cassie closed her eyes for a moment. It was a surprise that neither Jennifer nor Angela appeared to be able to hear the frantic ticking of her biological clock.

'Hey, Sammy,' she said, hoping that her voice sounded normal. He smelled so lovely and his skin was so soft. And he was pulling her hair. Hard. *Really* hard. 'Ouch,' she yelped.

'Sorry, should have warned you,' Angela said, disentangling Sammy's hand and holding out her fingers for him to play with instead.

Cassie smiled and shifted Sammy around in her arms and told him that he was very cute and very clever. She could *totally* act normally and non-broodily around a baby.

'You know, I feel I know almost as little about you as you did about me? Do you have children?' Jennifer asked, pulling champagne flutes out of a cupboard.

'No.' Oh no. A voice wobble. Hopefully Jennifer wouldn't have noticed.

'I'm so sorry. I shouldn't have asked. So insensitive of me.' She'd noticed.

Cassie shook her head. 'No, honestly, not at all insensitive. I don't have kids and I'd love to have them one day, if the situation ever arises, but equally I'm very happy with my life if it never happens. I don't currently have a partner, so it isn't really likely to. And I do have three alpacas and eleven chickens, so they keep me pretty busy.' Always a winner, mentioning the animals.

'Alpacas! Hey, that's so cool.' And bingo, off the 'do you want babies' topic. Although, Cassie had some questions of her own. Meeting Sammy had got her veering back towards going for the fertility treatment. She'd regret it if she didn't try. Maybe Jennifer and Angela had gone down the sperm donor route and would have some useful advice for her. It was a tricky question to bring up politely, though.

Angela took Sammy to put him to bed and, after some chat about childhood hobbies, Jennifer suddenly said, 'So how's it going with choosing a location for the books?'

Cassie only registered Jennifer's words when she realised that she was looking at her differently, and that she'd used her business-mode voice.

Business Jennifer was a lot less appealing than Friendly Dinner Host Jennifer, frankly.

'Not too bad,' Cassie lied. 'I've been researching all the different areas.'

'Okay. And how far have you got? Because time is of the essence.'

Sammy gurgled over the monitor. So cute.

'Cassie?'

Ow. That whole Listen-To-Me shrillness was *right* back. Cassie hoped for Angela and Sammy's sakes that Jennifer never got like this about domestic matters. She experienced a sudden wave of sympathy for Future Sammy when he hadn't made his bed or he'd dropped a grade at school.

'I'm thinking that it's so hard to choose a single area to focus on that I should have a different one for each book. So it's like a pan-London series, rather than a Hampstead Heath or Hyde Park or whatever series. So they could be set in different-seeming places. More of a something-for-everyone vibe,' she said, panicked.

'That's perfect,' Jennifer said. 'I'm sure they'll go for that. Great work.'

Oh, okay, no decision to make then. It would involve more research but that was cool because Cassie was going to enjoy being a tourist in London.

Jennifer had a few more work-related points that she wanted to make before Angela came back into the room and then she switched straight back into nice Home Jennifer mode and served their main course, a restaurant-standard sea bream dish.

'Do you both cook a lot?' Cassie asked. It was remarkably difficult to reconcile Jennifer's two personas. It was as strange as the recent change in James.

'Angela normally does more of the cooking but she's still breastfeeding, so it's more difficult for her at the moment,' Jennifer said.

'Yep. It's nowhere near as time-consuming as it used to be, except before bedtime, when he likes a long feed,' Angela said, 'so it's fine but it isn't great timing for evening meal preparation unless you do it a lot earlier in the day.'

'It must be lovely having those cuddles with him,' said Cassie, trying not to sound wistful.

'It is.' Angela's face lit up. 'But I tell you what, breastfeeding's a lot harder than it looks. And I had mastitis at one point, and that was horrendous. I've never felt so ill so fast in my life.'

'It sounds awful.' Cassie knew that it was awful because she'd had mastitis herself, after she'd lost the baby. Awful didn't begin to describe how bad that had been. 'Did you have any help from wider family after the baby was born?' Genius, almost the 'is there a sperm donor in the picture' question.

'No, not really,' Jennifer said. 'My family's in the States, and Angela's family's in Australia. And based on great but also bitter experience, we know that when either of our families stay with us, they're *high* maintenance, so we decided to be strict with them, and we didn't have anyone to stay until Sammy was three months old. So it was just the three of us.'

'Apart from Doug. The father,' Angela said. 'A friend who provided the sperm.'

'Yeah, we basically turkey basted,' Jennifer said. 'Doug's completely hands-off, though.' Dammit. They hadn't done the anonymous donor and IVF route.

'Lucky that he's hands off,' said Angela, 'because we don't really want to share Sammy.'

'Yeah, Doug's perfect,' Jennifer said. 'We know him, because with an anonymous donor of course you have no idea, and he's great, but he works all hours so, you know, he isn't around much. Ideal. In the nicest possible way.'

Cassie was beginning to be sure that from *her* perspective an anonymous sperm donor would be ideal. Prospective donors had to be rigorously screened for genetic health conditions, didn't they? And they had to give their details so that children could find their fathers when they turned eighteen. And if someone was public-spirited enough to donate sperm you'd think they'd be kind enough to agree to meet their eighteen-year-old child.

And, frankly, with her track record with men when she was younger, it wasn't like she'd be great at choosing an in-person sperm donor. This way, her child would probably get a *better* father.

Funny how sometimes when someone expressed a firm preference about something it made you realise that you felt quite differently. She'd have to make a 'Do IVF with sperm donor' pros and cons list later.

On her way home, Cassie read several more texts from Dina. Mega rain still on the island. Don Brown had seen a whale off Blue View Point. The more Dina thought about it, the more she was sure James could be The One. If he went to Amy's party she was pretty sure that something would *happen*. James was *really* nice. James was going to get someone to come to the island to try to improve the Wi-Fi. James had a great sense of humour when you spoke to him properly. James was amazing. Right.

Cassie finished her reply just as the taxi driver was pulling up outside the flat.

List time.

Pros:
DESPERATE to have baby
DESPERATE to be pregnant with own baby
If it works out would then HAVE A BABY TO LOVE
A lot to be said for not having a father involved. Simon would have been a shit father

Cons:
Heartbreaking if doesn't work out
Hard to be pregnant by self
Hard to bring up baby by self
Etc

Cassie could *always* be bothered to write a list out. But on this occasion there were just *so many* cons, big and small, it felt like a waste of time.

Frankly, it felt like madness to even be contemplating going it alone.

But the capitals said it all. *Desperate* and *have a baby to love.*

She was going to do it. She was going to bloody do it. She was going to try to have a baby.

Chapter Eleven

James

James waved at Dina as she walked past on her way to feed the animals, and carried on buttering his toast.

Maybe he should go and help her with the feeding. He needed more reasons to call Cassie, get to know her better, before he suggested buying her land, and the animals would be an obvious excuse for a call. He had the time to help with them. With no commute and close to no socialising, you could work north of twelve to fourteen hours a day and still not be that busy unless you needed a lot of sleep. And he'd be happy to hang out with Dina a little. She was good company plus she could put in a good word for him with Cassie; they were clearly close.

He finished his toast and grabbed shoes.

'Morning, Dina,' he said when he got to the animal enclosure. She spun straight round with a big smile on her face.

'James,' she practically purred.

Oh-kay. A little bit of flirting would be great, but he didn't want to end up in a situation where she'd be bad-mouthing him to Cassie. Maybe better if he looked after the animals entirely by himself.

A good twenty minutes later, he said, 'Great,' as she finished a lengthy demonstration, all of which he was pretty sure would be covered in Cassie's notes. 'Thank you so much. I'm sure I'll see you soon. With eggs I imagine.' He should definitely get involved with the eggs; he had the impression that Cassie was someone who'd enjoy an egg distribution anecdote.

'Great.' Dina kept her eyes on his for a lot longer than an animal husbandry conversation warranted. 'If you change your mind about the island dinner, let me know. And you're very welcome, it should go without saying, to come to Amy's party. We'll hopefully see you at both. Happy animal feeding.'

Yeah, he still wasn't going to the dinner but he'd maybe think about the party, whoever Amy was. Presumably another neighbour.

Feeding the alpacas and chickens wasn't so bad, it turned out. James had rarely had anything at all to do with animals other than a couple of school visits to zoos. During his childhood, they'd never had a pet – a fortunate thing, given that it would have either died from neglect or been yet another far-too-early responsibility for him and Ella. And as a single adult with a busy job and a smart London flat, you just didn't own animals.

You could in fact spend a fair amount of time watching them. This would be why zoos were a success and why people liked owning cats and dogs. Was he going mad or did alpacas have quite intelligent and kind faces? And the chickens; it was like they had actual personalities. There were definitely some who were bolder and some who were more timid. Who knew?

James scanned the index on Cassie's notes one more time. He needed a water-tight reason to call her; there wasn't a lot to say about the animals yet, and it clearly shouldn't be to discuss something that she'd covered in the notes. Whale watching. She hadn't mentioned that. It related to nature. She was clearly a nature lover. And it would be a good lead-in to discussing ecotourism and the financial benefits for locals.

'Cassie. Hi. How are you?'

'Good thanks. How are you?'

'Yeah, great, thanks. I was just calling to ask your advice about something. Take advantage of your local knowledge, something you didn't mention in your notes.' Nice. Strong implication there that he'd read them.

'Oh, okay. Of course.' She actually had a very attractive voice.

'I'd really like to do some whale watching and obviously I could just google it—' if the bloody internet worked '—but I thought it would be better to get advice from you.'

'I'm really sorry but I can't give you any advice.'

'Oh. Have you never been?' Whatever. It had still been a good excuse to start this conversation.

'No.'

'I suppose it's like I've never been to Buckingham Palace. You don't do the tourist things close to home.'

'Kind of. It's more of a considered choice, though. Not to say you shouldn't go if you want to, obviously, but I think a lot of conservationists are against it. I mean, you can do it safely for whales, but I think there's a lot of evidence that people *aren't* doing it safely. They get too close, in large boats, and it's affecting whale behaviour and migratory patterns and breeding cycles and so on.' Right. Probably not the moment to mention ecotourism. 'So my view is that it's probably best not to support it as an industry. I don't think there's anything in it for whales. And you can see them occasionally from the beaches, if you're lucky.'

'So what would you recommend?'

'Well, I mean, there's so much to do. As I mentioned, possibly at too much length, in my notes.'

James laughed politely. 'Not at all. They were fascinating.' He needed to get off the notes topic, fast. 'How have you settled? Is your work going well?' Whatever it was that she did exactly.

'Yes, it's great thank you. It's a fab location, obviously, and the flat's amazing. And, yep, work's good, thanks.'

'You said you were a writer?'

'Yep.'

'What kind of writing do you do?' Most people liked talking about themselves.

There was a long pause.

'I write books.'

'Oh, wow. Book books? Fiction, I mean?'

'Yep.'

'That's really interesting. I don't think I've ever met an author before. What genre?'

Another longish pause.

'Children's.'

'Wow. So what's your pen name?' She clearly didn't write under her own name, because he'd have found her when he was googling her. There was no pause this time.

'I can't tell you. I'd have to kill you. Not joking. No-one knows; I never tell anyone.'

'No-one?'

'Hardly anyone.'

'Well, wow again. I want to say congratulations, but that's probably quite patronising if you've been doing this for a number of years or published a lot of books.'

'I'll overlook the patronising thing and say thank you.' She had a smile in her voice but she wasn't biting on giving him any more information. 'What is it exactly that you do?'

'Private equity. Basically investing in businesses, turning around ailing ones, investing in start-ups.'

'Interesting. So what made you choose that career?'

'I guess I just love the human side of business, you know what makes people tick, behavioural cycles, that sort of thing.' Women always loved that answer. It wasn't up there with saying you were a fireman or a doctor, obviously, but it made his job sound better than it was. He never told anyone the real reason, that he'd needed to start earning as much money as possible as young as he could, to look after his mother and Leonie better, and this had been the best paid job going when he graduated from uni.

Woah. The heavens had suddenly opened. James flattened himself against the wall of the house to huddle under the porch thing that ran all the way along, to keep his phone dry. Not a good idea to stop the conversation now, when they were finally getting on well.

They ended up chatting for a good fifteen minutes longer. Cassie was a lot more fun to talk to than James had imagined she would be. She had a great line in sarcasm.

He managed to get another pleasant phone chat in a couple of days later, having struck gold in realising that he could eat some of Cassie's freezer meals and call her to thank her for them.

They were definitely on good enough terms now for him to ask her about the land.

*

The next time he called her, he made sure the forecast was good and his phone fully charged, and that it was 5 p.m. in the UK, which felt like an hour at which she might not be too busy. All bases covered, hopefully.

'Hey, Cassie. How's your day been?'

'Hello. Good, thanks. I'm just back from a guided tour of Buckingham Palace. How are you?'

'Also good, thanks. Was that work or pleasure? Sounds interesting?'

'It was for work and yes it was very interesting. You obviously don't see the queen's actual living rooms but it's still her house. Lots of history and beautiful things. And you see a bit of the garden, which basically seemed to be a lot of lawn and trees.'

'So not as nice as your garden?'

'Exactly.' Cassie laughed. 'How's my garden doing?'

'Looks nice. Lots of flowers coming out.' James knew literally nothing about plants. 'The gardener's been busy.'

'How're the animals?'

'They seem very well and, if I say it myself, they're being very well looked after. I genuinely know all their names now, and I'm pretty sure they recognise me.'

'Wow, listen to you. I really wouldn't have had you down as an alpaca whisperer.'

'Me either. Island living's bringing out hidden talents in me. I'm becoming very good at bartering with eggs as well. I got a great steak yesterday from Lonnie Duggan in return for half a dozen.'

'Impressive.'

'I know. So what hidden talents have you found in yourself since you moved to London?'

'That's a good question. I'm becoming expert at not catching anyone's eye on the Tube, head down, no smiling. And pushing really hard so that I get the last space in the carriage.'

'Excellent. Important skills.' James was smiling, even though there was no point because she couldn't see him. Was this some kind of age-related issue, now he'd hit thirty-five, a lack of control over his facial muscles?

'Exactly.'

'Cool. Well, I should probably leap straight into what I have to ask you. I have a business proposition for you.'

'Oh-kay. Interesting.'

'I've been exploring the island, obviously, and, equally obviously, I love it, because who wouldn't? It's stunning.' Always flatter people. Even hardened businessmen often fell for a bit of hyperbole. 'And I discovered your plot of land and beach, round the headland, which gave me a business idea.'

'Right.' Her voice was flat. Hopefully she'd sound more interested when she'd heard more.

He'd planned his pitch in detail, including planning permission research and points that would appeal to the woman he thought she was, like how building a tourist business on the plot would benefit the local community economically and enable urban dwellers to experience the enriching joys of rural living.

She listened to the whole thing in complete silence and then continued with the silence, so he ended up suggesting that if she didn't want to sell they could go into partnership, just for something to say. He couldn't remember the last time he'd displayed such poor negotiating skills.

When he'd lapsed into silence himself, she finally spoke. 'How did you find out that I own the land?'

'When I saw what a good opportunity this was, I did a little digging.' Yeah, okay, as he said it, he realised that if the tables had been turned he wouldn't have appreciated Cassie hunting him down. She'd clearly wanted to keep her ownership under wraps, for whatever reason. She clearly liked to keep a lot of things private, like her pen name.

'Right. Well, no, sorry, I have no intention of selling, or going into business with anyone. I bought that land with the intention of leaving it wild, for environmental reasons, and also slightly for selfish personal reasons, because I love the quiet there. And people travelling halfway across the world for eco holidays annoys me a *lot* as a concept. I mean, they wouldn't be rowing or swimming themselves there, would they?'

'True, but if people are going to fly to their holiday destination no matter what, it might as well be green when they get there. Still makes for a lower carbon footprint overall. Like it would be better for the environment if none of us bought new stuff, ever, but since we're going to, let's at least make what stuff we do buy environmentally friendly.'

'Yup, okay, so maybe I was being a little judgy there, but still no. I don't want a hotel at the end of my back garden and I do want my land to be a wildlife sanctuary, without even a very small number of guests. Sorry.'

'Hey, no worries. Just a thought.' He could carry on working on her over the next few weeks and months. He'd definitely made a dent in her argument about what was best for the environment.

'James. Can I ask you a question?

'Yep, sure.'

'Have you been calling me... *just* because you wanted to develop my land?' Bugger.

'No, not at all.'

'Oh my *God*. You totally have.'

'Really, no.' Was lying a good idea at this point? No-one wanted to go into business with a liar. 'I mean, maybe a little.'

'*What*? That's so cynical.' Okay, he should have gone with the lying.

'Okay, yes, a little cynical to start off with, but I've really enjoyed our conversations. And I do think my suggestion would benefit a lot of people.'

'Hmm.'

'Sorry?' A lot of women couldn't resist when he said *Sorry* like that. Whether or not he meant it.

'Oh-kay,' she said, sounding like she could totally resist. 'I'd better go. I have work to do. Nice to chat.' Little bit sarcastic-sounding there. 'Bye.'

That could have gone better.

Cassie's responses over the next few days to his messages about the animals and Laura were less chatty than usual; she definitely wasn't that impressed by his hunting her down and the business suggestion. Well, fine. Her land would be perfect for his purposes, but there were other plots on other islands in the area, some for sale, presumably with much more amenable owners. Or Cassie might come round in due course.

*

A few days later, the quiet of the morning was shattered by some kind of large vehicle beeping and crunching over the gravel in the drive. James pushed his chair out from the desk and stood up to investigate.

Life on the island was so quiet that he'd got to the point where he was mildly pleased at the possibility of a chat with anyone.

When he got round the side of the house, he found a large lorry coming to a halt in the drive.

'I have your marquee,' the driver told him as he swung down from the cab.

'Sorry, I think you've got the wrong address,' James said.

The driver's companion already had the back of the lorry open.

'It's the right address,' the driver said. 'We've delivered here before for Cassie.'

James shook his head. 'Nope, definitely a mistake. Cassie isn't here. Sorry.'

'It's definitely today.' The man showed James the booking form. Yep, it was today's date. Odd, because Cassie didn't strike James as someone who messed up in that kind of way. But she obviously had.

'I'm thinking she must have made a mistake with the date when she booked it.'

'I don't think so. She confirmed last week.' What?

The men didn't look like they were going anywhere. And presumably they'd gone to quite a lot of trouble to get the marquee here. Unless by some lucky chance there was a marquee business on the island.

'You local?' he asked.

'Pretty much. From the mainland. Just got off the ferry.' Yeah, not that local.

James was going to have to call Cassie.

She picked up on the third ring. 'Hi, James.'

'Hi. I have a lorry with a marquee on it in the drive.'

'Oh good. Thank you for letting me know.' What?

'Why? Did you actually order it for today?'

'Yes? I thought I told you it was coming today? Did I put the wrong date?'

'Erm.' When did she think she'd told him? Oh. Probably in her notes. 'What's the marquee for?'

'For the party?' She sounded a bit impatient, definitely sure that he *should* know what she was talking about. Given the level of detail she'd gone into about everything else, it did seem likely that she'd covered this party in her notes. So she was about to realise that he hadn't read them. But seriously, *who* would have read that many pages? The notes were practically book-length. And did he care whether she knew that he hadn't? He did recall a heading along the lines of 'social events' in the notes index, but he'd assumed that would just be elaborating in excruciating detail on things like the island dinner that Dina had mentioned.

'Party?'

'Amy's eighteenth?' She sounded properly annoyed now.

'Amy?' Who *was* Amy? This would be the party Dina had talked about.

'Her party's on Saturday. In the marquee. On the field. I definitely told you about it.' Right. Maybe at this point the best thing would be for him to go and check her notes.

'Okay. I need to go. I'll call you back.'

'Great. I'll be waiting on the edge of my seat to hear from you.'

James managed – with a fifty-dollar bribe – to convince the men to hold off for a few minutes on beginning the marquee erection.

Then he found and speed-read the party-related notes. Okay. Amy was Dina's daughter and she was turning eighteen today – Dina must have been very young when she had her – and on Saturday evening she was having a big birthday party in the marquee that was about to be erected in Cassie's field. The only access to the field was via Cassie's, or James's – depending on how you looked at it – garden, or by boat; and if he didn't want things to be delivered via the garden he should let Cassie know as soon as he arrived, so that she could organise for the deliveries to be made by boat, but she'd be incredibly grateful if they could use the garden, which would barely inconvenience James at all and would be cheaper.

There would be caterers. There would be portable toilets. There would be several hundred guests in total, because a lot of the islanders would be coming plus other friends. And James would be a very welcome guest at the party.

And she had another party planned for this summer. Laura's eightieth.

Right. If he was honest, James didn't really mind about there being a party in the field or about his garden being used for access. If you'd asked him before he got here or even at the weekend, he wouldn't have been happy at the thought of having his peace shattered and having to spend a lot of time with his neighbours, but as it turned out he wasn't loving the solitude thing, so, no, he didn't mind enormously.

He *did* mind, though, about the principle that she hadn't told him in advance about either the Wi-Fi or the party hosting. Was he going to get any more unpleasant surprises?

He went back outside and told the men that they were welcome to go ahead, and then he called Cassie back.

'Hi. So, I'm not convinced it's okay to rent a house to someone and then, after they've signed on the dotted line, in fact *arrived*, tell them that they're throwing an enormous, or indeed even a very small, party,' he said.

There was a very long pause. He was not going to fill it. Silence was always the best negotiation tactic.

Eventually, Cassie said, 'The party's in the field, which is not part of the rental agreement although obviously you can use it if you wish, and I left the notes asking you to let me know if you didn't want to allow access through the garden as then they would have brought it by boat. And while you might not want to attend or listen to a loud party at that proximity to the house, it isn't *that* close, and it isn't on the land you have rented and there are big events in venues in relatively close proximity to your flat here *all the time*. Like both the parks.' Oh, please.

'I'm sorry but that's a ridiculous comparison. You go to London, you expect noise. You come to an island in the middle of nowhere, you expect silence. I mean, obviously.'

'What, so people on islands don't have parties? You'd complain if your neighbour threw a party?'

'Maybe.' What James should probably do now was read *all* her notes, find out to what extent it could be argued he was in the wrong. 'Okay. Well, I've told the men to go ahead with the installation.'

'Kind of you.' *Very* sarky. 'Bye then.'

The notes were incredibly long. It took way longer to read them than it took to erect a large marquee on a somewhat uneven and still wet field. James took a break from the notes to see the men off and then got back to them.

On paper, Cassie was warm and friendly. Like she'd been during their few amicable phone conversations. Funny, too. And remarkably loquacious. You wouldn't think one person could have so many mini-anecdotes about their home and one smallish island. Or that all the anecdotes would be enjoyable to read. He almost wanted to meet some of the people she'd written about.

He should probably call her back.

'Hi.'

'I read the notes a little too fast initially and I missed the bit about the party. Apologies. Obviously I'm happy for it to go ahead and I'll keep an eye out for the catering deliveries.'

'You didn't read them at all before, did you?'

'No? In my defence they're extensive and I'm not a big reader.'

'You don't read work stuff?'

'Yes, I do, but I don't read for leisure. Anyway. I'm trying to thank you for leaving them for me. I enjoyed reading them and thanks for taking the time to write them.'

'Okay, well, no problem.' Sounded as though she was smiling.

Mid-afternoon, he decided that he'd better go and check on Laura. Strangely, he didn't object that much now to visiting her. Too much solitude could get to you.

There was no doorbell at Laura's. James banged hard on the door. It opened way faster than usual.

'Hey, James.' It was Dina. This was the first time he'd seen her inside. She was even more attractive when she wasn't soaking wet in a field. 'How are the animals? And have you made any progress on the Wi-Fi? Laura and I were just talking about you.'

James nodded. It was apparent that the arrival of a stranger on the island was big news.

'Come through.' She turned round and led the way to the kitchen at the back of the house.

'Good afternoon, James.' Laura pushed down on the arms of her chair to get herself onto her feet. 'I'll put the kettle on. You missed the dinner.' Wow. How long would it take for island life to get seriously claustrophobic?

'Yeah, stuff to do,' he said. 'Settling in. Unpacking. I was sorry to have missed it.'

'Next time.' Laura smiled at him comfortably.

'They're monthly. We could all go together next time.' Dina's smile implied that she had very X-rated plans for him. It was like James was a nineteenth-century eligible gentleman who'd turned up in a village full of marriageable young ladies and low on marriageable men.

'That sounds great.' He made sure his own smile was bland.

'Tea or coffee?' Laura asked.

'Tea would be great, thank you. Can I help make it?' James said.

Laura and Dina were good company together. Dina laughed at Laura when she went down the inquisition route, and Laura tsked at Dina when she overtly ogled James and suggested that they go to Amy's party *together*. Amy was apparently busy with her friends getting ready for this evening. Dina was going to go and join them soon and she'd love for James to *join* her later. James told her that he wasn't sure how his schedule was but he'd look forward to seeing her at the party.

The rest of the day wasn't bad either. He finished up some work, enjoyed reading the remainder of Cassie's notes and cooked dinner for himself. Turned out that a) there were some basic skills you didn't lose and b) you could enjoy cooking when you could afford whatever ingredients you liked and you didn't have your baby sister hanging round your ankles and your mother completely off her face and the feeling that your time would be better spent on seeing your mates or schoolwork.

At this rate he'd be knocking up a pecan pie to contribute to the next island dinner and polishing Cassie's lawnmower in pleasurable anticipation of the race.

*

'Hey, James.' Dina, looking good, very good, if a little scary, dressed in a tight, low-cut black mini dress and some impressively high heels, had knocked on his kitchen door and then opened it without waiting for an answer – James made a mental note never to be downstairs not fully dressed unless he wanted something to happen – and poked her head in. 'You coming over to the field now?'

'I'll be there in about half an hour if that's alright.' Probably not a good idea to go to the party *with* Dina. 'Couple of things to do first. Got to put the chickens to bed.'

'Sure. Look forward to seeing you there.'

Cassie and Dina had apparently organised the whole party together, with a lot of virtual input from Cassie, at awkward times of the day due to the Wi-Fi issue. Did *no-one* on this island know about hotspotting? James should tell them. And he should get back on the phone to the Wi-Fi engineer. Mid-week it had sounded like he had some good ideas about how to improve their service.

'So I've been using my Wi-Fi all day every day,' he told Dina over excellent mini-tacos and beers in a corner of the marquee.

'*No!*' Dina stopped with her taco halfway to her mouth. 'How? Why does it work for you and not for anyone else? Did you bring it with you?'

Explaining to Dina, and then to the several friends she dragged over, about the hotspotting felt like being in *Back to the Future* or something, like he was visiting the past from a time of greater technology.

'No, really,' he said in answer to a question from Laura, 'we do not have different or more modern technology in London.'

'Mom, everyone knows about hotspotting,' Amy said when her mother had brought her over to be impressed. 'Like everyone on the island under thirty. Probably some of the oldies too.'

'Firstly, over thirty is not old. And secondly, what? Why didn't you tell me? Do you think I *want* to set my alarm for two a.m. when I want to use the internet?'

Amy screwed her face up, like she was thinking hard. 'Did I know you did that?' she asked.

'Yes, you know I do. I mention it a *lot*. Like every day when I'm yawning over breakfast. Sheesh, Amy, I'm a *person*, not just a food-making, lift-giving, bathroom-cleaning voice of wisdom. Like, pay some freaking *attention* to me.' Dina smiled at her daughter as she spoke, softening her words, and pulled Amy in for a hug.

'Love you, Mom.' Amy grinned at her mother.

James could barely look. There was something so great but also alien about a fantastic parent-child relationship. When you'd never had a relationship of any kind with your father, and the one with your recently deceased mother had morphed early on into you, the child, doing any parenting that was happening, it was sometimes hard to witness a well-functioning family relationship. Normally he was okay with it. It was great that his friends had good families. But today it was touching a nerve. Must be because he'd stupidly opened the email from his father last week.

'So, James,' Dina said to him. 'Laura tells me you don't have kids. Are you keen to start a family?' Woah. Punchy question, and punchy timing.

'Yep, no kids, and, no, no plans for any.' That was an understatement. James was definitely not going to have children. One, he'd probably inherited some kind of terrible parenting gene from his own parents. Two, it had been too much responsibility for him and Ella having to bring their sister Leonie up and he'd totally messed up his part in it. Three, he liked his life as it was. His real life, his London life, when it didn't involve angry exes or ex-employees.

Amy smiled at them all and waltzed off to dance in the middle of the marquee with a group of friends of her own age.

Dina leaned closer to James so that he could feel her breath on his neck and had to twist his head to an awkward angle to avoid seeing straight down her cleavage. 'Maybe I could persuade you to rethink. I'm feeling broody again now that my baby's grown up.' Good grief. Hopefully that was just the many beers she'd downed talking.

'Ha,' he said, going for the treat-it-as-a-joke approach. 'Yes. Good one. Like to dance?'

Dina did like to dance and they did in fact have a lot of fun on the dance floor until James begged for mercy and extricated himself to go and chat to some of the other guests.

Around midnight, speeches started.

'And now I'd like to ask James to come up onto the stage,' Dina blared over the mic, at the end of a long and drunken speech, her arm round a smiling Amy.

James nearly choked on his lemonade, experiencing a strong, and not pleasant, feeling of déjà vu from Emily's birthday party. He shook his head slightly. Obviously Dina was not going to tell the room that he was about to propose to someone. That would be the most unbelievable coincidence ever. Plus Dina didn't seem at all delusional. This was going to be fine.

He walked over to the stage, receiving a lot of pats on the back from complete or near strangers on his way.

As he jumped up onto the stage, Dina mic-catcalled, 'Nice butt, James,' to a lot of cheering. James nodded and bowed. He'd take that; a lot better than her expecting him to propose. 'Amy and I just wanted to thank you for hosting in Cassie's absence.' She handed him the mic.

'My pleasure,' James said, smiling. Thank God no-one wanted to marry him. 'Really, I did nothing. Thank *you*, Dina and Amy, for inviting me. I've had a great evening and I hope you have too.' He looked at Dina and Amy and then he looked at everyone else, including the two-man band (trumpet and drums, the island electrician and odd-job man respectively, and genuinely at least as good as Emily's fancy band had been). Then he leaned into the mic, did a big conducting motion, and started singing 'Happy Birthday'. Might as well put his expertise to good use.

Everyone joined in and no-one booed or slapped him.

Not too bad an evening.

Chapter Twelve

Cassie

Cassie pushed the front door open with her back and heaved her shopping inside. She *loved* London shops. If you realised on a Sunday morning on the island that you might have all the ingredients you needed for a pre-afternoon-tea baking-fest but you didn't have any baking trays, you'd be buggered. In London, off you went to the nearby shops, and if one shop didn't have exactly what you wanted, you just went to another one. Or you could Amazon-Prime it. On Wednesday, she'd had some stationery delivered within six hours of ordering it. Deliveries took a lot longer when you were a ferry journey away from the nearest depot.

Her phone pinged. James. What now? Did he want to suck up to her again to try to persuade her to agree to his ecotourism plan – which was never going to happen – or was he going to have a go at her?

Hi Cassie. Party went well – marquee, loos, food, drunkenness levels – all good. Laura pretty much outlasted us all (directing the dancing from the sidelines with her stick...). Great evening. Alpacas and chickens not too traumatised – checked on them this morning.

Hmm. Sucking up.

Dina had sent a whole series of texts.

Party was a-maz-ing. My beautiful girl is eighteen. Can't believe it. Same age I was when she was born. Thank you so much for the field and all your wonderful help.

James also amazing. Sooooo HOT. Seems like we're taking things slowly (aka NO ACTION WHATSOEVER YET) but I'm thinking that's just because he's a gentleman, which is GREAT but I want something to HAPPEN…

HOTSPOTTING. Always thought it was a menopausal thing BUT NO: it's more expensive BUT you can get internet on your laptop through your phone!!! Any time of day obviously!!!!! Amy already knew!!! James getting Wi-Fi fixed.

Sending more photos from party later soon but here's one for now.

She'd sent a group one of herself, Amy, Laura, a couple of other good friends and James.

Cassie shouldn't be interested in checking out James in party gear.

She *was* interested. She stretched the photo into a close-up of him. So good-looking. His bone structure and the shape of his mouth. His hair had grown and was slightly wavy. Gorgeous. The photo showed him wearing a navy shirt and smart jeans, a very affluent-Londoner look. Exactly the kind of man she'd learned the hard way not to like. Exactly the kind of man who of *course* Dina was going to fall for if he had any kind of wit and charm at *all* and who was of *course* going to let her down. Not to judge a book by its cover.

Cassie now knew that he *did* have a lot of charm, when he wanted to. He was tenacious too – he must have put a lot of effort into finding that she was the owner of her land. Wasted effort.

He was probably used to getting his own way about everything. No doubt he'd have another go at schmoozing her.

Another 'James is soooo amazing' text came through from Dina.

It was a teensy bit annoying how everyone was so enamoured of James.

It looked from the photos as though the party had been great. And Cassie had missed it. *However,* she'd had a fab catch-up yesterday evening with a couple of old university friends, and there'd be other parties. Like Laura's – maybe she'd take a long-weekend trip home for that one and see everyone.

Right. She'd better get baking so that she'd be ready before Anthony and the neighbours from the floor above arrived. She sent some heart emojis and a 'Speak later – in baking crisis' message to Dina.

Baking was going to be a lovely, civilised way to spend a couple of hours.

Cassie hated baking. She was terrible at it. Cooking savoury dishes was no problem because they were really about the flavours, so you didn't have to follow a recipe slavishly. Baking *was* a problem because you needed to use the right ingredients in the right quantities and bake them for the right length of time at the right heat.

Cassie had messed up at least one of those things with *all* of the *four* bakes that she'd attempted. So now she had a lot of inedible food on James's previously immaculate granite worktops and a lot of burnt raspberry juice to clean off the inside of his no-longer-pristine oven, and *no food* for the afternoon tea.

But it was okay because she was in London and she could use Wi-Fi and Google to find Luigi's number and then buy cakes from him. And if he didn't have any cakes left she was going to call another baker until she found someone who did. London was great.

'This is delicious cake.' Anthony beamed at Cassie.

'Thank you.' She beamed back. He was lovely. As were the elderly woman and the young couple from upstairs. 'I say thank you... I didn't make it myself. I had a little baking disaster. So I bought these cakes.'

'Well, you bought very well.' Juliet, the older woman, was as sweet as Anthony. And the two of them seemed to get on remarkably well, to the extent that it looked like something could even happen between them now they'd met properly.

Speaking of which. Dina and James. Cassie should ask about him, on Dina's behalf, and also out of curiosity.

'What's James like?' she asked.

'James?' Juliet was frowning.

'James is apparently the owner of this flat.' Anthony accompanied his explanation with a little pat on Juliet's arm. She visibly fluttered at his touch. *Definitely* something could happen between them. 'I don't know him at all. He must keep very different hours from me. I might perhaps recognise him if I saw him. Did you say you'd seen him, Juliet?'

'Yes, I think so. I didn't know his name but I'm sure it was him,' Juliet said. 'Ever so dishy. Charming smile.'

'Think he's a banker,' Jack from upstairs said. 'Something like that. Looks like one.'

'Well, I don't know about that,' his wife, Chloe, said, in a much more gossipy tone, 'but I *do* know that he had a woman banging on his door and swearing away late at night about a month ago.' That had probably been Emily.

'Yes, I heard that,' Anthony said.

Juliet nodded. 'Me too.'

'Does he have a lot of partners?' Cassie asked. 'Asking for a friend. Genuinely. He's been a bit of a hit on the island.'

None of them thought that he brought a lot of women to the flat. In fact, the only one that they could describe sounded very much like Dee. Maybe he wasn't quite the smooth operator he seemed to be. That would make sense, given he hadn't jumped immediately into bed with Dina. Dina was very funny, and gorgeous in a brunette Marilyn-Monroe kind of way. Your average straight and single man did not say no to her.

An unwelcome vision of Simon came into Cassie's mind. He definitely wouldn't have said no, single or otherwise. He'd started seeing other women before they split up, after five years together, within a week of her miscarriage. It had been devastating, but, four years on, she needed to stop assuming every man was the same. There were plenty of decent ones out there.

The jury was still out on James, though.

'Thank you so much.' Chloe hugged Cassie as they were all leaving after their much longer than expected – in a good way – afternoon tea. 'You'll have to come up to us soon. Maybe dinner in the next week or two?'

'That would be fabulous.' Cassie hugged her back.

Jack, Anthony and Juliet all gave her pecks on the cheek as they left. As Cassie watched from her front door, Jack slung his arm round Chloe's shoulders, sweet, and *then* Anthony placed his arm kind of round Juliet in a chivalrous, ushering kind of way and she gave him a *look* from under her eyelashes. Would Cassie be flirting in her seventies? She hoped so. She wouldn't mind the opportunity for some flirting several decades before then too, if she was honest.

*

A few weeks later, back from lunch upstairs, Cassie flopped down into the one comfortable armchair in James's flat. She'd only been in London for a couple of months, but it was definitely beginning to feel like she belonged a little.

Her phone buzzed. James.

'Hello?' Cassie no longer expected an argument when he called. He hadn't been grumpy with her at all since the marquee conversation. She was fairly sure that it was because he was taking a long view on the ecotourism thing and trying to butter her up over an extended period, but she was still pleased to be on friendly terms with him.

'Hi, Cassie. Is this a good time?'

'Yep, I'm in the flat feeling fat after a large and long Sunday lunch with your neighbours.' Jack and Chloe had made a lot of delicious veggie sushi for Cassie, Juliet and Anthony, and it had been accompanied by a lot of great wine and great chat. Juliet and Anthony had definitely been flirting. Jack and Chloe were fully paid-up members of Cassie's 'Get Juliet and Anthony together' project – which was more in Cassie's head than an actual reality because they seemed to be getting themselves together pretty well and she'd done nothing to help, but she had plans to if necessary – and Chloe had sent Cassie a *Get in* WhatsApp before

Cassie was even back in her flat. Chloe was definitely going to have a hangover before she went to bed this evening unless she was a stronger woman than Cassie. Cassie had only had two glasses of wine and wasn't going to be drinking even a tiny amount from now on because she was starting her first IVF cycle a week tomorrow.

'Sounds good. I should probably feel bad about the fact that I've never met my neighbours, but that's London for you.' James might have stopped the grumpiness but from what Cassie knew of him it was a stretch to imagine him actually feeling bad about stuff. 'I *do* now know *your* neighbours.'

'I know you do. You're the island hero now you've got the Wi-Fi sorted.'

'Yep. I am. I've been given more blueberry pies than any one person could ever eat. No-one seems to realise that it wasn't exactly altruistic, because, as you know, it was driving me insane. My next job's trying to get better phone reception. I'm guessing that you heard that the engineers spent days and days trying to work out why the Wi-Fi was so slow and then tracked the problem down to Laura's old TV that she had on all day every day. Even when she was out. It was emitting a signal that interfered with the entire island's broadband.'

'Yes. Unbelievable.' Cassie had also heard that James had bought Laura a new TV to replace the old one. She'd wondered if he was sucking up to Laura, too, for business reasons. Laura's house stood in the middle of a very large plot that ran down to the sea. 'You know occasionally she switched it off if she knew she was going to be spending several hours out, which was usually dinner or something at someone else's house, and Dina and I used to joke that she was our mascot because the Wi-Fi worked better when she was with us.'

'Ouch – so near and yet so far.'

'I know. So how is Laura?'

'She's good. One of the alpacas isn't, though, which is why I'm calling. Donna's been behaving oddly.' James had a lot to say about Donna's symptoms. By the time he'd finished, Cassie was struggling not to laugh. 'Did you just *snigger*?'

'Yep. You've changed a lot since you arrived.' And it was hilarious that in order to suck up to Cassie because of her land, which she would never allow to be developed, he was going to all this trouble. 'In terms of animal interaction.'

'Needs must. So what do you think's wrong with her? You don't sound that worried?'

'I'm pretty sure that she just has a cold but, yes, definitely a good idea to get the vet out. I have insurance. Her details are in my notes.'

'Okay, great, I'll do that. There's something else that I wanted to speak to you about. I know that I'm being a little unfair putting you on the spot and asking you in person, so if you want to think about it, or just say no straight out, please do just say no, because I know it might feel a bit odd.' So he *had* just been sucking up to her again. Cassie felt her face drop. Stupid of her; she shouldn't find it disappointing. She should have known.

'Right,' she said.

'I'm going to be over in London next weekend for a christening. There are a couple of documents in the flat that I'd like to pick up and I'd like to come over to get them while I'm in town, if that's alright.' *Oh.*

'Yep, no problem.' She'd have to make sure the place looked *immaculate* before he arrived. 'If you could just let me know when you're coming, just in case?'

'So that you can clear away all the evidence of the debauched parties, marijuana-farming and illegal pet breeding that you have going on?'

'Exactly.'

'Yes, of course. And thank you so much.'

'Really, in no way a problem. A christening sounds nice.'

'Yes, it is. My best friend and his wife – their first baby. I'm going to be the proud godfather.'

'Well, congratulations.'

'Thank you.'

Cassie should probably finish the conversation and try to get another chapter of the first book in her series drafted, but weirdly she was enjoying their chat. They ended up sharing their top christening anecdotes and then the conversation turned to the animals.

'What inspired you to get them?' James asked.

'They both kind of felt like no-brainers. My mother's from Jordan and as a child I adored visiting her family there. They had chickens, so I'd always wanted some and it was the first time I'd had outside space as an adult. I lived in a flat in Glasgow. And I happened to read about alpacas and one thing led to another.'

'So it was a hankering after the outdoors that led you to move to the island?'

'Kind of. I mean, yes. Basically, I used to be a lawyer, and then I got my first book deal just as I had a bit of a difficult break-up, so I could work anywhere, and it just felt like the right time to move.' Woah. Why was she giving him so many details about her life? She never talked about leaving Glasgow. 'What about you? Have you always lived in London?'

'Yep. Boring.'

'Always in the same area?'

'Similar. Quite close by. Anyway, I'd better get on. Call the vet.' Apparently he had as little desire as she did to talk about his past life.

'Thank you for your alpaca knowledge. I'll let you know how Donna gets on and I'll message you during the week to agree a time to come over to the flat at the weekend.'

'Great.'

*

Cassie straightened up. Her back was *killing* her. Ralitza came three times a week and kept the flat spotless, but Cassie had been up at the crack of dawn today making sure that it was even more spotless than usual before James came round. She'd also put away every single thing that could possibly *be* put away and had, no joke – she couldn't even believe in her own head that she'd done this – warmed up some shop-bought bread in the oven just so that the kitchen would smell inviting. Like she was a desperate home-seller when in actual fact her effective landlord was just popping in for a couple of minutes and would then leave.

Should she stay and say hi, have a chat? Would that feel awkward because it was his flat but currently her flat? And because they'd initially argued but were now getting on well? In a distrustful way, because there was a good chance that he was only being polite because he wanted something from her. Would it be better if she went out? And if she did go out should she leave him a note? Would it look weird if she *did* go out? And was she in a state of gibbering internal indecision about a really small issue because it actually seemed like quite a big issue, and why even was that?

Maybe it would be a good idea to get out of her shorts and uber-baggy T-shirt and into a dress. Just in case she did see him. James had looked great – as in outrageously sexy, despite being cross and unfriendly – when she'd met him. And he looked good in each one of the steady stream of photos that Dina supplied in which he just happened to feature.

Dress on, she arranged herself nonchalantly on a bar stool.

Nope. She was going out. He'd been very frosty when she'd stayed to meet him when he'd arrived on the island, and there was every chance that he'd be unimpressed if she were here when he came today. He'd probably only been friendly to her recently because he wanted to develop her land.

She'd better get her skates on, otherwise she'd bump into him on her way out.

Chapter Thirteen

James

Notting Hill Gate Tube station. The traffic. The heat rising off the pavement. The smell of petrol fumes. The sound of engines, car horns, sirens. People jostling, bumping into you, but minding their own business. And the relative peace of the side roads. Fantastic. God, James had missed London.

Good to know that the concrete jungle existence really was for him.

Great to have experimented with living somewhere else, but he'd be pleased when he came home for good.

Although, to be fair, the island had grown on him somewhat. You had to love the beach and ocean. He'd learned some new skills. Like totally pointless alpaca husbandry. And much less pointless cooking. He was fairly sure he'd continue with that at least a couple of evenings a week when he got home.

He rounded the corner into his road.

Would Cassie be in the flat? Did he want her to be? There was something odd about being in your own city, your own street, and about to go into your own home, when it was not in fact currently your home. It would feel even odder if she were there, underlining the fact that it was currently *her* home. He wouldn't mind meeting her, though.

Since he'd started talking to her on the phone, he'd begun to enjoy their conversations. She'd grown on him. The way she lived – the way she seemed to be, the mad colour, the animals, the friendliness – had really annoyed him initially, but now he wasn't sure why.

A movement along the road caught his eye. A woman, hurrying away in the opposite direction. She had a lot of dark-brown curly hair and beautiful light-brown skin and was wearing an orange sleeveless dress. Was that… Cassie? When they'd met outside her house, her face had been largely obscured by her hood, so he didn't know exactly what she looked like. He'd seen her ID photos, but would you ever recognise someone from those?

It wouldn't be surprising if it was her. A woman with a house and garden furniture like hers would definitely wear orange.

He was genuinely going to be slightly disappointed if he didn't get to meet her properly today. Odd.

Right. Time to go inside.

He rang the doorbell first, just in case the woman in the orange dress hadn't been Cassie and she was in the flat. He should have just asked her earlier in the week if she thought she'd be home.

Once he was up there, he knocked and waited, but there was no sound, so he put his key in the lock and opened the door.

If he was being fanciful, he'd have to liken being inside the flat to walking through a child's nightmare. Everything was exactly as he knew it, except it wasn't; it was like a distorted view of his own home. It was immaculate, but with little Cassie touches around the place. He could see that she used the kitchen regularly: not a surprise. It contained coloured tea towels and bright flowers and a large bowl of fruit, and smelled of bread baking. There were books in the lounge area, of course.

He should stop looking around. It felt intrusive. This was Cassie's home for now. He should get his papers and go.

His study had had the full Cassie treatment. She'd added a bright-pink geometric velvet cushion to the chair. She had photos dotted around, including one of the bloody alpacas. There were a couple of jam jars containing flowers. Objectively speaking, it looked nice; but he didn't like being here. It was unsettling. Time to leave.

On his way out, he saw an elderly man wearing a pale blue V-necked sweater going into the flat next door. He must be his neighbour. How come it felt like he'd never seen him before? He must have done. He must just have been paying zero attention.

'Anthony?' James asked on impulse. During one of their phone conversations, Cassie had told him about the neighbours. He should probably talk to them sometimes.

'Yes? You must be a friend of Cassie's?' Yeah, objectively, London life could feel a little ridiculous. James had lived here for three years and Cassie had said Anthony had been here for decades. And yet, complete strangers.

'Yes,' he said. 'Well, no. I own the flat. We swapped.'

'*Oh.*' Anthony lowered the shopping bags he'd been carrying to the floor and walked down the corridor towards James. He held his hand out. James transferred his document wallet to his left hand and shook Anthony's hand. 'Hello, James. Cassie's mentioned you. Good to meet you.'

'Good to meet you too,' James said, not sure where he wanted to go with this. It was one thing saying hi to a neighbour; his London existence didn't allow time for full-on friendship.

Anthony smiled at him. 'Cassie's wonderful,' he said. And then he turned round and went back to his flat. Okay. Fine. That was an acceptable level of interaction.

James had some time to kill now. He had several godchildren – nothing like a well-paid job to make you an attractive godparent prospect – and was going to Bedfordshire this afternoon for the fifth birthday party of one of his god-daughters, but it wasn't starting until three, and it was still only eleven. Probably best to have a walk in the park and then grab a coffee and brunch at Luigi's.

He had one foot over the café's threshold when he realised that the woman in the orange dress was in there, sitting at a table in the window, *his* table, the table that he always sat at when he went there if it was free. She had to be Cassie. Her hair had been tied back in her passport and driving licence photos, and now it was down, but facially she bore a reasonable resemblance to her passport photo.

She seemed to register him at the same time that he saw her. She glanced up, did a somewhat comedy double take and then smiled at him. Wow. She had a great smile; it totally transformed her face. And of course she'd recognise him because he hadn't been wearing a shapeless raincoat with an enormous hood when they met, and his passport photo looked like him because he didn't have gigantic amounts of hair to do in different styles.

He smiled back.

So what now? Obviously she'd chosen to go out this morning and hadn't planned to speak to him. But since they were both here, it would be odd not to say hi.

He really couldn't join her at her table, though, in case she didn't want to chat.

Ridiculous: he was behaving like some kind of uncertain teenager.

Snap decision. He'd go and say hi first and then the ball would be in her court as to whether she wanted to leave.

And then Luigi shouted, 'James, *ciao*,' from behind the counter, squeezed himself out with difficulty and came towards James for some serious handshaking and man hugging.

When they'd finished catching up, James ordered brunch and turned to go and speak to Cassie while he was waiting for his food.

And she'd left the table and was standing only a few feet behind him.

'Hi.' She hoiked her large bag up onto her shoulder. 'I was just going. I thought I'd say hello first.' Bizarre how disappointed he was. Island living had clearly made him oddly needy.

'Hello. I wasn't one hundred per cent sure that you were you. Passport photos are never that reliable and I couldn't see your face at all when we met in the rain.'

Cassie laughed. 'Oh, yes, my hood. I love that coat. How was your flight?'

'Yeah, not bad, thanks. I watched some old episodes of *The Office* and managed to nod off for a couple of hours between meals.'

'Sounds like a pretty good red-eye. I always slightly envy and slightly hate the people who can sleep the whole time.'

'I know,' James said. 'Actual robots.'

They smiled at each other. James couldn't believe he hadn't realised before how stunning she was. Completely different from every woman he'd ever gone for in his entire life but beautiful.

What had they been talking about?

Luigi clapped him on the shoulder. 'You want your usual table?' No. He wanted to stay here and talk to Cassie. But she was clearly ready to leave.

'Yep, great, thank you,' he told Luigi.

'I'm going to get going. Lovely to see you. Enjoy the rest of your weekend.' She shot him another one of those gorgeous smiles and left.

James sat down at the table that Cassie had just vacated. He suddenly felt a little bit bereft. Ridiculous.

*

James shook his head slightly and tried really hard to concentrate on what the vicar was saying. He should be focusing on the service. That was the least he could do as godfather. It was hard, though. Matt had been right when he said the baby wasn't sleeping well at the moment. How the hell were he and Becca *surviving* this torture? There'd been screaming, *loud* screaming, almost every hour through the night. James should have stayed in a hotel instead of in Matt's spare room. He couldn't remember being this tired for a long time. And Matt did this *every night*. Wow. James didn't remember Leonie being like this when she was a baby but he'd been a teenager then and could have slept through anything. Or maybe his mother had just added a touch of vodka to her bottles. It really wouldn't have been surprising if she had.

The baby, of course, was now sound asleep in his mother's arms.

The vicar's voice was monotonous and it was hot in here. James closed his eyes for just a second and felt himself sway on his feet.

'James.' One of the godmothers, who'd been at Matt and Becca's wedding, a nice woman in blue called Anna, or maybe Emma – James had been too tired to concentrate when they'd been re-introduced – nudged him.

He opened his eyes wide, tried to blink his sleepiness away, smiled at her and mouthed, 'Thank you.'

*

Matt handed James the baby and took a glass of champagne with one hand and ran a finger round the inside of his collar with the other. 'Hot,' he said.

The baby was screaming blue murder. James cradled him horizontally and did some vigorous sideways rocking back and forth and miraculously the noise stopped. He'd discovered the trick from his brother-in-law when his twin nieces were babies. It was definitely another thing that upped his desirability as a godfather. People *loved* him for it.

'Thank you, thank you, thank you,' Matt said. 'That *noise*.'

The baby's eyes looked firmly closed. James eased the rocking down to a gentle sway. And stood still. The baby's eyes pinged *wide* open again. And his mouth opened wide too.

James started rocking again and the crying stopped.

He and Matt looked at each other. 'He's perfect,' Matt said.

James nodded. Perfect but really bloody loud and really bloody tiring. He was just the godfather and he'd been away for the past couple of months, but after one night he was knackered and had had enough. To be fair, he was jetlagged and the birthday party yesterday afternoon had been ear-splitting – a lot of little girls in princess costumes running around screaming – and he and Matt had had a late one last night. But still. Just one more reason that he never wanted a baby of his own.

Five minutes later and he was ready to stop rocking. But every time he stopped, the baby cried again and everyone turned to stare like he and Matt were murderers.

'Hello, my beautiful,' Becca crooned, taking the baby out of James's arms. Nothing happened. No noise other than a cute, snorty, satisfied little sigh. She wasn't rocking at *all*. 'I'm going to go and give him a feed.'

'And *we* can go and get another drink,' Matt said to James.

*

The other godparents all had children. And again, they all had stories that reminded James, if he'd needed any reminder, of why he absolutely did not want children himself.

'So James—' Anna/ Emma's husband, Richie, back from the very free-flowing bar, slapped him hard on the shoulder. The man had definitely had too much to drink '—you planning sprogs soon?'

'Nope. Very happily single and childless,' James said.

'You should have kids. They're fantastic. Emma has two. I have seven and counting.'

'Okay. Cool,' James said. He didn't want to ask why. Bad joke? Many ex-partners? Whatever.

'Do you want to know why?' Richie leaned in. James leaned backwards to get away from his beer breath.

'Sure,' he said. No, he didn't. No interest in a pissed idiot.

'Emma and I have two together but I'm a sperm donor.'

'Ah.' James nodded. He snuck a look at Emma. She'd just finished downing a full glass of champagne and was reaching for another one. 'Sounds great.'

'We wanted to give something back, didn't we, darling?' He nudged Emma. 'Em's eggs were duff, whereas my sperm are great little swimmers, golden balls, what can I say, so we had our two via egg donation and we thought we'd like to help people in the same way. So I did it because Em obviously couldn't.'

Emma said, 'Oh, piss off, Richie. Enough,' and walked off.

James walked off too.

*

'Apparently he's playing away,' Matt told James. 'Not for the first time. Poor old Emma. She and Bec were at school together. Such a shame that she married such a dickhead, frankly. Bec thinks she's going to leave him.'

James nodded. 'Not surprising.'

So many messy relationships out there. So many good reasons to stick to the single life.

So many shit fathers, too. Like James's own. Frankly, he'd probably have been a lot better off with someone like Richie. At least he owned up freely to his paternity.

*

In the end, it was a relief to leave the christening and head to the airport. It had been great to see his friends, but this weekend had felt like an odd blip in the middle of his summer. Being in London, seeing everyone, had made him feel like an interloper in his own life. It turned out that he'd adjusted a lot better than he'd thought he had to life on the island, and he wasn't ready for the experience to end. He had a lot of plans for the rest of the summer. Business, obviously, but leisure, too. He was going to go fishing, and sailing. Explore some of the nearby islands by bike. There was also genuinely the possibility that if Laura tipped her head to one side and asked him one more time to join her poker evening, he'd give in and go.

Seriously; he was getting sentimental. Carry on like this and he'd be begging Cassie to remain lifelong pen pals. And, peculiarly, that thought made him smile.

Chapter Fourteen

Cassie

Cassie waved the remote at James's enormous TV and flicked aimlessly between a few more channels. It was so hard to concentrate on *anything* when you just wanted to know if your IVF was going to work. It looked like they were on track to retrieve eggs soon. The waiting after that would be even worse. Although at least she wouldn't have to inject herself any more. It would definitely have been nice to have had someone to share *that* with. Pretty much everything else was better on her own, though, than her first pregnancy. Simon had been way more interested in his golf handicap – and flirting with other women – than in her and the baby.

She checked another couple of channels. There was nothing she wanted to watch.

The TV was huge. You actually had to turn your head a bit sometimes while watching it, it was so far from one side to the other. It was very flash – very James.

Was that the real James, though? It was hard to tell. He'd been a bit of an arse to start off with but recently he'd been a lot more pleasant. Was he still trying to get his hands on her land or was he genuinely nice?

What he *definitely* was, no question, was gorgeous. When she'd seen him in the café yesterday morning, just, wow. At her house, in the rain, grumpy as hell and mean, he'd still been undeniably handsome. But when he was smiling and friendly, he was something else.

She'd have to be careful if he tried to persuade her in person to go down the ecotourism route. If he did too many of his disarming slow smiles, she might give in. Good job she hadn't stayed to talk to him any longer yesterday.

For goodness' sake. She was *smiling* just thinking about him. Like she was developing some kind of idiotic crush. Better than obsessing about IVF but kind of ridiculous.

Her phone rang. It was her mum.

'Can we come and see you this weekend? I've managed to persuade your dad to move his History Club night.'

'Of course. That would be lovely.' It would be. One of the great bonuses of spending the summer in London was having the opportunity to see her parents. It was a lot easier for them to travel to London than to Maine from their new home in France. Next weekend wasn't *the* best timing, because she'd probably have had the embryo transferred by then and be feeling at least as hormonal as now, and even more stressed, but she could always just pretend she was feeling ill. And seeing them would be a distraction from the constant *thinking*.

She looked around the room as her mother told her about the new trees she'd just had planted in their garden.

Her parents were going to *love* this flat.

Good job her mother wasn't going to meet the flat's owner. She'd no doubt love James too and probably try to set Cassie up with him. Now that she'd retired, she was desperate to become a grandmother. Last summer when Cassie had visited them, her mother had invited two different 'eligible young men' over on consecutive days and had literally asked them, in front of Cassie, about when they'd like to start families. She had also let them both know, very explicitly, that they weren't required as long-term partners, just as potential fathers. Sperm donors basically.

At least she wouldn't be upset in the slightest if Cassie got pregnant via actual sperm donation. Cassie had been able to assure her implications counsellor that her family and friends would have zero problem accepting her choice to do IVF in this way.

Her parents would actually be *ecstatic* if Cassie got successfully pregnant now.

She definitely couldn't tell them about her IVF, though. They'd be too upset on her behalf if it didn't work out. One of the reasons she'd moved to the States after her miscarriage had been that her parents' grief on her behalf had made everything worse.

Her mum had finished telling her about the garden.

'Love you,' said Cassie. 'Can't wait to see you on Friday.'

She pressed red on her phone and picked up the remote again. The first channel she clicked on was showing a re-run of *Call the Midwife*. There was the most gorgeous baby on the screen.

She wanted a baby of her own *so much*. Oh, God, what if it didn't work out?

No. She wasn't enjoying sitting alone with the television and her thoughts. She was going to turn the TV off and get on with some work, maybe re-draft that last scene about the twins hiding in the grounds of Buckingham Palace.

*

Cassie's heart jumped as her parents emerged from the Eurostar Customs. Sometimes it was only when you actually saw people that you realised just how much you'd been missing them.

'Cassie.' Her mother swept towards her and enfolded her in a hug. 'It's so good to see my beautiful daughter.' She leaned back a little out of the hug and inspected Cassie's face. 'Have you lost weight since last month, *habibi*?'

Cassie had to fight hard to force back sudden tears. Oh *God*. These hormones were driving her *insane*. She was a complete mess – nearly in tears because it was so wonderful to see her mother. She was also a complete blob. Of *course* she hadn't lost weight. She was retaining water at the rate of what felt like several gallons a day. She was wearing a swing dress today because she hadn't been able to do up her favourite jeans earlier.

'Are you eating properly?'

'Mum. It's lovely to see you. And I'm thirty-seven and I can cook and yes I am eating properly and no I definitely haven't lost weight.'

'Hmm.' Her mum squished her back into another mammoth hug and Cassie nearly yelped out loud. Her boobs were *so* sore. It was four days since they'd transferred the embryo and *honestly*, she had so many bloody symptoms. It had to be a good sign, surely. A lot of the symptoms were very similar to ones she'd had the first time she was pregnant. All the information they'd given her at the clinic said that these symptoms were to be expected because of the drugs she was on, and not to read too much into them, but *surely* they had to mean something. Hopefully.

'Hello, darling.' Cassie's father had joined them, panting slightly, with all the luggage. 'You're looking very well. It's wonderful to see you.' Cassie's eyes filled *again*. Lucky that her mother had drawn her father into a three-way hug so that neither of them could see her face while she blinked the tears away.

'Hello, Dad.' She'd got rid of the tears, so she pulled away slightly, to get more comfortable. 'You look well too.' He looked *red*.

'That's what everyone says when I'm sunburnt. No-one should ever make Glaswegians live in hotter places.' He grinned at her and she smiled back. They both knew that the grumbling meant nothing; he'd always be happy wherever Cassie's mother was. He'd also always be scarlet for several months of the year, if that place was a sunny part of France, given that he could burn in Glasgow in April. 'Come on. Let's go and find this flat of yours.'

*

One of the great things about Cassie's parents staying was that they kept her very busy, which meant that she had a lot less time to lose her grip on sanity. It was hard to fit in too much secret googling of 'positive IVF stories – real life symptoms' around all the sightseeing her parents wanted to do.

They had almost nothing in common other than a strong enjoyment of each other's company. Her dad was a keen fan of military history. His top three London tourist choices were the Imperial War Museum, the Churchill War Rooms and the National Army Museum. Her mum had reached the point several years ago where she said she'd kill herself – or her husband – if she had to go to another war-related place of interest. She did, in fact, still often go with him, but she wore headphones and listened to 1970s music or audiobooks while tour guides talked.

On her parents' second morning in London, Cassie went with her father and Anthony and Juliet on a trip to see the pagoda in Kew Gardens in West London, while her mother went to the National Portrait Gallery.

'Your father's already spent forty minutes talking to me about the pagoda being used to test smoke curtains used to camouflage low-flying aircraft in the Second World War,' she told Cassie while her husband was in the shower. 'I can't take any more today so I'd have to ignore him if I went, and your neighbours need to flirt with each other without me being a gooseberry.' Cassie wasn't a huge fan of military history either, but she could definitely use the pagoda and smoke curtain thing in her second London book.

Annoyingly, she managed to leave her phone in the flat, but Juliet obliged by taking a lot of photos to help with her research. Anthony definitely featured in more of them than was necessary. Cassie's matchmaking was going fantastically well.

If her mum had gone with them, they'd have been in a cab both ways, but her father liked to 'see London properly' and that involved a lot of public transport. By the time they were on their way back, Cassie was almost beside herself with exhaustion. *Surely* this meant she was pregnant. Please let her be.

'Cassie, it's our stop.' Her father was shaking her gently while Anthony and Juliet smiled at her. Oh, okay, she might have nodded off a little there. 'Are you alright?'

'Just a little bit tired. I've been working hard.' She could use this tiredness as an excuse for not drinking any wine this evening when her mum's cousins came over. One less thing to worry about today.

As they opened the front door of the flat, the aromas of Middle Eastern cuisine and the sound of Cassie's mother talking – presumably on the phone – reached them, and Cassie felt a wave of nostalgia for childhood and arriving home from school on her mother's day off work. It was just *so* lovely having her parents around.

'Well, it's been wonderful to talk to you, James,' Cassie's mother said, blowing a kiss across the room at Cassie. *James*? Surely not *James*

James. 'Could I just ask you a question?' She winked at Cassie. Oh no. Please no. She had that look in her eye. 'Are you single?' She listened to the answer and then laughed. 'Saucy.' *Saucy*? Honestly. What had James *said*? And what would he be thinking? Her mother winked at her and Cassie sighed. Incorrigible.

Her mother was nodding and smiling and eyebrow raising now. 'I'll let Cassie know,' she said.

Cassie shook her head. *Why* had she left her phone behind today?

'Great to talk. Bye.' Her mother waved the phone at Cassie. 'I like his WhatsApp photo.' Yep, that was a good photo. 'He has a very nice voice. Good sense of humour. He works in private equity. He's good with your animals. Thirty-five. Single. No children. Straight. You know where I'm going with this. It's like it was meant to be.'

Cassie took her phone. 'Yes. Serendipity. Absolutely.'

'Exactly.' Cassie's mother nodded. 'I'm looking forward to meeting him in person.'

Cassie sighed again.

'Ach, that's enough teasing. I don't think Cassie wants to marry the man she swapped homes with.' Cassie's father sauntered over, picked up a spoon and stuck it into the dish simmering on the hob.

'I'm not suggesting marriage. That's so old-fashioned. But I'm serious. I have a sixth sense. I like him.' Cassie's mother swiped the spoon out of her husband's hand before he could get it to his mouth. To be fair, she'd never liked Simon, so she did at least have *some* sixth sense.

Cassie's father rolled his eyes and smacked a big kiss on her lips. Cassie's heart clenched as she watched them. If she couldn't find what they had, she'd be better off single.

'What did James want?' she asked. She genuinely wanted to know and she also wanted to divert her own thoughts, because she was feeling tearful *again*.

'He was just calling for a chat, to let you know how things are with Laura and the animals. But we had a *much* more interesting conversation than that.'

Honestly.

Chapter Fifteen

James

James was still laughing following his conversation with Cassie's mother as he made his way up the field to feed the alpacas, checking his phone for messages as he went. She'd been hilarious. And possibly only half joking when she'd propositioned him on Cassie's behalf, and he didn't even mind.

She sounded like a fantastic mother. Involved. Caring. Sober.

It didn't surprise him that Cassie seemed to have a good relationship with her parents. The way she lived, the homeliness of her house, the animals, the close friendships she evidently had with her neighbours, all seemed to point to someone from a stable family.

He thought of Cassie's mother asking him his height and shoe size, and chuckled again.

Wow. Island living was clearly doing something to him. A few months ago he'd have found her questioning annoying or – if she'd been like Emily's mother – terrifying, but somehow he'd been totally charmed, even if he was clearly being sized up as a potential father. So far off the mark it was untrue, but funny all the same. He could imagine how livid Cassie would have been if she'd been in the room.

His smile dropped when he saw that a text had just come in from Ella. Guilt was never a welcome emotion. And he so often felt guilty when it came to her.

Hi James. How's Maine? Early, I know, but we're just thinking about Christmas. Would you like to come to us? We'd love to see you! The girls are well. They loved the alpaca pictures!

Christmas. Seriously. Ella's invitation wasn't as early as last year's, granted, because it was already early August now and last year she'd asked him about Christmas in June, but it was still ridiculous. Although he couldn't criticise her; clearly it was just a different manifestation of the urge they both obviously had, to make their adult lives as organised and unchaotic as possible; as different as possible from their childhoods, basically.

He wasn't going to go. There'd be too much niceness and thinly veiled concern from Ella and her husband, and the worry on his part the whole time that the conversation would turn to their mother and Leonie. It would be much better to join a group of single friends skiing or go to Matt's.

He swung himself up onto a sturdy branch of one of the big trees in the field and took a couple of photos of the alpacas from above, and sent them to Ella with a message.

Hey. Here are a couple more alpaca photos for the girls. Thanks so much for the Christmas invite. Would have loved to come but already agreed to go to friends. Sending more chicken photos in a minute.

The photos might distract them all from the fact that he'd turned down yet another invitation. And the girls would like them.

Love the photos. No worries about Christmas. Offer's always open if you change your mind.

More guilt.

*

Fishing wasn't the best activity for when you didn't want to spend too much time with your own thoughts, and Don Brown, James's now-regular fishing companion, wasn't the best company when you'd like to be distracted. Don hardly ever ventured beyond a grunt in response to any conversation opener.

It had just occurred to James that one day Ella might stop asking him over. He never went any more, but he still wanted her to keep asking. Just in case one day he wanted to accept one of her invitations. Shit. He'd reflexively jerked his fishing rod. If Don's wisdom was right, he wasn't going to be catching anything for hours now.

'Why don't you join us at our poker evening on Tuesday?' Woah. Don had spoken when he didn't have to.

James opened his mouth to say no and then clocked Don's rare smile. He was a nice man. James didn't think he issued invitations that often. Couldn't do, given how infrequently he spoke.

It wouldn't hurt him to go. It wasn't a big deal like Christmas with Ella and it wasn't like he had other stuff to do in the evenings this week. He'd been down to Boston several times recently but he didn't need to go again for a while. Although, a poker night. Really? Was he that desperate? Don was smiling again. Okay, fine, he'd go once.

*

James looked around the room. Laura, Dina, Don and Isla Brown, and two other men, Harvyn Jones and Bax Marley. Harvyn was probably mid-fifties, and Bax a little younger than James. James was hazy on the actual rules of the game, but he was pretty sure that he was going to smash this out of the park. For a start, he'd be outstanding on the poker-face front. Years of high-stakes business meetings had to have been an excellent training. None of the others would have had the life experience that he'd had.

'Raise.' Laura was a different woman with a handful of playing cards and a pile of chips in front of her. Her eyes were fired up but they were the only mobile part about pretty much her entire body. She had the poker-face thing down to a tee.

Or did she? James leaned in very slightly. He was sure her eyes had flickered to the furthest left of her cards. Did that mean something?

Three rounds later, and a lot of chips down, mainly in Laura's direction, he was sure of two things. One, he'd under-estimated the likely skill level of the others. And two, Laura couldn't help sneaking too many little peeks at her hand when she knew she held a winning card. Now James just had to get on top of the rules.

So close. So bloody close.

'I nearly won that round,' he told everyone, in case they hadn't noticed.

Laura patted his hand. 'You did very well, sweetie,' she said. 'For a beginner.' What? He was being patronised by an eighty-year-old Jessica Fletcher-lookalike?

James narrowed his eyes. 'When's the next poker evening?'

'Tuesday next week,' Bax said. 'You got the bug?'

James considered. He was supposed to be going down to New York on Tuesday afternoon but he could switch it to Wednesday. 'I wouldn't say I have the bug. But I *will* be beating you all and I will *not* stop until I do.' He was going to look forward to next week.

*

'I hear you've taken up poker,' Cassie said the next time he called her. The gardener had told him there was a glut of greengages in the orchard part of the field and he had no idea what to do with them. Cassie had suggested either making jam and chutney, or freezing them for when she got back. 'And that you think you're going to beat Laura. That will never happen.' James shook his head. Not because of the gossip factor – he was used to that now – but because she was wrong. He'd totally beat Laura. He wasn't going to admit it to a living soul but he'd been practising online – thank God, for many reasons, that the Wi-Fi worked now – and he was definitely improving.

'We'll see,' he said.

'Have you been practising?'

'Maybe.'

'You know she came in the top ten in the over-seventies US poker championships last year and she's pretty sure that she'll be in the top three of the over-eighties championship this November? And then she'll qualify automatically for the over-eighties world championship?'

'I did not know that.' Wow. His fellow islanders were clearly a lot more interesting than he'd originally given them credit for. And a lot more of a challenge. 'How did she do all of that without practising online? Before you had working Wi-Fi?'

'She switches her TV off when she's playing online so that she can concentrate.'

'Wow. Feels like the mystery of the broadband could have been solved a lot sooner.'

'I know. Gutting.'

James laughed. He enjoyed these conversations with Cassie; it'd gone beyond just being about her land. He almost didn't want to ask her again about that in case it caused a barrier between them. He'd leave it for the time being. Maybe until he left. And, if they did agree a deal, maybe he could come back for a visit.

Chapter Sixteen

Cassie

Cassie wanted a baby *so* much. She stirred her de-caf latte again. She could murder a real coffee – insomnia had been just one of the *many* side-effects of the fertility drugs – but when you might be growing a baby inside you, you had to try to do everything right.

She looked out of the café window. Across the road, there was a little girl helping her mother brush the steps up to their house. The girl was maybe four or five and she was dressed in leggings and a T-shirt, a superhero cape and what were presumably her mother's high-heeled, leopard skin boots. The look of concentration on her little face was *so* cute. Even cuter was the way she smiled up at her mother when she finished each ineffectual push of her broom. And her mother smiled back at her like they were the only two people in the world. There weren't really enough words to describe how much Cassie wanted that.

Nearly time to go and take the test. Apparently some clinics advised you to have a blood test with them to find out. Cassie's was happy for you to do a home test, which was better because she'd rather be home, on her own, when she found out.

She wanted to know the result *so much*.

But, also, she couldn't bear to do it.

No, she was going. It was time.

Negative. Not even a hint of a super faint line that she could hold in a super-bright light and kid herself might be the shadow of a positive test. Completely, unambiguously, negative. She'd weed for the right length of time. She'd waited for the right length of time. She'd done everything right. She heard a horrible wailing sound and then realised that she was the person who'd made that sound.

She was so *stupid*. Imagining for the past twelve days that she'd been pregnant and for months before that that she was going to *get* successfully pregnant. Doing everything right for the non-existent baby. *So* stupid.

And so bereft.

This *wasn't* as bad as the miscarriage. This time she'd never seen a healthy baby on a scan before something went wrong. The whole thing from her first consultation had only been just over three months. She just needed to have an enormous cry and then get over it.

Except, God, it really *hurt*.

How did people cope with doing this several times? So unbelievably difficult. And *how* did they cope when they knew it was their last-ever attempt?

She sniffed, hard. She needed something to distract her, something else to think about other than her failed IVF and work.

She should take a wee trip home to go to Laura's eightieth next weekend.

*

Cassie looked out of the windows at the front of the ferry. The island was getting closer. She'd be setting foot on it in under twenty minutes. She'd been away for four months. Strange to be home when someone else was living in her house.

She was glad, though, that she'd come back now. How could she have missed Laura's big party? Laura had been the most wonderful friend to her over the past four years. They'd met the day that Cassie viewed the property and she'd been ecstatic that Laura was so friendly, because she'd fallen in love with the island and the house but living in such a relatively isolated place you did need to get on with your neighbours.

This weekend she was just going to have fun with her friends and put the baby thing out of her mind. She'd decide next week whether she was going to go for another round of IVF while she was in London.

'Honey, I missed you.' Dina had been waiting at the dock for Cassie, jumping up and down as the ferry berthed. 'I'm not going to lie, getting to know James has been great,' she said as they humped Cassie's suitcase into the boot of Dina's car, 'but I *really* miss you when you're away. Do *not* stay in London. You have to come back at the end of the swap.' They got into the front seats of the jeep. 'I'd like to think I can persuade James to stay, with me. I think tonight's gonna be the night.'

'Dina.' Cassie adored her friend. She already felt better for seeing her. And she suddenly couldn't believe she hadn't told her about the IVF. Maybe she'd tell her tomorrow before she went home on Monday. 'Of course I'm coming back after the swap. And you have *such* a dirty cackle.'

'Believe me, honey, if you knew what was inside my head, *then* you'd see and hear dirty.'

*

'Are you okay?' Dina handed a mug of tea to Cassie, who was sitting on the sofa in the corner of Dina's kitchen, and stepped back, hands on hips, and looked very closely at her.

'Yes. No, not exactly.' Why hadn't Cassie ever told Dina about the IVF? Why hadn't she told anyone? She was going to tell Dina right now, not tomorrow. 'I did IVF in London and it didn't work.' She heard her voice go all high and screechy on the word *work*. 'With a donor sperm.'

'*Cassie*. Honey.' Dina sat down next to Cassie and put her arms round her. 'Oh my God. That's huge. And so difficult. I'm so, so sorry that it didn't work out.'

Cassie felt tears start to trickle out. Dina pulled Cassie's head onto her shoulder and then Cassie just sobbed.

'I'm sorry,' she said eventually, sitting up straight.

'Hey, there's *so* nothing to be sorry about.'

'I'm sorry I didn't tell you about it. I'm sorry that I'm crying all over you now.'

'Do *not* apologise. It's a huge thing, and sometimes huge things are too hard to talk about. I know how affected you were by your miscarriage and what a shit Simon was. It took you a long time to tell me about that after we met, and I got that. And I get now that you didn't want to talk about this. And I'm honoured that you've told me now. You shouldn't ever have to talk about anything with anyone unless you want to.'

'Thank you.' Cassie sniffed. 'Love you.' She reached her arms round Dina and squeezed.

'Love you too. So, and please don't answer if you don't want to talk about it, is it too early for you to have decided whether you'll try again?'

'Yes, I'm not sure. I think I probably will. I think I'll probably regret it if I don't. Although there are obviously other options that I could explore, like adoption. And it was hard.'

They sat in silence for a few minutes, and then Dina said, 'So were the side effects horrible?'

'Yeah, they really weren't great. Physical and emotional. Bloating, sore boobs, bad sleep, all of that, but also I was *so* hormonal. One day going through a ticket barrier at a train station I was asked for my ticket and I yelled *Bugger off* at the ticket inspector. I was furious that he'd *dare* to ask me, because *obviously* I have a ticket, like *look at me*, I'm not a train-ticket-scammer. Honestly. Not exaggerating. But none of that was the worst thing. The worst was the *waiting*. Time passes so slowly. You analyse every single physical feeling that you have for possible pregnancy symptoms, even though you know there's a very strong chance that everything's actually down to the drugs you took. You count the days to when you're due to take the test. Time passes so slowly and it's so hard to think about anything else. And then of course if it's negative, you're devastated. Really not great.'

'I'm so impressed that you did it,' said Dina. 'I'm *so sure* that it'll work out for you one way or the other in due course.'

'Thank you.' Cassie sniffed again. 'Do you have any painkillers?'

'Headache from crying?'

'Yep.'

'Coming right up.' Dina stood up.

'Thank you. And thank you for listening. It helped.'

'Hey. No thanks necessary.'

'We have a couple of hours before we need to get ready for the party, don't we? I might just text James and check that he doesn't mind if I walk through the garden and then go and say hi to the animals.'

'It's so weird that you don't know him.'

'I know.' Cassie did feel as if she knew him, though. She wasn't sure why she hadn't really mentioned their phone chats to Dina..

Cassie stood still in her – well, James's – drive, next to where he'd parked her car. It wasn't where she normally parked it. It was really strange standing on her own property but it being occupied by someone else.

She should have decided whether or not she was going to knock on the door, speak to James if he was home. He'd texted 'Np' – still annoying – when she'd asked if he'd be happy for her to go through the garden to see the animals. He hadn't said whether or not he was around. If he *was* here, would it seem odd if she didn't say hello on her way past?

Eek. What if he was home and could see her standing here like a lemon? She needed an excuse to stand still while she thought. She took a few steps to the side and buried her face in the blossom of the nearest large bush. It was totally normal to stand and admire flowers for a few moments.

She should have chosen a different bush. This one was beautiful to look at but it did not smell good. It was cloying.

Anyway. To knock or not to knock?

She didn't *want* to say hello. After seeing him in Luigi's a few weeks ago and talking to him pretty much every day now, she'd thought about him a little too much, although he'd been a good distraction from the IVF misery. She was pretty sure she'd be a little awkward around him now that she'd registered all the raw masculinity that he had going. She was fine talking to him on the phone, but seeing him in person would be different.

She was going to be sick if she spent any more time sniffing this bush. Honestly, disgusting. She moved over to the next one along. Better.

Okay. What would she do if she were normal and did not have an irrational attraction to James that she really shouldn't have because her best friend was in serious lust with him? She would knock on the kitchen window as she went past and wave airily if he was in there, and then walk on past. Knocking on the door might be over-friendly.

So she was going to knock on the window and hope that he wasn't there.

It was very odd walking down the side of the path. It felt slightly intrusive, like she was spying on James or something.

He had the chairs arranged differently round her table outside the kitchen. She never left them like that. He had the cushions in different places too.

As she walked round the corner of the house and up to the window, her heart was actually thudding away. Ridiculous. She wasn't usually a nervous person.

And, oh no. He was in the kitchen. Okay, fine, not a problem. Np. As planned, she was going to knock on the window, wave and walk off.

With the best will in the world, if you were knocking on a relatively low window, it was hard not to look through that window and into the room. James was doing something at the table, with his back to her. Dina wasn't wrong about his physique. He was wearing a faded black T-shirt and as he worked at whatever he was doing – what *was* it? – she could see the muscles in his shoulders and upper arms flexing under the T-shirt. Rippling. Unlike on the other two occasions she'd seen him, his blond hair was appealingly un-styled and messy. His neck and arms were tanned. Gorgeous, basically. Exactly the kind of man who always appealed physically to Dina. And Cassie, if she was honest.

Except, while Dina kept going back for more, Cassie had learned not to from bitter experience.

Right. She'd better knock on the window immediately or she'd look as though she was just standing leering. Peeping Cassie.

She should really have thought this through before she left Dina's. She hadn't had a shower yet or changed after her journey and she also hadn't re-done her lipstick, re-brushed her hair, anything. Really quite stupid. James was looking sexily dishevelled and she was looking very *un*sexily scruffy. And she was still staring into the kitchen at him. What if he could see her in a reflection or something? Or sensed her there?

She whipped her hand up and knocked, really fast, and far too loudly. It was a good job the window was double glazed, frankly, or she'd probably have broken it. She'd *really* hurt her knuckles. Ow.

James turned round, very quickly – not a surprise – he'd probably got a big shock given that her knock had sounded like gunfire – and broke into a smile when he saw her.

She waved at him and then pointed in the direction of the animals, returned his smile and turned round.

She'd got a couple of steps away when he opened the back door and said, 'Hi, Cassie.' Bugger.

He was so ridiculously pretty to look at, if you could call large, masculine-looking rugby player types pretty.

'Hello, James.' She sounded very formal. So odd to be essentially strangers and yet to have been sleeping in each other's beds and using each other's bathrooms for the past four months.

Why was she thinking about beds and bathrooms?

The silence was too long.

'How was your journey?' Thank the Lord he'd said something.

'Good, thank you. I mean, lengthy, obviously, but I managed to sleep enough and there were no delays.'

'Feels a bit surreal being here, right? I have to say that I found it odd being back in London but not currently being resident there. A bit like a parallel universe.'

'Exactly.'

'Would you like to come in and check out Laura's cake?'

No. Cassie really didn't want to go into her *own* perfect kitchen that she'd designed herself and *loved* but which was not currently hers. What if James had moved all her stuff around?

He opened the door wider and stood to one side. Bugger. She was going to have to go in or look rude.

'I'd love to,' she said.

For a moment she thought he wasn't going to move out of the way and that they were going to end up in an awkward which-way this-way that-way moment, but fortunately he stepped back. He was tall. But not too tall. The perfect height. Also arguably the perfect width.

And now she was standing in her kitchen, with James. He hadn't moved too many of her things and he was very tidy.

And. Wow.

'The cake's stunning,' she said, moving forwards to look more closely at it. 'Laura will love it.'

'Thank you.' James beamed and Cassie realised two things: one that a beaming James was literally the most attractive man she'd ever seen in her life, and two that the room smelled quite strongly of baking and he'd just reacted as though the cake was his own work.

'Did you make it?' she asked. Mind-boggling given that his kitchen in London had given the impression of having been completely unused other than maybe one shelf of the fridge, the corkscrew and some glasses.

'Yep.'

'This is going to sound rude, so I'll apologise for that in advance, but did you make it *yourself*?'

'Yep. And I'm going to be honest. I am so goddamn proud of myself. I mean, look at it.'

'I am looking. I'm so impressed. That ganache is *smooth*. And the piping on top. I mean, *wow*. What kind of cake is it?'

'I thought I should do something for everyone. Working from the bottom tier up, we have carrot, Victoria sponge, fruit and chocolate. All with a butter icing filling.'

'Oh my *goodness*. That sounds fab. Laura's going to be delighted.' He was such a contradiction. 'Do you bake a lot at home, in London?' It was just so hard to imagine.

'Ha. No. Never. Yeah, I think everyone here was quite surprised when I volunteered to make the cake, but you must be absolutely astonished, given the lack of baking paraphernalia in my kitchen. Your kitchen, I should say. Yeah, no, this is a one-off, but not my first cake. I baked a lot with a much younger sister when she was little.'

'Wow. What a lovely big brother.' Ridiculously perfect. In the baking department, anyway. 'I always had shop-bought cakes. I'm an only child and my father's never baked and my mother, who of course you've spoken to—' so embarrassing '—only makes Middle Eastern pastries which are very different-tasting from English cakes and really weren't popular at Glaswegian kids' birthday parties. Fortunately she was always at work – not in a bad way, obviously, she was and is an amazing mum and a great cook, actually – but she rarely had time to bake. She's a doctor and she worked long hours. I say is, she *was* a doctor. Retired now.' Honestly. Verbal diarrhoea. Stop talking. 'I could have done with a big brother like you.' And that just sounded creepy.

'I was definitely not always a lovely big brother. I used to get very annoyed with my younger sister, a lot. But, you know, needs must. Our mother was—' James paused, as though he was searching for words '—busy and my other sister has never baked, and someone had to do it. You know, birthdays. Important to little girls. And it really isn't difficult.'

Cassie wanted to ask if James had had birthday cakes himself. It was like he'd gone somewhere sad in the middle of what he'd said. But oddly – given that they were only talking about cakes – it felt like that was too personal a question.

'Are you kidding?' she said. 'It's *really* hard. I can't bake to save my life. I had your neighbours over for afternoon tea and tried to make everything myself but absolutely all of it was a disaster so I had to get Luigi to cater it. The beauty of being in Central London, of course. Here we'd have just had to break our teeth on rock-like brownies or starve.'

'But you're a great cook. All the meals you left in the freezer were delicious.'

'I do cook but baking's a whole different thing.'

'You genuinely don't bake?'

'Can't bake.'

'Maybe it's a one or the other thing. I have to say, my cooking hasn't progressed a long way beyond the absolute basics. I'm excellent with toast and pasta and I can fry a steak and that's pretty much it.'

Cassie opened her mouth to say that they'd complement each other *perfectly* and then realised that she *really* didn't need to sound as though she was coming onto him.

'Well I think your cake looks spectacular, much more impressive than making a stew, and Laura's going to be a very happy eighty-year-old,' she said.

'Speaking of which, what do you think about candles? I ordered eighty but now I'm wondering if putting them all on could cause a fire. Or if the first ones we light will burn down before we get to the end.' He'd bloody ordered eighty candles. Honestly. Good at baking *and* thoughtful. *This* couldn't all be to try to butter people up, surely.

Cassie looked at the cake and tried to imagine. 'I think there might be a fire,' she said. 'How close would they have to be together?' She moved closer to it. 'Maybe not that close? It's big.'

James moved closer too. 'So eight rows of ten,' he said, making line motions over the top of the cake with his hands. He had great hands. Very firm-looking. They were standing very close to each other now. Cassie could see his chest rise and fall as he breathed. There were blond hairs just visible at the neckline of his T-shirt. Now she was imagining his chest naked. What was *wrong* with her? She looked up at him. And he was looking down at her, a small smile tugging at the corners of his mouth. Her own mouth felt very dry. What had they been talking about?

Candles.

'That would be a lot of flame.' Her voice sounded very hoarse. She swallowed. 'It would be very hot.' *She* was hot. 'It might melt the icing.'

He was looking at her lips. Never mind *icing* melting. *Cassie* was melting.

'It would be hot.' His smile was growing.

Cassie tried hard to force her mind back towards the cake.

'I don't think we should do all the candles,' she said. He was still looking at her with his gorgeous, slightly lopsided smile. 'I think they might ruin the decorations on top of the cake. And eighty's a *lot* to blow out.'

'I think you're right. What do you suggest instead?' He'd inched a little closer to her.

Cassie licked her lips. 'Um. Maybe just one candle?'

'One candle it is.'

They were still looking at each other. James still had that smile going and Cassie was fairly sure that the shape of her lips mirrored his.

'What do you…' he began, and then there was a beeping. A loud and persistent beeping. Cassie blinked. What was that?

It was her timer.

'Timer,' she said.

'Timer,' repeated James, still smiling.

'Is there something in the oven?'

'Oh. Right. Yes. Yes, there is.' He turned round and their arms brushed. The zing! Cassie felt it right to her stomach. No wonder Dina was so besotted. Honestly, Cassie's heart was beating *so* fast. Terrible. Dina was her closest friend.

James reached for oven gloves and went to the oven to take something out. Two trays, with an eight-shaped bake and a zero-shaped one.

'What is that?' Cassie asked.

'Shortbread.'

'Wow. Honestly. You're like some kind of baking *god*.' No. Not good. She *really* sounded like she was coming onto him and, in light of what had just happened – and she had no idea what it had been, but, God, it had felt strangely erotic – she should just leave the kitchen, now. 'Great to see you,' she said primly, like she was leaving a coffee morning or something, 'and I'll no doubt bump into you at the party. I should get going now. Animals to see. Dresses to change into.' Cringe, cringe, *cringe*. Why was she talking like that?

'Yes, great. I'll see you later.'

Cassie wondered all the way up the garden whether he was watching her as she walked. She was going to twist an ankle if she carried on walking like this, but it was really hard to move normally when you were wondering whether or not someone was looking at your bum and whether it looked okay in these trousers.

The good news was that while she'd been in the kitchen with him she'd completely forgotten about the IVF.

She was *so* pleased to see the animals. Chickens were like little people; they had definite personalities, as even James had spotted. As did the alpacas, obviously. Donna, Maisie and Fred ambled over to her and she hugged them all in turn.

'I missed you so much,' she told them. They *definitely* recognised her. Fred was nuzzling into her. So gorgeous. 'How *you* doing?' she asked him. Maybe she'd be better off doing her next cycle of IVF in Boston after all. Then she'd be home if and when it all went wrong. She could get drunk with Dina and hug the animals. It probably wouldn't be that hard to sort a Boston trip at short notice.

Donna came back over towards her and Cassie put her arms round her neck again. 'So, Donna,' Cassie said. 'I just had a very weird moment in the kitchen with James.' God, she couldn't believe she'd just said that out loud, even to an alpaca. She still didn't even know whether she liked him as a person and, more importantly, if anyone should be having any kind of moment with him, it was Dina. Donna lifted her head and looked at Cassie, unblinking. Yeah, Donna was right. Best to ignore what had just happened.

Chapter Seventeen

James

James lowered himself into the kayak and pushed away from the beach. It would be much better to be out here on the water when Cassie came back past the house so that they didn't have to speak again.

What the hell had happened just then?

Cassie was absolutely not his type. She wrote ridiculously lengthy notes and she used emojis. She adored her bright colours, apparently clothing-wise as well as with her décor and garden. She kept animals. She was friends with *everybody*. She clearly had a stable family background, very different from his. She'd *chosen* to live on this island on the edge of the world. She read a lot.

He paddled harder.

She did make him laugh out loud and she did have an excellent line in sarcasm. She was kind and he was pretty sure she'd be very loyal. She had a gorgeous Scottish accent. She was beautiful. When she'd turned up at the kitchen window looking both flight-weary and very cute, in a canary yellow – very Cassie – waist-length top, he'd just wanted to talk to her.

And *then* what? He paddled even harder.

First, he'd indirectly mentioned Leonie to her. He never did that. Second, when they'd been standing next to the cake, and he'd been breathing in her fruity, flowery scent, looking at her expressive face and her somewhat bonkers hair, all he'd been thinking about was how much he'd like to pull her into his arms, wind his fingers into her hair, kiss her until she was breathless. What was *wrong* with him? He didn't want to kiss the woman he'd swapped houses with and was now kind of friends with. Far too complicated.

Anyway, he'd literally been saved by a bell and now his head was clear.

He continued to paddle furiously around the headland and towards Cassie's perfect wild beach. Frustrating woman.

After about an hour, muscles satisfyingly stretched, he made his way back. He needed to check on the caterers and Laura, sort the cake out and get changed. Cassie should be long gone by now.

James locked the boathouse door, picked his towel up and put it over his shoulder and, as he walked up the steps from the beach to the garden, swiped his phone to check his emails.

A colleague had just sent through the numbers for a business model they'd been discussing. He turned his phone round to squint at a spreadsheet.

He only saw Cassie as she rounded the tree where the garden hit its L-shape. Though he didn't so much see her as bump right into her.

'Oops,' she squeaked, and tripped. *Shit.* She was a lot smaller than he was and he'd been paying no attention whatsoever and had barrelled straight into her. James shot his non-phone-holding arm out, encountered a lot of softness, and then found her arm and set her straight on her feet. God, that scent again. And some of her beautiful hair was in his face.

He took a step away from her to avoid a repeat of the kitchen madness.

'Sorry about that,' he said. 'You okay?'

'No, *I'm* sorry.' She looked up at him and smiled. Her gorgeous smile was so wide and generous that it went right to somewhere inside him. 'It was me. I was going at a semi-run. I suddenly realised that I'd been with the animals for far too long and I ought to go and say hi to Laura and then I need to get changed.'

He was still holding onto her arm. He let go, quickly, and took a step away from her. Her gaze snagged on his bare chest for a moment before she looked back up at his face. James had to fight not to smirk. Seriously. What was he? A teenager?

What had they been talking about?

Who'd bumped into whom.

'Nope, my fault. Reading my emails on my phone. Anyway. You going back this way?' He gestured towards the house. She'd been with the animals all that time? 'So you missed the animals a lot?'

'I really did, so, yes, I've been with them for ages.' Mind reader. 'I brought a carrot and broccoli snack for the alpacas and then I just sat and watched them all. And it's possible that I had a little snooze. That journey's a long one.'

'It is.' James nodded. 'I hope you found the animals well,' he said. 'I wasn't expecting a crash course in animal husbandry when I came here but I've genuinely enjoyed looking after them. Apart from Donna being ill, of course.'

'Yes, very well.' There was that wide smile again. 'They seem brilliantly looked after. And I saw that you've bought them some fancy snacks. They're going to miss you.'

'Yeah, I realised that the way to an alpaca's heart was via its stomach so I turned to Google and, yes, I did invest in some serious quantities of strawberries and green beans with handfuls of raisins thrown in.'

Cassie laughed and they walked on for a few seconds in what felt like very companionable silence.

'I'll see you later then.' She stopped for a second at the corner of the house.

Now she was facing him, he could see her properly. Her face was very expressive, with that gorgeous smile and beautiful dark-brown eyes. Her face was also green.

'Cassie.'

'Yes?'

'I'm thinking that this is like when someone has spinach in their teeth, you know, when you're doing them a favour telling them.'

'Oh, God. Did I go to sleep in alpaca poo?' She twisted round to look over her shoulder and James caught a glimpse of smooth, light-brown skin at her waist as her top lifted slightly.

He really should grow up. That should *not* have had any kind of effect on him.

'No. Your cheek. I'm thinking alpaca spit.'

She put her hand on her cheek and screwed her face up. 'Oh yes. They had a little fight over the food and there was some spitting.'

'Yep, I've been there. It's quite hard not to get caught in the line of fire.'

'I love how you're such an alpaca expert now.' Cassie grinned at him. 'Thank you for pointing this out. Not a good party accessory. I'll do some serious scrubbing in the shower.'

It was probably because he'd caught that glimpse of her bare waist that a momentary image of how Cassie might look under a shower flashed across his mind. Seriously.

*

Dina and Cassie arrived at the marquee together, twenty minutes before the party was due to start. James was doing some last-minute chair and table arranging with the caterers when they came in.

James stood up. 'Evening. You're both looking lovely.' Which was absolutely true.

Dina had on a very Dina-like dress. Black again, straight, knee length, tight and low cut. She was wearing it with bright-red high heels and lipstick to match.

And Cassie. She was wearing a very different kind of dress. Brighter, and kind of softer. It was emerald green, also low cut, but in a less revealing way, with a wide skirt and a big gold belt. Her shoes were softer than Dina's too. Gold to match her belt, and he was pretty sure that heels like that were called wedges. And her lipstick was orangey. Not so glamorous, but extremely attractive and very Cassie. She looked beautiful.

Dina walked over to him with her arms held out. No choice but to give her a hug and say a lot of effusive hellos.

'And I don't need to introduce you, of course,' she said, inviting Cassie over with a big smile and nod of her head. It felt odd, because, of the two of them, while Dina was the one James had spent more actual, physical time with, Cassie was the one he felt like he knew better. Which was ridiculous. He didn't. He'd partied with Dina, played cards with her, drunk tea with her, chatted to her. He'd had a fair few conversations with Cassie and had lived in her house, but was that enough to get to know someone?

'Yes.' Cassie sounded unusually clipped and her smile seemed strained. Not that he was an expert on what her smile normally looked like. 'Hi, James.'

'Evening.' For whatever reason, this did not feel like an easy situation. He pulled his shirt cuff back and checked his watch. 'I should go and get Laura. I'll see you both soon, when I have the birthday girl safely here.'

Cassie seemed to relax slightly. 'I can't wait to see her.'

'Ask her to tell you about when I went round earlier in the week,' James said. 'She was a good ten or twelve feet up a tree holding onto the trunk with one hand, trying to prune some branches with the other.'

'Oh my goodness,' Cassie said. 'Incorrigible. So dangerous. You have to admire her, though.'

'You do.' James nodded. 'I think we all need to aspire to being like her when we're eighty. Right. I'm going. I'll see you later.'

He hadn't bargained for how long it would take Laura to find her shoes, put them on (shoe horn required; but where was the shoe horn?), change her shoes (shoe horn required again; at least they didn't have to look for it this time), change her shoes back, decide on which coat she needed even though it was a very balmy evening, and finally consent to getting into the car.

She'd wanted to walk and had been remarkably stubborn all week in the face of much pressure, including Dina telling her, with all her usual subtlety, that they didn't need her to fracture a hip on the way. Eventually, Dina had called in the big guns, Cassie, and she'd managed to persuade Laura over the phone. Neither Laura nor Cassie had divulged what Cassie had said but James had been pretty sure it had been the same kind of seductive Glaswegian-accented, simultane-ously sarcastic but soft-voiced persuasion that had had him visiting neighbours, hosting parties, agreeing that of course he didn't really want to buy her land from her and so on.

*

Pretty much everyone else seemed already to have arrived by the time he and Laura made it into the marquee. James immediately cast his eye around the place to look for Cassie. For Laura's sake, obviously. Not on his own account.

Maybe a little on his own account. He really wanted to talk to her some more and he really wanted to know why her smile had seemed so strained earlier. He was pretty sure she was normally upbeat and it didn't really seem right for her to be miserable.

She was in the middle of a big group of islanders, laughing, her face alight. Okay. She clearly wasn't miserable. He must have imagined it. And there'd be no reason for the two of them to talk this evening, because she'd be wanting to catch up with all her friends.

'Hey, I brought you another beer. Thought you could do with one. Your hand's been empty for a while.' Dina's voice had gone full-on sultry.

'That's really kind, but I'm good, thanks.' James gave her his best non-committal smile. 'I'm going to drive Laura home later. And someone needs to look out for all the rest of you because I'm getting the sense that not everyone's on the wagon tonight.'

'Boring.' Dina pouted.

Not boring. Wise. When alcoholism was probably in your genes, you'd be stupid not to be careful around drink.

She put both the glasses she'd been holding down on the nearest table and took his hands. 'Let's dance.'

James did not need a misunderstanding, especially in a small community like this, where he was going to be living for another two months, and where he suspected he might like to return for holidays. Dina was showing all the signs of a woman who'd happily end the evening doing something very intimate with him. And since he thought of her as a friend now and she'd mentioned a few times recently that she was keen to settle down, and there was no way he was settling down, he was absolutely not going there.

The same two-man band that had been playing at Amy's party had just struck up a slow dance. 'Good idea,' he said. 'We should get everyone onto the dance floor.' He took Dina's hand and boogied across the tent with her, side by side, in a – frankly somewhat peculiar, but satisfyingly un-intimate – manoeuvre, inviting every single person he saw to join them as he went.

It was a remarkably successful move. By the time they'd done a circuit of the marquee, he had at least half the guests who were under eighty dancing, and apparently inspired by the dancing, the band had switched to a much more up-tempo song.

Clapping his hands energetically above his head with everyone else, anything to escape any one-on-one Dina-sultriness, James wondered where Cassie was. He'd thought they'd scooped her up into their dancing group but now he couldn't see her anywhere.

Finally he saw her, over in the corner by the bar, drinking by herself. She looked strained again. He wasn't close enough to see her face, but her shoulders were both a little stooped and a little rigid. Not a comfortable look.

He clapped himself all the way round the edge of the group until he got to Cassie.

'You okay?' he asked.

'Yes, thank you, fine.' She tipped her head back and emptied her glass. White wine. 'Totally fine.' She leaned over the bar and said, 'Todd, could I get another of these?'

'Sure.' Todd got a clean glass out for her. 'Give me a minute. Gonna have to open a new bottle for you.'

'That is not a problem.' Cassie slumped slightly against the bar. 'Todd. Have I told you that you're a very nice man?'

'Why, thank you.' Todd looked a little too pleased with that compliment.

'Could I get a large glass of water?' James asked.

'Sure.'

Todd handed Cassie her glass and she made to walk away.

'Wait for me?' James said to her, while Todd filled his water glass.

'Okay. Fine.' Cassie took a step backwards, turned her ankle and spilled some wine on the floor. 'Owww. Oh, no, s'okay. Doesn't actually hurt.' That would be the anaesthetising properties of alcohol.

'Come on.' James took her elbow and walked with her towards the marquee entrance. He was pretty sure that she wouldn't want to stay this drunk. 'Why don't we get some fresh air?' Hopefully a combination of a lot of water and the cool evening air would sober her up. She wouldn't want to miss the rest of Laura's party. They hadn't even done the cake yet, and, if he said it himself, that was going to be a good moment.

'Okay,' she said. 'You know what, James?'

'What?'

'Everyone keeps telling me that they love you. People like fishing with you. They like talking to you. They like shooting pool with you. All sorts. They're pleased to have met you. They wouldn't *have* met you if I hadn't left. It's unflattering.'

'They do miss you. They keep telling me they do. Plus rumour has it that *my* neighbours like you, and I don't even *know* my neighbours,' he told her.

'Oh yes.' She stumbled. 'That is a very, very good point. You must be very, very clever.'

James steered her round the side of the marquee a little way. 'Come and sit on this wall with me for a moment?' he said. 'Maybe look at the stars?'

'Look at the stars?' Cassie hiccupped. 'Are you the kind of person who looks at stars?'

'You know, I actually am.' He knew that he was smiling at her. He really didn't know why. He hated drunkenness. 'Let me take your glass.'

'One more sip first.' She pulled it away from him and it spilled. Really not a bad thing. 'James. We've made a mess on the grass.'

'Yeah. Drink some water.'

'The water's nice actually.'

'Drink more of it.'

'Are you trying to get me un-drunk? Because I can be drunk if I want to. And I'll tell you why.' She turned and prodded him in the chest. 'I can be drunk because I'm not pregnant. I'm un-pregnant. I'm very very very un-pregnant. Not pregnant at all.' She hiccupped again.

Should he say anything? This felt like a minefield. Had she met someone in London? Dina had definitely told him that Cassie was single, and he'd assumed from his conversation with her mother that she was. Plus, if she *did* have a partner, what had that been in the kitchen earlier?

'I like your shoes, James.'

'Thank you. I like your shoes too.'

'I like your shirt too.'

'Thank you.'

'Oh, God,' Cassie moaned. They'd been sitting there for a good half hour pretty much stargazing and she was clearly a lot more sober now.

Not sober-sober, but not do-stupidly-dangerous-things-drunk any more. 'Sorry. I had too much to drink.'

'No need to apologise. It happens. Are you okay?'

'Yeah. No.' She paused. James waited, sensing she had more to say. 'I know I was waffling about not being pregnant. Basically...' She was staring at the ground. 'Basically, I had IVF with a donor sperm while I was in London, and I found out last weekend that it didn't work.'

God. And, okay, so the kitchen moment hadn't been so bad.

'Cassie. That's huge. I'm so sorry.' Should he ask her any questions about it?

'Thank you. I'm sorry for being drunk on you.'

'Hey. You haven't been drunk on me. I mean, a little bit, but my choice. I saw you at the bar and I was worried about you, so I came over to see you. Totally my choice.'

'Well, hey yourself.' Cassie nudged him. 'Very nice of you to be worried about the pain-in-the-arse, nagging house swappee.'

'Did I say that?'

'Yes, pretty much, but quite a few weeks ago.'

James nodded. 'You've grown on me since then.'

'Like fungus?'

'No. Like something quite nice.' He thought for a moment. 'Nope, I can't describe it.'

'You've grown on me too,' Cassie said.

'Well, thank you.'

'Do you only talk to me because you want to buy my land?'

'No.' That answer had required no thought because it was the truth. 'I admit that initially it was my reason but now I just like talking to you. I know we aren't going to be doing business and here I am, still talking.'

'I'm very pleased about that.'

'Me too.'

They sat and looked at the stars again.

'Are you going to be okay?' James had to ask. It didn't feel right just to abandon the IVF topic, however difficult it was to know what to say. It felt like he'd be belittling her experience if he didn't show some interest. 'Are you going to do it again?' Was that a shockingly insensitive question? 'Obviously don't answer that if you'd rather not.'

'I don't know. I think so. Probably. I'm thirty-seven. Not a spring chicken. I decided to go it alone because, well, you know, as you do, basically because of a shitty ex. I'd love to have two children. I mean, I'd love to have a *lot* of children, but two would be amazing. *One* would be amazing.' She sniffed. 'Sorry.'

'Hey. Don't say sorry.' James wondered if the shitty ex was shittier than Richie from the christening, the sperm-donating father-of-seven. How would Richie react if any of those kids came looking for him when they were eighteen? Having a baby on your own was a big decision. It was hard, too hard for some women, like his own mother. Cassie was strong though. That was obvious. She sniffed again. 'You're going to be okay,' he said, 'whatever happens.'

'Thank you.'

He looked down at her. He was pretty sure she was crying. Yes, she was. He put his right arm round her as gently as he could and with his left thumb wiped away the tears he could see. 'You really will be.'

She gave a big gulping sound and he gathered her against his chest while she cried.

Was it wrong that he was enjoying holding her? Definitely. She was *upset*, for God's sake. He should absolutely not be registering how well she fitted into his arms. He kept his head up, resisting the urge to bury his face in her hair, and looked into the darkness.

'Oh my *God*,' she said eventually, pulling her head back. 'Honestly. Truly pathetic. That's the second time I've cried on someone in one day. I bawled all over Dina earlier. And in your case there's going to be mascara on your shirt.'

'Not pathetic. Totally understandable.' He squeezed her shoulders and she looked up at him. She was beautiful in the moonlight.

'Thank you,' she said. 'I'm going to apologise one last time.'

'And I'm going to refuse to accept that apology one last time because you have nothing to apologise for.'

'Okay. Thank you. I'm not normally this pathetic, honest. It brought back some difficult memories.'

'I'm so sorry.' He really didn't know what else to say. Ask what those memories were? Definitely not. But ignore what she'd just said? No; he couldn't do that either.

'I lost a baby a few years ago. I was five months pregnant.' Her voice wavered.

How truly awful. No wonder she was upset today.

'That's terrible.' James squeezed her shoulders again. It felt like a ridiculously small gesture in the face of something so huge. 'I think you're being remarkably brave.'

'I don't feel brave.'

'Are you kidding? Doing all of it by yourself? *So* brave.'

'Thank you.' From her voice it sounded as though she'd managed a smile. 'It actually feels good to say it out loud, a bit of a sharing of the burden. I mean, I'm not going to go back in there and stand on a table and shout it out to everyone, but a little bit of talking is a good thing. Sorry that you were the victim.'

'Ha. Really not a victim. I'm honoured that you chose to tell me.' He hugged her again and then pointed upwards. 'Shooting stars. That's got to be lucky. How often do you see that?'

'To be honest, I think we're lucky just seeing the stars at all. And I feel very lucky to live here and to have done a house swap into such an amazing flat and, actually, as it turns out, with a lovely person, and now I'm definitely sober enough to realise that I'm sounding hideously schmaltzy, so I think we should go inside and help Laura cut her cake.' Her neck as she looked up at the sky was so elegant. James took his arm away from her shoulders. For a moment of insanity he'd wanted to trace the line of her neck and her collarbone with his finger. So inappropriate.

'Good point,' he said. Definitely time to go inside. James squinted at the luminous tips of his watch hands. 'Yep. We said we were going to cut it at eleven o'clock, didn't we, and it's quarter to now.' He stood up, held his hand out for Cassie and hauled her to her feet.

'Crikey,' she said. 'When the alcohol's worn off a bit you realise that it's quite cold.'

James opened his mouth to say that he could warm her up and then shut it again because that would sound *really* off. Especially since he wasn't wearing a jacket, so the only way to warm her would be to hug her. He held his arm out. 'Come on. Let's get you inside. It's a lot warmer in there.'

'*Woah*,' Cassie said. It was lucky for her that she'd been holding his arm because her shoes clearly weren't made for walking across fields. This one had a particularly large number of small mounds dotted around.

'You okay?' he asked. 'Did you hurt your ankle?'

'Nope, all good. Thank you. Embarrassing. Like we're making a habit of you catching me.' She looked up at him and smiled. And it was like the moment in the kitchen all over again. For no good reason at all, he really wanted to kiss her. They were standing looking at each other, not speaking. He could so easily slide one arm round her waist, pull her softness in towards him, maybe put his other hand in her hair, cup her cheek. He could still remember how her skin had felt when he'd wiped her tears away.

Her lips were slightly parted. Oh, God, she was moistening them with her tongue. And now she was starting to smile a little.

He took a little step towards her.

And *what* was he thinking? How ridiculously complicated would it be to start something with the woman he'd swapped properties with? Who knew really far too much about his life. And yet also absolutely nothing about his background. And who was currently gutted because her fertility treatment hadn't worked out and understandably grieving for the loss of her baby. And who'd had a *lot* to drink earlier in the evening.

He took a step backwards.

'Cake-cutting time soon.' His voice sounded embarrassingly hoarse.

'You're right.' And Cassie's sounded very fake bright and breezy. 'And it's cold. We should go inside.' She pulled her arm out of his. 'Pretty sure I'll be okay. It's flatter on this bit. Thank you.'

'Pleasure,' he said. Still sounding hoarse.

What an idiot.

Chapter Eighteen

Cassie

It was a good job that the clouds had moved away from the moon. Cassie really didn't want to trip over again and land pressed up against James. Just now, she'd been *so* ready to kiss him. It had seemed so inevitable that something would happen that she'd almost made the first move herself. And then he'd taken a big step away from her.

Hopefully he hadn't realised that she was so keen. Or hopefully, if he *had* realised, he'd put it down to the serious amounts of wine she'd knocked back earlier.

Woah, nearly tripped. She needed to walk very carefully. Staying upright was totally doable. She just had to place her feet one in front of the other very precisely, and feel around to make sure that she didn't hit any surprise bumps on the ground. Right foot out. Ball of the foot on the ground, follow it with the heel, put her weight on. And then with the left foot. And back to the right. Easy.

Had she misjudged things with James just then? She'd been certain he was feeling what she was; he'd just had that *look*, like he'd had in the kitchen earlier. He'd been half smiling, his eyes on hers, and on her mouth, and on the base of her neck. God, she was shivering just thinking about it. Ridiculous. But it had felt so intense. And then something had made him stop.

Which was a good thing, obviously. They'd swapped homes and it would be weird to do anything even approaching also swapping bodily fluids, plus – and way more importantly – Dina was halfway in love with him. She *really* liked him.

Cassie really liked him too, if she was honest.

Anyway. Maybe in another life. In this life, she'd totally be up for meeting someone, one day, but realistically James was not that person.

She did like him a lot, though. He was much nicer than she'd thought. And it was good to know that he was no longer just trying to butter her up.

'Thank you again for listening to me,' she said.

'Seriously. Not a problem. Pleased to be of listening assistance.' He was definitely for real. No-one could fake that smile and the warmth in his voice, combined with a tiny bit of gorgeous *I don't normally have conversations like this* awkwardness.

And hooray. They were back at the tent.

'Hey, where have you been?' Dina hurried towards them from halfway across the marquee. 'Are you okay?'

'I just drank a bit much,' said Cassie, not looking at James. 'I felt a bit sick. James was kind enough to take me outside for a minute to cool down.'

'Always the gentleman.' Dina flashed a smile at James. Cassie smiled generally at everyone, still not looking at him. This was terrible. She felt like she'd just committed adultery or something. Dina would be so hurt if she knew that they'd nearly kissed in the field. 'You okay now?'

'Yes, all good,' Cassie said, grabbing a glass of wine from a passing waiter, one of Amy's friends from the mainland. 'Where's Laura? It's cake time!'

Laura was sitting in state on the Birthday Girl Throne that Dina and Cassie had decorated with flowers earlier while James was collecting her in his car. She was holding a non-alcoholic cocktail and a sausage roll, surrounded by lots of friends, and apparently asking Soraya, from the village, who had four adult children and was nearly fifty, if she was pregnant. From Soraya's reaction, it looked as though she *was* and did not want to tell anyone. And Cassie was not going to be affected by the 'everyone except me is pregnant' thing again. She was going to react like an averagely happy person, and focus on Laura.

'Honestly—' she took a big slurp of her wine '—I don't know how she gets away with it.'

'Well, speaking as someone who met her relatively recently and got the full Laura treatment within literally minutes of meeting her, I think it's her sweetness and her earnestness that get you,' James said. 'You really want to tell her to shut up, but you just can't. So you give her a little bit and then she takes a bit more, and half an hour later, she knows a lot.'

Cassie nodded. 'Yup. You gave in very easily. I know that. She passed a *lot* of information on to me about you immediately. Literally. I knew a *lot* about you by your second day here.'

James swivelled his eyes. 'I'm worried now. What did I *say*?'

'Ha. You're just going to have to wonder.'

Cassie loved the way James's lips twitched when he was amused.

'Hey.' Dina's voice cut through her thoughts. 'What are you two smiling at?'

What *were* they smiling at? Other than each other?

'We were talking about Laura,' James said, after a slightly too long pause.

'Yes, we were,' Cassie said. 'About how she drags information out of people and how they're powerless to resist.'

'She does do that. Now. Cake time.' Dina clapped her hands. It was a loud clap and it did cause everyone to turn to look. She cupped her hands round her mouth and repeated, 'Cake time.'

'You nervous?' Cassie nudged James with raised eyebrows as Laura pressed the point of the cake knife into the middle of the top tier.

'Yup.' He nodded. 'Genuinely am. I mean, a) Laura's the queen of baking and b) I don't want to poison people. And c) I really don't know whether it's going to taste good or not because I have no frame of reference because I don't eat cake.'

'What? At all?'

'Nope.'

'Wow. You know what you are?' The wine was making Cassie feel more chilled again. She poked James in his gorgeously wide and solid chest. 'You are a man of steel in the face of inquisition. And a man of mystery. Because Laura thinks you *do* like cake. She thinks you love her blueberry cake.'

'That,' said James, giving her an eyebrow waggle, 'is because I—' he leaned in and lowered his voice '—*told* her that I loved the cake.'

Cassie gasped. 'You *lied* to Laura.'

'I did.' James nodded very seriously. 'It was a white lie.'

Cassie smiled at him. He was so gorgeous.

He was so Dina's.

She should walk away.

Cassie downed the rest of her wine and moved over to join the others close to the cake.

'This is an awesome cake,' Dina told James. 'Moist. But not too moist. Great flavour.'

'Thank you.' He smiled at her, but really not in the way he'd been smiling at Cassie today. It was hard to know why not. Dina looked fantastic. She'd poured her hourglass figure into a black velvet dress, her make-up was still perfect five hours down the line and her hair was bouncy loveliness. And she was funny and loyal and kind.

And Cassie really wanted to go to bed and forget that she'd nearly betrayed Dina this evening. She was so, so glad that nothing had actually happened between her and James.

'I'm just going to go and chat to a couple of people I haven't seen in a while,' she told Dina and James, and left them to it. She took a quick glance over her shoulder when she was a few feet away from them. They looked great together. Blond James and dark Dina. Both glamorous in their party gear. They'd look incredible going to a black-tie event together, for example.

'James is great,' Don Brown told Cassie. 'Great fishing companion.' Cassie nodded. Don was the sixth person in a row who'd told her how much they liked James. Good job James had pointed out to her that his neighbours liked her too, otherwise her nose would be feeling seriously out of joint.

Dina was clapping again. Cassie had never really noticed before how loud her claps were. She must have very hard hands.

'Time for us to sing "Happy Birthday",' she announced. 'And I'm going to ask James to start us off.'

'I think Cassie should join me.' James beckoned her over. 'She set all the arrangements in train and booked everything and this is her field. Credit where credit's due. All I did was put a shirt on and turn up.' Very sweet. Apparently he was genuinely very kind under his initially hard exterior, and very self-deprecating because the cake must have been a lot of work.

Also genuinely very tuneless. By the last 'to you', Cassie was laughing so much she thought she might be sick. James was laughing even more than she was. So endearing.

'Cassie, honey.' Laura held her arms out to her. 'Thank you so much for travelling so far across the world for my birthday. You didn't have to but I'm so happy that you did.'

Cassie put her arms round Laura. 'I'm so pleased to have been able to come.' She felt Laura sway a little. This was a late night for an eighty-year-old. 'You ready for bed yet?'

'I think I might be.'

'Me too. Come on.'

'Right here with the car keys,' James said.

*

Cassie had moved firmly onto London time and was sound asleep in Dina's spare room within under five minutes of them rolling in through Dina's front door, so it wasn't until breakfast time that Dina started on the post-party analysis.

'What do you think of James in the flesh?' Dina poured more black coffee into a mug. 'He's gorgeous, isn't he? And so good to talk to. And from everything I've learned he seems like an all-round good guy. And he is so not interested in me.'

'Thank you.' Cassie took the mug gratefully. Her head didn't feel good. At least she'd been drinking white and not red last night. With red, she always started her hangover before she was even in bed. 'You don't *know* that he isn't interested.' She took a long drink. Should she have said that?

'I do know. I've given him a *lot* of opportunities and nothing's going to happen.' Dina shook her head. 'I should just accept it. And, you know, I've only known him for four months. I shouldn't be this upset.' Cassie looked into her mug and gave the coffee a little swirl. What should she say? She was pretty sure that Dina was right, because the way James had looked at her was definitely different from the way he looked at Dina. False hope was not a good thing to have. Like when you thought you were pregnant but you weren't. As a good friend, she should definitely not tell Dina about the moments she'd had with James yesterday, but she should also maybe encourage her to face reality.

'Maybe he just doesn't want a relationship at the moment,' she said.

'Yeah. Anyway. I can't believe we're talking about me and my unrequited lust for James after what you told me yesterday. I'm being self-centred.'

'*No*. Dina. Never self-centred.' Cassie put her mug down. This was awful. Dina was feeling bad when she, Cassie, if anyone, should feel bad. Although it wasn't like she'd chosen to feel that connection with James last night. Maybe it had been because they were living in each other's houses. Very intimate. 'Let's do something nice this morning when we've finished breakfast. Have a swim and sunbathe? What's Amy doing today?'

Cassie put her arms round Fred's neck and looked at his familiar, dopey face. 'I'm going to miss you,' she told him. 'But don't worry. I'll be back in a couple of months' time.' Donna and Maisie wandered over.

There was a bit of throat clearing behind her. She turned round, leaving an arm round Fred's neck.

'Afternoon.' James was wearing shorts – he had *great* legs – and a T-shirt and carrying a bucket. He stopped a good ten feet away from her, which was an extremely good thing. 'Hope I'm not disturbing you. I thought you were leaving this morning.'

'I'm catching the ferry soon and then driving down to Boston and catching the last red eye. Just thought I'd have one last cuddle. With the alpacas.' Honestly. Just the word *cuddle* had her thinking about last night in the field and what hadn't happened.

'They are great for a quick cuddle. I've been known to sneak one in myself. I just came to collect eggs. Hannah and Holly in particular have been laying later in the day recently and I don't like leaving them because I did once by mistake and they pecked into them and ate them.'

'James Grey. You've become a devoted chicken farmer.'

'I really have. I think I'll miss them when we swap back. Not joking. You'll have to send me news of them.'

'Yeah, I'm going to miss your neighbours when I leave London.' She was going to miss James too.

'Maybe we should make it an annual thing. For a holiday. Again, not joking.'

Cassie nodded. 'That does sound like a plan.' And then she and James would have to stay in touch.

'Okay, great. So I'm going to go over to see the chickens. Have a good journey.'

'Thank you.'

'Probably speak soon about something.'

'Yes, probably.' Cassie smiled at him and he walked round her, giving her a *wide* berth.

James had demonstrated that he was a lot lovelier than she'd ever have expected, but Cassie still felt a little awkward about having a full-on one-sided chat with the alpacas within possible earshot of him, so she just gave each of them a kiss and left.

*

Cassie thanked Henry fervently for his help with her luggage and closed the door of the flat behind him. Arriving here after the long journey from the island felt different this time. It genuinely did feel like a second home.

This time, she had food, she had towels and she had friends, and this evening she was going to the cinema with Chloe, Juliet and Anthony. Juliet had suggested a film based on what was apparently a great example of nineteenth-century German literature, and Cassie had invited Anthony – he read a lot of quite serious books – for another good opportunity to try to get him and Juliet together. A lot could happen under cover of the darkness and noise of a film auditorium.

*

'Hi, Jennifer.' Cassie put her phone on speaker and turned the volume down. The cinema last night had been one of those fancy ones with a lot of velvet and a wine bar, and she'd had more glasses than she should have done because the film had been dull, so she had a headache this morning. She could increase the volume if it turned out that Jennifer was in Friendly Home Jennifer mode rather than Business Bitch mode.

'How's it going? We have a meeting with the TV people lined up for next Tuesday.' Business mode. Cassie adjusted the volume down further.

'Okay, so all great then,' Jennifer wound up. 'And now I'd better go. Gotta try to find another babysitter. We have tickets for *Hamilton* this evening, which we don't want to miss, and our babysitter just fell through. Teenagers. She got asked out on a date with the boy she's been into for months and she said yes and binned us. And you know what, you can't do that.' Screechy but fair. 'I'm not going to be asking her again. Disappointing because we know her mother and that's why we felt confident leaving Sammy with her, but, you know. You do need a babysitter to be reliable.'

'And you wouldn't want her date to help her babysit?'

'So she can make out on the couch and ignore any sounds from the baby monitor? No. I'm actually really pissed at her, which is why I'm talking to you about it now and mixing business and displeasure. It's our anniversary and it was the first time since Sammy that we were going to venture out beyond Barnes. Anyway. Maybe I'll find someone. I'm going to call around.'

'Why don't I do it?' Cassie heard herself say. What? She didn't want to be alone all evening with Sammy. She'd be beating down the door of the IVF clinic again by the time Jennifer and Angela got home.

'I couldn't accept your help. I hope you don't think I was asking you.'

'No, of course I don't. But, honestly, not a problem. I was only planning to work this evening. I can bring my laptop with me.'

'Are you really sure?'

'Totally.' Not. But Cassie couldn't avoid babies for the rest of her life just to stop herself feeling broody. That would be ridiculous. And how rubbish if Jennifer and Angela had to miss out on their anniversary evening.

'Well, then I will accept very gratefully but on one condition.'

'Mmm?' Never say yes to Jennifer until you knew exactly what the question was.

'You have to accept whatever very OTT thank you present I buy for you with no quibbling.'

Cassie laughed. 'No present OTT or otherwise is necessary but, yes, should there be any such present I will accept it quibble-free.'

'Perfect. Thank you *so* much.'

'Bye. Have fun.' Cassie closed Jennifer's front door and turned to look at Sammy. She could totally, no question, do this. Of course she could. She was a competent adult. He was a very small person. How hard could it be for her to look after him?

He started crawling away from her along the hall towards the kitchen, really quite fast. He had a *gorgeous* kind of commando action, not your classic crawl, and it looked so determined and so *cute*. And, woah, he was about to go headfirst down the two steps that led to the kitchen.

Cassie pulled a very quick short sprint out of the bag and picked him up just before he reached the first of the steps. He was so soft and chubby and just adorable.

And wriggly.

'Head,' he said and hit her – remarkably hard for someone so young – on the side of her face.

'Ow.'

'Head.' Bang.

He got three more massive hits in before she got him into his playpen. She'd always thought they seemed a little mean, in an animal-in-a-zoo way, but, yep, less than five minutes into an evening's babysitting and she could totally see that as a full-time carer to a baby you'd need some significant breaks from being smacked round the face and constantly having to run after them while they crawled into danger.

*

'Hey, Cassie.' It was Real Jennifer, not Scary Dream Jennifer who'd been yelling in Cassie's dream that Cassie should not move back to Maine. Cassie had just been asleep on the sofa in Jennifer and Angela's kitchen. Really quite sound asleep. It was hard work looking after a baby. He hadn't gone to sleep until about ten. 'How was he?'

'A delight,' Cassie said. He'd been gorgeous. Also, way more tiring than she'd expected. 'I have to tell you that I messed up his first nappy change and put the nappy on back-to-front. It was a *lot* more complicated than I'd thought. Anyway, he weed out of the side all over his sheets. I found clean sheets in the wardrobe and put the wet ones through the washing machine. I wasn't sure whether to tumble dry them so I hung them up.' He'd actually needed *four* nappy changes, and three of them had been messy – what had he been *eating*? And thank *goodness* the one when the nappy had been on the wrong way had only been wee.

'Thank you so much,' Angela said.

'My pleasure. He's lovely. How was the show?'

'OMG. Sensational. Lin-Manuel Miranda's a genius.'

'It was brilliant,' Angela agreed. 'Thank you again.'

'Honestly, it was a lot of fun. I should thank *you*.'

A little snuffle came over the baby monitor. Cute. The snuffle turned into a little cry, which was no surprise to Cassie; Sammy was clearly not a good sleeper.

'I'll go,' Angela said. 'We must have disturbed him when we came in.'

'I'm going to get going,' Cassie said. 'Great to see all three of you and I'm so glad that you enjoyed the show.'

'I have a bottle of wine for you for now and I have another something coming for you, which should arrive in a couple days' time.'

'Honestly, there was no need. But thank you. I love the label.'

'Hey. I'd be taking advantage otherwise.' Hilarious, given that Jennifer was *very* ready to take advantage of a lot of people in a professional environment.

The cab arrived quickly. Cassie sat down in the back and took a lovely deep breath. She was genuinely worn out. Every time she'd relaxed, Sammy had woken up. The evening had been a strange mix of her heart cracking at the gorgeousness of him, loving the cuddles, clapping with him and laughing with him as they played together, and worry that he ought to be asleep. And all the nappy changes, of course. She hadn't totally *loved* dealing with Sammy's dirty nappies but he'd laughed so much at the faces she'd pulled and the nursery rhymes she'd sung while he was on his changing mat that she'd ended up in stitches too. There weren't many sounds better than a baby giggling away.

She looked out of the window at the trees on Barnes Common. Such a wonderful place to bring a child up.

Not as good as the island, though. Now *that* would be a great place to bring a child up.

She nodded to herself. Yep. There was no question. Even if she was hopeless at getting him to sleep, she had loved every minute with Sammy. She now knew more than ever that she wanted to try again at least once more to have a baby of her own. Not in London again, though. Yes, it would be really awkward having to book a hotel room and go down to Boston at the drop of a hat, and London with the hospital on her doorstep had been way more convenient, but if it all went wrong again, she'd rather be at home. She wanted her friends nearby.

Why did James pop into her head when she thought about friends?

Chapter Nineteen

James

James was going to have to phone Cassie. Hopefully she wouldn't be in bed yet.

'Hi, James.' She sounded pleased to hear from him.

'Hello. You sound wide awake so I'm hoping that this isn't too late to call.'

'Nope, all good, not in bed yet. I've just got home after babysitting my agent's baby.'

'How was it? I'm not the biggest fan of babysitting, if I'm honest.'

'I actually really enjoyed it. Although I'm knackered now. He took a *long* time to get to sleep. But no, I had a good time. He was gorgeous. Emotionally, it was a great thing to do. I've avoided being around babies for the past few years, but it was fine. I coped. I more than coped. I had a lovely evening. It made me realise that you should confront your phobias, or maybe slay your demons, more often. Anyway, I'm waffling. How are you?'

'Not waffling and what you say makes a lot of sense.' It did. Maybe James should consider attempting to slay some of his own demons. 'I'm good except I'm worried about Fred. He hasn't been himself for the past couple of days. I just wanted to talk things through with you before I call the vet again.'

'Oh my goodness. What's happened to him?'

'He just doesn't seem right. The vet already checked him out today and couldn't find anything wrong. But I *know* him.'

Was he, James, really saying these things? Mad.

Twenty minutes later he was standing next to Fred holding his phone out to Fred's ear with the volume on high while Cassie crooned to him.

'No *way*,' he said to Cassie after she'd eventually croon-shouted to him that there was a limit to how long she could phone-monologue to an alpaca and could they maybe stop. 'He looks happier. I'm pretty sure he's been missing you. He's wandered off now and is chomping away. He's been quite off his food.'

'I'm *ridiculously* flattered,' Cassie said. 'Also *ridiculously* amused about how much of an animal-lover you've become.'

'I know.' James nodded even though she couldn't see him. 'It's like some kind of reality show experience. Swap lives with someone and see if you become more like them.'

'You're right. And generally whether you learn stuff about yourself. During *my* reality show experience, I've slain one demon and I might confront my other one. Plus, if I'm honest, I've learned not to judge a book by its cover.'

'I'm not going to ask what your other demon is but I'm here if you'd like to tell me. I *am* going to ask if I'm the book you judged.'

'Yep.'

'Ha. I might have judged you a little too.'

'So what's your reality show transformation been? If you'd like to say?'

'Really just being open to stuff. I mean, when I made the sudden decision to do the swap it didn't enter my head that I'd live like this. I thought I'd carry on like I live in London, but here. No interaction with neighbours, no alpaca and chicken feeding, no fishing. No poker. But it's been great. I genuinely think I'm a nicer person.'

'Wow. On behalf of my house and the island I'm going to say, "You're welcome".'

'It isn't just the house and the island. It's you too. Leading by example. Anyway, I think this conversation's getting a little sappy, so I'm going to thank you and leave you, but I might need to call you again very soon, maybe tomorrow, so that you can give Fred another pep talk.'

Old James would have been on the verge of vomiting from a chat like that. New James just put his phone in his pocket, gave the alpacas some sugar beet shred, dodged some spit and carried on back to the house.

Maybe he should tackle some of his own demons. Specifically, his father and sister.

That evening, one beer, three games of poker and about twenty dollars down, he came to a sudden decision.

'Guys, I'm going to shoot,' he told the others. 'Something I've got to do this evening. I'll see you next Tuesday.' He'd miss poker when he got back to London. Maybe he'd try to find a similar group there.

'You'd better prepare to lose big next week.' Laura was gathering up piles of chips. She really was a seriously good player. James needed to practise more.

*

An hour later, he leaned back in Cassie's uber-comfortable desk chair, rolled his shoulders and flexed his fingers. He was going to do this. He was going to send both emails. Demon slaying.

To: Dougie Finegan
From: James Grey
Subject: Relationship

Dougie,

We both know that you're my father.
    My mother died nine months ago and you have not mentioned her death to me.
    My sister died five years ago and you have not mentioned her death to me.
    In the five years since Leonie died you have asked me for money eleven times.
    I'm not going to give you any money.
    If you'd like to attempt a father/ son rather than investee/ investor relationship, I'd be happy to talk.
    Otherwise, we should probably call it quits.

Best,
James

He pressed Send. Good.
The next one was going to be harder to write. It meant more.

To: Ella Marshall
From: James Grey
Subject: Hi

Hey Sis,

I just wanted to say that I'm sorry I haven't been around much recently. Would you and the kids like to come to London for a weekend sometime soon?

James x

He pressed Send. Wow.

The email to his father would likely only result in a possible reduction in requests for money. The one to Ella might be the first step in re-building a proper relationship with his older sister.

*

'Hi, Cass.'

'Fred chat time?'

'Yep.' It was the third day running. Fred had been moping like nobody's business. Understandable. James missed Cassie too and he barely knew her, nor had she been feeding him treats every day most of his life. 'Question. How long have you had the alpacas and how old are they?'

'Donna's four, Maisie three and Fred two. I got them as babies and fed them initially from a bottle.'

James could imagine her doing that. She'd have a similar expression of concentration to the one she'd had when he'd seen her chatting to them.

'How's your day been?' he asked when she'd finished giving Fred his pep talk for the afternoon.

She told him about a visit to the London Dungeon – she'd wanted to check whether her characters could feasibly get trapped in there overnight – and then asked him how his own day had been.

He hesitated for a moment and then suddenly decided to take the plunge. Confide in her a little. 'Following on from our conversation the other day, I wrote a couple of big emails to family members on Sunday. I haven't been properly in touch with my sister for a while and I invited her to come and stay when I get back to London. I heard back from her today and we've set a date.'

'Wow, that's great. What... happened? If you want to say?'

'Nothing serious. You know, just life. We just drifted apart.' Turned out that there was only so much soul-baring he could manage in one conversation.

Cassie waited for a second, maybe to see if he had more to say, and then said, 'I'm going to address my other big thing. I'm going to go to Glasgow for the weekend. I left soon after I had the miscarriage, and I haven't been able to face going back because of the memories. It's been four years. I'm going to go just before we swap back.'

'Wow. Congratulations on taking that step. That's huge.' He'd had no idea that she had any of that going on in her head. Funny how they knew so much about how the other lived and a fair amount about their current lives but so little about their backgrounds. Well, not that unusual when it came to him. He generally didn't tell people stuff.

*

'Fred's looking good today. The girls too. And all the chicks. Basically, I'm a farming genius.' James settled in on the tree stump he often sat on when he was talking to Cassie about the animals.

'Be honest. Fred's stopped missing me, hasn't he?'

'Yep. He's shockingly fickle.' It was true. There was no need for James to call Cassie every afternoon any more, but it was what they did now, every day, even if it was just a few words. They'd been doing it for several weeks. He liked their chats, and he was pretty sure she did too. They'd fallen into a habit of taking it in turns to call each other and neither of them ever made an excuse; and he suspected that Cassie made sure she was free for the call every day, like he did. 'So what've you been doing today? Did you get your draft to Jennifer?'

'I did, thank goodness.'

'How's the plan going for the next one?' So restrained on his part. He *really* wanted to know what books she wrote. Why didn't she want to tell anyone her pen name? Did she really write extreme erotica, not kids' books? Had she written something so famous that people would be beating down her door if they knew who she was?

Cassie laughed. 'You really want to know my pen name, don't you?'

'Well, obviously yes.'

'Okay. Promise you'll never tell anyone.'

'Absolutely.'

'It's going to mean nothing to you. Milly Moore.' That *did* mean nothing to him. So disappointing. For a moment he'd genuinely been expecting to hear her say a name as famous as Enid Blyton or J.K. Rowling.

'Cool,' he said. 'Very interesting.'

'Yep, I knew you'd never have heard of me. You might have heard of a couple of my characters.'

'Probably,' he said. Of course he wouldn't have. Not having been a big reader as a child he hadn't heard of any characters other than Harry Potter, Stig of the Dump and… that was about it. He couldn't think of any others off the top of his head.

'The MacDuff Twins.'

No way.

'No *way*. What, the ones in the TV series? Which are on US TV as well as UK TV? That all adults including even me have heard of. Wait, they're from *books*?'

Good God. She had to have made an absolute fortune from those if her agent was remotely competent.

'Yep. And that's why I don't tell anyone my pen name, because I don't want people putting two and two together and beating down my door. Though, actually, I didn't tell anyone to start off with because I didn't want my ex to be able to get in touch with me, and then when we did the TV deal, it turned out to have been a very good thing.'

'Wow.'

Cassie laughed. 'I enjoyed that. You were *totally* expecting not to have heard of my characters, weren't you?'

'I was. I was wondering whether or not I was going to fake recognition, to be polite.' He really wanted to ask more about the ex, but baby steps with the revelations.

'Confessions for a rainy day,' Cassie said.

'It isn't rainy here. We have blue skies and a bright sun. I'm wearing shorts and sunglasses.'

'Lucky. So what have you been up to?'

'Work. Went for a swim. I'm playing poker with the guys and Laura this evening. She'll fleece us.' He squashed a sudden urge, from nowhere, to talk to Cassie about Ella. 'And I'm going to eat another of your freezer meals. I'm thinking another portion of the hashweh. That's seriously delicious.'

They talked for ages, about nothing, until James realised that he was going to be late for poker if he didn't go.

*

'Thank you, all of you. I'm genuinely choking up a little.' Incredible, against all his initial expectations and impressions, that he'd be sad to be leaving the island the day after tomorrow. 'This is a great place and you're great people, and six months ago I really wouldn't have believed that I'd have felt so attached to being here. I'll be back.' James finished his best Arnie-as-Terminator impression amid cheers and whistles, and leaped down from the table he'd been standing on.

'Another beer?' Dina asked.

'I'm good, thanks.' James indicated his glass of water.

'You're very good at staying sober,' she slurred.

James nodded. She was right. He really was.

'Can I talk to you?' She had a hand on his forearm and was sliding it up.

He moved a little away from her and said, 'Sure,' in his most off-putting voice.

She wasn't put off. 'Could we go outside?' They were in the village hall's function room.

'Yeah, sure. Or maybe into this corner.' He walked over to a table set apart from everyone else but in full view of the room, and sat down at one of the two chairs there. Dina followed him over and sat down on the other chair, pulling it closer.

'Here's the thing,' she said. 'I really like you.' Okay. Excruciating.

'I'm going to leap in right there,' he said. 'I could be completely mis-reading the situation but I get the impression that you might be looking for a relationship. I'm the opposite. I'm really not looking for one. You know. That's part of the reason I came here. Romantic relationships really aren't for me. I really don't want one. For various reasons.'

'What are those reasons?' She was still slurring and still sitting too close to him. He was so not going there. He didn't talk about this with anyone and he couldn't really imagine anyone he *would* like to talk to about it. Certainly not Dina. He didn't feel any kind of deep connection with her. Which was a good thing. An image of Cassie sitting next to him on the wall in the field came into his head. And another of watching Fred while Cassie talked to him. Maybe there was someone he could talk to. Although he wasn't going to.

'They are… complicated.' What to say? He just wanted this conversation to be over. And when she was sober tomorrow, if she remembered this, she wouldn't be happy. 'It's basically a genuine case of "It isn't you, it's me". I like this song.' He didn't. Some kind of rap was blaring out of the speaker and he really wasn't a fan. 'Want to dance again?'

'How would you feel about a one-night-only thing?' Dina was practically sitting on his lap now. James shook his head and started to stand up.

'I'm really flattered, I really am, but I feel that we have a great friendship – we do from my side, anyway – and I really wouldn't want to ruin that.' And there was another image of Cassie in his head now. Standing in the field together, under the stars. He shook his head. 'Come on. Let's dance.' He stood up fully, held his hand out to Dina, pulled her off her chair and led her over right into the middle of a group of people jumping up and down, still to the same ear-splitting rap.

On the upside, he'd managed not to have to say a bald *No*. And he'd managed not to go outside with her. On the downside, he did really like her as a friend and that had been *awkward*.

'Dance with me, James?' Laura leaned her sticks against the wall and held out a hand to him. The rap song had finally finished and a much easier-on-the-ear, slower one had come on. 'There's still life in the old girl.'

'I'd be honoured,' James told her.

The rest of the evening was a blast.

*

The next day he had a lot to do.

'Morning, Dina.' She was in her back garden hanging up sheets. 'Great evening last night. I thought I'd just catch up about the animals and their feed. I probably won't have time to speak tomorrow morning because I'm leaving early. Call me someone who Cassie's had too much of an influence on, but I've made some notes for you.'

'Thank you.' She smiled at him from round the side of a large patchwork duvet that she'd just thrown over her washing line. 'I probably owe you an apology for last night. I was a little drunk.'

'No, no apologies. If anyone should be apologising it's probably me. I'm pretty sure I did some terrible dancing.'

Dina laughed. 'Okay.' Good news. Not too much awkwardness.

The rest of the day was full of packing, clearing up, writing notes for Cassie (really – what had happened to him?) *and* stocking up the freezer for her and arranging a delivery of fresh food for her in ten days' time for the day she was going to get back.

*

This was great. The wind in his hair, the open road ahead of him, country music blaring out of the car radio. James had almost had a lump in his throat when his ferry had left the island, which was why this road trip had been such a good idea. Something to look forward to rather than the anti-climax of just going straight home. He was driving from Maine down to Chicago and then following Route 66 to Los Angeles before flying home from there.

Time for a break. James had seen the signs for this viewpoint for the past few miles and had decided he should stop. One, he was tired. Two, it would be ridiculous to do this trip without taking in the sights regularly. And three, if he didn't stop now he might not get another opportunity to call Cassie while she was still awake. It would feel strange now not to talk to her on a daily basis.

He got out of the car and walked up to a viewpoint facing towards Montreal.

There was a lot to tell Cassie. The staggering vastness of North America. The fact that right now he wasn't far from the Vermont house he could have rented instead of Cassie's, and how he was very glad that he'd rented hers. The meat, meat and meat menu at the diner where he'd had lunch.

'Hi.' She sounded sleepy. Good job he'd called now.

'Howdy.'

'You gone American cowboy already?'

James smiled and settled in on his rock for their chat.

Chapter Twenty

Cassie

Cassie smiled and snuggled herself into her duvet to listen to James's gorgeous voice telling her about views and the Vermont scenery and ranting about his lunch. She'd have been asleep half an hour ago if she hadn't carried on reading in the hope that he might call. They'd fallen into the habit of one of them calling the other at this sort of time pretty much every day, before his evening started and just as hers ended. They talked about all sorts. Big stuff, small stuff.

It had probably been her turn to call him today but she didn't know if it'd seem strange. He was on his road trip now, so the swap was pretty much over. But he'd called her and now she was feeling warm inside.

'So what are you going to do this evening?' she asked.

'I'm going to drive on for another hour or two until I hit Montreal proper. I've got a hotel room booked. I'm going to have dinner and walk round the city this evening.'

'Sounds like the road trip was definitely a good decision.'

'Yeah, it really was.'

'I booked a little trip of my own today. My Glasgow weekend.'

'Wow, congratulations.'

'Thank you. I'm feeling good about myself just for booking it. Demon slaying's the way forward.'

'Yeah, I think you're right. I'm genuinely looking forward to seeing my sister and her family when I get back.'

It was nice to feel like they were confiding in each other.

*

Cassie shivered. She should have brought a thicker coat. Glasgow was not warm in the summer. She should have remembered.

'How does it feel to be back?' her cousin Meg asked her as they drove away from the station. Strange how when you grew up somewhere you didn't really clock much about it on a daily basis. Now, after having been away for four years, Cassie was really noticing the imposing height and darkness of the stone buildings lining the city centre streets.

'A bit weird, but good, actually. Like, it's just a place of which I have mainly good memories, and I'm very unlikely to bump into Simon but if I do, whatever. He's firmly in my past. The main thing is that I'm seeing you and everyone else.'

'Good. Fecking taxis.' Meg honked and middle-fingered a Toyota Prius driver who'd just cut her up. 'Your mum and dad are arriving this evening.' Meg's husband was a vicar – Cassie adored the fact that the sweariest person she knew had married a very sweet and mild-mannered man of the cloth – and they lived in a large (and cold and ramshackle) vicarage in Hillhead, which was able to accommodate a lot of guests. 'Your mum's going to freeze.' Very true. Cassie's mum had spent the entire time she lived in Glasgow mentioning the cold at least once a day. She was a lot happier weather-wise in France.

To be fair to Cassie's mother, Glasgow was a lot colder than London. And a lot rainier. It had been moderately sunny when they'd left the station but now the sky was grey and the car windows were splattered in large rain drops.

'The sodding central heating's broken down again.' Meg turned right into busy traffic, causing several cars to slam their brakes on. 'I'm wondering whether we should stop in town now, have lunch and then buy some extra blankets.'

'Good plan. We should probably also buy my mum a couple of jumpers. She won't have brought enough warm clothes.'

So this was okay. Cassie and Meg were sitting in a hidden-gem-style little Chinese restaurant in the city centre eating dim sum. It was better than okay. Cassie should have come back to Glasgow before now.

'I did an unsuccessful round of IVF with a sperm donor this summer,' she told Meg. If there was one thing she'd learned over the past few months it was that you felt a lot better when you were open with the people you were closest to.

'I'm so, so sorry that it didn't work out,' Meg said when Cassie had finished telling her the details, succeeding in only sniffling a bit. 'But two things. One, you're only young still. Plenty of people have babies well into their forties. And two, I'm *so* pleased that you're finally over that bastard.'

'I think I was over him almost immediately. I mean, once someone's behaved like that you really don't like them any more.'

'Not the same as being over them, though. Not necessarily over *him*, but over how he behaved. He's such a shit.'

Cassie nodded. 'Yep, you're right. I honestly think I could see him now and feel nothing.' A lot of which was due to her stay in London. And maybe a little to do with getting to know James.

Meg opened her mouth and then closed it again.

'What?'

'Nothing.' Meg signalled at the waiter. 'Let's go and hunt down those blankets and jumpers.'

Cassie and Meg had found a lovely soft polo neck jumper for Cassie's mother and were trying to decide whether to buy it in cream or emerald green when a woman with a baby in a pram interrupted them to say, 'Meg. Hello. I thought it was you. How *are* you?'

'Good, thank you. So sorry, we're in a bit of a rush.' Meg took both the jumpers and started walking towards the till. Like she really didn't want to talk to the woman. Odd. Meg never behaved liked this.

'You dropped your umbrella.' The woman held it out and Cassie, not having been as quick off the mark as Meg, and therefore still near to her, took it.

'Thank you,' she said.

'No problem.' The woman smiled at her and then looked more closely at her. 'I'm Sophie. I feel as though we've met before. Not surprising, I suppose, given that you're a friend of Meg's. Glasgow's a small place.' Strange, because Cassie didn't recognise her at *all*. She was tall, slim and blonde with a warm smile and startlingly blue eyes. Quite recognisable, really.

Meg had only half-turned round. 'Glasgow *is* a small place. Great to see you.'

She turned away again and started to move away as Sophie said, 'Have you seen Archie?' Meg turned back round as Sophie pulled back her pram cover to give them a better view of her truly gorgeous baby. 'Eight weeks old. My third,' she told Cassie. 'I'm *sure* we've met before.

It's going to annoy me until we work out where. Do you work with Simon perhaps? Simon Grant?'

Cassie froze.

Meg sprang into action, looking at her watch with an exaggerated circular motion of her arm and saying, 'Oh my goodness, Cassie, we're *late*. Great to see you, Sophie. Archie's beautiful. Love to all. You know what, I don't think either of these jumpers are right. Bye.' She put the jumpers down on the nearest display table, took Cassie's arm and marched her towards the escalator.

'So that's Simon's wife?' Cassie said.

'Yes.'

'And baby.' The baby had actually looked quite like Simon. God. The pain. That was maybe what *her* baby would have looked like. Cassie felt a tear trickle out and opened her eyes really wide to stop any others following. She wasn't bloody doing this. It was four years ago. It was sad but it was in the past and she had a lot of great things in her life and she was *not doing this*.

'I was going to get tissues out,' Meg said as they got off the escalator, 'but you don't look like you need any.'

'I don't. It's in the past.'

'I am *so* proud of you.'

'Is that what you were going to tell me when we were finishing our lunch?'

'Yes. Wish I had, now.'

'Hard to predict that we'd bump into her. Also, honest truth, how old are her other kids?'

Meg screwed up her face. 'The oldest is about four. She's the person he was having an affair with when you split up.'

'Right.' Cassie waited for the wave of emotion to hit her. It didn't. 'Wow. What an arse. How many times has he tried to get in touch with me? And the whole time he's had at least one child.'

'Yes.'

'Wow. Thank you for not telling me when I couldn't have coped with it and for giving it to me straight now. Do you know what I want to do?'

'Castrate him?'

'Nope. Better than that. I'd like to go back up and buy both those jumpers because Mum'll love both of them and they're a great price and I don't want Simon to have any effect on my life whatsoever any more. And then let's get on with having a fantastic weekend.'

*

'We're going to miss you.' Juliet took a delicate bite of one of Luigi's mini lemon tarts. Cassie had cooked the main course for their dinner but she wasn't going near any baking – apart from anything else it had taken her three days to clean the oven last time she'd messed up and she was leaving tomorrow – so she'd bought in their puddings.

'Yes, we are,' the others chorused through full mouths.

'I'm going to miss you too.' Cassie looked round the four of them, Juliet, Anthony, Jack and Chloe. Such lovely people. She wished she'd had more time to try and get Juliet and Anthony together. 'We have to stay in touch. I'll be back in London from time to time, so I'll email and we can make a date, I hope.'

'Definitely,' Chloe said. She put her cutlery down. 'Jack and I have news, which we wanted to tell you in person before you leave. We're too excited to wait.' Going by Chloe's recent sudden abstention from alcohol it was kind of obvious what it was going to be; in fact, Cassie had been going to make a goat's cheese starter and had changed her mind because pregnant people couldn't eat goat's cheese. 'We're expecting. Our due date's in May.'

That was around when Cassie's due date would have been if her IVF had worked out and she was *not* going to think about that *at all* now because this was Jack and Chloe's news and it was thrilling for them. Cassie could not spend her whole life avoiding situations like this and she had in fact learned that this summer. If she could go to Glasgow and deal with hearing about Simon's family, she could totally deal with this.

'Congratulations. That's fantastic. I'm so pleased for you.' Cassie meant it. Good. Very good. She was a nice person after all. Maybe she'd just have a little slurp of her wine. Just to hide her face for a moment.

Fifteen minutes later, the excited pregnancy and baby-preps chat was dwindling.

'We have news too,' Juliet said into the conversational lull, looking coyly at Anthony.

'Oh my goodness,' Cassie said. 'Oh. My. Goodness.' Yes. Maybe her matchmaking efforts, all the dinners she'd cooked, had paid off. Anthony was returning Juliet's look in a, frankly, somewhat nauseatingly fond manner.

'We?' Jack was looking backwards and forwards between Anthony and Juliet like they were playing an Olympic table tennis final.

'That's right.' Juliet reached her hand out and Anthony took it. *So sweet.* 'I feel as though we should possibly put a little misconception straight.'

Cassie frowned. What?

'Cassie, dear, I think that you might perhaps have been attempting a little matchmaking.'

Cassie screwed up her face. This was a bit embarrassing. 'Maybe,' she said. She must have been a bit too obvious. Although, it had clearly achieved its desired effect. Maybe they'd get married. She hoped they'd invite her to the wedding if they did.

'Juliet and I have been married for twenty-seven years,' Anthony said.

'Are you… joking?' Cassie said tentatively into silence. His delivery hadn't been particularly joke-like.

'No, dear.' Juliet lifted her hand from Anthony's and stroked his cheek. He leaned his face into her palm. Yep, that looked very familiarly intimate. *Wow*. 'It just hasn't really come up in conversation before now. And then, once you haven't mentioned something, it becomes a bit awkward. And it felt even more awkward once we realised you were trying to get us together.'

'Woah,' said Chloe.

'Congratulations?' said Jack.

'Yes, congratulations,' said Cassie. Honestly. All that effort for nothing. Although she'd had a lot of good evenings with them. She *really* wanted some detail now. Why did they live separately? Or maybe they didn't. 'Are your flats linked inside?'

'No, the flats aren't linked. We live separately. We like it. It works for us. We started out like this because we'd both experienced sticky divorces and then we just carried on. And it's great.'

'That's right. And it makes certain things easier.' Anthony finished his glass of red and Cassie re-filled it.

'Yes. We're swingers.' Juliet popped another dainty mouthful in.

Cassie, Jack and Chloe all looked at each other.

'Oh,' said Cassie eventually. Juliet did not look as though she'd just made a joke. On the other hand, she'd just said, very conversationally, that she and Anthony were swingers. Nothing wrong with swinging, obviously, if everyone involved was happy about it and you enjoyed it, but Juliet had possibly the primmest demeanour of all people that Cassie had ever met. And yet again, apparently, you should not judge a book by its cover.

'Yes. Excellent lemon tart, Cassie. It works perfectly with the berries.' Anthony put his spoon down and dabbed at his mouth with his napkin. 'Yes. It works wonderfully well having two separate flats. It means we can bring people back to ours with so much less awkwardness. And we both have little alarm buttons in our flats, you know, in case of danger, but nothing's ever gone wrong.'

'Well, that is *great*,' said Jack, a little too heartily. Cassie pressed her lips together so that she wouldn't laugh. It was very funny seeing cool, hipster Jack looking thoroughly uncomfortable.

'Don't worry.' Anthony leaned in. 'Neither of us likes doing it with *young* people. We aren't going to proposition you.'

Jack choked a lot while Cassie, Chloe and Juliet all laughed so much they nearly cried.

It was weird going to bed on the last night before she started her journey back home, not least because there was no call with James as he was already on his flight back from LA. Cassie was leaving at the crack of dawn to do the whole journey in one day, so she'd just miss his arrival by a few hours. Which was probably a good thing. It would be too strange to see each other in the flat.

The big question was, would they carry on speaking once they were back in their real lives? Realistically, probably not.

*

'Hi.' Shit. She'd said that too quietly, kind of moonily, like a lovestruck teenager, while smiling. It did feel *great*, though, that James had called her.

'You on the boat? I just heard seagulls and a foghorn.'

'Yep. My flight was a bit delayed this morning. I just made the last ferry of the day, thank goodness. Imagine if I'd missed it.'

'Yes, that would be gutting. So near and yet so far. You'd have had to swim.'

'Exactly. So you must be back? Does it feel good?'

'You know, it is nice, although I'm already missing the States, but what's made it really great is the food and the notes you left for me. Dinner was fantastic, thank you. I love the mansaf, as you know, and a pistachio and orange cake from Luigi is one of the few desserts I really like. And I'm about to read your notes before I go to sleep. So thank you. That's why I phoned, to say thanks. But now I'm here, tell me about your journey?'

Not only had Cassie not finished telling him about the people she'd met during her day, she'd barely had a chance to ask him anything about his first day back at home when it was time to leave the ferry.

'I haven't heard about your day but I'm arriving,' she said.

'Happy homecoming and let's speak tomorrow. I'm going to read your notes in bed now.'

Cassie was still smiling from their conversation when she saw Dina waving manically at her from the jetty.

*

Cassie turned her key and then the front door handle, and pushed. *So* lovely but also weird to step inside and have her own house back.

There was an A4 envelope with her name on it on the kitchen table. She opened it and pulled the contents out. James had written notes for her, by hand. A lot of notes. So many that she wasn't going to read them all now because it would take too long.

Oh. Okay. Yep.

They weren't anywhere near as long as the ones she'd left for him at the beginning of the swap.

Of *course* she shouldn't have expected him to have read them all straight off.

She was going to save these and read them this evening, when she got into bed.

He had great handwriting. At a guess, if an expert analysed it, they'd say he was very strong-minded, purposeful, pretty goddamn sexy, in fact.

She put the kettle on and opened the cupboard where she kept the tea. Wow. Someone had restocked it.

She opened the fridge and there was a large note in James's handwriting. *Look in the freezer.*

She opened the freezer door and saw that every drawer was full.

She pulled open the one that was just below her eye level. Everything in there was labelled in James's writing. Soda bread. Carrot cake. Cookies.

The next one down was shop-bought soups.

The one below that was portions of lasagne, which looked homemade.

Wow.

She was so glad that she'd done the house swap with James. It had certainly been valuable from a work perspective; she'd achieved even more than she'd hoped with regard to writing the London series and was well into her second book now. And even more importantly, it had been great from a personal perspective. She'd done her first round of

IVF, which was a huge achievement, she'd been back to Glasgow and would now have the courage to go whenever she wanted to, and she'd made some wonderful new friends.

Particularly James. He'd morphed from one of the most annoying people she'd ever met into someone who she *adored*.

Chapter Twenty-One

James

'You're doing what?' Matt leaned his golf club against his bag and stared at James. 'Mate. You're having your neighbours over for dinner? And you're cooking for them? It's like you've been on some self-discovery retreat or something.'

'I know. I barely recognise myself,' James said. 'I'm also having Ella and her family to stay for the weekend in two weeks' time.' He'd never confided fully in Matt about his family – he was a great friend but it was too hard to explain his own family set-up to someone from a solid background with sober, together, caring parents – but Matt did know that James and Ella didn't see each other a lot. 'I was thinking I could maybe get you all over for Sunday lunch. With them. With the kids.'

'Wow. Mate. We'd love to.' Matt nudged the ball onto the tee and looked up. 'Would you cook the lunch yourself?'

'Yes, I think I would.'

'Wow.' Matt took a swing. 'I'll bring a takeaway menu as a backup. Just in case.'

*

'Thank you so much for inviting us. This has been such a wonderful weekend. You're a super popular uncle.' Ella smiled at James. They were walking together in Hyde Park while Ella's husband Patrick ran ahead with their eight-year-old twin daughters. 'It's a mark of how little time that we've spent together in recent years that I was gobsmacked when we got back and you'd baked with the girls.' In the end, James had bottled inviting his friends to meet his family, and had instead suggested that he look after the girls to allow Ella and Patrick to go out for a relaxed lunch, just the two of them, and they'd jumped at the chance. 'I didn't think you did that any more.' She hesitated for a moment, and then continued. 'You used to bake with Leonie.'

'Yeah,' James said. Oh God. Choking up.

'Do you…?' Ella cleared her throat and then said nothing. She stopped walking and said, 'Could we sit on this bench for a moment?'

'Sure,' said James, not pleased. She was blatantly going to carry on talking about Leonie. This was why he'd avoided Ella so much for so long.

Ella sat down at one end of the bench. He sat down at the other. He sensed her turn to face him. He carried on staring straight ahead.

'I totally get that you don't want to talk about Leonie,' she said. 'I have talked about her, to Patrick and to some of my closest friends. It helped. But I understand why you wouldn't want to and I respect that. I want you to *know* that I respect that and that if you and I start to see each other more regularly again I will not try to talk about her. I think we could acknowledge she existed, like for example just now mentioning about how you used to bake with her and how cute—' her voice wobbled '—she was when she wore her apron and stood on the chair next to you. But we don't have to talk about her if you don't want to and we never have to talk about the rest of it. Ever, if you don't want to. But, James, we've both lost one sibling, and our mother. We don't have to lose each other. We could do this again. When we were young, we were together against the world. I've missed you.'

James stared straight ahead of him at two squirrels playing together. Rats with tails. If he told Cassie he thought that, she'd probably get annoyed.

'I saw red squirrels over the summer,' he said eventually. 'In Maine. I don't think I've ever seen a red squirrel in London.' He carried on watching them for a while and then looked round at Ella. 'I don't think I can talk about Leonie but I'd like to spend more time together,' he said. 'I've missed you too.'

She shuffled along the bench a bit and reached her hand out towards him. He took it and squeezed, hard.

'Love you, sis,' he said. He had a lump the size of a boulder in his throat.

'Me too,' she said. She took her hand out of his and wiped under her eyes with her fingers. 'Sorry. Getting sentimental in my old age.'

They sat in silence for a couple of minutes.

Then Ella said, 'So what made you invite us for the weekend? If you don't mind me asking.'

James didn't mind her asking, in fact so much so that he was going to give her a straight answer, with almost full information.

'At the risk of sounding as sentimental as my older sister—' he smiled at her '—my few months in Maine had quite an effect on me. Different pace of life. I was bored at the beginning, to the extent that I decided I might as well spend time with the neighbours. It's a very neighbourly place. And, you know, the animals.' He'd shown his nieces, Daisy and Lottie, more videos of the alpacas and chickens this afternoon. They'd *adored* watching them. Daisy had immediately decided that she was no longer a horse but an alpaca and had stopped galloping around the flat, a relief, and instead had started trying to extend her neck and twitching her face, which would definitely get annoying quickly if you lived with her. 'It all just made me think, I suppose.'

Cassie had made him think, too, if he was honest, but he wasn't going to mention her because Ella might misinterpret what he said and think he was interested in Cassie romantically. Ella and Patrick had met at medical school and had got married when they were twenty-five and had the girls when they were twenty-nine. James was pretty sure that Ella would like him to settle down too. But he wasn't like her. Their mother had always said that she didn't know who Ella's father was, and, given that she'd contacted both James's father and Leonie's and had done her best – however limited that was – to assist them to develop relationships with their fathers, it seemed likely that she really hadn't known who he was. It also seemed likely, to James, that Ella's remarkably steady temperament had come from her father. It certainly hadn't come from their mother.

James knew that both his parents were incapable of great relationships, his father because he was an arse, and his mother because she'd been an addict, so it didn't seem likely that he himself would be a great candidate for a long-term relationship. Or being a good father. So he wasn't going to go down either route. But no point ever mentioning that to Ella because it would just upset her. People who were happily loved up usually seemed to think that everyone else around them would be better off if they were loved up too.

'Well, I'm grateful then to your Maine trip,' said Ella into the silence, 'because this has been great. Thank you. Would you come and stay with us for a weekend soon? The girls and Patrick and I would all love to see you.'

James nodded. 'I'd like that.' He genuinely would.

*

'Hi, Cassie.' He hadn't spoken to her over the weekend while Ella and Patrick and the girls were staying. He'd told her before they came that he probably wouldn't be able to chat. Really, they should probably stop talking so regularly. Although there was always a lot to say. 'How was your weekend?'

'It was lovely. We had our annual pumpkin festival and, drum roll please, I won the "best oddly shaped pumpkin" prize.'

'I'm impressed. I must also be a new person or mad because I genuinely think that sounds like fun.'

When James had finished telling Cassie about his weekend, she said, 'So I have a question for you. My big meetings with my editor and the TV company are next Thursday and Friday, so I'll be in London for a long weekend, and I wondered if you'd like to meet on Saturday and come with me to the exhibition that Jennifer gave me tickets to for my thank-you-for-babysitting present?'

'That would be great.' No thought required. 'Where are you staying?'

'I'm not sure yet. A hotel somewhere.'

'Why don't you stay here?' Now that he'd started having guests, why not? It seemed a little ridiculous having two en-suite spare rooms that never got used.

'Oh, no, I didn't mean for you to invite me.'

'I know you didn't. But it would make sense, wouldn't it? You know your way around London from here. You know your way around the flat itself. It's central. I'd be very happy to have you. And no pressure to spend the entire weekend with me. I mean, just use it as your base as you did when you were living here, and if you have any spare time we can just hang out a little? And the neighbours would love to see you. If you have a spare evening we could ask them if they're free for dinner?'

'Okay. Well, that's a lovely and generous offer and I'd love to.'

James felt himself smile. He was already looking forward to seeing her.

Chapter Twenty-Two

Cassie

Woah. Cassie pressed the red button on her phone and tried hard to stop grinning. So she was going to stay with James while she was in London. *Woah*. If she was honest – which she wasn't going to be with anyone except herself – *how exciting*. And unnerving, because, again being honest – and again only secretly – she *really* liked him.

Like she hadn't *liked* anyone for a really long time.

Since Simon.

In fact, she liked James a lot more than she'd ever liked Simon. She and James had great, lengthy, satisfying conversations. They were *friends*.

She needed to do some serious online shopping immediately – it was a good job that the Wi-Fi worked now. She needed some good nightwear. If there was even the smallest possibility of bumping into James at night – and, yes, all his bedrooms had en-suites, but what if there was a fire – she needed to be wearing something a lot better than small pyjama shorts and a huge *Friends* T-shirt.

*

'How's Amy doing at college?' Cassie leaned back so that she could see the stars better above the trees surrounding Dina's garden, and took another sip of her coffee. 'And how are you coping now she's been gone a few weeks?'

'I've got to be honest, it's hard. I know that you live alone and you're cool with that, but I never saw myself alone, you know? And she's just great company. But you don't want to hold your kids back. She's having the best time. And I'm just going to go and visit a *lot*, you know, "Hi, honey, I just happened to be passing, because you're only a ferry ride and a seven-hour car journey away. Why don't I take you out for dinner? And if you're willing to speak to me, I will do all your laundry and buy you a *lot* of food." You know, your typical stalker mom.'

'I can imagine that it must be so hard.' Cassie pulled their blanket closer round them – it was seriously chilly this evening – and hugged Dina.

'Thank you.' Dina squeezed her back. 'And, since I'm sharing, I'm kind of feeling lonely on the man front too. It felt like now might be a good time to meet someone, now that Amy's hit eighteen. I spent far too much of the summer trying to chase James. I offered myself on a plate. And he really wasn't interested. And really, he isn't exactly right for me. I mean, he's great. He's gorgeous, obviously. He's a nice person. He's funny. But there wasn't really a spark. There'd be other people each of us would gel with more.' Yup. Cassie and James definitely gelled. 'For whatever reason, I can't really imagine sleeping with him. So I need to move on and find someone else. That does *not* mean, obviously, that when James turns up here on holiday next year with a gorgeous blonde in tow I won't hate her.'

Cassie nodded. She was pretty sure that she'd hate any gorgeous girlfriend of James's – blonde or not – too.

But sheesh. Two things. One, was it awkward to mention to Dina that she'd agreed to go and see James when she was in London? Not just agreed, she was looking forward to seeing him. And she was going to be *staying* with him. Definitely awkward. Especially since she hadn't mentioned their daily evening phone chats. And two, what if James *already* had a new partner and introduced Cassie to her? No, he probably didn't have a girlfriend yet, because if he did it would be a bit odd to be inviting another relatively new female friend to stay.

That thought should not be making her feel *this* relieved.

'What are you thinking about?' Dina asked. It clearly wasn't a secret that Cassie was going to stay with James, but it felt like it would be better to mention it another time.

'Just about the constellations,' Cassie told her. 'I love Orion.' That was the only one she could reliably spot. Funny how James had much better knowledge about constellations than she had, even though he'd spent his entire life living in London.

*

'Good morning.' Henry was double-taking like nobody's business, with some serious side-to-side eye action. 'I think I just saw Mr Grey this morning?'

'Yep. I'm just in London for the weekend. I'm staying with him.'

'Oh, okay.' Henry bent down and picked one of her cases up. 'Makes sense. For some reason I thought you wouldn't be here at the same time.'

'No, we're friends,' Cassie said. They were. It was nice. She indicated the case. 'Thank you so much but I think James is on his way down so we can probably manage the cases between us in one go.'

And the door to the lift pinged open and James stepped out.

Gorgeous, gorgeous, *gorgeous*.

He was wearing faded jeans and a navy T-shirt, and, if you liked your men smiling, tall, blond and handsome, then he'd be exactly the man for you. Cassie's heart was beating far too fast for good health and she definitely had an alpaca-style inane smile on her face. Apparently she liked her men the way he was.

'Hey,' he said. 'Good journey?'

'Not bad, thank you.' She was still standing stock-still. He reached her and leaned down for an air-kiss, except she leaned a bit at the same time, so they brushed cheeks. Such a tingle. It felt like there should be some schmaltzy music in the background.

'So how does it feel to be back?' he asked her as they got into the lift together. During the entire six months that she'd been here she hadn't noticed that the lift was this small. She'd definitely been in it with other people at times, and it had seemed more than big enough for two. You could actually get three people in here. But right now, it felt like she and James were standing unusually close together, a bit awkwardly close. She could see the contours of his chest through his T-shirt and the blond hairs on his forearms. Where should she be looking? Down? Up? Straight ahead? At him? She was going to stare straight ahead. Although the lift doors were mirrored, so now she had the choice of watching herself trying not to watch him, or just watching him. *He* was watching her now, and smiling. She smiled back. Yep. Inane.

He'd asked her a question.

'Um, good,' she said. Totally out of words.

Finally, the lift stopped and the doors started to open. It took ages for them to get out because they both waited for the other to go first, until Cassie said, 'Thank you,' and moved ahead of James and then hung back awkwardly until he was out; and then they walked along the corridor together.

Space-wise, it was less awkward inside the flat once they'd negotiated some backwards and forwards round each other through the door and in the hall.

'You got new sofas,' Cassie said.

'Yeah. Once I got used to the comfortable ones at your house, I realised that I could do a lot better here. Substance, not just style. They were delivered on Tuesday. They have excellent squish.'

'Cool. I'm going to look forward to snuggling into one of them.'

There was an awkward silence. Why had she used the word *snuggle*? You sat on or sank onto sofas and neither of those sounded so… odd, really. Or possibly innuendo-laden.

'Great.' James walked over to the door that led off the sitting room onto the bedroom hallway. 'I'll put your case straight in your bedroom.' He'd chosen the one closest to the sitting room, which was the one further from his room.

'Thank you.' Cassie should take the opportunity to pull herself together. 'I might just pop in there and have a shower and get changed if that's okay. I always feel a bit grimy after a long journey.'

'Good plan,' he said. 'There's a towel on the bed, and I have croissants for you whenever you're ready.' Honestly. First the word *snuggle* had done all sorts to her, and now she was thinking smutty things about towels. A long journey, no sleep and seeing someone who you fancied the pants off were a bad combination.

Who knew eating could be so bloody stressful? Cassie took another bite of her croissant and tried to chew normally. Given how well it felt that she and James knew each other, they'd spent remarkably little time actually together. They'd definitely never eaten together before. She was spraying crumbs *everywhere*. Normally, she was a perfectly competent eater.

Fortunately, she wouldn't be sharing any other meals with James today. She had a big lunch with her publisher to look forward to, which was exciting on two counts – one, finally meeting them in person was a big deal, and two, they had the cover designs for her first London book ready – and then dinner this evening with Jennifer, which she was also looking forward to.

'I need to make a move.' James stood up as Cassie finished her second coffee; she was going to need a lot of it today after close to zero sleep on the plane. 'I'm out this evening too and busy during the day tomorrow so I'm not sure whether we'll be home much at the same time, but I'll definitely see you at the pub tomorrow.' They were both having dinner with their own friends tomorrow evening, and had agreed to meet at a pub afterwards for late-night drinks.

'I'll see you there.' Cassie attempted a chirpy and non-flirtatious tone and ended up with a squeak, which turned into a choke. Bloody croissant crumbs.

'You okay?' James asked when he'd finished whacking her on the back.

'Yep. Thank you.'

'I thought I was going to have to do the Heimlich manoeuvre there for a moment.'

'I'm obviously so tired from my journey that I've forgotten basic skills like swallowing.'

James laughed. 'I'll see you later. Hope your meetings go well.' He got up from the table, picked up a jacket and left.

Cassie realised that she was smiling at his departed back.

He'd be a great housemate. Cassie and Meg had shared a flat together in Glasgow for a few years. Meg had been a fab housemate. They'd had a *lot* of fun. Then Meg had met her vicar and when they'd got married Cassie had got herself a flat of her own, which had been a lot less lonely than she'd expected, because she'd worked long hours and been out a lot in the evenings. Then she'd met Simon and moved in with him and she'd found that living with someone who wasn't the ideal housemate was much worse than living alone. Since she'd moved to the island, Cassie had enjoyed her space. She had her friends and the animals and she'd been pretty certain that it would be hard to find someone she'd like to live with.

Take Dina. A great, great friend. And would Cassie like to live with her? Definitely not. She was an excellent next-door neighbour.

James, though. She could imagine happily spending a *lot* of time with him. Eating together, coming home to him, talking through their days, like they'd been doing on the phone for the past few months.

This was stupid. She really hardly knew him.

Anyway, it was ridiculous to be sitting around thinking about James; she was making herself late.

*

James was sitting on a sofa with a paper and a mug of something when Cassie crept into the flat at midnight, convinced that he'd already be in bed.

'Evening. How was your day?' He put his mug on the floor and leaned back. She was pretty sure from their phone conversations that he normally went to bed earlier than this.

'Very good, thank you. It was great to meet my editor in person finally, and I love my cover, and we're on the same page about the rest of the books in the series.'

'Liking your pun there.' James smirked, but in a nice way.

'Thanks for noticing,' Cassie joked back. 'Yes, so, those meetings were great and then I went to this very cool restaurant in Covent Garden with Jennifer for dinner. So all in all a very successful day. Being a writer can be quite solitary so it's exciting to actually talk to the people you work with in person occasionally.' Cassie was ridiculously pleased that James was still up, and ridiculously ready to have a long chat with him.

'So tell me about your book cover. Cup of tea or coffee?'

Half an hour later, Cassie looked at her watch and said, 'I'm keeping you up on a work night. We should go to bed.'

'You're right. We should. You must be exhausted after your journey and then a full day's work. I shouldn't have started talking to you. Come on.' He stood up and held his hand out to pull her up to standing from the other end of the sofa. 'I think you're sorted for everything but if there's anything you need, you know where I am.' Yes, like she was going to go and knock on his door in the middle of the night.

He smiled at her and her breath caught. It was a good job she was so tired because she was fairly sure that if she hadn't been she'd have had a hard time not lunging at him.

James had left for the morning by the time Cassie surfaced, fully showered, dressed and made-up, just in case she bumped into him, which was a little bit disappointing.

*

The door to the pub opened and Cassie glanced over. No, not James. More disappointment.

She hadn't had this feeling for a *long* time. Very teenage. The sensation that, yes, she was having a good – no, a *great* – evening with her university friends, she absolutely was, but there was something missing. Or not exactly missing, but something that would make the evening even better. Specifically, James.

He'd said that he and his friends would arrive about ten thirty. She really wanted to check her watch but that would be *so* rude.

Maybe she'd just pop to the loo. Then she wouldn't need to go again for the rest of the evening and she could check her watch while she was there. No, bad idea, because obviously James wouldn't recognise Neeta, Claire and Rach.

'Cassie?' Rach was staring at her like she was nuts. 'Do you want another one?' Did she? Cassie had no actual idea how much was left in her glass. She looked down. Still almost full.

'I'm good, thank you. My round after this one.' She smiled at Rach and picked her glass up and took a sip.

Men's voices came from over by the door and she looked behind her. Yes.

Honestly, her heart had sped up far too much at the sight of James, and the evening suddenly seemed a lot more interesting. This was like being sixteen and having a mega crush on the most gorgeous boy you'd ever seen. But instead it was being thirty-seven and having a mega crush on the most gorgeous *man* you'd ever seen. Maybe not everyone would like him as much as she did, but when you'd talked to him, and seen the wicked humour behind his smile and got to know how his face creased when he was about to laugh, and discovered that you just *got* each other, it was hard not to have a full-on crush.

He broke into a smile when he saw her, and it was like the whole evening had brightened up.

And when he leaned in for a cheek-kiss to say hello, it felt like her entire insides lit up.

He was just as great in a group as he was one-on-one, perfect company – lively but he didn't dominate the conversation.

'Time to go home?' James suggested at about half eleven. 'Shall we walk?' The flat was about a mile away from the pub.

'It's such a beautiful night,' Cassie said as they strolled up Exhibition Road. 'There's something so special about a warm evening in November. The first autumn I was in Maine, we had a really hot week and I remember just *loving* it.'

'Not a lot of warm autumn evenings in Glasgow?'

'Nope.'

James smiled down at her and turned slightly and his arm brushed her shoulder. Immediate goosebumps. 'At the risk of repeating myself from the night of Laura's party, although I have a slight suspicion that you might not remember everything we talked about then, look at Cassiopeia. You don't often see it this clearly in the London skies.' He stopped and pointed. 'Look.'

Cassie looked up. She had an excellent view of the left side of James's jaw and cheekbone, and his strong neck. Way more worth looking at than the sky, which she could see any time.

Could James tell how she was feeling?

His gaze moved from the sky down to her face. A smile played at the corners of his mouth.

Cassie shivered. At this moment in time, all sorts of wrong though it was, she wanted him *so much*.

'You're cold. We should go home. Take my jumper.' He pulled it off over his head, giving Cassie yet another excellent view, this time of the stretch of his chest muscles and biceps through his shirt.

'Thank you.' Cassie really couldn't tell him that she wasn't cold at all.

His jumper was warm from his body. Something that had so recently been touching his body was now touching hers. And she was surrounded intoxicatingly by his musky smell. If she could just be wrapped in his actual arms and pressed against his chest, she'd be a very happy woman indeed.

She really needed to get a grip.

The walk back was lovely, and not long enough. Cassie could happily have worn James's jumper and walked arm-bumpingly along with him for hours.

Maybe it was the wine she'd had, but this time the lift didn't feel awkward so much as like the perfect opportunity to be close to James in their own little world, just the two of them. As it chugged slowly upwards, James leaned against the back wall of it, smiling lazily at her while she told him about her plans for the couple of days she was spending in Glasgow after the weekend. She could totally have launched herself right at him, there and then. It was, frankly, a huge disappointment when the doors opened.

Once in the flat, Cassie put her bag down and walked over to the windows. 'I love the view from these at night.'

'Me too.' James joined her. Even if she hadn't been able to see how close he was from their reflections in the window, she'd have sensed his – magnificently solid – shoulder above hers. 'When I viewed the flat before I bought it, it was December and about seven p.m., so fully dark, and I walked in and saw the park lit up by the streetlights, and even a couple of stars – it was a clear evening – and I was sold.'

'You do like a star.' Cassie turned so that she was facing him and smiled up at him. They were standing very close to each other but not touching.

'I do.' He wasn't looking at the sky, though, he was looking at *her*. Very intently. He'd been smiling but the smile had gone. His eyes were very serious. And very blue. She'd never really gone for blue eyes; she'd always much preferred brown ones. But, actually, the right blue was gorgeous. His were a light navy. Like a clear inland lake.

His pupils were definitely dilating. He was looking at her eyes. And her mouth. And her chest, possibly because she was taking some very deep breaths.

Her mouth was so dry. She licked her lips and his gaze returned to them.

She took another deep breath and he inhaled sharply too.

Oh God. Something was going to happen.

She inched a tiny bit closer to him. Their chests were almost touching now.

A small part of her brain told her that this was maybe not the best thing to be doing and her entire body shouted *Shut up*.

James lifted his hand and cupped the back of her head. Oh, God. This was really, really it.

Chapter Twenty-Three

James

Cassie's hair felt beautifully soft. And there was so much of it. James wound his fingers through her curls, put his other arm around her waist and leaned down towards her.

He brushed her lips with his, very lightly, just for a second.

It was like the world stopped for that moment.

And then he drew back.

Cassie had both her hands on his chest, her head tilted up towards his, her lips slightly open, her eyes half closed.

There was only one thing that James wanted to do at this point, and he was pretty certain that Cassie felt the same way.

But.

She was his guest, and it was Friday night, and she was staying here until Sunday, and what if she regretted it in the morning? She had nowhere else to go. It would be a nightmare for her if she wanted to leave but couldn't.

They really shouldn't do it. It was really unfair on Cassie.

He looked down at her face upturned to his, her beautiful generous mouth, her deep brown eyes.

He really, really wanted to kiss her. Undress her. Explore her body. Slowly. A lot.

And, no, he was really, really not going to.

God.

'We should go to bed,' he said.

Cassie smiled, a languid, beautiful, 'I'm about to have sex' smile.

No, that was not what he'd meant. 'I mean, separately. It's late.' Oh God. How crass. How incredibly crass. His whole reason for not doing anything was *not* to embarrass her. 'I really like you.' Oh, okay. Way to go. Tell her he liked her but... But what? 'But you're my guest and I...' *What?* 'I think we shouldn't do anything we, *you*, might regret. Would you like a glass of water to take to your bedroom?'

Cassie's smile had dropped. 'Yes, a glass of water would be great, thank you.' Her voice was a little squeaky.

James was still holding her. Why was he still holding her? He let go of her and walked over to the kitchen, took a glass out and filled it with water.

'There you go,' he said, taking great care not to touch her fingers with his when he handed the glass over.

'Great! Thank you!' Still squeaky and far too bright.

Seriously. Great job, James.

He cleared his throat. 'So I'll see you in the morning whenever you're ready for brunch and the exhibition? Before our cooking fest.'

'Perfect!' Still fake brightness. 'I'm looking forward to seeing your baking skills in action. So good night then.' She spilled a bit of her water in her hurry to get away from him.

So uncool of him.

*

After some highly awkward extreme politeness in the flat, they went to Luigi's for Saturday morning brunch. Mistake.

'My two favourite people together.' Luigi enveloped them both in a big hug and then drew back for some serious raising and wiggling of his monobrow. '*Together.*'

James went for big fake laughing while Cassie said *No* a lot.

'Your favourite table is free,' Luigi said, ushering them over. 'It's like a movie, no? You take it in turns to sit at the same table, never meeting. And *then*….'

'You are *so* right,' Cassie said, while James floundered. 'We still haven't met. One of us is a ghost.'

Luigi laughed uproariously and wagged a finger at her. 'Yes, and soon you might make little ghost babies.'

Cassie rolled her eyes at James as Luigi returned to the bar to torture some other customers, and then, thank God, she laughed. James didn't spend a lot of time having personal conversations with people other than, very rarely, longstanding friends like Matt. He hadn't been sure how okay Cassie was going to be with the baby reference.

'He means well,' James said. Clearly Luigi was not to know that the two of them had had a near possible-baby-making experience last night.

'He does. He's lovely. And he makes a mean pastry.'

And, in fact, the rest of their brunch was great. You could get over a lot of awkwardness with some people-watching. Soon, the conversation morphed into their usual wide-ranging chat and everything felt okay again. Almost.

'So who's paying?' asked Luigi, holding his machine out.

'Me.' Cassie bent to rummage in her bag.

'Nope. Me.' James whipped his wallet out and had his card on the machine before her. 'My treat. You're the one who got the exhibition tickets.'

'Well, firstly,' said Cassie, 'you're hosting me this weekend, so I should pay, plus Jennifer *gave* me those tickets. And secondly, how did you even do that? It was so fast. You'd have made an amazing cowboy. It's kind of sad that there isn't a lot of call for that kind of speedy reaction nowadays.'

'Actually, there is. Kids' card games. Have you played Dobble? I took no prisoners with my nieces a couple of weeks ago. They were seriously impressed.'

'I haven't met your family,' Luigi said. 'You should bring them here.'

'I will.' He would not. He didn't need Luigi telling his sister and her family about his romantic brunch with Cassie. Ella would start harbouring hopes that he was about to settle down.

Cassie nearly tripped as someone jostled her in the doorway – maybe she should stop wearing those wedge heels so much, although they did look great – and James put his arm out to steady her.

'Too cute,' Luigi called after them.

'I'm still thinking about the exhibition.' James separated his third egg white and yolk. 'If I'm honest, I wasn't really expecting to love it, but there was a lot of interesting social history there.' The exhibition, at the V&A, had been about the role of the high heel throughout history.

'I know. There've been some seriously weird people through the centuries.' Cassie was doing something with herbs and spices and chickpeas.

'You thinking about the bondage thing?' James looked over her shoulder and sniffed. 'That smells mouth-watering. Have I eaten that before? Did you leave some of that for me in my freezer?'

'I did. And, no, you can't have any now.' She nudged his arm out of the way with her shoulder before he could sneak a mouthful. 'You get on with your pavlova.'

James smiled. This was the kind of day you could get used to.

There were a lot of hugs when Anthony, Juliet, Jack and Chloe arrived. All between them and Cassie. James shook hands and air-kissed instead. It felt too strange to leap from three years of having ignored people – purposely, if he was honest – straight to hugging. It was genuinely good to see them, though. There was something to be said for knowing your neighbours.

'I'll get the drinks,' James told Cassie. 'You have a lot of catching up to do.' She was in the middle of a detailed conversation about how Juliet's ninety-three-year-old mother was recovering after the hip replacement she'd had a couple of weeks ago. Juliet had been worrying that her mother would get depressed during the post-operative phase but apparently she was doing brilliantly. James had had no idea about any of that, which felt slightly odd, given that the operation had happened while he'd been living here, in the same building as Juliet, and Cassie had been back on the island.

James handed Juliet and Chloe their drinks and asked Anthony and Jack what they'd like. Juliet had finished talking about her mother and Anthony was now telling Cassie all about his latest wood carving.

'He's so talented,' Cassie told James. 'You should see his flat. All sorts of wood sculpture, everywhere. Beautiful to look at. So impressive.'

'You're flattering me.' Anthony was beaming away.

'I'd love to see them.' James said. Anthony beamed even more.

James couldn't decide whether he adored Cassie for her ability to become very close to people, fast, or slightly put out that maybe he was just another friend; did she feel there was something special to their friendship, as he did? No, she must do; of course she did. He definitely hadn't imagined the moments there'd been between them. Also, all these people had confided in Cassie but they didn't really know a lot about her life other than the superficials. He was pretty sure that she hadn't told any of them about her IVF cycle, for example.

'And there you go.' He handed Anthony and Jack rhubarb and ginger gin cocktails – Cassie had decided they should go fancy on the drinks – and sat down with the others.

'It's just so exciting. I keep buying more and more baby stuff. It's all so *teeny*. And cute. And gorgeous. And lovable,' said Chloe. She pointed to one of her scan photos again and said, 'Look at its beautiful little face. I just can't get over how perfect my little bean is. Pregnancy is *the* most amazing thing.'

James glanced at Cassie on the other side of the table. Her normally animated face looked somewhat stone-like. Not surprising. At a guess, this had to be excruciating for her.

For a sober person, Chloe was behaving with a remarkable lack of tact given that she and her husband were at a dinner party with four people, all older than them, all childless. Any one, or all, of the four of them might have wanted children. One of them might have just bloody had an unsuccessful IVF attempt this summer.

'Very cute,' he said, smiling at Chloe and standing up. 'Can I get anyone some more pudding? More wine? Coffee? Tea? We have several herbal ones.'

'I'd have liked to have had a baby. My mother would have liked to have been a grandmother. One of the great sorrows of her life is that she doesn't have a grandchild.' Apparently Juliet wasn't going with James's subject change. Her voice was harsh, really different from its usual softness. 'But I didn't meet Anthony until I was too old.'

Anthony's face dropped. 'We've had a wonderful time, though, haven't we, darling?' He frowned. 'All our travel? We couldn't have done that with a baby.'

'No, you're right, you're absolutely right.' Juliet patted his arm. 'Extremely right and extremely childless.'

Okay. Subject change required.

'I'll put the kettle on,' James said. 'In case anyone does want tea or coffee.'

'On the upside,' Cassie said to Juliet, 'we non-pregnant people can get as drunk as we like.'

'Absolutely right.' Juliet downed her wine and said, 'Could you make mine an Irish coffee, James? We have had a lot of fun, haven't we, Anthony? I think children would have ruined our sex life. I doubt you could safely keep sex toys in the house with young children around.'

Good Lord.

'Good night,' they chorused one final time as Jack and Chloe got into the lift and Anthony led a now very giggly and tactile Juliet into his flat.

'Wow. So these are the neighbours I've been missing out on all this time,' James said when he'd closed and bolted the door.

'I know. I wasn't expecting that level of entertainment.' Cassie started to carry plates from the table to the dishwasher. 'It's usually all very friendly. I think maybe we had too much pregnancy chat and too much alcohol involved this evening.' Cassie herself hadn't actually had that much to drink.

'Is it, um, difficult for you seeing a friend like Chloe?' he said, and then did an immediate internal eye roll. How was he going to finish that question without upsetting her? *Are you jealous or upset because she's pregnant and you aren't?* Obviously not. What an idiot.

'You mean because she's pregnant? Yes and no. Yes, I did go through a phase of struggling not to be, I don't know what, not envious – or not in a bad way, because I'd always be happy for a friend – but, yes, I suppose in some ways envious. And that is not good. It makes you feel like a bad person.'

James knew all about the envy thing. When he was young, he'd been envious of his friends' families. Especially the ones with the mother, father, two point two kids set-up. A father who acknowledged and was remotely interested in his children. A sober mother. Food on the table provided by an adult instead of one of the kids. He'd been happy for them, but he'd have liked that for himself and his sisters too.

'And no,' Cassie continued, 'because actually I really *am* happy for her and she *should* be able to be bubbly and excited and obsessive about her pregnancy, of *course* she should. Really, it was a lot worse seeing Juliet. Maybe I'm scared that I'll be bitter like that in thirty years' time. Anyway—' she pulled the cutlery rack and started loading it, fast, like she wanted a physical outlet for her feelings '—that's a lot of blether about me. What about you? Have you ever wanted kids?' She straightened. 'Sorry. I don't know what I was thinking. That's a very personal question.'

'No, it's okay.' He *really* didn't want her to feel bad on top of everything else. 'We're friends. It isn't too personal.' It kind of was. He really didn't talk about this stuff. Maybe he should. 'No. I don't want kids.'

Her eyes widened, a lot, and then she blinked, hard, but she didn't say anything. Instead she took a dishwasher tab and put it into its compartment and pressed the 'on' switch.

'I guess that's unusual,' he said, walking over to the sofas.

Cassie followed him, but keeping her distance.

He suddenly really wanted to explain. 'But, no, I don't. I suppose I don't have a role model. My parents were only together very briefly. I do know who my father is and he has no interest in me. And my mother was great from the maternal love perspective but not so good in practice because she was an alcoholic so she wasn't brilliant at looking after us.' Wow. He'd just told Cassie about his parents. He never told people. It felt okay. Good, even. 'My older sister, Ella, is two years older than me.' Now he wanted to tell her about Leonie, but he couldn't get the words out. How no *way* was he going to have kids because it was like he and Ella had brought Leonie up and he'd totally failed Leonie and she'd become an addict like their mother, and died. He just couldn't talk about that at all.

Cassie's eyes had filled and she had a hand stretched towards him. No. He couldn't deal with sympathy.

'I'll tell you something funny about my father,' he said. 'He's fallen on hard times financially since, but he was quite a famous singer in the early eighties, before he met my mother. You might have heard of him. He did quite a well-known Christmas song that still gets played. Dougie Finegan.'

'Dougie Finegan is your *father*?' Cassie gave a tiny, muffled snort. *Yes*. A very successful change of topic. 'He's got a lovely voice.'

'Yep. I inherited my musical abilities from my mother.'

'Wow.' Cassie had her lips pressed really hard together like she was trying really hard not to laugh.

'You thinking about me singing?'

She laughed out loud. 'Yes.'

He kind of wanted to tell her about singing 'Happy Birthday' to a hostile audience at Emily's party, except he didn't want to remind her about Emily.

Wow. Emily and Cassie. So different from each other.

Cassie was different from any woman he'd ever dated, actually. She was still sniggering a little, her eyes alight. He was laughing too, just because she was.

She looked beautiful, sitting at the end of the sofa, her feet curled under her, in a soft blue dress this evening, more muted than the bright colours she usually wore but great against her warm skin tone.

James really wanted to sit down next to her.

He sat down at the opposite end of the same sofa.

Why had he bought such large sofas?

He really, really did not want to go to bed right now. Not alone, anyway. And obviously he wasn't going to go to bed *with* Cassie.

'Some late-night TV? Maybe a film?' he asked.

'Sounds good.' She really did have the most stunning smile. He loved it when it grew gradually, like it was doing now as he watched her.

'Great.' He looked around for the remote.

'It's here.' Cassie leaned forward and picked it up from the coffee table. James applied superhuman effort and kept his eyes above where the low neckline of her dress gaped for a moment. She pointed the remote at the TV.

'Oh, of course. Obviously you know how to work it.' Really, it was so strange to think of her having been here in his flat for several months. Also, nice. Intimate.

'To be honest, I don't *totally* know how to work it. I always thought there was some interaction between it and your Fire TV stick, and I never really worked out exactly how to do it, so I had relatively limited viewing options while I was here.'

'Yeah, I can imagine. I struggled with it myself initially, and I had the instructions. Yep. I should have left you some instructions.'

'You should.' She smiled at him. 'At least I had you writing lists by the time we swapped back.'

'Yep, you listed me into submission.' He was sure the word *submission* had sexual connotations. Pretty much everything did right now. They should really switch the TV on and get watching something.

He shifted along the sofa to take the remote and she moved towards him. Their hands touched briefly when he took it and he caught a sharp intake of breath from Cassie. That should really not have made him want to smile so much.

She reached up and gathered all her hair into a high ponytail for a moment, exposing the delicate line of her neck.

She glanced over and saw him looking at her. 'It's a bit hot in here.' She sounded a little breathless.

James nodded. He was feeling hot himself.

She let her hair down and stretched.

James swallowed. 'So what do you fancy watching?'

'I've seen a lot of films on planes recently.'

'Yeah. Me too. What about a classic film?'

Astonishingly, Cassie had never seen a single Hitchcock.

'What? That's insane,' James told her. 'You have to watch one.'

'But aren't they scary? I don't want to get frightened.'

'You'll be fine. I mean, I'm here. It isn't like you're on your own.'

'Hmm.'

'Okay. What about a deal? You let me introduce you to the master of cinema this evening and when you come back on Wednesday evening we'll watch the least scary film of your choice.' He put his hand out. Cassie looked at him, eyes narrowed, for a moment, and then shook it.

'We'll be watching something very different on Wednesday evening,' she said. 'Maybe a cheesy nineties rom-com.'

'And I will watch it with a very open mind. Right. *Psycho*. I'm thinking lighting down for the full movie experience.'

'Oh-kay.'

'We can turn the lights on if you get scared.'

'Okay. You're on.'

'You're going to love it. It's so well crafted. There's a reason that films become great classics.' James sat back with his arm along the back of the sofa behind Cassie and prepared to enjoy the movie.

'No, no, no, no, no, oh my *goodness*.' Cassie was pressed right up against his side and was holding his knee as though her life depended on it. James hadn't expected her to have this level of terror. If he was honest, he'd had more than the odd moment where he'd thought about some close contact with Cassie but none of his fantasies had involved her being terrified.

'We can stop now?'

'No! I need to know what happens. But could we have a light on?'

When the credits rolled, and Cassie had calmed down, she was still pressed right up against him. He had his arm round her shoulders and she was gripping his hand genuinely painfully.

'Oh. My. Goodness,' she said. 'Amazing.'

'I *knew* you'd love it in the end.'

'Love it? I hated it. There's a reason that normal people don't like horror movies.'

'What? Normal people *do* like horror movies. Especially well-constructed ones like that.'

Cassie shook her head. 'No. I'm never going to sleep again. I'll dream about it tonight.'

'I'm kind of feeling as though I should apologise. But also I'm *sure* you'll look back on this evening and be grateful. You know, when you're in the pub and someone refers to this film and now you'll know what they're talking about.'

She let go of his hand and turned within the circle of his arm to face him. 'Firstly, I was very happy in my Hitchcock innocence and secondly, I'm thirty-seven years old and no-one has ever talked about the film *Psycho* in front of me before.'

'How is that even possible?'

'Because my friends have great taste in films?' She smiled up at him and it felt like his heart actually lurched inside him. Suddenly, his powers of speech were gone. His entire mind, and body, were focused now on where they were touching, his arm round her shoulders, their thighs pressed together.

Her expression got more serious and her lips parted slightly.

This time James was all out of willpower. He pulled her in closer with his right arm and his left hand found her face, while she put her hands on his chest. He cupped her cheek very gently and lowered his lips to hers.

She tasted of raspberry pavlova and peppermint tea and the *weird* cocktail that they'd concocted at the end of the evening, and she also tasted perfect and right and like he was *home*, and he was lost.

*

James woke up before Cassie did. He raised himself on his elbow and lay watching her for a few moments. He really couldn't remember ever waking up feeling more contented. Which was possibly a little stupid, because this felt complicated.

Cassie stirred and rolled. The duvet fell away from her bare shoulders and James nearly groaned out loud with lust.

Cassie opened her eyes and smiled at him. Maybe he *had* in fact groaned out loud. Her smile was slow and then wide, and definitely inviting.

'I don't think I'm going to have time for brunch. I'll miss my flight.' Cassie scrabbled around next to the bed. 'I can't find my phone. Maybe I left it in the sitting room?' She'd almost certainly left it in the sitting room. They'd left a lot of their clothes there. 'What time is it?'

James checked his watch. Apparently he hadn't had time to take that off. 'Wow. Twelve fifteen.'

'No way. Oh my goodness. Wow.'

They grinned at each other like complete idiots for a few moments and then James reached for Cassie again.

'I really can't,' she said between kisses. 'Those flights to Glasgow get really booked up. I can't miss it.'

'You could stay another night?'

'Mmm. I would really like to but I'm having a family dinner this evening. And I really want to go to Glasgow again. You know. Facing my fears and all that.'

'You haven't told me what it is about Glasgow that's so bad. Is it because of your ex?' They'd spent the whole night having sex. He could ask that question.

'Well.' She'd taken a long time to start her answer. 'Simon *was* awful. Basically, he was rubbish when I was pregnant, he didn't come to the scan where I found out that the baby had died, and when I told him, he seemed almost uninterested, certainly not particularly upset, and, within a few days, he said oh, by the way, could I move out because he wanted to move someone else in.'

'Tosser. *Tosser.* Unbelievable.' James wanted to punch something, or someone, but right now he had to hold Cassie. 'Cassie, that's so awful. You did so well to leave him.' He wrapped his arms all the way round her, as though he could protect her like that.

'Tosser's right. After I left, he kept trying to get in touch with me through friends, a serious case of only wanting something when you can't have it. And then I discovered this summer that the other woman – who he's now married to and who presumably would not be happy if she knew he'd tried to get in touch with me – must also have been pregnant then, when I was.'

James held Cassie even more tightly. 'I'm beyond furious with a man I've never met,' he said. 'I'm glad you're now able to go back to Glasgow. One man's terrible behaviour shouldn't stop you from visiting your hometown.'

'It wasn't actually entirely because of him that I left or couldn't go back. I got my book deal around the same time, and left my old job, so I could work anywhere, and I just had a big urge to go and live somewhere else. A lot of it was because I couldn't bear being around my family and friends who were all grief-stricken for me, and there were just too many memories.'

'I get that.' James nodded. That was pretty much why he'd avoided Ella for so long. 'And for what it's worth I think you've been incredibly brave.'

'Thank you.' She smiled at him and then she reached up and kissed him again. 'No, I shouldn't have done that. I *have* to go soon.'

In the end, James accompanied Cassie into the shower, so they didn't even have time for lunch before they dived into a taxi.

'Are you sure you want to come all the way to the airport?' she asked.

'Yep.'

They held hands and talked about nothing and everything in the back of the cab.

When it was time for Cassie to go through airport security, James took her hands and kissed her full on the lips.

'Can't wait to see you on Wednesday,' he said.

'Me too.' Cassie looked gorgeous when she'd just been kissed, her eyes hazy and her lips plump and red.

She turned round to leave, and as she moved away, James said, 'I love you.'

Her back stiffened and she turned round, her mouth forming an O shape and her eyes wide.

She looked stunned, frankly.

As well she might. He was pretty stunned himself.

He'd just told her he loved her. And they'd only been in each other's lives since April, what, seven months ago. And, yes, they'd talked a *lot* and they'd spent some time together, including this whole fantastic weekend, and they'd spent last night having a lot of fantastic sex. But what the hell had he been *thinking* saying he loved her?

He was pretty sure he *did* love her.

Certain, actually.

But you didn't tell someone you loved them when you barely knew them. Or when there was no chance of things going anywhere because you didn't live in the same place and one of you was never having kids and the other was desperate for a baby.

She didn't even know the full story of why he didn't want kids. He'd have to tell her, as soon as possible. He couldn't say he loved her with all that that might imply without giving her the full facts about himself. He'd broken his own rule of not letting anyone think he was more serious about them than he was.

Although, in fact, he was serious about her. But he did not want kids and she did. He should not have told her he loved her.

What. An. Idiot.

She was still staring at him.

Oh, to hell with it. He'd talk to her about it properly later in the week.

'I love you,' he repeated.

Chapter Twenty-Four

Cassie

Cassie's tote was swinging uncomfortably from her elbow from when it had fallen down when she'd spun round to stare at James. She hitched it back onto her shoulder.

He'd just told her he loved her. Twice. She should definitely reply. Unfortunately, it seemed that she couldn't speak.

'Excuse me.' A tall woman in extremely pink lipstick and a heavily shoulder-padded power suit gestured at the door behind Cassie and the handful of people behind herself. 'A queue's forming.'

'Oops, yes, so sorry.' Cassie tried to move to one side to let people through, but there wasn't space. And she was supposed to be boarding any minute. And she had no idea what to say.

So she lifted her non-bag arm and gave James a little wave, said, 'Bye,' and scuttled through the door with the tall woman close behind.

What? What? What? James had told her he loved her, twice, and she'd told him *Bye*. She stepped onto a travelator in a daze, thinking about James's face as she'd left him. He'd been smiling when he spoke but the smile had faded significantly when she'd just walked off.

What should she do now?

Phone him? Text him?

To say what?

She could maybe say she was looking forward to seeing him on Wednesday.

She pulled her phone out of her bag. Oh. Text from Dina. *Dina*. Gaah. Last night. *Guilt*.

Hey, how's your weekend been? I've had a great time visiting Amy. Just got out of bed. Hooked up with one of her college professors last night!!!! How bad is that??? GREAT night though :)

Wow. So great news that Dina had hooked up with someone. Fantastic news. But, oh, God, *Cassie had slept with James last night and he had just told her he loved her*.

Ow. *Ow*. Woah. End of the travelator.

Cassie managed to save herself from what felt like possible death or a broken ankle at the very least by grabbing the nearest person.

'Are you alright?' The lipsticked, shoulder-padded woman looked pointedly at Cassie's hand scrunching her suit sleeve.

'I'm fine. Thank you.' Cassie wiggled her ankle – again, *ow* – let go of the woman and bent down to pick up her bag and all the things that had fallen out of it.

Right. Sorted. Hopefully she hadn't actually sprained her ankle.

There was a lesson there. Never read texts on a travelator.

It looked like she had a couple of minutes before her row was going to be called to board. She had to call James.

'Hi.' He was smiling. She could hear it in his voice.

'Hello.' Oh, for God's sake. No words. She should have thought this through before she called. Say something. 'I've had a great weekend. I'm really looking forward to seeing you on Wednesday.'

'Me too.'

'Okay. So bye then,' she said.

'Bye. Safe flight.' Still that undertone of a smile. Gorgeous.

*

Meg was waving manically when Cassie got through the gates after sending a quick text to James to say that she'd arrived safely.

They were still mid-hug when she said, 'Cassie Adair, you are *glowing*.'

'Am I?' And *that* was a stupid way to have reacted. Of course she was glowing, though. Distracted, anyway. This afternoon the most gorgeous man in the world had told her he loved her. Clearly they had no future together, but she'd still spent the whole flight daydreaming. Not just about the L-word, either, but about all the sex.

'Cassie, your eyes are practically glazing over.'

'Big night last night,' Cassie said. 'Out with friends. I'm just tired.'

'Hmm.'

Finally Cassie had a moment to herself. It had been great having dinner this evening with Meg, her husband, their friends; of course it had. She just really needed more time to process what had happened over the weekend.

She closed the loo door behind her and pulled out her phone. James had left a voicemail for her a couple of hours ago and she *really* wanted to know what he'd said.

She had actual goosebumps as she heard his voice say *Hi, Cassie*. He'd just called to say hello. She was smiling just listening to him. Honestly. Moonstruck. She checked her watch. It was only quarter past eleven. He'd probably still be up. She could give him a quick call.

Not from here, though, because anyone walking past might hear her. The garden would be best.

'I'm just going to pop my head outside for some fresh air,' she told the others on her way past the sitting room.

'Good idea.' Meg stood up. 'I'll join you.' Bugger. Maybe Cassie would find a moment to call James tomorrow.

*

'Hi, James.'

'Well hello. How's it going? What are you up to?'

'I'm on my way to meet a friend, just walking down the road from Meg's house. It's raining. It rains a lot in Glasgow.' This was good. This was what they did; they chatted on the phone. They did not have sex and tell each other they loved each other. Mundane was the way forward. 'I didn't bring an umbrella. I should have remembered one. I have my hood pulled up.'

'Is that the one with the blue fur?'

'No, a different one. I have more than one hood.'

'I'm guessing you're looking beautiful whichever hood it is.' James's voice was low and gravelly and Cassie's insides were turning to jelly.

'Why thank you,' she said, trying to sound normal.

'Talk me through what else you're wearing.' Oh, God, this was not going to be a mundane conversation. Cassie was fairly sure she was already blushing.

*

'Hi again.' This was the third time in two days that James had called her. Their last two conversations had completely avoided any L-word discussion but had been *filthy*, frankly.

'Hi, James. I can't talk because I'm just on my way into my aunt's house.'

He murmured a couple of things to her. And now she was hot all over just as she was about to sit down for afternoon tea. Honestly.

*

Cassie took a bite of her – somewhat cardboardy – tuna and sweetcorn sandwich and looked out of the window. They were already halfway down England. They'd be landing in not much over half an hour and James was going to be meeting her at the airport.

She couldn't remember the last time she'd experienced such a fizz of anticipation. From what he'd said on the phone this morning, she was pretty sure that he'd be very keen for another night like Saturday night, and she was equally sure that she'd be very keen herself.

On the one hand, at her age, it was nuts to start something with someone who'd told her he didn't want kids. Who Dina – her neighbour and best friend – had been hung up on for months. And who'd become a good friend who she'd miss if they stopped seeing each other.

On the other hand, they'd already pretty much put paid to the 'we're just friends' thing on Saturday night and another night wouldn't make any difference to that and would, almost certainly, be incredible.

She took another bite of the sandwich. Honestly. The bread was so stale. At least she'd get good food later. James had suggested that they go out for dinner. Just the two of them. Very date-like. And they were supposed to be watching a film of Cassie's choice afterwards, although maybe they'd have better things to do late at night. He'd also suggested that they go for a walk in Hyde Park together this afternoon, also very date-like.

So stomach-churningly exciting, however stupid it might be.

*

Cassie saw James as soon as she was through the automatic doors. He was a good half head taller and a lot broader than all the people around him, so he was easy to spot.

His chin kind of wobbled as he smiled at her, like a wave of emotion had washed over him. Cassie's eyes pricked in response.

And then she was clear of all the other passengers and they were standing facing each other.

'Good flight?' James asked.

'Not bad. Had some tepid water and an almost edible sandwich.'

'Good to hear that you won't have ruined your appetite for later.'

'I definitely haven't done that.'

A slow smile spread across James's face and he held out his arms. Cassie walked straight into them and they had a long hug. Which was lovely. Yes, this, whatever this was, had no future, but they might as well enjoy today. Before she went home and planned her next solo IVF attempt.

'Right.' James released her and picked up her suitcase. 'Better get going. I have a cab waiting outside.'

It was kind of weird being in the back of a taxi – with, therefore, a taxi driver in the same enclosed space and presumably listening with at least one ear to their conversation – when they obviously had so much personal stuff to say to each other.

Cassie went down the route of talking about her stay in Glasgow and James told her a couple of work anecdotes.

They carried on with the inconsequential chat the whole time through taking Cassie's bags up to the flat and until they were walking in the park, surrounded only by trees, with no other people in sight.

'So I thought we should talk.' James scuffed a little pile of orange and brown leaves with his foot. 'I kind of wanted to leave it until tomorrow, but I thought we should do it today, so that we have time to say whatever we like, without a plane departure deadline.'

'Yes.' Cassie nodded.

'Actually, if you don't mind, there's something I'd like to tell you. I never tell anyone this. Ever.' He scuffed more leaves.

'Of course.' Cassie wanted to hug him but he seemed to have withdrawn into himself physically. It didn't seem likely that he was going to tell her anything good.

'The sister I baked with. She was twelve years younger than me.' God. Past tense. He was going to tell her something really terrible.

James stopped talking.

'Yes,' Cassie said, to fill the gap and to prompt him to speak because now that she knew he was going to tell her something awful she just wanted to know immediately.

'Basically, none of our fathers were around. It was our mother, my older sister, Ella, me and Leonie, my little sister. As I told you before, our mother was an alcoholic, and from when Leonie was little she got worse and worse. Ella and I were terrified that we'd get taken into care, so between us we did everything at home and looked after Leonie. Ella and I were also both determined to have better lives, and we both worked hard at school and she ended up doing medicine at university and I did economics. She went to Bristol University and medicine's a very full-on degree, obviously, so she didn't really come home much, and then she met her husband when they were in their second year. So then it was really just me looking after Leonie by myself a lot of the time. I went to university in London so that I could carry on living at home and then I went for the best paid job I could find, which was in finance, so that I could earn enough to buy a flat and support us all properly. Anyway, to cut a very long story somewhat shorter, I really didn't do a great job of looking after Leonie. She ended up addicted to heroin. I was working long hours. Our mother was completely out of it by then. Ella had got married and had twin daughters, who are eight now. I did my best but I just wasn't up to the task of parenting Leonie. She died of an overdose five years ago. Our mother died last year.' He carried on walking, looking straight ahead. This was probably why he didn't drink much and why he seemed so obsessive about everything in his home being new, tidy and perfect.

'James. I'm so, so sorry.' Cassie hurried to keep up with him.

'I don't tell people this, ever.' He was still walking and looking straight ahead. 'I wanted to tell you to explain why I'm not going to have children. A guilt I have to live with forever is that I hated the burden of having to help parent when I was so young. And a greater guilt is that I failed Leonie. I am categorically not going down that road again.'

'James. No. You didn't fail her. You really didn't. It sounds as though you were a wonderful brother. I mean, for example, your baking. That's so lovely and caring. You chose your university and your job so that you could look after your family. That isn't failing them.' Now was really not the time to talk about his decision not to have children. Maybe there'd never be a time to talk about that. It wasn't important right now. What was important was trying to find *some* words to try to absorb *any* of his pain.

'It doesn't feel that way.' His voice shook. 'Sorry. Emotional. This is the first time I've ever told anyone this in such detail. Ella and I have never talked about it. I can't talk about Leonie with her. My best friends from university don't know either. I never invited them over.'

Wow. Huge. Cassie really couldn't think of anything else to say. 'Could I hug you?' she asked.

'Okay.' James had been walking with his arms folded across his chest. He stopped walking and lowered his arms to his side.

Cassie put her arms round him. His entire body was rigid. She stood and held him for a long time until eventually he started to relax.

'It doesn't sound like you're ever going to believe this,' she said, 'but I can't think of a time when I've heard a story of greater family love. I think you're amazing.' She reached up and touched the side of his face, his stubble scratching her fingers.

James lifted his arms from where he'd been holding them at his sides and put them round her.

'You're wrong, but thank you,' he said, his voice rough. 'And thanks for listening. Come on. Let's walk again. I know it isn't exactly the weather for it, but they do great ice creams at the café along here. What's your favourite flavour?'

'Salted caramel, *obviously*, because it's the best. I just want to say one thing. I think maybe you should tell Ella what you told me about Leonie. And now let's go and get the ice creams.'

It was dusk by the time they got back to the flat. They'd got their ice creams and walked miles round the park and talked a lot about very unemotive topics. They'd laughed a lot too, and at some point they'd ended up holding hands as they'd walked. It was probably the most memorable walk of Cassie's entire life. And oddly the best. Except for the fact that they still hadn't discussed James's weekend L-word bomb and the fact that this felt like something big except it wasn't going to go anywhere.

'I'm *knackered*.' Cassie pulled her boots off and flopped onto the sofa. 'How far do you think we walked? I feel like I've done actual exercise.'

James sat down next to her and pulled her feet onto his lap and started on some very skilled foot rubbing. 'I'd say at least five or six miles.'

'Really? That's a long way for an afternoon stroll.' Cassie leaned her head against the back of the sofa. Unbelievably, because these were just her *feet*, whatever he was doing with his thumbs was causing her all sorts of sensations in all sorts of other parts of her body. 'You're an excellent foot masseur.'

'That's not the only body part I'm good with.' He did an exaggerated wink.

'Ooh er.' Cassie laughed.

And then he kissed her and she stopped laughing and kissed him back.

'The only reason that I'm not going to suggest cancelling the restaurant and getting takeaway,' James said two hours later, checking his watch, 'is that obviously that's very inconsiderate towards them. We should get dressed and go. And it's a great restaurant. I think you're going to love it.'

They were only about fifteen minutes late in the end for their reservation. The restaurant was a French bistro, tucked away in a side street in Notting Hill.

'Dessert?' asked James two hours later.

'Delicious as they look,' Cassie said, 'I'm going to pass because I'm very, very full already.' She wasn't *that* full but she would be if she ate pudding, and a full stomach wouldn't help if the evening panned out the way she hoped it would. 'Shall we maybe have our coffees… back at the flat?'

They held hands all the way back, apart from when they stopped a few times for some kissing.

By the time they got inside James's building and into the lift, Cassie's ability to think was completely gone. There was something gut-punchingly wonderful about watching themselves kiss in the mirrored walls of the lift, and when she simultaneously watched and felt James's hands move under her top, it was like she might actually die of lust.

The lift was ancient and slow, and by the time its doors were open, they were both a little dishevelled.

They almost fell out of the lift, laughing, and nearly knocked Anthony over.

'Well, good *evening*.' Anthony was smiling broadly when James had set him back on his feet. 'I thought as much but Juliet was having none of it. I'm sorry to steal any thunder you may wish to keep to yourselves for future announcements, but I'm on my way up to see her now, and I shall be reporting this to her in great detail.'

'Eek.' Cassie screwed up her face and tried to un-screw up her top. 'Nothing, *really*, to report, Anthony.'

'That's right. Absolutely.' James was also making some clothing adjustments. 'Best regards to Juliet.'

'I hope you have a lovely evening, Anthony,' Cassie said.

'I hope *you* have a lovely evening, my darlings.' Anthony did a pantomime wink and Cassie and James both winced.

The corridor was wide and they both kept very carefully to their own side of it as they walked from the lift to the flat. Anthony was up there with a bucket of freezing water in the effective mood-breaker stakes.

'Coffee?' James said when they were both in the sitting room, still standing several feet apart from each other.

'Great!' Hard to stop yourself being over-exclamatory when you felt awkward. Probably best to address the elephant in the room. One of them, anyway. 'I'm guessing you might be avoiding Anthony and Juliet for a while.'

'Yeah. Or maybe not. Maybe better to tackle them head on. Deny everything. I mean, not that there's anything to deny. Well, there is something.'

Cassie nodded. There was something. And now they were probably going to get onto the bigger elephant.

James took mugs out of the cupboard and began to fill them from his fancy boiling water tap.

'I told you on Sunday that I love you,' he said with his back to her. 'I do love you.'

Cassie *really* wished that they'd stayed in the restaurant and had pudding. Being too full for great sex would have been a lot better than bumping into Anthony and ending up having this conversation.

'We don't really know each other that well,' she said.

'I think we do.' James turned round to face her. 'You know, in a kind of quality-not-quantity way.'

Cassie's breath caught in her throat. The serious look on his face, and his words – had there ever been such a beautiful declaration of love? A love which almost certainly couldn't go anywhere. Heart-rending.

She had to reply, and she had to be honest with him.

'I love you too,' she said, not smiling.

James took their mugs over to the island and sat down on one of the bar stools. Cassie joined him and perched on the other one, careful to sit far enough away that their legs wouldn't touch.

This was one of those conversations that you never wanted to have, but they were going to have to have it.

'So obviously I live on the island and you live here,' Cassie said. 'And, obviously, we both know that I would love to have a baby and you would not, and so, really, I'd like to thank you for the most amazing weekend and the most amazing day today.'

'And you're going to go back home tomorrow and that's that?' James was staring at his mug and on about his fiftieth stir of it.

'Well, I mean, I suppose so.' Extraordinary to feel so devastated about saying goodbye to someone she'd known for, really, not that long. But, yep, he was right. Quality not quantity. They'd got to know each other very well, in a very unique way, in that short time.

James looked up. 'I really never thought… I mean, I've never felt this way before, and I've never believed that I would settle down.' He let go of his spoon and put his hands flat on the island, one on either side of his mug. 'That I would want to settle down. Turns out I'd just never met the right person before.'

Cassie's eyes were heavy with tears. 'I can't imagine ever meeting anyone I could love as much as I love you, even though we've only known each other a few months,' she said. 'And I feel as though you're my perfect man. Except we aren't perfect for each other, are we?' So indescribably sad.

'We could be?'

'But I don't see how. Obviously I don't know whether or not I'll ever have a baby, but I want one so much. And you're here, and I really love you.' She really did. So very much. 'And I can't bear the thought of ending up like Juliet and Anthony. That look that she gave him when she was talking about them not having had kids.'

'They're happy, though.'

'I'd be so scared that I'd resent you, even just once, in the future.'

'I think maybe I'd have a baby for you. I know you'd be a great mother. Maybe a baby doesn't need two great parents.'

Cassie shook her head. 'You said at the weekend how awful it is not to be wanted by your father.'

'But I love you.'

'I love you too. But sometimes love isn't enough, is it? If you want diametrically opposed things.'

'I think I'd have a baby for you,' James said.

'I would want you to want to have the baby for the baby itself.'

'Maybe I would.'

'That isn't true, though, is it?'

James stared ahead for a few seconds and then shook his head.

They both sat there, not speaking, for a long time. Then James stood up and poured their cold drinks down the sink.

'We should probably go to bed,' he said. 'You have a long journey tomorrow.'

They went to bed separately, which at the start of the evening Cassie would not have believed possible.

In the morning, she felt like total crap from lying awake crying for so much of the night. James didn't look a lot better. She should have had the bloody pudding in the restaurant and they could have had fat-stomached-person sex last night and had this conversation over breakfast and she could have cried on the plane instead.

They ate croissants and compote very politely together and then James insisted on carrying Cassie's bags from the bedroom out to the hall and then she suddenly said, 'James. Please could we have a hug? I can't bear you to look so miserable.'

Unfortunately, the hug felt desperately sad. Unbearable to think that this was it.

'I'm going to come with you to the airport after all.' James said the words into her hair. 'If that's alright?'

'Yes, please.' While he was still there, with her, there was still the chance that maybe he'd have an epiphany and realise that he did want a baby. Or they'd bump into Juliet and she'd say how glad she was that she'd never have kids and Cassie would be able to bin this feeling that she *had* to try for a baby. Or *something*.

They didn't hold hands in the back of the cab but they did sit quite close together, their knees touching. They talked about London sights and history that Cassie had gleaned during her stay.

At the airport they did the walking version of the same sad experience.

Cassie's last sight of him was him looking no longer his friendly rugby player type but like a serious, handsome City man again, all rigid jaw and drawn cheeks.

Turned out she hadn't run out of tears last night. She got through a lot of tissues on the plane.

*

Cassie looked out of the window at two squirrels playing on her lawn. So gorgeous. Actually quite heart-rendingly gorgeous. She'd disturbed a bobcat tracking a squirrel last week. It was awful when animals preyed on each other. She sniffed and wiped a stray tear from her cheek.

Four weeks on from saying goodbye to James, you'd have thought that she would have moved on from the tears phase. But apparently not. If anything, she was getting more emotional. Yesterday she'd cried because she'd run out of yoghurt and the island store didn't have the flavour she wanted.

She was starting to wonder whether she should just call him and tell him that she loved him more than she loved the idea of a baby. Yeah, she probably should. It felt like it was true. Maybe she'd just needed a bit of distance to work that out.

She closed her eyes for a moment. All the emotion was making her a lot more tired than normal. Very sluggish.

Okay. She needed to shake this off. She really couldn't work at the moment. Maybe she'd walk round to see Dina, see if she was up for a little coffee break. Or tea maybe. She'd been drinking a lot of herbal recently. She wouldn't mind a ginger and lemon one this minute.

She'd been struggling a little bit spending time with Dina since she got back, due to the guilt she felt over sleeping with James. Rationally, there was nothing to feel guilty about. Dina and James had never been together. Dina had told Cassie before she left for London that she knew that she and James weren't right for each other anyway. Dina had had more hot sex with Amy's professor. And Cassie and James weren't really in touch any more. But it still felt bad. *Really* bad. And since she and James *weren't* in touch – oh, God, just thinking about it she was welling up again – there was no reason to tell Dina about any of it, because the last thing she'd want to do would be hurt Dina. Of course, if she called James and told him she loved him and something happened, *then* she'd have to tell Dina. Something to think about later.

She stood up. She was definitely going round to see Dina. Dina was a great, great friend and neighbour.

'Hey, stranger. Haven't seen so much of you the last couple weeks. Flat out with work?' Dina hugged her.

'Yep, very busy.' If you could call it busy sitting at your desk staring into space and crying quite often and sleeping the rest of the time.

'I'll put the kettle on. And I have pastries.'

Five minutes later, Dina said, 'Here you are,' and put Cassie's coffee down in front of her.

'Thank you.' Cassie hadn't even got the mug halfway to her lips before she realised that Dina had made it far too strong. Dina was not an absent-minded person, but she must have absent-mindedly put about three times too much coffee in. Just from the stomach-turningly disgusting smell wafting out of the mug, Cassie could tell that it was undrinkable. In fact, she was gagging slightly just from the smell.

She put the mug back down on the table and pushed it away as subtly as she could and leaned backwards in her chair to get away from it.

Dina put a plate of pastries in the middle of the table and sat down opposite Cassie.

Cassie took a plain croissant. The others looked too sugary.

Now that did taste good. Lovely and carby. The coffee still smelled grim, though. She pushed it a bit further away.

'So how's Amy?' she asked. She was a terrible friend. She should have been around more now that Dina was on her own. Oh no. Her eyes were misting over thinking about Dina being lonely.

'She's good.' Dina leaned forward and looked closely at Cassie. Eurgh. Her *breath*. It *stank* of coffee. 'Honey, are you okay?'

'Yes. Great. Just got something in my eye.' Cassie turned her face away from Dina's and breathed only through her mouth. Should she *warn* Dina that she shouldn't go out in public with such severe coffee-breath? Would that be really rude? Or would it be being a good friend?

Dina's coffee had to be mouldy or something. Cassie pushed her mug further away and inched her chair back from the table.

'Something wrong with the coffee?' Dina had a strange look in her eye.

Honesty or a white lie? Honesty. She'd be doing Dina a favour.

'Yes.' Cassie raised her eyebrows, scrunched her face and nodded.

Dina reached for Cassie's mug and took a big sniff. 'Honey, there's nothing wrong with that.'

Cassie was feeling really shaky from hunger and from the disgusting smell. She took another croissant.

'Honestly, Dina, the coffee smells hideous. Vomit-level hideous.' She did actually feel quite sick.

Dina was studying Cassie with an even stranger look in her eye now.

'What?' Cassie said, munching her croissant.

'Okay,' Dina said. 'Right.'

'Seriously? What?'

'Honey.' Dina paused and Cassie gave her the evil eye. Like, just get *on* with whatever she was going to say. 'Okay. I don't want to say this because I don't want to intrude.'

What? When did Dina ever not want to intrude?

'But I kind of feel I should say it because if it's true and you don't know then you really do need to know so you can look after yourself properly. And if it's true and you don't want to talk about it then I'm so sorry for intruding. And if it isn't true, I'm also very sorry. But you're very tired. You're very emotional. You think my coffee's off. Basically, do you think you could be pregnant?'

'Pregnant?'

Pregnant.

Woah.

Cassie put her elbows on the table and her head in her hands and thought.

Yep. When she thought about how she'd felt in the early days of her first pregnancy and compared that to now, and thought about the fact that she and James had definitely been pretty stupid once or twice on the contraception front, and did period maths, there was a very definite chance that she was pregnant. Her period was *really* late. How had she not noticed?

Pregnant. *Woah.*

'Honey. Have I upset you?' Dina pulled her chair next to Cassie's and put her arm round Cassie's shoulders. 'Did you do IVF again? I'm so sorry if it didn't work out or if you're feeling this way because of the drugs and you're waiting to do the test. I'm *so* sorry for being so insensitive.'

'Not IVF,' Cassie said through her hands.

'You haven't done IVF? So do you think you might be ill? Should you see a doctor?'

Part of Cassie really wanted to pretend that she thought she was ill. Actually, most of her wanted to pretend that. Also, a little bit – the sane bit, if she was honest – knew that she should tell Dina the truth. Except, oh God.

'I think I might be pregnant,' she said, still through her hands.

'I'm so sorry, I misheard. I thought you said you didn't do IVF. Oh my God, Cassie. This is so exciting.'

Cassie took her hands away from her face. 'I think I might be pregnant but I didn't do IVF.'

'What? You mean?' Dina gaped. 'An actual *penis* was involved? For basically the first time in four years?'

Cassie winced. 'Yep.'

'*Whose* actual penis?'

Oh shit. Cassie screwed up her face. She couldn't say it. She should say it.

She couldn't say it.

'Oh my *God.* Did you have sex with *James*?'

Chapter Twenty-Five

James

James hunched his shoulders in response to the November drizzle that had just begun. Rain was the wrong weather for today. He was pretty sure that he was taking a positive step and when you took a positive step the sun should shine.

God, he wasn't looking forward to this. It was one of those things where you really wished you could fast forward to afterwards.

His phone vibrated. Hopefully it was Ella saying she couldn't make it after all. They could perhaps do it next weekend instead. Or in a few weeks' time. Years maybe. Maybe just never.

It was Cassie.

Ridiculous, and uncomfortable, how his heart leapt at the sight of her name. It was a month now since she'd left and they'd spoken once in that time, when he'd called to check properly that she'd got back safely. It had been so excruciating that he'd decided not to call again for a while, and she hadn't called him either.

In the meantime, he'd decided to carry on trying to sort his family life out. It felt like something positive – not just, frankly, heartbreak – should have come out of the house swap experience.

'Hi,' he said.

'Hello.' Pathetic that just the sound of her voice sent a little thrill through him. He should really be doing better at getting over her.

'How are you?'

'I'm well, thank you. How are you?' She actually sounded a little odd.

'Yep, also well. I'm doing something pretty huge this afternoon.' Cassie's call felt quite serendipitous, given that she was the only person who he'd ever talked to properly about his background and was the one who'd encouraged him to talk properly to Ella again. He had a sudden overwhelming urge to confide in her now. 'I'm on my way to meet Ella and we're going to visit Leonie's grave together for the first time.'

'Oh my goodness. Oh, James. That's huge. I should go. I'll call another time.'

'No, don't go. I'd like to talk. If you'd like to.'

'Of course I would. So you and Ella…?'

'Yes. It's hard. When my phone rang I was almost on the brink of bottling it.'

'You know what? I totally get that it's scary and that you'd probably like *anything*, like sudden vomiting or a minor injury, *anything*, to happen to get you out of it. But, actually, I'm sure that it will be a very good thing to do. Cathartic.'

'Yep. You're right that I would like to do pretty much anything else, and, yes, you're probably right that it'll be a good thing to have done. But right now it feels like an almost insurmountable step. I can't really imagine getting from here to later in the day. Like I might *have* to walk away.'

'No. You can do it. Break it down. Just one thing at a time. At the moment, you're on the phone to…' she paused '… a friend. And you're walking somewhere. I can hear the noise of the traffic. So you're just going to carry on with that walk. And then when you get there, you'll say hi to Ella. And so on. You can totally carry on walking while you talk to me. One step at a time.'

'You're right. I can do that.' God, he missed talking to her every day. Maybe they could start doing that again in due course.

They ended up talking for the whole of the rest of his walk to the cemetery. He told her about how Patrick was taking his nieces to the cinema in Leicester Square while he and Ella met, and how they were all then going to stay the night with him again and he was going to babysit while Ella and Patrick went out for dinner. Astonishingly, Cassie even managed to make him laugh a couple of times.

'I'm here,' he said eventually. The cemetery was very flat and he could see Ella in the distance. Even at a good couple of hundred metres he could tell that she didn't look relaxed. Something about the way she held her body. He checked his watch. No, he wasn't late. Ella was early. 'I'm sorry; I've been talking about myself for the past fifteen minutes. How are you? Was there something specific that you wanted to talk about?'

Cassie paused infinitesimally, before saying, 'Nothing, just a chat, really. I hope it goes well now, with Ella. I'll be thinking of you.'

'Could I call you later? Or tomorrow? Hear your news?'

'Of course. Any time. Don't feel that you have to, though. You might not want to talk this evening. Or you might. Any time.'

James would definitely like to speak to Cassie almost any time. He *really* missed her. 'I hope it isn't too difficult now.'

'Thank you. You're a good friend.'

'So are you. I'll be thinking of you. Speak soon.'

'Bye.'

*

'Hi, Ella.'

She turned round and he saw that his sensible, organised, solid, unemotional older sister had tears running unchecked down her face.

He really didn't want to do this.

He wanted to turn around and walk away *so much*.

His feet were almost itching with the desire to run.

It was all too much.

He was going to go. He was going to let Ella down because he always let family down and he just could not do this.

And then Cassie's words echoed in his mind. One step at a time.

Maybe he *could* get through this like that.

Okay. Give Ella a hug.

He moved closer to her and put his arm stiffly round her shoulders.

Ella whispered something.

'I'm sorry. I didn't hear that.' He leaned his head closer to hers.

'I failed her so badly,' Ella said in a barely audible voice.

'What? No.' In contrast to Ella's, James's voice rang out ridiculously loudly, from the shock.

'Yes.'

'No,' he said, 'I was the one who failed her. You weren't even there. It was all down to me and I messed up. I just couldn't manage it. I was too young. I had work. I wanted to make a good life. I tried so hard but I just really, really messed up.'

'But that's the whole point. You *were* there and I wasn't.'

'But you couldn't be. You were at uni. You did a fantastic degree and you have a fantastic job. You're a *doctor*. You help people.'

'I didn't help my own brother and sister, though, did I? I left. I was so desperate for a better, saner, more structured home life that I basically deserted you when I was eighteen and left the daily responsibility for Leonie and Mum to you. I can't believe you don't hate me for it.'

'I…' James stopped to think. He'd learned from talking to Cassie that honesty was a good thing, even when it hurt. 'Yeah. I did. A little. But also, I was so proud of you. I mean, medicine. So impressive. And you did come home in the holidays and your example really inspired me to work hard at school and get myself to uni too. And I had the same sense of being desperate to make a better life. That's why I chose to work in private equity. It really wasn't my vocation. I mean, it's fine, I'm not complaining, I do enjoy a lot of it because I like being busy and it's interesting, and I also love that the world of smart-suited high finance is so far away from a dirty, shabby, empty-bottle-filled flat in a horrible estate. But the only reason I did it initially was the money. I can't rationally hate you for leaving. Really, the big difference between what we did is that you're two years older, so you left first. If I'd been the older one I'd probably have chosen a university away from London not realising that that would mean that you'd *have* to stay.'

Ella did an almost alarmingly gigantic sniff. 'We should have had this conversation five years ago. If not before Leonie died. You know what? You know who failed whom? If we're being magnanimous, we could say that life failed Leonie. And if we're pointing fingers and speaking ill of the dead, we could say that Mum did. And all three of our fathers. Our neighbours. All the adults in the situation.'

'I don't want to think that Mum failed us. Her alcoholism was an illness. She couldn't help it.'

'Moot point. It's too fatalistic for my taste to think that people can't help themselves. But, yeah, maybe. The fact remains, though, that someone should have helped us. I mean, you and I were carers from when we were so young. People must have known about that.'

'We were very good at hiding things.'

Ella nodded. 'We were. But even so.'

'You still good at hiding things? I am. My best friends don't know about my background.' That wasn't one hundred per cent true now, in fact. Cassie did. James's other friends didn't, though.

'Similar. I tell people, but in a very potted-history kind of way.' Ella smiled at James and he smiled back and hugged her properly, this time because he wanted to. 'Leonie would be pleased to see us back together like this,' she said. 'We are properly back together now, aren't we?'

'We are,' James confirmed. He stepped forward and pulled a weed away from Leonie's gravestone. 'She was beautiful,' he said. He heard his voice go all wobbly like a heartbroken child's.

And then they both cried, a lot, which was much better than it might have been because this time, unlike when Leonie had died, James and Ella were very much crying together. They were standing close to each other, their arms round each other's shoulders, instead of several feet apart, each of them with their arms clasped across their own chests, the way they'd been at the funeral.

In the end, Patrick babysat the girls in the flat, while James and Ella went out for dinner together and talked a lot more. And then when James and Ella got home, they played poker with Patrick, and James put his Maine-gained skills into practice and thrashed both of them, ending up with a hundred and thirty-seven extra-long matches to Patrick's three and Ella's ten.

*

James looked out of the windows towards the park. He wasn't appreciating the view as much as usual. You couldn't pass an entire Sunday evening just sitting on a sofa. He hadn't planned anything this evening, imagining that he'd be grateful for some peace and quiet after Ella, Patrick and the girls had left. But now they'd been gone for fifteen minutes and the flat, and the rest of the day, just felt remarkably empty.

Right. He was going to call Cassie. Let her know how yesterday had gone and ask her how she was.

No. He was going to text her. He couldn't deal with any more emotion this weekend.

He really, really missed her.

He wished so much that they could be together. But they couldn't be. Cassie wanted children. And babies needed to be adored and *wanted* by both their parents. Like Ella's girls. And not like Leonie. Babies should never be let down in any way by the adults in their lives.

Of course, if he and Cassie got together and tried for a baby, maybe it wouldn't happen. But that would be awful too. Cassie would be devastated, and James… wouldn't be.

Yep. Best just to stay in touch in a relatively distant way.

Hi Cassie. Thanks so much for the chat yesterday. The one step at a time thing really worked. I got through the whole day and, to my surprise, it was great. Ella and I have got a lot closer again. We talked a lot about Leonie. Thank you. Demon slaying works… Planning to talk properly to my friends more too. How are things with you? What have you been up to? How are the animals? Laura? Dina? Jx

And now he was going to see if Matt and their friend Josh were up for a quick Sunday pint. Since they were his actual best friends and he had not had sex with them, nor was he wondering whether he would or would not ever want to try for a baby with them.

*

'And, yeah, that's basically it.' James finished summarising everything about Ella, Leonie and his mother and father for his best friends, and took a big gulp of his lager.

'Mate.' Matt was shaking his head. He'd been shaking it for a while. 'We were all just getting pissed the whole time and had literally no responsibilities and you were doing all of that? I'm so sorry that you didn't feel you could tell us before. And that we didn't realise. I mean, I suppose I kind of did, a little, but, you know, you get used to people being a certain way, and never talking about certain things, and you never really investigate further. Sorry, mate.'

'And if at any point I took the piss out of you about you never once having been drunk in the seventeen years we've known each other, I really want to apologise.' Josh had spent over a decade trying to persuade James to get even a fraction as trashed as he got at least once a week, until he'd ended up with stitches in his head from falling off a pavement at Matt's thirtieth and had decided to tone things down on the alcohol front himself.

'You should meet my sister Ella and her family. What about if you all come over for Sunday lunch the next time they come for the weekend? And this time we'll actually do it,' James heard himself say. And he didn't regret it.

This was good. He was grateful – hugely grateful – for the fact that he'd done the house swap, and met Cassie, but this was his actual life, and he and Cassie clearly did not want the same things, so it was a good thing that he'd texted her rather than calling her back, because he should definitely move on from her. He had a busy life, so he'd stop missing her soon.

He really bloody missed her right now, though.

Enough. He was going to get the next round in and he was going to stop thinking about her.

Chapter Twenty-Six

Cassie

'How did your conversation with James go on Saturday?' Dina wasn't even through Cassie's door before she asked. It was great that Dina was okay about Cassie having slept with James, a huge, huge relief *but*, right at this moment in her life, Cassie could have done with a bit of space from Dina. From anyone knowing about this whole pregnancy thing.

'Good. I mean, I didn't actually tell him. It was an important weekend for him, so it didn't seem like the right time.' And now it might never be the right time to tell him again that she loved him.

'Cassie.'

'I know, but I *really* couldn't. He had a lot of family stuff going on and it really wasn't the time. And you know what, I now realise that it's *insane* to tell him before I've actually done the test. I don't know what I was thinking. I might not actually be pregnant.'

'You said you were sure? Period two weeks late and counting? Nearly three weeks now? Every symptom under the sun?'

'Yes, but who knows? Maybe my body's playing tricks on me because of the IVF treatment earlier in the summer. Or because I had sex for the first time in so many years.'

'Honey. The only trick your body plays on you when you have sex is to get you pregnant.'

'Yep. Fair enough. Probably I'm pregnant. But I don't know for definite and it really wasn't the time to talk to James. Now I realise that it was a blessing in disguise because even if I *am* pregnant, it might not be viable given that I lost the baby before, and there's no point going through that whole conversation with him if it isn't going to work out. And I *know* that he doesn't want children. So that would not make him inclined to want to be involved in a surprise pregnancy.'

'Obviously it's entirely your decision but I kind of think that you should give him the option of whether or not he wants to be involved. You don't want to regret anything later on. I also kind of think that you should find out for definite *right now* whether you are in fact pregnant or not. And, on both counts, when I say "kind of", I mean I really do think that. To clarify: you should take a pregnancy test now and if it's positive you should tell James. In my opinion. Which is always correct.'

Cassie gave her the evil eye for a moment, while she thought. Dina was partially correct, actually. 'I do agree about doing a test. I don't agree about telling James. I'm going to do a test now and if it's positive I'll tell James in a few weeks' time.'

'Okay. So *yay*. We're doing a test. This is exciting.'

'We?'

'Do you really want to do this by yourself?' Dina was jumping up and down like an excited puppy. After briefly going alarmingly quiet after the Cassie-had-slept-with-James news, she'd been brilliant about it. And she was a fantastic best friend. And it would be great to have her support, whatever the outcome of the test.

'No, I'd love you to be with me. But I'm doing the actual weeing alone.'

*

'I'm going to be sick. This is terrible.' Cassie stared straight ahead trying to do that eyes-on-the-horizon thing that idiots maintained helped. It didn't. She was definitely going to throw up. 'I hate ferries.'

'It isn't far,' Dina said. 'And it also isn't that choppy. Keep your eyes on the horizon.'

'Oh, please.' Cassie whipped a sick bag out of her tote and had it open just in time to catch the contents of her stomach.

'I'm sorry that you feel so rough,' Dina said, rubbing her back, which actually made Cassie feel worse, except she had nothing left in her stomach to come out, 'but this is probably still better than going to the island general store and having Mrs McGinty telling the whole world that you bought a pregnancy test.'

'Yep.'

*

'Oh my gosh oh my gosh oh my gosh oh my gosh.' Cassie had three different pregnancy tests from the drugstore nearest to the ferry terminal, and *finally* they had a table in a – somewhat downmarket – Mexican restaurant, because she really needed spicy food, and now she was finally going to find out for definite. 'Here I go.' She took a deep breath, and stood up, and then sat down again. 'I don't think I can do it.'

'Yes, you can. Or do you mean you haven't drunk enough? Have a glass of water.'

'No, I mean I think I might be about to have a nervous breakdown.'

'Okay. Let's go. Come on.' Dina took her jacket off and put it on the back of her chair, moved out from behind the table and took Cassie's arm and gave it a gentle pull. 'The restroom's over there in the corner.'

It was really small. Dina waited, squashed up against the wash basins, while Cassie squeezed herself into one of the two, remarkably small, cubicles.

'So are you gonna do it?' Dina said after a while.

'Just reading the instructions again.'

'Which one are you doing first?'

'The expensive one. Dina, I don't want to hurt your feelings, but I *hate* weeing in front of people and these cubicle doors are *small*. Could you maybe wait outside?'

'Sure. But call me as soon as you're done peeing because I want to be here for the big reveal.'

'Okay.' Bloody hell.

This was a lot worse than when she took her test the first time she'd got pregnant. She'd done the test in the swish en-suite bathroom of the master bedroom in Simon's swanky Glasgow townhouse. There'd been no need to spread loo paper around the seat of the loo, because it was obviously clean and strangers did not sit on it. It hadn't smelled vomit-inducingly strongly of urine mixed with grim air freshener. And it hadn't had a cracked loo roll dispenser or sticky floor tiles that you really didn't want to touch at all.

Okay. She'd done it. She'd weed for the right length of time. Two minutes to go.

She was out of the cubicle, holding the test flat, carefully not looking at it and calling to Dina still with one minute to go according to the timer on her phone.

Dina hurried back in, looked down and said, 'Oh my God, oh my *God. Oh my God.*'

Cassie looked down too. 'But it shouldn't be ready,' she said.

'You're pregnant,' screamed Dina. 'Honey, I'm so, so happy for you.' She flung her arms round Cassie.

'I'm pregnant. I'm bloody pregnant.' Cassie knew without a shadow of a doubt that if this worked out, she was keeping it.

She also knew that if it worked out she'd be the luckiest woman in the world. And that James was really *not* going to feel the same way.

'Congratulations. Such wonderful news.' Dina was kind of running on the spot in excitement.

'Thank you. I can't believe it. Oh my goodness.' To hell with worrying about James. She was going to enjoy this moment. This incredible moment. This was actually *so* much better than when she got her positive test the first time she was pregnant. Yes, this loo was *scummy*, but Dina was here and she was happy for her and she was a great friend and she'd be a great support, whereas Simon had been spectacularly unimpressed by the news.

Yep, she wasn't going to tell James yet. She didn't need to talk to an unenthusiastic father-to-be in the near future, even if he was the one person in the world she couldn't stop thinking about, and who she so often wanted to talk to so badly. Now, she was going to let herself be absolutely bloody *ecstatic*.

'I'm having a *baby*,' she squealed.

And then she joined in with Dina's jumping and speed running on the spot until it made her feel sick.

Chapter Twenty-Seven

James

Christmas Day. Ella's sitting room. An enormous tree covered in silver baubles and tinsel. A roaring log fire. Ella and Patrick, Daisy and Lottie, Patrick's parents and his brother and his wife and kids. It was one of those happy family scenes that James had never imagined himself in. He'd even less imagined himself enjoying such a scene. But he *was* enjoying himself, hugely. He adjusted his paper hat and turned to look at Daisy.

'Uncle James?' she said. 'I said how many bones are there in a giraffe's neck?'

'This is your fault.' Ella pointed at James as she hauled herself off the sofa. 'A giraffe obsession was the natural next step from the alpaca one. You deal with cervical vertebrae questions. I'm going to get mince pies.'

'Yes, because no-one's eaten anything for at least an hour,' Patrick said.

'You have to over-eat on Christmas Day.'

'Uncle James. How many?' Daisy had her head tilted to one side. James had a sudden rush of memory of Laura looking at him that way, which naturally led him to think of Cassie. He didn't want to think about Cassie. He pondered the question. He had no idea. Giraffes' necks were definitely very long.

'Maybe about a hundred?' he said.

'No!' Daisy was grinning from ear to ear. 'Seven. Lots of mammals have seven neck bones. Humans. Mice. Whales. Platypuses.'

'Wow. That's genuinely interesting and it's also some seriously good knowledge for someone who's just turned nine,' James told her, his heart swelling with, what was that, extreme fondness? Love?

It was love. He did love his nieces. He loved them a lot. Could he love a child of his own?

Maybe. Definitely. But could he look after it satisfactorily, love it *enough*? Well, yes, he could definitely love it enough. But could he love it *right*? Probably not. He'd have no idea how to be a father.

He needed to stop thinking about Cassie.

'Do you want some more giraffe facts?' Daisy asked.

'I certainly do.' And he really did. Just to watch the way she chortled when she caught him out.

'Thank you so much for reading the kids a story. The perfect Christmas present for tired parents,' Ella said, handing James a glass of pink champagne as he came back into the room after a riotous bedtime.

Patrick's brother and family were also staying, and they had three lively children, all under ten. Five kids in one bedroom didn't seem like a recipe for a lot of sleep but it did seem like they were going to have a lot of fun tonight as long as their parents turned a blind eye.

'Time to celebrate them all being in *bed*, and some peace and quiet.' Ella took a sip of her own drink.

It had certainly been a noisy day. Strangely, James hadn't minded the noise and chaos. In fact, he'd enjoyed it.

'Not a problem. I'm actually feeling very smug at the moment. Lottie has some seriously impressive Harry Potter knowledge. And apparently I'm outstandingly talented at doing different Harry Potter characters' voices.' He'd genuinely enjoyed it. Who'd have thought? 'What about a Christmas game of poker?'

A couple of hours on, they all pushed matchsticks towards Ella while she sucked her cheeks in the way she always had when they were kids and she'd beaten James at something and was trying to look nonchalant.

'You've been *practising*,' he said.

Ella stopped sucking her cheeks and laughed out loud. 'Yes I have. Poker's very addictive. Also, I'm never going to let my little brother beat me.'

James shook his head. 'So ridiculously competitive.'

'Said the most competitive man ever.' Ella shook her head right back at him and they both laughed. 'Hot chocolate before bed, everyone?'

'And a couple more hands of poker?' James said.

A good hour later, everyone downed cards and matchsticks after the others begged Ella and James for mercy, and Patrick went off to make the hot chocolates.

Watching the fire's embers wane, lazily enjoying the others' conversation, James reflected that this was the best Christmas he could remember. Probably the best of his life. Last year, he'd spent Christmas skiing with a group of single friends, who he wasn't even that close to, basically to avoid Ella and his thoughts in the aftermath of their mother's death; and he'd spent New Year at a party with Emily and a group of near-strangers.

This year he was here for Christmas and he'd agreed to go to Matt and Becca's for New Year's Eve. Both immeasurably better. And he wouldn't be with Ella now if he hadn't done the house swap and met Cassie.

He wondered what she was doing for Christmas. Knowing her, she'd probably have made special Christmas food for the alpacas and chickens, and be spending the entire festive period surrounded by family and friends in person and online. He'd love to hear her Christmas stories. He'd love to hear her voice. He'd love to tell her about his own Christmas. He'd love to call her full stop. Probably better not, though.

Chapter Twenty-Eight

Cassie

Cassie picked her phone up and looked at it. Then she put it down and looked out of the window at the white-blanketed garden. The first massive snow dump of the season was always breathtaking. Every year, she was stunned anew by its beautiful, sparkly smoothness. And next year, all being well, she'd have a baby to introduce to snow. A baby who she'd seen on her twelve-week scan yesterday. A baby whose father deserved to know about its existence.

She picked up her phone again.

So this was it. She was finally going to tell James about the baby. She should probably have told him after her eight-week dating scan but she'd been too paranoid that something might go wrong.

'Cassie. Hi.' That lovely, gravelly voice. He sounded quite surprised to hear from her – understandably – the only interaction they'd had since he visited Leonie's grave had been a few texts. But he also sounded pleased. Soon he was presumably going to be a lot more surprised and a lot less pleased.

'Hello.' Eek. She couldn't just go straight in with it. *Hi, James. I'm twelve weeks pregnant. I thought you should know.* No. She needed to find some small talk from somewhere. She should have planned this.

'Happy new year.' It was definitely okay to say that even towards the end of January.

'Happy new year to you too. How are you?' he asked.

'I'm good, thank you. How are you?'

'Yep, great. I'm seeing Ella and her family a lot more. We spent Christmas together. It's great. All good.'

'I'm so pleased to hear it. Everything's good here. We have our first big snowfall of the winter today. Later than usual, so it's been particularly exciting. The animals are all well. Dina and Laura are well.'

'Great.'

Okay. This was silly. She was just going to go for it.

'I called because I have something to tell you,' she said.

'Okay.'

'It's actually something really big. So what I'm going to do is I'm going to say it and then I'm going to end the call to let you digest the information. And then there's no need for you to say anything at all, ever, if you don't want to. I mean, it will be entirely up to you. I'm not expecting anything from you. I mean, I'd be very happy to hear from you if you'd like to get in touch, but there's no obligation.' For *goodness'* sake. She really should just stop babbling and get on with it.

'Okay.' He sounded as though he was laughing slightly. He probably wouldn't be laughing in a couple of minutes' time.

'So. The reason that I called is…' Woah, this was hard to say. 'It's that I'm three months pregnant and you're the father, and I'm keeping the baby. And no need to say anything. I'll go now.'

She pressed the red button and ran to the loo and threw up.

Chapter Twenty-Nine

James

The phone had gone dead. James moved it so that he could see the screen. Yes, Cassie had in fact hung up. She had told him that she was pregnant and she had ended the call. She had told him that she was pregnant *with his baby*.

Pregnant.

Pregnant.

He'd genuinely thought for a moment that she was going to say that she loved him and could they try a relationship of some kind. Pretty arrogant of him. Good job she hadn't realised that he'd thought that.

Anyway, focusing on the essentials, she was pregnant. She was going to have a baby and he was the father.

Wow. Just. Mind-boggling.

If you were going to get this kind of news, you really didn't want to be in the back of a taxi on your way to an important client meeting. You'd want to be home alone, or in the middle of the park or the countryside or somewhere, alone. Alone, basically. With time to think, to react, to try to get your mind working again. Right now, James's mind was completely stunned. He had no idea what he thought.

The taxi was pulling up outside the client's offices. Maybe he could cancel the meeting. Pull a sickie. Go home and call Cassie back. Yep. That was a good idea. He'd go with food poisoning. That could come on very suddenly and didn't have to last long so you could be back in action the next day totally unsuspiciously.

'Actually, mate.' He leaned forward to speak to the driver to ask him to take him home, and his colleague Pranav knocked on the window, grinning away at him. James contemplated for one second spinning the food poisoning yarn to him and then realised that without any vomit or green features as evidence, he wasn't going to look particularly convincing. Okay. He was going to have to do the meeting.

He got out of the cab, had his hand pumped up and down a few times by Pranav and paid the driver.

'I just need to send a quick message,' he told Pranav. He couldn't leave Cassie hanging completely.

Got a meeting. Will call later.

Also, congratulations.

Okay. That had sounded a bit odd, but he couldn't not congratulate her, could he? Given that she'd been going for IVF with a sperm donor, this had to be good news for her. She was bound to be pleased. Unless she thought an anonymous sperm donor would be better than him.

Good grief. She was pregnant with his baby.

They should have been more careful.

They were inside the building now and Pranav had definitely just said something to him but James had no idea what.

'Sorry, mate, I think I misheard what you just said. Could you tell me again?'

It was extremely difficult to concentrate on the answer and it was also extremely difficult to concentrate in the meeting.

'Are you alright?' Pranav asked him on the way out.

'I've got a bad headache,' said James, making a snap decision. 'I'm going to take the rest of the day off.'

He put in some calls to cancel the other two meetings he'd had lined up for that afternoon and started to walk the couple of miles back to the flat, to clear his head.

The walk didn't help. By the time he got home, he still had no idea what he thought about the baby.

Well, that wasn't strictly accurate. He did know some things. He knew that he was happy for Cassie, because she'd wanted a baby so much. He knew that he was going to have to be involved in the baby's life because there was no way that he'd be able to live with the knowledge that there was a child in the world who *could* have an involved father but didn't because he, James, had made the decision not to be involved. That would be doing to the baby what his own father had done to him, and he wouldn't be able to live with himself if he did that. He also knew that he wanted the absolute best for the baby, and for Cassie, obviously. And that, even though he was of course going to be involved, he had no role model in his life and he'd probably inherited shit-parent tendencies from both his own parents and he'd probably mess up repeatedly, so it was a good job that he was going to be involved from afar.

And he also knew that he had absolutely no idea what to say to Cassie.

No idea at all.

He really couldn't speak to her.

He'd send her a quick text to let her know that he *was* thinking of her, but was busy. And then he'd get on with some work in his study, the mind-numbingly boring number-crunching kind, that you did have to concentrate on because otherwise you'd make a mistake.

Maybe while he was working his subconscious would figure out for him what he should say to Cassie.

He put the kettle on and tapped out a message.

So sorry, manic day. Speak very soon. Congratulations again.

One grey tick, two grey ticks.

It didn't help his number-crunching, or his subconscious, that he kept glancing at his phone to see if the ticks had turned blue.

They went blue about an hour in. And then he got a reply.

She'd sent a photo, with a caption.

It was a scan photo. Easily recognisable because they all looked the same. Friends and colleagues liked to show them to you and, really, as a non-parent-to-be, it was hard to be that enthralled by them. Just a black and white grainy picture of the inside of a uterus, which was always a bit weird if you knew the owner of the uterus – probably not a very New Man reaction, so he'd never say it out loud, but definitely weird. And a blobby thing which was the start of a baby.

He read the caption.

The baby. Picture from 12 week ultrasound. Next one will be at around 20 weeks, to check for anomalies.

God. Anomalies. That was when they'd discovered that Cassie had lost her baby. She'd be beside herself with worry until then, presumably.

He should send her a message to try to comfort her in some way. She'd been a great help when he'd confided in her.

Am guessing that this will be a worrying time for you and that you'll be nervous until the next scan. As you said to me when I visited Leonie's grave: one step at a time. One day at a time.

When he'd pressed Send, he took a proper look at the scan picture.

And, in fact, *this* blob, *his* blob, didn't look exactly the same as the other blob scan photos he'd seen. It looked… It actually looked quite beautiful. It was going to grow into a person. It was going to grow into *his* baby. And Cassie's baby, obviously. *Their* baby.

He needed to google to check exactly what the twelve-week scan showed.

Yep. Wow. There was a lot you could see, it seemed. Nowadays some scan machines could even see the sex at twelve weeks.

Woah.

He needed a glass of water.

Wow.

He should really send another message to Cassie.

The baby looks beautiful in the scan. Speak later.

He still didn't know what he was going to say to her. He'd have to leave it until tomorrow to speak to her. Maybe the day after. He needed some time. He needed to speak to her soon, but when he did speak to her, he was going to have to get it right.

Chapter Thirty

Cassie

It was eleven o'clock in the morning. Cassie took her book and sat down on her cushion on the bathroom floor to begin her daily four hours of nausea. She knew from friends and the internet that a lot of people had randomly timed morning sickness, but hers was like clockwork, almost to the minute from ten past eleven to ten past three. Sometimes she vomited, sometimes she didn't, but she always felt like she had gastric flu for the entire four hours. It had happened every single day for the past couple of months since she was about six or seven weeks pregnant. This was a time when she was hugely grateful that, as a writer, she could choose what hours she worked; she'd been doing a lot of evening writing recently, when she was nausea-free.

The best thing to do was to hang out on the bathroom floor with some cushions and books and then if she *did* vomit the loo was right there, which was necessary, because the vomit was often quite projectile. It was just one of the many spectacularly unglamorous things about pregnancy. She'd happily take every one of those things, though, if it resulted in a baby to love at the end of it.

This was a great book. She was really enjoying it. It was very engrossing.

Three chapters in, she suddenly realised that she was… three chapters in. And she did not feel sick. What time was it? The chapters were quite long. It had to be after ten past.

It was actually nearly twenty to twelve. As in, nearly half an hour after the nausea usually started. Had she got the time wrong?

By half twelve she was still reading and she was really hungry. She hadn't managed lunch at actual lunchtime for two months. She had a late – and large – lunch every day at about half three, when she'd recovered from the nausea.

Shit, shit, shit, shit, shit. She wasn't feeling sick at all. Had her pregnancy symptoms all just gone? Had the same thing happened again? Was it her? Did her body kill her babies?

She needed to do something.

Dina answered immediately, thankfully. 'Honey, don't panic. We're going to get the next ferry and we're going to get you to the clinic for a check-up.'

Cassie messaged James, through tears, while they were on the ferry. The bastard had said he'd 'speak later' and then she'd heard nothing, for *three weeks*, the arse, but she couldn't bear the thought that he'd be thinking that she was still successfully pregnant if it was all going to go wrong.

Sudden diminution in pregnancy symptoms. Having scan this afternoon.

There were double blue ticks immediately and then her phone rang.

'Cassie. Oh my God. I'm so sorry. I hope so much that it's okay. I'm so sorry also that I haven't phoned. I picked up the phone so many times and then I just didn't know what to say other than I love you and I know that wasn't the right thing to say. But of course I should have phoned. I'm so sorry. And more importantly right now I hope so much that the baby's alright. And I want to be involved. If it is alright. I should have told you that three weeks ago.' James sounded hoarse.

Cassie was crying too much to be able to speak. 'Thank you. I'll let you know,' she said between gulping tears, and pressed red.

*

'Everything's fine. You're a couple weeks into your second trimester. It's very common for early symptoms to reduce or disappear after the end of the first trimester. Your baby's looking very well. I'm printing photos for you.' The sonographer was a very jolly, smiling woman called Ore, and Cassie could have kissed her, except she was busy crying again, big, snotty tears.

'Are you alright?' Ore asked.

'Yes.' Cassie nodded through the snot tears. 'I was just really scared. I had a bad experience before.'

'I'm so sorry. Everything's looking exactly as it should be now, though. So focus on that and try to be happy.'

'Thank you.'

Dina squeezed Cassie's hand and Cassie smiled at her.

'I should tell James,' she said. 'He sounded really worried. At the moment he'll be thinking the worst.'

Her message with the photo attached went straight to blue ticks and her phone rang seconds after that. She mouthed *Sorry* at Ore and Dina, and swiped to answer with one hand while she tissue-wiped the scan jelly off her tummy with the other.

'Hello.'

'Cassie. Thank God. I'm so relieved. I've been so worried about you. And the photo's great, thank you. If you have others, I'd love to see them.' He sounded genuinely interested. If he really *was* properly interested, what an idiot not to have been in touch before now. Or maybe she was being harsh. With his family background it was understandable that he would have panicked somewhat.

'Yep, I'll send them all through.'

'Thank you so much. I hope you're okay. You must have been so stressed. I certainly was. And it's obviously worse for you. Could I ask a huge favour? I mean, please feel free to say no, obviously, but I wondered if I could come to the anomaly scan with you?'

'But the hospital's here in Maine and you live in London.'

'I'll fly to Boston and drive up.'

'Are you sure?'

'Of course I'm sure.'

'Okay.' Cassie didn't know whether to beam with happiness that he wanted to come to the scan or throw her phone out of the window with frustration that it took a scare for him to be able to express his interest. 'So I'll see you then.'

Wow. She was going to see James again soon.

He was still talking. 'I'd love to know your due date, too. I should have asked about the exact date before.'

Wow, again. Would he want to come over for the birth?

She was going to have to develop emotions of steel to deal with seeing him from time to time, if he wanted involvement in the baby's life.

Shit. What if he wanted some form of custody? *Shit.* She should *not* have got pregnant by James. They should not have got so carried away. An anonymous sperm donor wouldn't want custody. Bloody *hell.* This was going to be so complicated.

She pulled her skirt waistband back up over her tummy and swung her legs over the side of the bed. 'I'm going to have to go. We'll speak later.' She was pretty sure that any more talk with the gorgeous, wonderful, infuriating father of her baby and she was going to be in tears, so it would be better to be alone.

Chapter Thirty-One

James

James wiped his clammy palms against his jeans. Sweaty hands were never a good accessory, especially when you were about to see the woman you loved – he was always going to love her – for the first time in nearly four months.

He checked his watch. All good. They still had fifteen minutes before the scan was due to start. Cassie would have texted him if they were going to be late.

A large jeep, Dina's – he recognised it – screeched round the corner of the medical centre and came to a very sudden stop just in front of him.

And there was Cassie sitting in the passenger seat on the right of the car, looking slightly wide-eyed and clutching the dashboard. Probably most of Dina's passengers finished journeys looking like that.

James stepped forward and opened the car door. Good grief. His heart rate was sky high.

'Hi.' He knew that he was beaming like a madman, but it really was so great to see Cassie. He held his hand out to help her down and wondered immediately if it looked patronising or sexist. He hoped not. But she was pregnant and the car was high and it was icy underfoot.

She placed her right hand in his and her left hand on the door and clambered down.

He was truly pathetic. It felt fantastic to have her hand in his, support her weight for a moment.

Cassie had to be really nervous about this scan. He was nervous too; you probably would be in any pregnancy, but it was particularly nerve-wracking given what had happened to Cassie before.

'Thank you,' Cassie said, standing up straight next to him.

They both kind of hovered for a moment, and then James leaned in and kissed her cheek.

'Hi,' he said again. 'How are you feeling? You look great.' Her skin was glowing, she seemed to have even more hair than usual – was that a pregnancy thing? – and her rounded tummy was beautiful. She was wearing a long, tight orange top over dark skinny jeans with boots, under an open woollen coat, and she looked perfect.

'Bit nervous.' She looked down at where they were still holding hands and wriggled her fingers. James let go of her hand immediately. 'But a lot less nervous than I might be because something amazing's been happening.'

'What?' asked James and then Dina walked round the car.

'Hi, Dina.' He smiled at her.

'Hey, James.' They shared a quick cheek kiss. 'Congratulations on the pregnancy.'

'Thank you. I'm very excited.' Also nervous and confused.

'Great.' She gave him a hard stare. 'So I'm going to leave you both to it. I'm going shopping, Cassie. Just call me whenever and I'll come straight back. Any time, however long it takes. I can shop all day, or not. Okay, honey?'

'Thank you so much,' said Cassie.

Dina pulled her into a big hug and said, 'It's going to be okay, I'm sure it is.'

James waited until Dina was back in the jeep and revving the engine and then said, 'So you said something amazing had been happening?'

'Shall we go inside?' Cassie turned towards the building's entrance and started to walk. 'I can feel the baby kick. Which I never did with my first one. So I know it's alive.'

'Wow. That *is* amazing. Wow. So what does it feel like?'

'Well. People, and books, tell you that it's like butterflies in your stomach, like there's something light moving in there. So you imagine what it might feel like. Then when it *does* happen it doesn't feel like you imagined at all *but* if you were describing it you'd absolutely say it's like butterflies in your stomach or something light moving in there.'

'Right. So what you're trying to say is it's indescribable?'

'Exactly.'

They went inside the building and Cassie gave her name at the reception and they got buzzed through into a waiting area.

They sat down and after a minute or two, Cassie said, 'It's kicking now.'

'Wow. So… you're feeling butterflies right now?'

'Kind of. Little squiggles of sensation.'

'Wow.' This was making it all feel remarkably real.

'Would you like to feel it?'

'Sorry?'

'If you put your hand on my tummy you can feel it from outside. Only a tiny bit because it obviously isn't very big yet, but you can definitely feel something.' She looked at him goggling at her. 'My jeans have a very large elastic waistband that starts at the bottom of my bump, so you can feel through that. No undressing required.'

James cleared his throat. 'Great.'

'So, it's still moving. Right here.' She pointed low down on her tummy. Oh, God.

James placed his hand there tentatively. And felt something squirm against his hand.

'That was it! That was actually it! I'm pretty sure I felt the baby! I felt the actual baby!' He'd never felt so exclamatory in his life.

'Yes, that was it.' She was beaming at him.

James wanted to put his arm round her shoulders and kiss her to high heaven, holding onto her tummy and their baby the whole time.

But he couldn't do that, so he said, 'Wow,' again.

'I know.' She was still beaming.

They sat there, smiling at each other like loons, with James's hand on Cassie's tummy, until they were called for the scan.

'Oh my God oh my God oh my God,' Cassie babbled. 'Now I'm scared. There could still be something wrong.'

They stood up together and James clasped her hand. 'I'm sure everything's okay,' he said. Please God he was right. 'And I'm here.' Yeah, not such a helpful thing to say. Where had he been the rest of her pregnancy to date? Sitting in London, worrying about her, thinking about her but not knowing what to say to her. What an idiot.

They held hands right into the room, Cassie gripping his like it was the only thing keeping her standing.

By the time she'd lain on the bed, rolled down the – frankly peculiar, but also clever – large, stretchy waistband on her jeans and had jelly smeared all over her tummy, and the sonographer had done some chat, James was feeling pretty jittery himself.

'And everything looks great,' the sonographer told them a few minutes later. The relief was immense. 'Let me talk you through all the different things we check for.'

James leaned forward so that he could focus better on the screen. Apparently he and Cassie were holding hands again.

The baby had grown so much since the last scan. There was a miracle going on inside Cassie.

'Would you like to know the baby's gender?'

'No,' Cassie said. 'Yes. I don't know. James?'

'I don't know,' James said. It had to be her decision. Common courtesy. He might be the father but she was the one doing all the hard work here. He *really* wanted to know, though. Right now. All his friends, *all* of them, who'd had babies, had chosen not to find out the sex. And he did get that, totally, because obviously surprises were cool. But equally, this sonographer woman *knew* whether or not the baby was a boy or a girl. So James wanted to know too. 'You choose,' he said.

Cassie was still thinking.

'Yes, please,' she suddenly squealed.

'You sure?' James asked.

'Are you certain?' the sonographer asked.

'Yes. I am.' Cassie spoke so loudly that both James and the sonographer jumped a little and then they all laughed.

'Okay, so here goes.' The sonographer paused. Cassie squeezed James's hand so hard that he wondered if it might be possible for someone to break a bone like that. 'It's a girl.'

'Oh my goodness.' Cassie turned to look at James and he leaned down and hugged her, hard, with the arm that didn't have the possibly broken hand.

'Oh my goodness,' she said again when he finally sat back up.

'Yup.' No other words. James would never have believed you could love a baby so much before it was even born.

'I'll print the photos out for you now,' the sonographer told them

'Could we get two sets of all of them?' Cassie didn't look at James as she spoke.

When they left the room, Cassie carefully gave one set of the photos to James, again not looking at him.

'Thank you.' He took them equally carefully.

This was awful now. They couldn't just part like this. They needed to talk more.

'Would you like to have lunch with me?' he asked. He looked down at Cassie. She was pressing her lips together, like she either didn't know what to say or was about to say something she didn't think he'd want to hear. 'We're having a baby together,' he said, not quite sure even as he said it where he was going with that.

'Lunch would be great,' she said, after a few seconds. 'Is Mexican okay for you?'

'Mexican's great.'

They didn't chat much on the way to the restaurant, because Cassie kept nearly falling over, so they were both occupied in keeping her upright.

'Is it rude of me to ask how it is that a woman who lives at the end of an island in the Atlantic, which by all accounts gets several hefty dollops of snow every winter, doesn't have the right footwear to deal with conditions on the somewhat tamer mainland?'

'Well, that's the point.' Cassis clung onto James as her right foot slid on the ice. If he was honest, he was enjoying this. Lots of close contact for a very legitimate reason. 'During the winter I don't have a lot of opportunity to wear anything other than serious boots with serious treads, so I save my nice grip-free boots for the mainland. I just hadn't bargained for the change in my centre of gravity due to pregnancy.'

James nodded. 'Fair enough.'

When they were seated in the restaurant – Cassie still in one piece fortunately – and had menus, James said, 'I have a really big question for you.'

Cassie's head jerked up from studying the menu, her jaw somewhat dropped. Damn. It looked like she'd misinterpreted what he'd said.

'Not *really* big,' he said. Damn, that sounded bad too, like he thought she thought he was going to ask her to marry him or something. 'But quite big. I wondered whether you had any ideas about names for the baby.' Now he thought about it, he did of course want to marry Cassie. Except he couldn't ask her, could he, because he'd messed up big time when they had the baby conversation in London. And then he'd messed up even more by not calling her for three weeks. Why had he done that? How was it okay? He'd been thinking about her and the baby pretty non-stop the whole time, but Cassie didn't know that, did she? She probably just felt that he didn't care.

'I hadn't thought of any names.' She put the food menu and the drinks menu down on the table one on top of the other and patted their long sides together and then their short sides. All very neat and tidy. Unlike their relationship, such as it was. 'I was feeling superstitious before the scan, so I didn't want to think about it then. Now, though, I'm thinking that I might be investing in some baby name books.'

'So are you thinking traditional? Out there? Jordanian? Scottish? American? Just something that takes your fancy? Do you care about the meaning of the name?'

'I would say that I do care about the meaning of the name and I'd like a name that I *like* and that ideally all my relatives on both sides of the family would like. So, yes, although my Arabic is *bad* – I mean, I speak it with exactly the same Glaswegian accent that I speak English but with a much smaller vocab – I'd like one that's good in Arabic as well as English. What about you?'

'Me?' It didn't feel like James should be making any choices here.

'Yes, you. You're her father.' It sounded huge, vocalised like that.

'I think I'd agree with you, on all counts.'

'Okay, cool.'

'I mean, obviously we might not agree on what's a pretty name and what isn't,' James said, 'but it should obviously be your decision.'

'Why is that?' Cassie was looking him right in the eye, and she wasn't smiling. Confusing, because wasn't he just being polite?

'Because you're the one growing her and that's a lot of hard work?'

'I'd still like you to like her name. And I'm sure she would, too.' Still not really smiling.

'Okay, well, great then. I'd like to like her name too.' James felt like there was a subtext to this conversation that he really wasn't getting. Like it symbolised some bigger stuff. Oh, okay, yep. It symbolised all the bigger stuff. 'I'd love to help you choose it.'

'Great.'

Luckily lunch morphed into a great experience after that, because they spent a *long* time talking about girls' names, some good suggestions, some not so good, on both sides.

By the time they were finishing their desserts, they'd laughed a lot, they had a very long longlist and an empty shortlist of names, and James was in utter despair about the fact that he loved Cassie, and their daughter, so very much but he just didn't have the words to communicate that properly.

Maybe it was for the best. Maybe they'd be better off without him.

*

'I love you,' he blurted out, just before Dina was due to drive into the parking lot to pick Cassie up.

'I love you too.' Cassie's beautiful deep brown eyes misted over.

Maybe James should say more. Maybe he shouldn't, though. Maybe he wouldn't be a good enough partner and father for Cassie and the baby.

Cassie broke the silence between them to say, 'You know what? We haven't discussed your involvement in the baby's life. You're welcome to be as involved as you'd like. She's *our* daughter, not just mine. And you need to understand that you aren't either of your parents – you're *you*, just like the baby isn't me, or you; she's already a perfect mix of both of us, her own person. You're totally capable of being a great father. You didn't let Leonie down. You were her brother and you were a great brother to her. You'll be a great father. I'm really happy that you're my baby's father. *Our* baby's father.' A couple of tears slid down her cheeks. 'Although I do want her to read and I do not want her to watch as much football as you do.' She smiled a lopsided, teary smile at him. 'Or any Hitchcock films.'

James's heart squeezed. He so much wanted to say something. But he had to get it right. And it was so hard. Having opened up to Cassie about Ella, and then to Ella herself recently, he knew now that something had closed off inside him when Leonie died, like he'd just shoved all his emotions away. He'd got better at talking. He'd been able to tell Cassie more than once how much he loved her. But this just felt huge. This wasn't just saying *I love you*. This had to be more than that. And should he even say anything when he couldn't even work out whether or not he could be the man that she and their baby needed. And there were practical considerations too. They lived on opposite sides of the Atlantic for a start.

He did have to reply to her.

'Thank you,' he began.

And then there was a massive screeching of brakes behind them and Dina's voice called out through the window of her car.

Cassie paused for a moment and then said, 'Thank you for coming.'

'My pleasure. Great to see you.' And what the hell was that? He'd spoken as though they were strangers instead of two people who'd created a baby together. And who loved each other.

Watching the car drive away was pretty bloody depressing.

*

This was when a good book would come into its own. James was in the dining room of his hotel, eating dinner by himself, and it would be nice to have something to do instead of just staring into space thinking about what an idiot he was. Idiot was an understatement.

If he wasn't going to say anything further to Cassie, he should have gone home this afternoon straight after lunch, but he'd booked the hotel for tonight and his flight for tomorrow evening, not knowing how long the scan would take.

So. He was an idiot. He watched a waiter carrying seven plates along his arm. The waiter plate-carrying thing was always impressive, but this man was *really* good.

God. He was sitting here, staring at waiters carrying plates, on his own, while the woman he loved, who was pregnant with his baby, was nearby but also very far away, on the island.

How had this happened? He loved Cassie. She said she loved him too and she believed him. So they loved each other. She was clearly going to be a devoted mother. He was very keen to be involved in the baby's life.

So why wasn't he with her right now? Why had he not found the words? Why hadn't he just wrapped his arms round her and said he wanted to be together, forever? They could sort out the practical considerations like where they would live.

It wasn't that, obviously. It was all about Leonie. How he'd failed her.

But Cassie had told him that he hadn't let Leonie down. That was what Ella had said too. When they'd said it, both of them, it had felt like it really made sense. It still felt like it made sense, now. And when he thought about it, Cassie was right that their baby was going to be a mix of them both and she might be quite unlike either of them. So the same could apply to him. He definitely wasn't like his father. He took a sip of water and looked at his glass. And he certainly wasn't like his mother either. At his age, she'd *always* been drunk by this time of day.

Maybe he could be a good father and a good husband. He did know one thing. He really, desperately, did want this baby. He knew another thing. He really, desperately, did love Cassie.

Chapter Thirty-Two

Cassie

Cassie slapped houmous on her bread, picked it up, thought about taking a bite, decided she didn't feel like it, put it down and pushed the plate away. She couldn't be bothered to cook and she couldn't be bothered anyway to have lunch at the moment. Maybe she'd have something spicy in a bit.

Everything was so boring. She couldn't be bothered to do *any*thing. She had edits to do on her second London book and normally she loved this stage of writing, and would happily spend hours on end at her desk, but she just couldn't get into it today.

She *should* be really happy today. She *was* really happy. The baby was well. That was wonderful news. In fact, it was doing a little jig in her tummy at this moment and that was *so cool*. In fact, just thinking about the baby was very calming, very lovely.

If she was honest, though, it was hard not to think about the baby's father, and that was not calming or lovely. He was an idiot and she loved him *so much* but obviously, despite the fact that he'd kindly flown from London to America to attend a scan, presumably out of some misguided sense of duty, he still didn't really want to be a father or part of a family with her and their daughter. Or he did now want to be a father but he didn't want to be with Cassie. Both of which were great, fine, his prerogative. But also, sad for Cassie and the baby.

Okay. Enough. She wasn't going to cry again. She'd done enough of that last night and this morning. She couldn't concentrate on work now. She was going to get stuck into some admin later, but first she'd do something useful that would distract her from her thoughts. She needed to get the snow and leaves and twigs out of the gutter outside the kitchen.

It was hard to remember to take your belly into consideration when it was constantly growing. This was a *lot* more difficult than it had been last time she'd done it, in the autumn. All good though. She had the ladder wedged very well. She just needed to go up another step and then she'd be able to reach properly.

'Cassie. For God's sake.'

Cassie jerked at the unexpected sound of a man's voice and the ladder wobbled. And then she saw James running towards her and her heart jumped and she and the ladder *really* wobbled. Shit, she was going to fall. She was going to hurt the baby. Help, help, help. No, it was okay. She was fine. Totally fine. Her heart was going like the clappers. Thank goodness the gutter was stronger than it looked. And she was pretty sure she hadn't dislocated her shoulder or anything, probably just a pulled muscle or something. Everything was alright.

Except, what was James doing here?

'What are you *doing*?' He was at the bottom of the ladder now looking up at her.

'Clearing snow and leaves out of the gutter. What are *you* doing?'

'Are you *insane*?'

'No. I'm very sane. I don't want a leak in my kitchen.'

'Are you stuck? Shall I come and get you?'

Cassie fantasised for a moment about James coming up to help her so that she wouldn't have to haul herself out from the roof and back onto the ladder and down it, because, frankly, it felt like a *huge* undertaking and her shoulder *hurt*. Then she shook her head. 'I'm good, thanks. Just going to finish clearing it and then I'll be back down. If you want to talk, why don't you wait inside? The door's open.' Again, what was he doing here?

'Oh, yes, okay, I'll go inside and put the kettle on and put my feet up in the kitchen and sit there wondering whether or not you're going to break your neck or your back or just your leg. If I sit at the table, I'll have a good view of you falling when you go past the window.'

Cassie took a deep breath. Her shoulder was really sore now and she hadn't even started cleaning the leaves out.

'It's lovely to see you here,' she said. It wasn't. He'd given her a big shock and now he was having a go at her. 'But could you maybe move a little so that I can scoop the leaves and snow out without them landing on you?'

'Nope. I'm staying here so that if you fall I can catch you.'

Cassie took a deeper breath. She'd been right the first time she'd seen his photo: he really was an incredibly irritating man.

'Fine.' She started scooping. 'I hope that expensive-looking jacket's machine washable.' *Damn*. It *really* hurt her shoulder when she leaned on it without the support of the other arm. She scooped harder, to speed things up.

Finally done. Thank goodness. This was an awful job when you were pregnant. Now she was going to have to get properly back onto the ladder. She looked down. James, his hair and shoulders covered in gutter gunk and dirty snow, was looking up at her.

'Finished?' he asked.

'Yes.' She beamed at him. 'So if you move I can come down.'

'Obviously I'm going to stay here to hold the ladder.' He sounded like he was speaking through gritted teeth. His problem.

'Fine.' With her non-hurting arm she launched herself away from the roof and back onto the ladder. The ladder wobbled a *lot* for a couple of seconds until James clamped it against the house with his weight.

'You idiot,' James shouted while Cassie descended with as much dignity as a woman could find when she had a sore shoulder, a bigger tummy than she was used to and the knowledge that she'd just been shown to have been utterly in the wrong.

'Thank you,' she said when she'd let him completely unnecessarily help her off the bottom rung.

'Cassie.' He was still holding onto her arm. 'You have to look after yourself and the baby. You could have hurt her. You could have hurt yourself. Have you done something to your shoulder?'

Cassie blinked to get rid of sudden hot tears. 'I'm sorry. I agree that it was a little bit silly. I should have asked someone else to help. I will not clear a gutter again, or go up a tree again, while pregnant. Or cycle. I would like to make the point, though, that I *would* have been fine.' She was pretty sure that she could have steadied the ladder with her legs when the big wobble happened. 'I wouldn't even have wobbled in the first place if you hadn't surprised me.'

'Okay, so I'm going to try really hard *not* to make the points that *who knows* whether or not you would have been fine plus you do seem to have hurt your shoulder a little. I'm also going to try really hard not to *shout* about the "up a tree" thing and cycling. And I'm also going to say I love you and that's why I'm here.'

'Oh.' Cassie stopped walking and blinked back more tears. 'Thank you.' She suddenly wanted to hurl herself into his arms and tell him she loved him too. But if they were going to have another serious conversation, they had to get it right. They had the baby to think about. And maybe he wasn't expecting the I-love-you thing to lead towards any hugging. Maybe he only wanted to talk about how they were going to share their parenting duties. She started walking again. 'Would you like a drink?'

'That would be great, thank you.'

'Tea? The smell of coffee still makes me feel sick.' She opened the kitchen door and stepped inside, bending down to pull off her boots.

'Can I help? Your shoulder?' James was bending down too. Cassie straightened up.

'Thank you.' There was no point in being obstinate for the sake of obstinacy.

There was something strangely intimate about someone helping you off with your boots. And a bit embarrassing when you remembered too late that you were wearing your favourite fluffy purple socks. And her trouser leg had ridden right up. Had she shaved her legs in the last couple of days? Eek.

This was *nice*, though. Did she have some kind of ankle fetish that she hadn't previously discovered? She *really* liked the feel of James's firm hand around her leg.

'Thank you again.' Her voice sounded oddly prim. 'My shoulder is a bit sore. And that was more difficult than I expected while pregnant. I've still got four months to go but I'm definitely not having a tiny pregnancy.'

'Pleasure.' He smiled up at her. 'I think you're having a gorgeous pregnancy.'

Honestly. It was silly how that made her feel warm inside and how she couldn't stop a big smile of her own spreading across her face. She did a mouth scrunch, to stop herself smiling any more stupidly, and went over to the kettle.

She made a lot of noise splashing water and clattering crockery so that they couldn't really talk while she was getting their teas.

And then they were sitting one on each side of the kitchen table with their drinks and one of Laura's blueberry tarts between them and they were going to have to talk or they'd be sitting in awkward silence. Except Cassie had no words.

'I should have been here to know that coffee made you feel sick,' James said.

Cassie said nothing, sniffed and cut two big slices of tart.

'And I should have been here to clean the gutter for you,' he said. 'And to get food for you if you had cravings. Or hold your hair out of your face if you had morning sickness. I'm sorry that I wasn't here for any of those things. I'd like to be here for the rest of them if you'll let me.'

Cassie's eyes were fixed on James's face. She loved his eyes, his cheekbones, his mouth, the line of his jaw. So much. She'd like to spend the rest of their lives looking at him, sharing things with him. Of *course* she'd like him to be here for the rest of her pregnancy. But it had to be right for him and it had to be right for the baby. Did he mean he wanted them to be together forever? Or just for now?

'I'd like that,' she said. Oh, God. Had that been the right thing to say? She put one of the slices of tart on a plate and pushed it across the table. 'Here you are,' she said. 'Even though you don't like most cake.'

'I did finally eat some of Laura's out of politeness and it was better than I'd expected. Not that sweet. Anyway—' James shook his head

'—not here to talk about cake.' He stood up. 'I have something for you. Alright if I go to the car and get it?'

Cassie nodded.

'Okay, great,' James said.

He was back from the car within a couple of minutes carrying some large shopping bags.

'Please stop me at any point if you don't want to hear what I'm about to say.' He sat down and picked up the first bag. 'Or if you'd like to say anything.'

Cassie shook her head.

'Okay,' he said. 'So the last time we saw each other we agreed that we loved each other. I don't think I'll ever stop loving you. I hope that you still love me.'

Cassie sniffed and nodded. Maybe this conversation was going in the right direction.

'Okay,' he said again. 'And we agreed that our relationship had nowhere to go because I really didn't want children and you really did. And you didn't want to end up resenting me if we got together and we never tried to have a baby, and neither of us wanted to try for a baby together if I wasn't enthusiastic about that.'

Cassie nodded again. His face was so serious that she wanted both to cry and to reach out and touch his cheek.

'Yep. So I don't really know how to convince you of this now, but I'm going to have a go. I went shopping. Myself. No concierge company involved.' James pulled something out of the bag.

It looked like he was holding a pack of… nappies?

'When you told me you were pregnant, I was very shocked. I was pleased for you and stunned on my own behalf, but I immediately felt that I wanted to do my best for the baby. Except I thought that

my best was bound to be pretty bad, because I'm my parents' son.
He pulled something else out. It looked like a box of… nappy bags.
'I spent quite a long time, too long, thinking.' He pulled out cotton
wool. 'And demon slaying.' He pulled out a tub of… nappy cream.
And folded that now-empty shopping bag up. 'Not to sound too
ridiculously corny, but I think I've grown as a person.'

Cassie took a deep breath to try to steady herself. Her heart was
beating insanely fast.

James picked up the next bag and took out the most gorgeous teeny
tiny navy corduroy pinafore. 'What I'm trying to say—' he pulled out
a tiny lime-green cardigan with a navy trim '—is that I love this baby
as much as I love you. And I want this baby as much as I want to be
with you.' He pulled out tiny lime-green tights. And some pale-blue
long-sleeved Babygros. Adorable. But his words were even better.

James picked up the next bag and took out a very soft-looking
ivory-coloured blanket.

'Alpaca wool,' he said. 'I've seen newborns in movies. Babies get
wrapped in blankets when you bring them home from hospital. I'd
like to be there when our daughter's born and when she comes home.'

Cassie could only smile.

'Final bag.' James picked the fourth one up.

Cassie loved his hands. They were strong and capable-looking, with
hard, tidy nails. He pulled out a beautiful soft blue toy elephant, a
classic mid-brown teddy with a bottle-green bow round its neck and
a pink alpaca.

'They're beautiful,' Cassie said. 'All of it's amazing.' *James* was
amazing. 'When did you get all this?'

'This morning.'

'Wow. I had no idea that you'd have such good taste in baby gear.'

'I know. What can I say?' He moved closer to her. 'The reason that I got all this stuff is that I love this baby so much and I want her so much and I want to be her father. And I've started to believe that I can be an okay father. I'm looking forward to trying to be a fantastic father. And I'd be incredibly honoured if you'd agree to us doing this together.' James was holding the blue elephant very tightly and looking into Cassie's eyes. He was smiling, but only a little bit, like he was apprehensive.

Cassie was apprehensive too. Her heart was starting to swell with hope. But what if he didn't want them to be *together* together? What if he just meant that he wanted to be an involved father? And if he *did* want them to be *together* – could they manage that? Could James actually deal with family life? Could she deal with him not dealing with it?

'I'm so pleased that you're happy about the baby.' She chose her words carefully. 'And of course you're going to be a fantastic father. And I'd like to try to parent together, yes.'

James was still torturing the elephant with his hands.

'So could I maybe stay for a little? With you?' he asked. 'And we could work things out gradually? The two of us? Together? You and me? With an end goal of us never being apart again?'

Cassie's heart lurched. He had meant *together* together. Her eyes filled.

'One step at a time?' he added.

'Sounds pretty good to me.' She was crying now and also smiling.

James put the elephant down and moved round the table, took her hands and pulled her to her feet.

He smoothed her hair away from her face, very gently, and then cupped both her cheeks with his hands.

'I love you, Cassie Adair.' He brushed her tears away with his thumbs. 'You've been driving me insane since the moment we first spoke on the phone and I don't think I can live without you.'

'*I've* been driving *you* insane? Honestly.' Cassie smiled some more and sniffed. 'I love you too, James Grey.'

His beautiful blue eyes were on hers and then on her lips. He leaned a little closer to her. She could see the fine lines at the corners of his eyes crinkling as his smile grew. She inched nearer to him.

'I love you so much,' he said. And then he leaned down and kissed her, gently at first, and then very urgently, like the world was ending.

Epilogue

James

James looked out from the stage at the sea of expectant faces below him, gave the mic a little tap, nodded at Bob and Ken in the band, did a big conducting motion with his arms towards the guests, and started singing, '*Happy birthday to you.*'

Leila, the birthday girl, leaned out of her mother's arms, made a grab for the mic and yelled 'Dadadadada.'

When everyone had finished singing and clapping, James spoke into the mic again. 'Just so you know,' he told them all. 'Our daughter's a genius. Not a lot of people take their first steps *and* say Dada on their first birthday.'

While everyone cheered again, James felt in his pocket for the box.

He was going to do it, right now. It was the perfect time, with all the people they loved the most here together in the marquee in the field.

The box was there. Solid, square, Tiffany.

He turned and looked at Cassie. She was busy planting kisses all over Leila's face while Leila laughed and laughed. Could a man's heart actually burst from happiness?

He was going to go for it. He cleared his throat and people looked up.

'So thank you, everyone, for being here. Thank you to all our friends on the island, obviously.' He caught Laura's eye, and Dina's, and those of his fishing and poker buddies and grinned at them all. 'And to everyone who's flown over here from Scotland, and England, and France, and Jordan.' A big cheer went up from the European and Middle Eastern contingents. Now was the time to say it. Ask them if they'd come again, maybe next summer, maybe around Leila's second birthday, for a wedding. He looked at Cassie and imagined saying *My wife and I*. And then he imagined how awful it would be if she *didn't* want to get married. She'd been adamant that they should take things slowly, apparently terrified that he'd leave her otherwise. Obviously having a baby and spending your whole time living together between the island and London was not in practice taking things slowly, but in theory they hadn't made anything official. He felt the box again. Nope. He couldn't go through with it. Stupidly high-risk strategy doing it in front of everyone. 'Have a fantastic afternoon and evening,' he told them all, and raised his glass. 'To Leila.'

'Are you okay?' Cassie asked him when they got a moment together after they'd all had cake – a gigantic, sparkly caterpillar one, which had been pretty spectacular if James said so himself – while Ella was supervising her girls playing with their little cousin on the bouncy castle they had set up on the flat part of the field. 'You seemed a bit distracted during your speech.'

'Yep. All good.' James hugged her and kissed the top of her head.

'Okay. Great. If you're sure.'

'Yes. Really.' That ring box was burning a hole in his pocket. He really didn't have the courage to do it, though. Maybe it would end up sitting in a drawer in the house for the rest of time.

*

Bob and Ken finished belting out Bruce Springsteen – they were men from a certain era and they liked to play music from that era – and switched to Jennifer Rush's 'The Power of Love'.

James detached himself from Matt, Josh and the rest of their boisterous group and held his hand out to Cassie for a slow dance. He still got a new thrill, every single time, when he took her in his arms. He was so very certain that he'd feel like this for the rest of their lives. And he really wanted to marry her. And he was too much of a coward to tell her.

'Got to love Bob and Ken,' he said in her ear. 'I'm pretty sure that this song was released in time for *our* first birthdays.'

'I know. But everyone's having a fab time.' Cassie yawned.

'You okay? Why don't we go and sit down?' It had been a lot of work organising this party and if he was honest Cassie had done more of it than he had. Plus they were juggling Leila and work, including their new ecotourism venture involving an island further down the coast. Not surprising that Cassie was tired. 'Some stargazing?'

They held hands walking across the field until they were sitting on the wall, pretty much exactly where they'd sat the night of Laura's eightieth.

James was about to point out Cassiopeia to Cassie when she nudged him, put her finger to her lips and pointed.

Two joined-at-the-hips-and-at-the-lips figures were making their way across the field towards the tents. They fell over and rolled around laughing. And then one of them rolled on top of the other.

'Eek,' Cassie whispered. 'I think we might be about to witness something very X-rated.'

'Evening,' James called.

'Evening, mate.' Josh stood up and heaved his companion up by her hand.

'Good evening,' Dina said.

And then she pulled Josh inside one of the tents Cassie and James had set up near the bouncy castle for their guests to stay in, and Josh did the zip up.

'I hope that's Josh's tent,' Cassie said. 'Oh my goodness.' The tent was in no way soundproof.

'Mate,' yelled James. 'Might as well be right next to us.'

The tent shook a bit and Josh and Dina emerged.

Cassie giggled as they disappeared off in the direction of Dina's house.

'Could be the start of a beautiful relationship,' James said. 'His divorce came through this week.'

They sat very close together, arms round each other, and looked at the stars for a few minutes.

'Remember Laura's party?' James said.

'So embarrassing.' Cassie snuggled further into him. 'I was so drunk. Want to know a secret?'

'Mmm.' James was enjoying the snuggling. He was also thinking. He was pretty sure that she'd drunk *nothing* today. Which was unlike her. She liked a glass or two of wine.

'I *really* wanted to kiss you that night.' She angled her face up to his and he leaned down to her, loving the combination of familiarity and temptation as their lips met.

He sat up suddenly and Cassie nearly fell off the wall and said, 'Oh.

'Sorry. But are you...?' Really, how to ask? But she was tired, and not drinking. They hadn't been outstandingly careful. They'd basically relied on natural contraception from Cassie's breastfeeding, and even when she'd stopped a couple of months ago and had a period they hadn't really taken too many precautions.

He saw in the moonlight that Cassie had squeezed her eyes shut. 'If you mean am I pregnant, I think I might be,' she said. 'I need to do a test. I was thinking maybe do it tomorrow but I wanted to tell you before I did it but then I didn't want to tell you in case you were either disappointed or happy at the outcome but then I did want to tell you because we should do it together. Shouldn't we?'

'Yes, we really should.' He looked at her more closely. 'What do you mean either disappointed or happy at the outcome?'

'Well, do you *want* another baby?'

'Yes.' It was a really easy question to answer, as it turned out.

'That's a relief.'

James nodded, still a bit stunned at the possible baby news.

'I have a question for you,' Cassie said.

'Mmm?' He shifted round a little so that he still had his arm round her but they were facing each other a bit more.

'I'd like you to answer this immediately without thinking: five minutes ago, did you *know* that you wanted another baby? Immediate answer.'

'No, I didn't.' Good question. 'But now I do know. I really do. I love you and adore you and am definitely very excited at the thought that we might be pregnant again and if we aren't I'd love the opportunity to spend a lot of time trying to make another baby.'

'Good. I love you too. So much.'

Okay. This was it. He was going to do it. He was going to go for it. Good job he still had the ring in his pocket.

He fastened his fingers around the box and Cassie said, very fast, 'James, I really love you and will you marry me?'

What? *He* was just about to propose to *her*.

'I'm sorry?'

Cassie looked down at the ground.

'Oh my *God*,' James said, panicked. 'I didn't mean I'm sorry in a bad way. I meant I'm sorry as in what did you just say, because…

He had the box firmly in his hand now. He let go of her and knelt down on the grass in front of her and opened the box. 'I would love to marry you, Cassie.'

'Oh my goodness,' she said. 'Oh my goodness, *James*. Oh my goodness. We're getting *married*.' She leaned down and kissed him and he put his free arm round her waist, pulling her in towards him. He would never tire of holding her in his arms. He really wanted her to try the ring, though.

He drew back for a moment, took her left hand and slid the ring onto her wedding finger.

It fit her. Serious relief.

'I *love* it,' she said. 'It's beautiful.' Clearly, she liked it. An even bigger relief.

'Not as beautiful as you,' James told her.

And then they kissed and kissed under the stars.

A Letter from Jo

Thank you so much for reading *The House Swap*. I really hope that you enjoyed it!

If you did enjoy it, and would like to keep up to date with all my latest releases, just sign up at the following link. Your email address will never be shared and you can unsubscribe at any time.

www.bookouture.com/jo-lovett

I had a lot of fun writing Cassie and James's story. I loved accompanying them as they changed from near-enemies to lovers, and exploring London and Hawk Egg Island with them. I also enjoyed following their journeys, beginning with Cassie's desperation to start a family and James's desperation *not* to… Trying for a baby is such a hugely emotive issue, shared by so many people in so many ways.

I hope that the story made you smile or laugh, and that you loved Cassie, James and their friends and family as much as I did!

If you enjoyed the story, I would be so pleased if you could leave a short review. I'd love to hear what you think.

Thank you for reading.
Love, Jo xx

 @JoLovettWrites

Acknowledgements

Thank you so much to Bookouture – such a supportive group of people, both the team and the authors. I owe an enormous thank you again to my wonderful editor, Lucy Dauman. She's extremely lovely to work with and everything she says makes incredible sense as soon as she says it (always in a very nice way!). Thank you so much also to Celine Kelly, Donna Hillyer, Sarah Hardy and Kim Nash and all the other in-house people who work so hard (a lot of above-and-beyond) to make every book as good as it can be.

I owe big thanks to many of my friends, but a particular thank you to Nadine Gourgey – she knows why! Thank you also to my friend Ghadir, who's cooked a lot of amazing hashweh for me over the years.

And thank you as always to my family. My sister Liz is a fantastic best friend. My husband Charlie has got *much* better general knowledge than I have and has had the misfortune to be working from home since March last year, so I've asked him a *lot* of questions, because he's so much easier to ask than Google. We're in London and a lot of this book was written during various tiers and lockdowns, so I have to apologise to my children again for the fact that I've had a lot more interest in my characters than in their home-schooling. Thank you to all of you for being so understanding and for eating so much pasta again (still no time for actual cooking).